GW00771855

Gillian E. Hamer

THE

CHARTER

Jane.
With thanks for your
support over the years!
With love,
Gillian
x.

TRISKELE BOOKS

First Edition, June 2012.

Copyright © 2012 by Gillian E. Hamer

The moral rights of the author have been asserted.

All rights reserved. No part of this publication may be
reproduced, distributed or transmitted in any form or by any
means (including photocopying, recording or other electronic
or mechanical methods) without the prior written permission
of both the copyright owner and the publisher, except in the
case of brief quotations embodied in critical reviews and
certain non-commercial uses permitted by copyright law. For
permission requests, write to the publisher, addressed "Attention:
Permissions Coordinator," as the email address below.

Cover design: J.D.Smith.

Printed in the United Kingdom by Lightning Source.

Published by G.E Hamer.

All enquiries to contact@gillianhamer.com.

ISBN   978-0-9571932-0-8

Acknowledgements

Heartfelt thanks to every single person who in some small way has helped make The Charter happen.

Huge thanks to my mum and dad for introducing me to North Wales and for all the opportunities you've given me. With thanks to Adrian, for his loyalty, patience, and for being my anchor in often stormy seas. And to my agent, Shelley Powers, for the trust she has shown in me, and her superb advice and commitment.

I'd also like to thank all the talented writers at the Writing Asylum who have given their time and energy in improving this story from its very humble beginnings. Particular mention must go to Kat Troth, for her invaluable support and Anglesey knowledge; to Sheila Bugler for her wisdom, warmth and enthusiasm; and to my wonderful muse Amanda Hodgkinson for understanding me. Thanks also to the uber-talented Jane Dixon-Smith for ... everything!

And finally to my partners in crime, my fellow Triskys. Liza Perrat and Jill Marsh. I could not have done this without you, ladies – together we've turned the dream into a reality.

Thank you.

Prologue

October 26 1859

ow can it be?
I stand on the edge of a high cliff. Holding back hair that whips across my face, I shield my eyes and squint through the stinging wind. Lifeless bodies dash against the rocks beneath me.

The ship disappears beneath the surface, battered by one huge wave after another. Rain mixes with tears that burn my eyes, and I feel as if I have woken from a nightmare of such terror my whole world has become horribly distorted. I know the sea. I have lived with the ocean all my life. I have been raised to respect Mother Nature, and to underestimate at my peril the power of the ocean. But I have never witnessed such a storm as this.

How can it be?

I have no memory of reaching this cliff. The last thing I remember is being wrapped in mother's arms on the rolling deck as my da strapped a belt around my waist.

"Women and children first," he said. "Now, hush! You keep your hand on this belt; it's all we own in the world, my angel. My precious angel. You keep it safe for Da. And you take good care of your mam. I'll see you on the other side."

Cold lips press into my cheek. Calloused palms cup my face for the merest of seconds. *The other side of where?* I want to ask. But he's gone and the ship is lurching violently beneath my feet.

"Da! Help … help me!"

A sound like a gunshot rips through the air.

"Port anchor's let go!" someone shouts. "Sweet Lord! Brace the yeards, lads, starboard won't take the strain, else!"

I bury my head in my mother's bosom; she wraps her shawl around me. The shrieking wind carries away the sounds of crying children, sobbing women, men barking orders. I cover my ears as strong hands lift me, push me towards the lifeboat. I grasp my mother's hand tighter.

Bang!

"Starboard anchor's gone! We're heading for the rocks! Get Captain Taylor!"

Seconds later, a ripping noise shakes the whole ship. The wooden deck shudders, and the bow gives out a loud moan. The ship tilts and I lose my footing, screaming as I slide towards the inky blackness, pulled by the weight of the leather pockets about my waist.

Water engulfs me.

Coldness engulfs me.

Darkness engulfs me.

How can it be?

I watch from the cliff edge as a pale dawn breaks. No golden rising sun, no blue skies, no welcoming warmth – just a gradual fading of blackness into misty grey.

The Royal Charter – the steamship that has carried my family from Hobson's Bay, Australia to a 'better life' in England – is still being pounded by the storm. With every massive wave that crashes over her, I expect the ship to disappear, but after each surge of the tide she reappears as if trapped by the jagged rocks and unable to find release.

Bodies pulled and tossed by the furious tide, pushed inland

one minute and dragged back into the white foam the next. Men I'd seen issuing orders; women I'd spoken to; children I'd spent many hours with over the past weeks. I close my ears to the screams and cries that circle my head like squawking gulls.

I stand there for seconds, minutes, hours, days … I know not.

The spray of the ocean is on my face. I hear the roar in my ears. I taste the salt on my lips.

But I know it cannot be. I know this cannot be real.

The truth hits me. Bile fills my mouth; I double over and retch.

When I straighten, I stand in silence and calmness. The storm still rages all around me, but I am protected. As if in the eye of the hurricane, my own space is quiet and still.

The answer is suddenly clear.

My name is Angelina Stewart.

I am eleven years old.

And I am dead.

Chapter One

November 2011

"Earth to earth, ashes to ashes, dust to dust – in sure and certain hope of the Resurrection into eternal life."

As the breeze carried away Reverend Thomas's closing words, Sarah Morton raised her coat collar and stepped towards her father's open grave. Knowing what was expected of her, but hating the ceremony of it all, she flashed a look at the mourners, lined up like crows on a power line. She shuddered and gave a weak smile, hoping to see even the tiniest glimmer of warmth in one of the pale faces. She saw none. They were all strangers, even the faces she vaguely recognised. Nothing had been voiced loud enough for Sarah to hear, of course, but she could well imagine the whispers and knowing looks passing among the small group.

The plaque on the mahogany casket gleamed as Sarah bent and lifted a handful of earth, pressing her fingers into the cool dampness before letting it drop. It rattled the coffin lid, making her wince. She lifted her other hand, kissed the single red rose and allowed it to fall.

"Goodbye, Father. I love you," she whispered.

It was terrible to think of her father lying inside that wooden box, cold and empty, lifeless as carved marble. He wasn't there, she knew that. He'd be the first to tell her he'd already gone to a better place … but he wasn't here to ask.

And it was his name, Owen Williams, (1942 – 2011) embossed on that small, bronze square that moved her now more than anything. It made it too real. It hurt too much. Seeing his name inscribed there as if he'd won some prize or been presented with a trophy.

She turned away, unable to bear the rattle of soil on the coffin lid, like the tapping of her father's fingernails trying to attract her attention. An icy tide rushed through her veins, and she stumbled as her heels snagged in the green baize surrounding the grave. The ground spun suddenly nearer. She squealed, biting down on the noise, stirred by a wave of panic. Strong hands grabbed her elbows, pulling her away from the grave mouth.

"It's okay, Sarah. Come on, now."

Warm breath and the reassuring voice of her husband grounded her. Her head swam with the aromas of roses, lilies and freshly tilled earth, and the overwhelming need to cry burst to the surface, even as she tried to regain her composure.

"Take me home, Dom. Get me out of here. Please."

Wrapped in his arms, she allowed herself to be led away. Keeping her eyes fixed on her patent leather boots, she concentrated on each step – but as she stumbled along, she couldn't stop herself snatching another glance at the grave beside her father's. She saw the grey marble, with years of green mould along edges that had once been white. The gold lettering had faded, so it was unreadable in parts, not that she had any desire to read the name. A clump of blackened flowers hung limply from a rusty wire vase, like twisted fingers reaching through from the earth beneath.

Dom's arm tightened across her shoulders. Sarah knew he thought it was grief – accepting, if not fully understanding, the strength of her emotions. And partly it was. But mostly it was a sense of deep regret that made breathing, walking – functioning – difficult for her right now.

There were mumbled condolences and passing handshakes that Dominic handled with quiet authority. The weak, damp hand extended by Reverend Thomas offered little in the way of comfort, but Sarah managed a watery smile that failed to reach her eyes. She closed her ears to the meaningless string of words. Not once had she ever found solace in the church, and today was unlikely to be the day she found religion.

She kept her head down, chin tucked into her collar, trying her best to be invisible. No doubt someone would comment on her ignorance. For sure, it would be all around the village by nightfall that the young Williams lass was nothing more than a stuck-up London snob these days, too good for the likes of Moelfre. But she really didn't care, not now. She was way past caring.

The strength of her antipathy astonished her and she questioned why she felt the need to protect Dom. Probably because she could imagine the hissed remarks. Back for a few short hours, and scarily, she could already see through Moelfre eyes. The cut of his navy suit – which even if they didn't know was Armani, screamed expense – the Rolex, the sparkling smile and deep tan. Everything about Dom's appearance that made Sarah's pulse quicken, would count against him to this unforgiving breed. He was an outsider; a foreigner in their eyes, to be viewed with equal measures of suspicion and scorn. But then, so was she now, she remembered with a feeling of relief.

They reached the front of the small church. Sarah's breathing returned to normal, calmed by the sight of the slate roof glistening in the damp autumn morning, and spiders' webs, that laced across the ancient stonework like delicate ice crystals. A peal of bells rang out the hour; the chimes snatched by the wind and carried out to sea. Above the jutting spire, the sky hung in ashen ripples over mist that clung to the valley, and in the far distance the peaks of Snowdonia rose above low cloud. Even on a bleak day, the views across the island were enough to take her breath.

Sarah's love of the island and its beauty had always worked in direct conflict with how she felt about her father. She was shocked to find the breakdown of the relationship still hurt more than a decade later. Surprised by how much she'd missed Anglesey. It felt good to be home, despite the circumstance.

Dom guided Sarah along the cobbled pathway, holding her tightly as she regained her strength. Her legs worked on their own, ploughing through the autumn leaves, the sanctuary of their BMW taking an age to arrive. She rummaged in her bag and fished out the keys. Soon, she'd be safe, cocooned inside, the outside world shut away.

"Mrs Morton! Excuse me, wait up. Mrs Morton!"

Sarah turned to see a man in his late thirties, tubby with ginger hair, trotting down the path. The bulk of his body strained against the shiny grey material of his double-breasted suit as he jogged. He swapped his briefcase into his left hand and came to a stop in front of them.

"So … so sorry to intrude at such a time. My sincere condolences." He breathed deeply. Reaching into his inside pocket, he produced a business card. "Adrian Carter. Your father's solicitor. I have a matter of some urgency to discuss with you and I wondered if I might arrange an appointment?"

Sarah took the card; the address was in Llangefni. From memory, her father had always used an old, established practice in Holyhead. He'd not mentioned anything about changing solicitors.

She cleared her throat and kept her voice low, aware of the dispersing mourners, who seemed to have slowed their departure. "Yes, obviously, the Will reading. But I'd appreciate leaving it a few days –"

"I'm afraid that's not possible, Mrs Morton. Your father left specific instructions. As I said, it's a matter of urgency. So, could I expect you in my office at eleven tomorrow?"

Sarah met Dominic's eyes. He shrugged and nodded.

"Okay, yes. We'll see you tomorrow," she replied.

"Oh." Carter flashed a look at Dominic and back again. "I'm afraid you have to attend alone." He returned the briefcase to his right hand as he backed away. "Very sorry and all that, but it was one of your father's requests. You have the address, Mrs Morton. I'll see you in the morning. Good day to you."

With that he marched towards the car park, scattering the last of the lingering mourners. Their gazes joined hers as he squeezed himself into a shiny green MG and reversed out onto the road.

Sarah re-read the business card as she settled into the car seat.

Carter, Carter & Sons (Solicitors – Cyfreithwyr) Llangefni.

"Okay now, babe?"

Pulling off her winter gloves, she ran the back of her fingers across Dom's cheek, hoping to erase some of the worry lines embedded there.

"Get me through today and I will be. I promise."

* * *

Red watched the BMW speed away, engine throbbing loud enough to dislodge late migrating starlings from the trees above. It sounded so out of place here in the middle of nowhere – even the cows paused in their chewing, turning to watch the car racing past their field. He listened, eyes closed, head tilted back, revelling in the throaty roar until it finally died out in the distance. He'd always wanted a car like that, dreamed of it, in fact. But if he had sixty or seventy thou in loose change, he wouldn't choose a Beamer; he'd go for something classier. An Aston or a Maserati perhaps, but maybe still a convertible. He'd always fancied the thought of a soft-top – zooming along the country lanes with the sun on his shoulders and a hot bird at his side. One day.

He took a last drag on his cigarette, ground the stub underfoot, and stepped from the shade of regimented fir trees that marked the western boundary of the graveyard. Other than the call of a distant pheasant in the woods, the only noise came from the two gravediggers, already covering old Owen in a good few feet of rich Welsh soil.

The scrape and chink of their spades, and the occasional phlegmy cough, kept Red company as he skirted the church car park, heading for the stile that took him across Caer Felin and out onto the side road where he'd parked. He didn't think it a good idea to leave his car among the regular mourners', and he'd congratulated himself on his decision even more so when he'd seen the chunky dude in the green MG pull up. His first impression – police – was soon discarded when he saw the briefcase. Solicitor was his second guess. But from what he knew of matters of the law – admittedly not that much – it seemed a bit unusual to turn up at a client's funeral. He'd strained his ears to pick up a snippet of the conversation – along with half the village, nosey sods – but to no avail. He had, however, made a mental note of the car registration, so he should be able to put that to use later.

He unbuttoned the collar of his dark grey shirt as he followed the public footpath, dodging muddy puddles and slippery leaves. He was very particular about his clothes; he might not own that many decent pairs of shoes, but the ones he did he travelled all the way to Chester to buy, and he didn't fancy getting them covered in mud. He detested funerals. Hated the whole experience of either genuine or pretend grief. He knew some people, usually the old duffers who'd nothing else to do in life other than count the passing of friends and associates, who made it a virtual hobby. Not him. He'd only been to two before today – and that was two too many.

He stepped out onto the lane, pausing to wipe his shoes carefully on the grass verge, and headed for his car. He hoped it had been worth the effort. He'd had no more than twenty seconds alone with the husband while Sarah was talking to Dreary Thomas. But he'd pushed his mobile number into the outstretched hand as he'd offered his condolences, then quickly hissed the words he'd spent all night rehearsing into the guy's ear, and shook hands with a meaningful look as he backed away and disappeared behind the vestry.

He'd seen the anxious glances trying to search him out in the crowd during the interment, but he'd made sure to blend into the shadows. He just hoped the guy got the message; he'd gone out of his way to appear as unthreatening as possible – no easy feat for a bloke like him. But there'd been a flash of something like panic in the other man's eyes. Still, no point in worrying. He'd know soon enough. If he didn't get a call later that day, then he'd have no option but to put Plan B into action – and who could blame him then if things went wrong and people got hurt? It wasn't like he hadn't tried Plan A first, was it?

He climbed behind the wheel and lit up another ciggie. If nothing else, at least he'd had the opportunity to see Sarah Williams for the first time in God knows how many years. She still had the ability to render him speechless, even after all this time. No other woman, before or since, had made him feel fourteen again, made his tongue stick to the roof of his mouth so that words failed him even if he plucked up the courage to attempt speech. He recalled that deceptive fragility about her from her teenage years – just before she smacked you in the gob or aimed a kick at your nuts.

He smiled at the memories; he'd teased the bejesus out of that girl, he knew that, but only because he fancied her rotten and was desperate to make her notice him. The porcelain complexion, huge blue eyes and glossy blonde hair that he'd dreamed of grabbing hold of in the height of passion. Christ, she was head and shoulders above anything else he'd ever seen on the island. Just a shame she had inexplicable taste in men …

Red pulled his mobile from his pocket and checked the screen, just in case. No missed calls. Patience, my boy, he warned himself. Play this right, and his Maserati dream could be one step closer. He opened the window and blew out a stream of smoke, recalling Sarah's tears at the graveside, the few words she'd spoken in church about her father. A shiver ran through him. Christ, she still had it. Whatever *it* was.

He hoped she'd come to understand he was doing this for her, to protect her and the family name. He'd do anything for Sarah Williams. Anything. He checked his mobile one last time before dropping it onto the passenger seat and starting the engine.

Come on, boyo, don't let me down. Don't let Sarah down.

Ring, dammit. Ring.

Chapter Two

The office door ricocheted against the wall, leaving yet another dent in the grey plaster. Lewis tumbled into the room, arms loaded with files balanced at a precarious angle.

Detective Sergeant Daniel Buchanan looked over the top of his newspaper and smiled. Danny had been with Bangor CID less than a month, but already DS Lewis's reputation as a 'walking disaster zone' had been highlighted several times.

"Bastard. Stupid. Pissing … pig-headed … imbecile!" said Lewis as he stomped across the office, one step per adjective.

Danny pulled himself out of his chair and deftly caught the top two files just before they hit the floor.

"Who's that then?"

"His Honour-Judge-Justice-Bleeding-Connors, of course. The old fool."

"Ah." Danny laid the files on Lewis's desk and headed to the coffee machine.

"I mean," said Lewis, yanking off his tie. He balled it up and lobbed it across the room where it hooked onto the end of the Venetian blind, dangling like a hangman's noose. "What does he want? A blood-signed confession witnessed by the sodding Pope?" He flashed a look in Danny's direction. "Sorry."

"No problem."

Danny emptied an extra sugar into Lewis's tea, amused to

see the auld Irish prejudices were still going strong: you came from across the water ergo you had to be a practising Catholic who beat your wife, only used the rhythm method and sought absolution at least once a week.

"So," Danny said, stirring the tea as he crossed to Lewis's desk. "You lost?"

"We're appealing. It took me two years to get that Polish drug-dealing piece of scum off the streets." Lewis closed his eyes for a second, drew a deep breath, and pulled off his jacket. He added in a low growl accentuated by rich Welsh tones. "If Connors thinks I'm going to sit back and let some 'legal loophole' by some fancy-arsed brief see the bastard get off." He slung his coat onto the back of his chair. "Well, he's got another think coming."

Lewis ran a hand through his hair, trying, and failing, to get the natural quiff to lie flat – a stress-related trait Danny recognised in his new partner. Not one they shared, he thought, running his own hand across a baby-smooth scalp.

Lewis took a long drink of tea before replying. "He thinks we set Symanski up."

Danny frowned. "Am I missing something? I thought you did?"

"No. Not the sting. Connors was all for using a student as a decoy, was even happy to agree to the circumstantial evidence. No, he believed Symanski's QC. In fact – get this – he more or less accused us of planting Class As in his flat."

Danny whistled through his teeth, at once understanding and sympathising with his colleague's anger. That was below the belt, the worst accusation you could level at a good copper, and he knew exactly how that kind of punch felt.

"Christ …"

Lewis took another sip of tea. "Well, as good as. Symanski had receipts – can you believe it? Sodding receipts! He had a little black book – a sodding LBB – with the dates of every fucking consignment he got from his bloody fuck of a supplier. And guess what? Court ruled the bastard supplier was to remain anonymous." Lewis took a deep breath and flexed his shaking hands. "And then, just to hammer the final nail into the coffin, Connors agreed to allow as critical evidence the fact Symanski could prove he was able to tie up purchases with bank statement withdrawals. Talk about leading the jury. He might as well have pierced their noses and strung them along like cattle."

Danny shook his head. "Couldn't he have just botched up a set of accounts? Who'd expect the book-keeping skills of a drug dealer to be up to scratch?"

Lewis grimaced and undid the top button of a once navy blue shirt, now badly washed to the shade of dark denim. Danny recognised the mistake in water temperature, one he'd made himself too many times, ruining a good many 'best' shirts.

"The emphasis was on us to prove it, and Connors swallowed the whole deal that Symanski was *so* very fastidious with his records. And because there were no bank withdrawals near the date of the sting, and not forgetting this bleeding witness statement from the secret supplier, Connors agreed with the defence that the amount of drugs found in his flat just didn't add up." Lewis shook his head. "I don't know if I'm more angry or insulted."

Danny knew exactly how his partner felt; he'd been on the wrong end of false allegations back in Dublin. One of the reasons he'd made the move across the Irish Sea was to escape the sideways glances that seemed to accompany him everywhere he went. It was hell to have the stench of corruption following you – especially when it was unwarranted. From what he'd already learned, Danny would stake his career on Geraint Lewis being a straight cop.

Danny sipped his coffee as he crossed to his own desk. "I'm sorry. I know how shite you're feeling. But appeals work in our favour more often than not. Stick with it."

Lewis nodded. "I'll stick with Symanski that's for sure. I'll be like dog shit on his fucking trainers – he'll smell me wherever he goes. He won't start trading in this town again on my watch,

I promise him that. If nothing else, I'll hound him out of Bangor."

"And I'll be at your side bud, no fear."

"Fancy doing me another favour?"

Danny stared for a moment. "You think I'm telling Thompson, forget it. I've had one bollocking this week, that's more than enough thanks."

If there was one hiccup in Danny's smooth transition from the Gardaí to North Wales CID, it was Detective Chief Inspector Rhodri Thompson. Despite Danny's best attempts at Irish charm, sheer dedication to his job, or even brown-nosing – all efforts to appease his senior officer had so far been in vain. Danny was determined not to take his DCI's apparent disdain personally, agreeing with other colleagues' advice that Thompson was making an example of him for some reason. And until he knew what reason, Danny figured he had no choice but to suck it up.

This week's *example* had highlighted Danny's incorrect use of procedure at a recent crime scene, and how his failure to set up a suitable chain of command had compromised an important enquiry. Thompson had flown into a volcanic rage, in front of most of the plain-clothed officers on the force. But, despite his face radiating heat like a fireball, Danny had taken it on the chin, accepting – if not agreeing – with the DCI's points.

"I'd do it for you," said Lewis, interrupting his flow of thoughts.

"Like feck you would." Danny drained the last of his coffee and crushed the polystyrene cup. "Drop it. I will, however, treat you to a meat feast pizza after work and even allow you to accompany me to The Shamrock to partake of a couple of shandies and watch the mighty United in action. There. Can't say fairer."

"Football again … great." Lewis dropped his head into his hands. "If I'm still alive. I used up a whole month's overtime on the Symanski hit. This is going to go down like a fart in a lift."

"Actually, I might have something to take your mind off your woes." Danny picked up the Daily Post and flicked through to page nine. "Do you remember that bloke we visited, my first week here, lived in that spooky auld place on the cliffs out Moelfre way?"

Lewis gave a blank stare.

"You do. He was a retired professor, history or some such bollocks, and he was right weird, remember? You reckoned he wrote to you weekly with imaginary death threats."

Lewis looked up, gaze clearing. "Ah. Yeah. Williams?"

"Well, he's hit the bull's-eye."

"What?"

Danny folded the paper inside out, held it out to Lewis, and tapped a small paragraph on the left hand side of the page. "It's his funeral today."

* * *

Sarah settled back on the sagging leather sofa and took in the surroundings of the hotel lounge. There was nothing wrong with the atmosphere; it was warm, friendly and traditional, but the whole place looked tired and in need of some modern touches. Small floral arrangements masked the smell of stale ale and cigarettes. A long buffet table dominated the room, sparsely laden with curling sandwiches and bowls of peanuts.

Nursing a cup of lukewarm coffee, she listened to the buzz of conversation. The cheerfulness of the small bunches of people huddled around the horse-shoe bar annoyed her, although she couldn't be exactly sure why. Dom was trapped in a corner of the room by a football fan who clearly recognised him. She thought about rescuing him but was glad he'd found a friendly face among the crowd. He looked in his element, his expression animated and cheerful. At least he had a way to fit in, unlike her. No, she'd leave him be; no need for him to share her misery.

The sound of the surf rolled through the inch of open French window, and she took a lungful of sea air. The familiar smell of dried seaweed lingered on the breeze, mixing with cigarette smoke from a group of men shivering on the patio. Her father had spent many hours drinking in this hotel, overlooking the vast expanse of Lligwy Bay, one of his favourite spots on the island. It seemed appropriate to hold his reception here. Besides, she couldn't bear the thought of this army of invaders taking over the beloved, remote, rambling house on the cliffs at Point Lynas. Charter House.

Sarah tuned into a conversation between the elderly ex-postmistress and local busybody, Mrs Ruthie Parry, and Reverend Thomas.

"Hadn't been well, not himself, the past twelve months," said Mrs Parry, brushing cake crumbs from her huge bosom as she spoke. "I was saying only the other week to someone, Owen Williams isn't himself nowadays. Troubled, he was. Worried bout his heart. I think it plagued him more then he'd admit. Someone – I forget who – told me he'd been having some kind of angina attacks. Aye, it's a damn shame."

Reverend Thomas nodded and took a sip of tea.

"For years I'd see him out walking. From one end of island to t'other, carrying his metal detector or his sketch pad. Always so active. But he lay dead for a week in his bed," whispered Mrs Parry. "Imagine that. A whole week before somebody found him."

Reverend Thomas began coughing and nodded towards Sarah. Mrs Parry's mouth formed a silent 'O' and she covered her embarrassment by helping herself to another portion of Victoria sponge.

Sarah bent to put her coffee cup back on its saucer, hoping the gesture hid her eyes. Talk about hitting a nerve. She rummaged in her handbag, dug out the compact and checked her reflection. No way would she let Ruthie Parry know she'd hit a nerve. Every disdainful glance or seemingly inconspicuous comment – and she'd seen and heard many that day – made her insides shrivel as she reproached herself for not being there in her father's final days.

She couldn't shake the thought of her father alone and dying. Did he know what was happening? Why hadn't he called her and told her his health was failing?

Because he wouldn't have wanted fuss.

Sarah could almost hear his words as if he stood beside her.

Can't be doing with fuss, my girl. All these people so bloody pampered and nothing more than hypochondriacs, the lot of 'em. When your time's up, it's up. And not a damn thing you can do about it. So, why all the fuss?

She looked out across the bay. Weak November sun had broken through the clouds, and yellow light glistened off miles of wet sand as the tide retreated. Another few hours and the sand would be covered. On this flat beach the sea swallowed a vast area in a matter of minutes. Nothing could stop the pull of the tides - just another of the things she couldn't change, things she had no control over. Of course, she wished she'd been by his side; wished she'd had a chance to talk to him, try to explain one last time why she'd had to leave. Why it was impossible for her to stay. But she hadn't, and that was that. She couldn't turn back time; no more than she could stop the next high tide.

"Sarah?"

She turned and saw Luke Evans – a childhood friend ... and her first love.

He leaned across to squeeze her shoulder in an awkward show of affection, and gave a gentle smile that at one time would have produced a whole swarm of butterflies in her tummy.

"Hello, Luke."

"How are you, Sarah? I only made the interment, I missed the service, I'm sorry. My shift didn't end till lunchtime and the boat was late getting into dock."

"It's fine, don't worry."

"I'm just so sorry. He was a good man."

"Thank you." Sarah gestured for Luke to join her.

"Well, he was," said Luke. "I had a lot of time for your father."

The sofa dipped in the middle as he sat. Sarah pulled her knees away from the warmth of his thighs, flushing as she wedged herself against the leather arm.

Luke continued, appearing not to notice. "He put up with my old man for years. My dad took more notice of your father than anyone else, even his own doctor. I'd have gone mental without his help." He paused, looked down at the carpet between his feet, his voice thick with emotion. "He was a good man," he repeated. "I'm going to miss him, for sure."

Tears welled in Sarah's eyes. "Last time we spoke, he said you'd taken him shopping. I know you've been a big help to him. I'm grateful."

Luke sniffed and shrugged. "It's nothing. I took him round a few DIY places in Bangor, that's all. After my old man died, he kind of took his place. Dunno what I'll do with my Sundays now."

"Is there no Mrs Evans, then?"

Luke shook his head, eyes scanning the room. "Round here? You kidding me? There's no single women left – not under the age of sixty anyways. All the good ones have been snapped up … or moved away."

He met her gaze for a second, before lowering his eyes to his lap. "There's a girl in Dublin. Nothing serious like, but she's a good laugh and I see her whenever there's a stop-over. But with the job and the small-holding to look after, I don't have a whole lot of time for romance."

"You're running the farm alone now?"

"Well, since Dad died, I see less and less of my beloved brother. David only hung around to appease the old man. Once he got his share of the inheritance, he did a bunk. Sometimes, I don't blame him … wish I'd thought of it first."

"What's he doing now?"

"Bit of this, bit of that, he says. Import and export. Something to do with antiques and old books and the like. Can't say we're close anymore to be honest."

"That's a shame."

Sarah's mind wandered back to teenage summers. Still light at ten pm as she strolled along the cliff path to Charter House, she'd pause to watch the final tip of sun swallowed up by the purple horizon. She could remember the smell of smoke from the small beach fires, the aroma of fried sausages; hear the sizzle of shrimps in butter. They'd spend hours catching them in homemade nets in rock pools around the Point.

In earlier years, aged nine or ten, she recalled their obsession with pirate games and how Luke had kissed her one day, hidden under the canvas cover of their pirate ship's sail, taking her completely by surprise. She'd relived that moment many times over in later years; the realisation of his boldness and the confusion and power of her own feelings. At the time, the most important thing in her life was their swash-buckling adventures or treasure hunts buoyed by local legend – until one by one each of them grew out of such frivolity and turned, in David's case at least, to music and marijuana - or in her case, books and boys.

Luke and David had been the brothers she'd never had, and their mother, Maud, like the perfect aunt. Maud often joked that Sarah was a welcome break in a house full of men – right down to the tom cat, Dai. It kept Sarah from under her father's feet in the holidays, and gave her more of the freedom she craved. While Luke was quiet and a loner, a strong character who kept his problems close to his heart, David had been gregarious and loud – a joker who was always the life and soul of the party, and could charm the girls with a cheeky smile and a sexy wink.

But it was always Luke for her. Luke and his gentle, smiling eyes attracted her in a way she couldn't explain. Just hearing his voice again gave her a feeling of warmth deep down in her stomach. But it was impossible to turn back time; not that she wanted to, what was she thinking? She had Dominic now. She glanced across to the bar, noting he'd attracted another couple of the younger men into the conversation and was revelling in his new found popularity.

As if sensing her thoughts, Luke leaned across and squeezed her hand.

"Must be odd, being back here, like," he said. "An awful lot different to down London?"

"Chalk and cheese."

"What's it like being the Posh and Becks of … is it Watford Dominic plays for? Sorry, I'm more of a rugby guy myself."

"Yeah. Watford. But we live in the city – an apartment on the Thames, near Canary Wharf. I don't get out to Watford all that often. Football's not exactly my thing either." She sighed and looked out across the bay again. "I miss Anglesey, though not much changes, does it? Not even after ten years. Although, there are a few faces I don't recognise –" She nodded towards a group of men in the far corner.

"Well, you know Reverend Thomas and Dr Davies," said Luke. "He's been here since the Domesday Book. And you must remember his youngest son, Craig? He was in our year at school?"

Sarah nodded. "Dickhead Davies."

Luke smiled. "That's him. The tall chap with the beard is the local policeman, Conrad Hughes. He's a nice guy, fairly new round here, and does a lot for the community. He's an amateur archaeologist in his spare time. I think your dad got on pretty well with him. They used to put a few pints away over the weekend, discussing their finds.

"And the sturdy guy with glasses over at the bar is young Martin Cole. The family moved into the village about six years ago. His parents died in a house fire about a year later, when the cottage they were renovating burned down."

"How terrible," said Sarah. "Does he have other family here?"

"Nah, he's a loner. Recently he'd started doing gardening and odd jobs for your father. He's a bit on the slow side, bit simple like, but a gentle soul. It was him that found your father's body actually –" Luke broke off as his face reddened. "I'm sorry."

"That's okay."

"He missed you, you know." Luke's gaze met hers. "Oh, he'd never have admitted it, but it very nearly broke his heart when you moved away. He was proud of you too. Always telling me what you were doing, where you were in the world. Boasting to his mates in here how you were a famous writer, working for all the big magazines. He kept your postcards pinned to the kitchen door for weeks. Proud as punch he was that you were such a success."

Sarah sniffed and tucked a strand of hair behind her ear. "He never said."

"He wouldn't have. You know what he was like."

Yes, she did. Stubborn, bullish, selfish and bitter. Her father had been all those things. A heavy drinker, saying it was her mother's death that had led to his drinking when he had always been a drinker. A man of many dark moods, always ready to blame anyone and everyone for his problems, never himself.

But ... still her father.

Back then, she'd felt forced to move to the other end of the land to finally escape his grip on her life. And although he'd never shown anything but resentment towards her new life, her career in travel writing, or her marriage to Dom, she could imagine he might have been proud in front of his friends.

"Well," said Luke, brushing off his trousers as he stood. "I'll go and get a bite to eat and head on home. Are you going back to London or staying on awhile?"

"Um, not too sure. I want to visit Grandma Ruth while I'm here, and I have to see the solicitor tomorrow, then I'll make a decision."

"Okay, well I'll maybe see you around before you leave."

"Sure, I'd like that. Thanks for coming, Luke."

Sarah watched Luke head towards the buffet table. There was a time when the very sight of Luke Evans' tanned, muscular arms sent her blood pressure up. His love of rugby and years of outdoor manual labour on their small farm had bulked him up even more.

Following the line of the far wall, her eyes met with Dominic's. He raised his eyebrows and gestured another fifteen minutes. She nodded and gave a weak smile. With effort, she could just about hold out that long.

"Hello … Miss Williams?"

"Yes." Sarah jumped and the reply came out sharper than intended. "Er, well, no, Mrs. Morton actually. But I am Owen's daughter."

A small, balding man held out a hand. "Nice to meet you, I've heard a lot about you."

She shook the outstretched hand. It wasn't much of a grip, and his skin was clammy. "I'm sorry … I can't repay the compliment. You are?"

He pulled a business card from the pocket of his tweed sports coat. "I'm Miles Harvey-Barnes, your father's agent."

"My father's what?"

"Agent. Did he never mention me?" He pushed his gold-rimmed glasses up his nose with a slender finger.

"A literary agent?" she asked, reading the gold print on the card.

"Yes, that's right. Fullard and Barnes from Manchester." The man puffed out his chest as he spoke. "You may have heard of us in your line of work. I understand you're a travel writer?"

"Yes, I am, but I'm based in London. I'm sorry I've never heard of you. I didn't know my father had acquired an agent. I know he's tried for years to get some of his work published, but he never mentioned any success."

Mr Harvey-Barnes peered through thick lenses; a frown played across his features. "It happened relatively recently, so perhaps he never had chance to talk to you about it. We'd secured a two-book non-fiction deal for him with a major publishing house. I believe there were good things to come for your father, a lot of interest in his findings. But now … tragic circumstances. Tragic."

Sarah knew her father had spent his retirement years researching local history and archaeology and had long had hopes of publishing some of his work for posterity. But he'd once said he'd had his fill with publishers, was planning on papering his study with rejection slips. So, why no mention of Miles Harvey-Barnes?

"… the decision of the estate, assuming you are the executor?"

She realised the man was still talking.

"Sorry, what?"

"I apologise, I was thinking aloud, about where this leaves the book deal. I presume the rights will pass to the estate and assuming you are the sole executor, it would be your decision to grant the right to proceed."

Sarah studied his flushed face, squirming under his keen, expectant gaze. She didn't like this man.

"Are you?" he prompted.

"Am I what?"

"Sole executor? With the rights to your father's work?"

"I'm sorry, Mr Harvey-Barnes, I really have no idea. My father never discussed his Will with me – and we've established he never mentioned any book deal. And, as his funeral was less than an hour ago, you'll understand the Will is not my top priority right at this moment."

Harvey-Barnes took a step backwards; his face turning a deep pink, he held up his hands.

"So sorry. No offence intended. None. Not at all. We can discuss this another time. Excuse me."

Before she could find a response, he'd doffed an imaginary cap and hurried out of the French windows, leaving Sarah open-mouthed. She shook her head, not quite believing what the day had so far thrown at her – secretive solicitors, impertinent literary agents, not to mention hostile locals and her own insecurities.

She'd no clue about the Will and certainly didn't want her father's money. She had her own – that had been one of the major aims of the past decade, to ensure she was financially independent. All she wanted were a few sentimental pieces from the house belonging to her mother, and some school stuff she'd left in her old room. She must ask Grandma Ruth if there were any keepsakes she wanted, and then she'd have to see about putting Charter House on the market.

"Hey, babe. You ready to go?"

She looked up at Dom, yawned and nodded. "You've finished talking football, then?"

"Yeah, sorry I took so long. Some of these guys are actually okay, you know."

Sarah rolled her eyes and Dom smiled.

"Who was the weedy guy?"

"Miles Harvey-Barnes."

"Who?"

"Exactly. My father's literary agent apparently. I want to go back to the house now."

Dominic took her hands and pulled her to her feet. "Are you sure you want to go back to Charter House? We can easily book a hotel."

Sarah shook her head, sighing as she relaxed into his embrace. "No, it's okay. It's my home, well … it was. I feel I want to be there one last time." She pulled away and looked into his face. "You don't mind, do you? I mean, I know my father never welcomed you with open arms."

"Time to forget about the past, Sarah." Dom held out his hand. "Come on."

She picked up her bag and followed Dom out through the bar, thinking of the old house, standing high up on the cliffs, proud and watchful as ever, and shivered with a mixture of emotions.

Home.

It had been a long time since she'd thought of Charter House as home.

Chapter Three

Through balding branches of tall trees lining the drive, the house came into view. Grey stone walls, decked with glossy strings of green ivy, like permanent Christmas decorations. Dark windows, whose lintels had looked like heavy eyebrows to an over-imaginative child. Beside the greenhouse, Sarah caught the first glimpse of her mother's beloved cottage garden. On hot, sunny days, the wonderful aroma of mint and thyme would drift through the open window. Despite the drizzle of an autumn afternoon, she could almost smell it.

She felt Dom's hand on hers.

"You okay?" he asked.

He slowed the car and she could see him studying Charter House, as it stood proud on the cliff overlooking Point Lynas.

"Lots of memories," Sarah said. "My mother loved this place, especially the gardens. Father rarely set foot in them – but it was her life. She planted those sycamores. 'Sentries,' she always said, 'standing guard along the drive.'"

Sarah recalled winter months, lying in bed listening to the creaks and groans of the old house, when westerly's howled around the Point, sleeping safe in the knowledge the sycamores were standing firm, protecting them from danger.

She looked over the lawns, out to where a grey strip of ocean met a dull sky and remembered playing on sun-dappled grass beneath the sycamores while her mother gardened nearby. The soft smile that lit up her face whenever Sarah called; the blonde hair breaking loose from her head scarf in the breeze. So many memories, built up over the years like a barrier against her loss until she'd almost feared Charter. It was time she learned how to love the old house again.

"My mother was a painter as well as an avid gardener," Sarah said, aware of the pride in her voice. "You'll see. In the house there are lots of her paintings. Or at least there used to be. She spent hours sitting here, or on the cliff path, painting the landscape, the sea and the sky. I wish I had just a quarter of her talent, but that was one gene she failed to pass on."

"You were named after her, right?"

Sarah nodded, for a second too choked to speak.

"Well, it's a beautiful place made for beautiful women." Dom smiled and selected first gear. "And, wow, look at those stunning colours."

He pointed to a towering tree in the centre of the grassy island that marked the end of the drive. The tree shone with a golden intensity even the thickening drizzle couldn't mask.

"That," Sarah said, grateful for the diversion, "is an Italian Maple. My father had it imported from Naples after my mother fell in love with them on their honeymoon."

Dom moved his hand from the gear lever and squeezed her knee. "Like on our honeymoon - those wonderful sapphires we got in Barbados, remember?"

"Of course. Trust my mother to prefer to bring a tree back."

Through the shimmering reflection created by the maple centrepiece, the house looked ancient and mysterious.

"My mother believed in ghosts," she said, and wondered briefly how she had told Dom so little about her mother until now. "She said the cliffs and the shore below were full of ghosts, had all sorts of stories about shipwrecks and pirates. She always insisted Charter House was haunted."

"Is it?"

Sarah shrugged. "I never saw or heard anything. Not that I

can remember, at least. I think Mother just liked the stories." She paused, feeling a smile break through. "Although, I do recall one night, my father came rushing out of the bathroom, wrapped in a bath towel. He tried to convince us later his tot of whisky caused him to be spooked by his own reflection in the mirror. But Mother wasn't buying it. She just smiled and winked at me in that enigmatic way of hers."

"Well, I hope we don't get to meet the resident ghost," said Dom, wide-eyed.

"I'm sure it was just a figment of Mother's over-active imagination." Sarah looked away, feeling the threat of tears. "It doesn't seem right, somehow."

"What doesn't?"

"Talking about my mother, thinking about her so much, on the day I've buried my father."

"Hey." Dom parked the car and leaned across to plant a soft kiss on her cheek. "You're raw. It's natural. Talk as much as you need. That's what I'm here for."

Sarah sniffed. "I'm fine. Shall we brave the rain and make a run for the house? I can give you a guided tour of my childhood."

Dom pushed open his door. A gust of damp, sea air rushed into the car. He slammed it shut again and shivered.

"God, it's windy up here. I can't believe you grew up in this house. It's beautiful but so isolated."

"I know. But we never thought of it. Mother never seemed bothered we were so far from a main road, or that it took her half a day just to get the shopping in. It was our home and I don't think I was ever afraid here. Not once. Not while my mother was still alive, anyway." She turned and gave him a quick smile. "Come on, be brave."

Sarah climbed out and stretched. Breathing in the cold, fresh air, feeling the rain stinging her face, she took a deep breath, glad to be away from the village. The house was the same as ever except for the newly constructed garage with bright red doors. A summer addition, her father had told her on the phone, following a freakish storm that sent one of the loyal old sycamores crashing through the roof of the building. Other than the garage, everything looked just as it had the day she'd left more than a decade earlier. The flower beds weren't up to her mother's standards, and the lawn was well overdue its final cut of the year, but effort had been made to keep everything neat.

Dom was struggling with their overnight bags, shoulders hunched against the persistent wind that tugged at his collar and inflated his overcoat. She was tempted to tell him this was a mild day compared to some up here on this rugged coastline, but he looked stressed enough.

"Come on," she raised her voice above the wind, "let's go in."

She gave one final glance up at the façade; at the symmetrical rows of windows like soulless eyes watching, judging her. She shook her head to clear the ridiculous image, and chided her imagination, as she scooped the bunch of keys from her handbag. Why was this so hard? Why did she feel she had to justify herself now for God's sake? It was a house – brick, wood and mortar – not a living, breathing member of the local community.

It had to be the effect of *Moelfre vision*, a term she'd coined during one of the more heated arguments with her father, not long before she'd packed her bags and booked a one-way ticket to London. How seeing things through the eyes of the people of Moelfre was like looking through the wrong end of a telescope, narrowing the whole world down until eventually everyone shared the same insular views. Where now, it seemed, her imagination would have her believe houses could pass sentence as easily as humans.

She turned the key and the door swung in with a creak; the lingering smell of open fires and stale cigar smoke greeting her. Dom dropped their bags onto the polished oak floor. The sudden silence after the roar of the wind unsettled her for a moment, and, as Dom made his way into the kitchen, she paused to glance at one of her mother's paintings hanging in the hallway. Most of the landscapes were vibrant and full of life, matching her mother's personality by depicting the colour and beauty of the island. But this one, beneath the curved staircase, was different – an eerie scene of sea mists creeping across the bay; the old house looking bleak and neglected.

A crash from the kitchen shattered her daydream.

"Dom?"

"Yeah, I'm okay. But you'd better come and have a look at this."

"What?"

Sarah turned to close the front door, pausing as a silver Volvo appeared through the mist, tyres crunching on gravel as it came to a stop under the Italian maple.

"Sarah!"

With a quick glance back at the car, she hurried along the corridor and pushed the kitchen door wide.

"What is it? Someone's just pulled up out front." She stopped, took another step forward. "Oh. Good God. What the hell is that?"

Splashes of crimson were smeared like graffiti across acres of white tiles, streaks of blood dried mid-trickle on the dusty window pane. Finally, her eyes settled on the twisted blackened form on the kitchen table.

She stumbled backwards, one hand covering her mouth, holding back a surge of bitter coffee. Her head spun and her knees buckled. She knew she was going to faint or vomit. Both. Her eyes connected with the grey painting, the angry brush strokes and the distorted image of Charter House.

Then there was darkness.

A gentle breeze caressed my face, carrying the salty smell of the ocean and the lingering sweet scent of honeysuckle. Soft fingertips brushed my forehead, and warm breath tickled my ear.

Sarah ... Sarah.

A voice called my name over and over in a sing-song lilt, like the repetition of a well-loved playground rhyme. The words were far off and fading, like the cry of a distant sea bird.

An image appeared, grey and blurred. A figure standing in the middle of an open field, surrounded by swaying grass and bathed in an aura of sunlight, and somewhere in the distance the crash of waves against rocks. My throat was dry and the air was thick with tension; I shivered in the certainty danger was close, but had no clue how I knew.

Sarah ... Sarah.

I frowned and reached out towards the image.

"Yes. Who's there? Mother? Is it you?"

The only response was the echo of my own heartbeat. I wanted so badly to believe it was her, willed the indistinct shape to clear. But there was no response, and I couldn't feel my mother's presence.

"Hello. Please. Who are you?"

The words were carried away on the breeze. I squinted, trying to force the hazy form into focus. My movements were clumsy. Everything was a struggle, like running up hill on the soft surface of sand dunes. The image faded away like the retreat of a morning mist, but the words remained, clear and focussed.

Sarah ... Sarah

I knew I had to follow the voice.

"Sarah ... Sarah! Come on, wake up."

Sarah swallowed and opened her eyes, confused as to why they were closed in the first place. Two strangers stared back at her. She squealed and pushed herself backwards as arms tightened around her shoulders, struggling until she recognised Dom.

"Wh-what?" she mumbled, trying to sit up.

"You fainted," said the stocky, bald-headed stranger. "Take a minute."

Sarah accepted the glass of water that floated into her vision, and several sips later, the whirling merry-go-round in her head slowed down enough to let her get off. She looked around, recognising the sitting room at her father's house, with its huge bay window overlooking the orchard and glimpses of ocean beyond. She drained the water and her pulse settled as she tried to co-ordinate her thoughts. A voice. Someone nearby calling to her. It had sounded like a child, she realised. A child's voice – a nursery rhyme. The memory was quite vivid. And then ... puddles of crimson ...

"Oh God, the kitchen ..."

Dom's arm tightened and he spoke over her shoulder. "No need for you to worry. I'll go and clean it up now you're okay."

"Clean it up?"

The younger man spoke, kneeling to make eye contact as he brushed a hand through straw-coloured hair. "I've checked it out, ma'am. It's not as bad as it looks. It's just a crow, must have come down the chimney on the range. Made quite a mess trying to get out. That's all. Nothing to worry about."

"Oh, I see, thank you. I feel so foolish now. But the blood ... I thought ..." She pushed away the image that gripped her on entering the kitchen, of her father dying a brutal death, alone here. She knew that was ridiculous; knew he'd passed away peacefully in his sleep. But the image had been so strong. She shook her head. "Nothing. Sorry."

"I've checked round the rest of the house, ma'am," said the other man in a heavy Irish accent. "Everything's in order."

Sarah nodded, relief rushing through her. Just a crow. Thank God. Just a bird, not a massacre or a crime scene. But that didn't explain the voice. And ... she frowned. Danger. There *was* danger. She began to shake. And these men ... they called her ma'am.

"Who are you?"

The pale-faced blond dug his hand into his wax jacket and opened a small black wallet. "Detective Sergeant Lewis. And this is my colleague DS Buchanan."

The Irish-man nodded an acknowledgement.

"Police? What's happened? Is it something to do with the child?"

Lewis frowned. "Child?"

"Yes. I thought I heard someone –"

Dom shifted his weight and the sofa dipped as he got to his feet. "Detectives, I'm not sure if you know but we've just come from my father-in-law's funeral. It's been a long and emotional day; understandably my wife's nerves are pretty shot. What she really needs is rest right now ..."

Sarah sat upright and held up a hand; she was still gripped by an inexplicable lingering fear. "No, why are you here? I want to know."

DS Lewis got up from the carpet, brushed his knees and sat in the armchair opposite. "We came to pass on our condolences about your father's death. I'd got to know him over the past year, and I was shocked to read the report of his funeral in today's paper."

Sarah studied the pale complexion and clear eyes, reading nothing in the man's face. But his partner looked uncomfortable; his cheeks had taken on a pinkish tint, and as hard as she tried she couldn't force him to maintain eye contract.

Dom spoke first. "Well, that's good of you. I'm sure we're very grateful."

"No. I'm not buying it."

"Sarah?" said Dom.

"Surely it's not normal practice to pay a visit to a grieving relative." Sarah looked from one detective to the other. "At least not one who isn't involved in a current enquiry."

The room stayed silent.

"So, how did you get to know my father, DS Lewis?" Sarah persisted.

The blond detective sighed and held up both hands in a gesture of surrender.

"Okay. I read about his death today, that much is true. I was curious about the cause of death?" He paused. The expectant look died within seconds when it was clear there was to be no response. "I've had cause to visit Charter House on quite a few occasions over the past year."

Sarah frowned. "Really. My father never mentioned that. Why?"

"He reported several cases of trespass and attempted burglary, none that were ever substantiated. He ..." Lewis paused again, glancing at his colleague, before continuing. "He'd wound himself up into a bit of a state, truth be told. He'd got it into his head someone was trying to cause him harm."

"Cause him harm," said Dom. "What kind of harm?"

"Well, there's no easy way to say it but he believed someone was trying to kill him and reported receiving death threats."

A snort of laughter escaped before Sarah had chance to contain it. "Death threats? You are joking?"

DS Buchanan cleared his throat. "Afraid not, ma'am. Jokes aren't in our job description. That's why we're here. Like DS Lewis said, we're keen to know your father's cause of death and also – although you've pretty much answered it already – whether you knew anything about your father's concerns?"

"No, of course I didn't know. I'd have come back in an instant if I thought his life was in danger. But it doesn't make sense. Who would want to kill my father? And why?"

Lewis clasped his hands between his knees as he leaned forward. "That's what we're trying to establish, Mrs Morton, whether or not these events were real or imaginary. We've not spoken to his GP as yet. But I wondered if there may have been a medical explanation? Some illness that might have caused bouts of paranoia?"

Sarah shook her head. This didn't make sense, none of it made sense. The only thing that sprang to mind was his drinking, but in all the years he'd drunk heavily he'd never been prone to paranoia. Moods swings and the occasional violent outburst, yes. But nothing like this. For some reason, Sarah wasn't ready to divulge such intimate details of her father's life or sully his memory.

"None, as far as I know, but I live in London and I have doubts my father would have told me even if there were. It might be best if you check with his doctor."

"Could you tell us who that was, ma'am?" said DS Buchanan.

"Dr Davies at Moelfre Surgery. I believe he handled the death certificate too. I'm afraid my father was self-sufficient to the extreme. I wasn't involved in organising the funeral; detailed instructions had been left with Dr Davies and my father's solicitors."

"I see." Lewis looked up from making notes on a tiny notepad. "And your father had no other family living local?"

"Only my gran on my mother's side. My mother passed away many years ago. Gran's frail and elderly and estranged from my father." Sarah bit down on her lip, trying to form some order in her thoughts. "God, I wish I'd known what was going on. I wish I'd had chance to see him. Or even just be here to take care of things. What a mess."

"It's the way with families," said DS Buchanan. "They drift apart. There's nothing you could have done differently, ma'am. No point in punishing yourself."

Sarah hesitated at the detective's words, knowing instinctively he'd experienced this same barrage of emotions. She looked up, met his gaze, and understood the mixture of pain and empathy she found there. Yes, he knew.

"I only found out he'd died two days ago. I just keep wishing things had been different." Sarah dug a tissue from her pocket. "When I got the call from Dr Davies to say he'd passed away I was in Italy. I got the first flight home and there was a letter from the undertakers informing me about the funeral arrangements – as if I were some distant relative rather than his only daughter. It's been so difficult to accept and I keep thinking how I carried on as normal while …"

Dom squeezed her hand as tears choked off the words. "It's been a tough few days, detective. Is there anything else we can help you with?"

Lewis shook his head and got to his feet. "Not at this stage. We'll pay a visit to Dr Davies, make a few enquiries. Even if there was no diagnosis, paranoia can creep in all forms with the elderly. I had it with my own mother. I'm sure it's no more than that."

Sarah stood up, the icy memories of the dream still vivid. She'd sensed danger, had her father sensed it too?

"I don't think my father was suffering from paranoia, detective. I know … knew him. He was as level-headed as you or I. What if the death threats were genuine? We've just buried him, that has to count for something, doesn't it? We're surely doing him a disservice if we just stand around nodding and bemoaning old age. Detective, promise me, this will be fully investigated. I wasn't here for my father when he was alive. I have to live with that. I don't want to let him down now."

It was Detective Buchanan who stepped forward, resting a hand on her elbow.

"You can rest assured we'll be following every line of enquiry, nothing will be overlooked." He handed across a business card. "If you need us or anything occurs to you or whatever. You call, okay?"

Sarah nodded, resenting the sting of fresh tears. "Thank you. As ridiculous as this all sounds, I have to know his death was peaceful, natural." She thought again of the distant voice, her reaction to the dead bird, and the heaviness that had weighted her down since she'd stepped foot inside Charter House. "I have to know."

Both detectives nodded, and after assuring them she would be in the area for the next few days, made their goodbyes.

As she stood on the doorstep watching the silver Volvo melt into the deepening dusk, she pulled up the collar of her jacket and let her mind roam. What had been happening at Charter House? Discounting her father's mental frailty, which she didn't buy for a second, what else could have possibly put him in danger? She stared at the row of sycamores, melting into the darkness one by one as the Volvo's headlights disappeared down the drive. In the grey light, she could almost imagine the swaying branches were moving forms, beckoning to her. Was it this kind of loneliness that had sent her father into a different reality, or had his life been in serious danger?

Perhaps, she thought, as she stepped back into the hallway and secured all the bolts behind her, the mysterious solicitor held the answers.

* * *

Red pressed himself flat against the bark of the tree trunk as the silver car crunched in a circle, headlamps sweeping towards him like searchlights. He held his breath until it passed, and was about to step out into the red glare of the rear lights to get a look at the number plate, when he realised Sarah was standing in the doorway, staring right at him. He flattened himself back against the tree, panting hard.

The thump of adrenaline through his bloodstream, partly from fear and partly the effect of Sarah's proximity, made him as edgy as a crack addict. But he willed himself to stay still and not do anything he'd regret. Christ, last thing he needed was for her to see him now. He waited, keeping one eye on the slim figure as she stood deep in thought. He was close enough to read the troubled expression on her face as she unconsciously wound her wedding ring round and round her finger. He'd love nothing more than to comfort her, pull her into his arms and keep her safe.

Was it only grief that troubled her? Or something more? He'd put a month's wages on these pair of Herberts being coppers. He might have been wrong back at the church, but these had the stench of arrogance – copper's perfume he called it. He'd only seen them for a matter of minutes as they'd climbed into the car. But that was more than enough. He'd seen a flash of fair hair, tall and lithe, while the other guy had looked more the English bulldog type. The archetypal good cop, bad cop pairing.

His pulse quickened as he chided his impatience. He'd had his face pressed against the back door window of the Volvo – making out only a pair of mud-covered walking boots and an Ordinance Survey map – when he heard voices and realised the visitors were leaving. He'd just made it into the shadows of the garage, when the first footstep crunched on the gravelled drive. Christ that had been a near one. What he should have done, what he'd now failed to do, was take down a note of the registration number and run a search later. There'd been no need to creep round and risk getting caught.

It was this kind of impulsiveness he was doing his level best to overcome. He started as the front door slammed and he heard the heavy bolts – one, two, three – slide into place. Sarah had disappeared; it was time to move, while it was safe. There was nothing to be gained hanging around here any longer.

The husband had failed to call, so this was his last attempt at friendly negotiation. If the note got no response, then it was straight onto plan B. He rubbed his hands together as he hurried down the driveway, keeping in the lengthening shadows along the verge, trying not to think about the damage the sodden grass was doing to his shoes. When he reached the lane, he crossed it in seconds and melted in the trees, heading along the unmarked public footpath through the woods. His car was tucked away next to a disused forestry commission hut, and he reached it in minutes.

Knowing the island as intimately as his own dick was one of his greatest strengths. Having a tender spot that no amount of years seemed to harden was his biggest weakness.

He smirked at his own wit, started the car and kept the lights off until he reached the lane, and then turned left towards the main road; a few pints and maybe a nice Madras calling.

If there was to be a response this time, it wouldn't be until the morning, or whenever Sarah's hubby next came to drive his precious BMW and wondered who'd been sitting in his seat –

like the Daddy-bear to Sarah's Goldilocks.

He laughed and accelerated away into the night.

Chapter Four

"Mrs Morton? Would you like to follow me? Mr Carter will see you now."

Sarah gave a grateful smile to the receptionist, glad to escape the oppressive magnolia room, with its dusty potted plants and two-year-old Tatlers. There was always a sense of foreboding about waiting rooms. Dentists and the fear of fillings; doctors and the fear of incurable diseases. And then places like this, anything to do with *officialdom*, always took her outside her comfort zone.

She followed up a flight of narrow stairs, and through a labyrinth of corridors, all decorated in the same muted tones. She imagined Dom in the supermarket, where she'd sent him for supplies, walking the aisles as agitated as she was. He'd been insistent, to the point of bullying, about driving her into Llangefni, declaring that her nerves needed time to heal and what else was he supposed to do kicking his heels alone at the house. Sarah was more convinced that he was uneasy letting her take control of his beloved motor down Anglesey's infamous lanes.

The girl rapped on the door at the end of a long corridor, and without waiting for a reply, pushed it open.

Adrian Carter greeted her with a limp handshake, and indicated a chair in front of a desk that half-filled the small room. He wore the same tight-fitting suit as yesterday, this time co-ordinated, or perhaps not, with a mint-green shirt and grey and emerald striped tie. It seemed the ruddy cheeks and cheap aftershave were also permanent features.

He pulled open a desk drawer, removed a folder and slid out a white envelope.

"Right, well then, let's get down to business," he said, nudging his chair closer to the desk. "I'm carrying out instructions issued by your father, Professor Owen Williams, on May 10th this year. A signed copy of his witnessed statement is enclosed in this file."

He slid the envelope across the desk. Sarah's eyes locked on her father's signature, scrawled in his usual elaborate style across the seal. Her heart quickened as the reality of his death caught her unawares, and she was struck again with the sense of falseness. As if she were going through the motions, each step carefully pre-planned, but still none of it seemed real.

She forced herself to listen to the solicitor.

"Your father left a series of instructions to be carried out in the event of his death occurring within twelve months of the date of our meeting. As that has subsequently been the case, I'm carrying out his wishes in accordance with his instructions. He asked that his only daughter, Sarah Jane Morton, nee Williams, be contacted immediately – as soon as we received notification of his death. Unfortunately, the mobile number we had on file wasn't recognised, and you failed to reply to the letter we sent to your home address … so I had to hope you'd be at the funeral service. Again, apologies for my presence yesterday, it's not normal procedure to track down a grieving relative at the cemetery, I can assure you."

"But I didn't receive any post from you. Perhaps it arrived after we left London? And I lost my mobile phone a couple of months ago, and had to have a new number. I'm sure I passed it on to my father though."

"It could be that he simply forgot to notify us." Adrian Carter frowned as he flicked through the pages in the file. "Or, I suppose we could have omitted to amend the records. I'll look into that." He scribbled a few notes on the pad in front of him. "So, let us take a look at your father's instructions –"

"I'm not sure I understand any of this …"

"It's not normal procedure admittedly, but it is still legally binding. So, I'll read aloud your father's statement. If you have any questions at the end, I'll be happy to answer them to the best of my ability. Okay?"

Sarah nodded and crossed her legs. A weird sense of unease passed through her body; the same sensation she'd had yesterday. Something was wrong. She couldn't put her finger on what it was exactly, but the solicitor's words, added to the police visit and the secrecy of this meeting, made her deeply uneasy. Her father may well have had his faults, but the more she thought about it, the more she determined that paranoia had never been one of them.

Adrian Carter cleared his throat and smoothed a sheet of paper, covered with bold typeface, on the desk in front of him.

"I, Professor Owen Williams, of able mind and body, have on this day made a list of requests to be carried out by my legal advisors and executors Carter, Carter & Sons (Llangefni) in the event of my death occurring within twelve months of the date of this document.

I hereby request that my daughter, Sarah Jane Morton, be contacted within twenty-four hours of my death, and given the sealed envelope contained within this file. I wish her to attest that the envelope is still in a perfect, sealed condition on receipt, and sign to validate this fact.

In the event of Sarah's death occurring before my own, I ask that Luke Evans, of Ty Nant Farm, Llanallgo, be made my sole executor, and asked to handle all dealings henceforth.

Under no circumstances must the contents of this file be passed to any other person – be it family or professional or legal.

This is my legal undertaking on this day."

Sarah cleared her throat. "Is that it?"

Adrian Carter nodded. "I'm afraid so. I understand it may be a bit of an anti-climax, but your father was determined to make it legally binding. There's nothing else in his instructions, other than it was signed by himself and witnessed by the young lady who attended the appointment with him."

"Young lady?"

"Yes." He held the sheet of paper up close to his nose. "Can't quite make out the signature. I or J ... G ... something."

"And she attended with my father?"

"Yes. I assume she knew him well as she was with him on both occasions we met. And he was adamant she witness the statement, and she was also given another sealed envelope, I assumed a copy of the letter he left for you."

"That's really odd. I've no idea who that could be. I didn't know my father knew any young women. It could have been a student, I suppose –"

"She was very young. Early to mid-twenties, I'd say. Slim with long blonde hair, looked quite similar to you actually. But younger, of course."

Carter's face went a deeper crimson as he shuffled the papers on his desk. Not one for the compliments certainly, but the mystery girl seemed to have left a lasting impression on the young Mr Carter.

"So, let me get this straight," Sarah said. "Despite my father requesting complete secrecy about this matter, he was willing to divulge everything to a young girl who is a stranger to both of us?"

Carter gave a brief shrug. "It would appear so."

"But it makes no sense."

"Perhaps the contents will enlighten you."

He nodded towards the envelope. Sarah glanced at it, not missing the look of keen expectation in the man's eyes. Her father's words came back to her; she could almost hear the gravel of his tone ... *contents passed to any other person – be it family or professional or legal.*

"Perhaps."

She touched the clear plastic strip, tracing her fingertips along her father's signature.

"It is still sealed," Carter said.

"Oh, yes, I can see that. I was just wondering if I'm expected to read it here on your premises, or take it home with me."

"There's no mention of that in your father's instructions, so I doubt it matters either way. I will admit I'm intrigued by the contents, but that's on a purely personal basis. There's nothing to say the contents will require any legal assistance."

She picked up the bulky envelope. "So, do you think it's his Will?"

Again, the solicitor shrugged. "I've really no idea. It seems an odd thing to do if it is, but it's possible. And as long as it's been independently witnessed, it would still be legally binding."

"But he's not made any other Will … besides this document, I mean?"

"Not that I'm aware of. He could of course, have used another law office, but I would very much doubt it. He said he'd lost faith in the last practice he dealt with in Holyhead. I can't imagine him going back there, but you might want to check."

Sarah nodded and mulled over what she'd learned. Little of it made sense. As she looked up into the intense brown eyes of Adrian Carter, she made a decision based more on gut instinct than anything else.

"Then, I think I'll take it home and deal with it there. Do I need to sign anything?"

With a sigh of barely concealed frustration, Carter slid a sheet of duplicated paper across the desk and indicated the space for her signature.

As the appointment with Morton had taken less than half an hour, Sarah headed for the café on the opposite side of the High Street. Dom would be at least another hour; there was no way she could wait till she got home. The envelope burned her fingers. Besides, her father's words replayed in her head like a stuck record ... *contents passed to any other person – be it family or professional or legal.*

Sarah grabbed a bottle of fizzy water, the quickest thing on the menu, and settled at a secluded table at the rear, away from chattering OAPS and grizzling babies. With trembling fingers, she tore open the envelope. Four sheets of thick writing paper slid onto the table, along with a small silver key. She picked up the key and examined it. She'd never seen it before. It looked like some sort of safe key.

Three sheets were covered in her father's neat black script. The fourth was an old map of the island, yellowed with age. She turned over the pages and began to read.

'My Dearest Daughter,

If you are reading this, cariad, then my fears have been realised. I am sorry. So heartily sorry. If you could see me now, you would laugh and tick me off, no doubt. Or maybe you'd say nothing and walk away? That would certainly be nothing less than I deserve.

For a seasoned old fart historian, I'm finding this very difficult. Or perhaps that should be seasoned old drunk. I sit in my bed surrounded by crumpled papers and empty bottles. At first, I welcomed the glorious May sunshine flooding the room, but I've closed the curtains now. Shut it out. The empty bottles look better in the dimness. Inebriation seems to find me too easily. You must think me a disgrace, and rightly so.

I am so sorry.

But this is not about me, Sarah. This letter is extremely important. I need you to understand that. This letter is a key to a lot of things, but most of all it is your only chance of safety.

You know I have spent much of my life tracing our family's ancestry. I know you have never shared my love of all things antiquated, and have learned to accept this. But you must remember stories of why Charter House was built on its current position, and the tales still told about the shipwreck around Ynys Mon to this day.

Well, since my retirement, I have researched the history in detail. A few months ago I discovered something new. Something startling in fact.

Since then, attempts have been made on my life, and yes, I'm old and the whisky runs through my veins and I deserve to tumble down the stairs. I accept that. I can well imagine your look of disbelief. Probably contempt. But the truth is above me. This is not about me. This is for you, Sarah.

The possibility I have been murdered is extremely high. I have enclosed a documented list of previous incidents. But my fear is thus. The probability you may be next is even greater. I know how this sounds. But believe me, Sarah, it is the truth. I don't want to frighten you, but if that's what it takes, maybe I should. Tell not a living soul about this letter. I shall make sure the solicitor is sworn to secrecy, and if I think they have betrayed my trust, I shall go elsewhere.

There is a difficult and dangerous journey for you ahead – but trust me that it is one worth taking. This is for you, Sarah. Your safety. Your future. You have the right to your family's inheritance. Trust no one. You are an intelligent woman, but it will be a hard task for you to distinguish friend from foe.

I will be with you every step of the way.

Remember your mother's favourite lullaby? Remember the code?

Go to my safe as soon as you can. Inside you will find instructions.

Sarah, I've messed up a lot. Ruined lives. Some you already know, more you have yet to learn. I apologise for it all. I lost your mother, lost my beautiful daughter.

I lost both my Sarahs – and it has been a hard price to pay.

I'm sorry for pushing you away. Even as a child, I thought only of myself. Sending you away to boarding school was easier than watching you blossom every day into a replica of your beautiful mother. *So selfish, I see it all now. I'm sorry for stifling, where I should have been encouraging such a gifted young mind.*

My own beautiful daughter and I turned you against me. I'm not the monster I see in the mirror at times, but I know you see it too.

May God forgive me.

I know I'm selfish. Stupidly stubborn. Boorishly bad tempered. So why would you listen? M'yn Diawl, YOU MUST! I do this now to make up for all my failings. It's all there is left to do. To try to put right some of my wretched wrongs.

I love you so much, Sarah.

So much. I need to tell you that I'm crying. Damned selfish again, yes, and I will most likely be damned for it all. But I'm damned right now if I don't get this right for you. My heart is torn apart. I'm sobbing like a sad old fool. You're reading this and I am dead. Dead! That hurts. In fact it sounds all wrong. But it isn't wrong. It's too late to make up. Too late for forgiveness. But not too late for you.

Please Sarah, trust me now – get to the safe!

With any heart I might have, I love you so much, cariad.

Dad x

Tears clouded her vision as she came to the end. Sarah dropped the sheets of paper onto the table, cupped her face in her hands, and let them come.

* * *

A polyphonic ringtone shattered Red's dream. Kings of Leon was probably not the most soothing sound to start the day, but it worked for him, and certainly cut through the fug of sleep pretty fast. He yawned and stretched, blinking as he reached out in the gloom towards the flashing blue neon. He scratched his scalp and propped himself on his elbow as he squinted at the screen. It was a mobile number he didn't know.

He coughed and accepted the call. "Hello."

"Who is this?"

"Er …" Red frowned, checked the display again. "You rang me, pal. Who are you?"

"Dominic Morton. You seem to be making a bit of a pest of yourself and I'd like an explanation. And I'm not your pal."

"Ah." Red sat upright, shaking his head to get his brain working. He groped around on the bedside table, trying to find his watch. Pale grey light streamed through the gap in the curtains, so he'd clearly slept in. He hated dark mornings; he couldn't seem to function without daylight.

"Ah … what?" The voice sounded tetchy on the other end of the phone. "What's with the cryptic bullshit? And who are you? Don't play games with me, I warn you. You don't want to mess with me or my wife."

Red cleared his throat. "I've no intention of upsetting anyone, Dom. May I call you Dom? I'm actually trying to do you a favour. You and your wife."

"Go on."

"I think it would be better if we were to meet in person. You name the time and place and I'll be there."

"Look, I've no intention of arranging any meeting unless you tell me what the hell this is all about. You could be a bloody maniac for all I know. It's certainly not normal to accost someone at a funeral or leave cryptic notes inside my car. Have you never heard of trespass?" Red bit back the sarcastic response. "Either you start talking or I pass your phone number onto the police." Static hissed. "And you can call me Mr Morton."

Red paused, needing a moment to consider how to redress the balance of power. He didn't know much about Dominic Morton, other than he was a professional footballer, drove a flash motor, and was probably well minted. But weren't all football players supposed to be as thick as pig shit with brains in their feet? Or their trousers? Well, this guy certainly wasn't stupid. But then, neither was Red. It would serve no purpose to antagonise *Mr*

Morton at this stage, but he had to regain control. And fast.

"I totally get where you're coming from, but believe me, there is good reason. I didn't make a big deal at the funeral as I'd no wish to further upset your wife at such a delicate time. I thought you'd want to protect her, which is why I've suggested a meeting in private. Once you've heard what I have to say, I'll be guided by your judgement as to how to handle things going forward. If you decide you want to tell Sarah, then that's your call, but personally I think at this stage she's got more than enough to contend with."

The silence hung, thick and oppressive.

"How do you know my wife?" Dom asked eventually.

Red swallowed and ran his tongue across his teeth. Lager and Madras. Never such a good idea the morning after.

"Who said I did?"

"The familiarity in your tone for one thing."

"Perhaps I did know her, in another life. And perhaps that's why you'll believe I'm trying to do her a favour. Look, what's to lose? I'm no maniac, but I'm sure you're more than capable of handling yourself anyway. Meet me and see. Then decide."

The other man sighed and Red punched the air. He slid open the bedside drawer and helped himself to a cigarette. Flicking his lighter, he drew in, closing his eyes as the nicotine surged through his bloodstream. He deserved it. His controlled approach was beginning to work. He could feel it.

"I still need to know more."

Red inhaled again, taking his time. The glowing tip illuminated the shadows of the room in an orange hue.

"What if I told you I had evidence Sarah's father had been murdered?"

He heard a sharp intake of breath. The pause lengthened.

"What evidence?" said Morton.

"I can't say. Not now."

"So, why not go to the police?"

"I have my reasons."

"Go on."

"That's your lot for now."

Another deep sigh. "Okay. Where?"

Red mentally scanned the area, guessing the other man's knowledge would be limited.

"The public footpath that leads along the cliff from Charter House towards Point Lynas. There's an old disused Trinity House lookout halfway. I'll meet you there first thing in the morning, about 9am. How does that sound?"

"It sounds like I could be signing my own death warrant."

Red laughed. "You're not. I promise. Believe me, I just want to help."

"Okay. Tomorrow morning. But I'm doing this for Sarah, and any funny business and I'm straight to the police. You understand?"

"Totally. See you tom –"

The dial tone cut him off. But he'd got the meeting. It was a start. Time to formulate the next stage of Plan A.

* * *

Danny checked his watch for the third time. Lack of punctuality was his pet hate. He was rarely, without the strongest of reasons, ever late for anything. He hated that panicky pressure that tightened his chest until he couldn't breathe. He would always be early for any appointment. Always set out an hour too soon for a long journey. Always arrived at an airport before check-in opened. Better to be early than late. It was a sign of manners, good up-bringing, so his ma always said, and she was right. But the consequence of this trait was that he detested being kept waiting himself. A ten minute delay would leave him as edgy as if he were the guilty party.

And so it was that their appointment with Dr Davies at Moelfre Surgery was pencilled in for one pm. The secretary – herself an ex-MI5 agent he'd no doubt – had made it perfectly clear that the ten-minute slot was the only space in the doctor's schedule. And if that were missed, well, they could kiss goodbye to an appointment this year.

And so, here he'd sat in his car, for the past twenty-two minutes, waiting for Geraint Lewis. It was now 12.38pm and they had at least a forty minute drive to Moelfre – which meant the whole arrangement had been shot to pieces because Lewis had been called to Thompson's office as they were leaving.

Just as he'd made up his mind to go find Lewis, his mobile trilled like an old 1970s telephone. He unclipped his seat belt and dug into his coat pocket. He hated mobiles, and this was the simplest, most basic phone he could find. Lewis's number flashed.

"About bloody time. Where are you?"

Lewis sounded breathless as if he'd been running. "You're going to have to go without me, sorry, mate. Thompson's had Cheshire CID on. I've been called to a shooting, a suspected contract killing no less, in Ellesmere Port."

Danny frowned. "Why you?"

"It's a Pole. Janus Novak. Symanski's right hand man until he turned informant. Mine."

"Shite."

"Yeah. Symanski has to be behind it and I have to prove it. I've *got* to go." Danny heard a car door slam. "I don't know how long I'll be away, so will you follow up the Williams' case? I'm feeling bad that I dismissed the old guy now, after meeting his daughter. You can handle the doc, can't you?"

"I could if I'd had chance to review the file; I don't even know the details of these supposed death threats –"

"Suspected tampering of the brakes on his Jaguar … twice. Suspected tampering with house electrics. Suspected tampering with an ancient tree that demolished his garage. Suspected poisoning. Suspected murder of his pet cat, Percy. Four reported break-ins, not one of which ever resulted in missing items. And, last but not least, nine reports of suspicious person or persons unknown trespassing in the grounds of his house."

"Christ, how am I supposed to remember all that?"

"You'll be fine, mate. Good luck. I'll speak to you later."

Danny tossed the phone onto the passenger seat. He glanced at the dashboard clock. 12:45. His rib cage began to contract and his heart rate doubled as he started the engine and headed for the dual-carriageway. Hopefully the journey would calm his nerves.

Half an hour later he sat, sweaty and flustered, in a bright white waiting room, flashing an apologetic smile at the receptionist every few seconds. He scan-read the notices about regular checks for various cancers and the risk of high blood pressure. Christ, this was a hypochondriac's heaven, but Danny couldn't wait to get out. He hated these places, second only to hospitals. The doctor was taking a phone call and would be with him shortly, he'd been told, with a look from *Herr Nurse* that implied he should be more than grateful. He checked his watch. 1:18pm. God, he couldn't remember the last time he'd been eighteen minutes late in his life –

"Detective Buchanan?"

Danny looked up. Gold-rimmed spectacles, white hair, a yellow short-sleeved shirt, and a deep golden tan were his first impressions. Danny shook the outstretched hand and followed the stout man into his office.

"Can I get you a tea, coffee, anything?" said Dr Davies as they settled into chairs either side of his desk.

"No. Thank you."

"You don't mind if I carry on, do you?" Dr Davies gestured to the remains of a cheese salad baguette and a mug of tea. "I have house calls to start at two. It's a fallacy GPs have an easy life, you know." He smiled and took a bite.

"Of course. I'm grateful for your time." Danny dug out his notebook. "I'm not sure how much your secretary told you but I wondered if I could ask a few questions about the death of one of your patients –"

Dr Davies swallowed, wiped his fingers on a napkin and tapped a yellow folder that matched the colour of his shirt.

"Yes. Bronwen brought me the file. Mr Williams, is it? Owen. I was shocked to hear of his death, I must say, but I'm not sure how I can help?"

"First off I wondered if I could see a copy of the death certificate and if you could clarify the cause of death?"

Dr Davies pulled his chair closer to the desk. "Righto. Why's that? Is there a problem?"

"Not necessarily. We're just looking for information at this stage."

"Well, see, I didn't actually issue the death certificate for Owen Williams."

"You didn't?"

"No, he passed away while I was on holiday; a cruise for my silver wedding anniversary. I only got back a couple of days ago and managed to get in contact with Sarah when I heard. Damn shame, but there you are." Dr Davies popped the last of his baguette into his mouth and pulled his keyboard towards him. "Let me just check the records. I presume the death certificate was posted straight to the undertakers at their request, but let me see if we have a copy on file. Bear with me. I'm not great with computers."

Dr Davies typed with two fingers. "Ah, yes, here it is. It was our locum, Dr Fisher, who attended the scene and issued the certificate. Cause of death, pneumonia and heart failure." He frowned. "That's odd …"

"What?"

"I didn't know Owen had contracted pneumonia, but for an instant diagnosis to have been made, then I'd expect them to consult his medical history. Let me come out of this and find his records."

"How was Mr William's health in general?"

Dr Davies looked up from the computer screen. "Strong as

an ox, old Owen. He did suffer from Type 2 diabetes. He was a drinker which played havoc with that - but I've lost count of the arguments we had on that subject. Last time I saw him was for a chest infection a couple of months ago. Other than that he had a routine repeat prescription for indigestion relief and another for his insulin and diabetic medication." Dr Davies continued to press keys. "God, I hate these things, be quicker to call Bronwen. Ah, here we go … let's just double check his records."

Dr Davies fell silent as he scanned the notes. "Well, it all seems in order. Dr Fisher must have looked at the chest infection details from September and matched them with the symptoms on the body. Perhaps Owen hadn't been taking care of himself and it had developed into pneumonia."

"And heart failure?"

"It's pretty standard on a death certificate, detective. I've yet to see a corpse whose heart still beats."

"But, if you don't mind my saying, it all seems a bit generic. Shouldn't there have been a post mortem?"

Dr Davies shook his head. "No. Not in a natural causes death. Not with a person in their mid-seventies who has a medical history that ties up with the GP's findings at the scene. Post mortems are only carried out for unexplained deaths, or where there is no medical history to refer to, as I'm sure you know."

"But what if there was a chance it wasn't natural causes?"

Dr Davies sat back in his chair. "Detective, can I ask, where's all this going?"

"We're simply following up enquiries at this stage. Mr Williams had some concerns before he died –"

"Concerns? What kind of concerns?"

"We're led to believe Mr Williams feared for his safety. He'd been receiving threats –"

"Death threats?" Dr Davies pulled off his glasses and stared at Danny. "No."

Danny nodded. "He contacted CID on numerous occasions. I think you've already answered my next question, but was there anything in Mr Williams' medical history that might point to this kind of behaviour?"

"Paranoia, you mean?" Dr Davies shook his head. "No history of Alzheimer's and no sign of dementia. Owen was as sound mentally as physically. And yet ..."

"Yes?"

Dr Davies rubbed the bridge of his nose, deep in thought, before slipping his glasses back on.

"Now you mention it, he did seem troubled. No. Distracted. And he looked exhausted the last time I saw him. He came about his cough, keeping him awake, he said. I asked if he wanted me to prescribe a short course of sleeping tablets as well as the antibiotics and he looked at me in horror. As if ... oh, I don't know, it sounds crazy ... but as if he didn't want to sleep."

"And did you give him the pills?"

"No. He wouldn't hear of it. I thought he might have been drinking more than usual – he had a grey, unhealthy tinge about him, you know? I told him to get some fresh air, take more exercise if he could, to build his strength and make him physically tired. He seemed content enough when he left. But not quite the robust man I knew. Old age creeping up, maybe."

"But definitely nothing that indicated onset of a mental illness?"

"Well, at Owen's age, you can never rule anything out totally. But certainly nothing that gave me cause for concern."

"One final point – you said you were shocked by Owen's death, without wanting to cause any offence, are you satisfied with the death certificate?"

Dr Davies sipped his tea and took several moments before answering. "I was shocked when I heard, yes, and knowing what I know now, I would probably have requested a post mortem. But I don't attribute any blame to Dr Fisher, he did everything by the book."

"Could you speak to Dr Fisher? Satisfy yourself of his conclusions?"

"It's a little late for a second opinion, Detective."

"Not necessarily. There are such things as exhumations."

"Of course, but that would seem a little extreme at this stage." Dr Davies checked his watch, rose and pulled on his jacket. "I'll speak to Dr Fisher and report back to you. But honestly, detective, if both he and the police officers in attendance were satisfied the death was natural, why should we doubt them?"

Danny slid back his chair and got to his feet. "Perhaps because a man who believed someone was trying to kill him is now dead?"

Chapter Five

As soon as Sarah heard the rumble of the hot water cistern, and Dom's singing coming from the shower, she pressed play on the tape deck. It had been her stereo originally, bought as a present for her tenth birthday, but had soon become outdated, outgrown and abandoned. Her father had used it to record speeches for his seminars and also to indulge in his love of Mozart and Gershwin.

She took a long swallow of Chardonnay and replaced the glass on her father's desk with a shaky hand. Everything was so surreal. From the moment they'd arrived in Moelfre. And now … what was she doing? Why couldn't she discuss the meeting with the solicitor with Dom? And why had she hidden her father's letter? She couldn't yet fathom it even to herself. Dom had seemed pacified – if not exactly happy – with her excuse she needed a bit of time alone, and the promise they'd talk later that evening after the dinner he'd offered to cook.

The cassette was where she'd known it would be, behind a bottle of Scotch, shoved to the back of the top drawer of her father's desk.

Static crackled as the old machine whirred into life, then suddenly, the sound of her mother's voice filled the room.

'Summertime and the living is easy,
Fish are jumping and the cotton is high,'

Her mother had loved to sing, another of her talents; the choir at the local church was the only passion to ever steal her away from family and her garden. They became famous after winning local heats and performing at the Eisteddfod in Llangollen. Sarah could still feel the surge of pride as her mother stood centre stage, to a spellbound audience, singing the lullaby which had always been just for her.

Hairs stood up on Sarah's arms, and her eyes filled with tears as she remembered the awful time after her mother's funeral when she'd refused to even close her eyes to attempt sleep until this tape was playing on a loop.

'Your daddy's rich, and your ma is good looking,
So hush little baby, don't you cry.'

In Sarah's nine-year-old brain it was the only memory she could still hold on to. By that time, even the smell on her mother's dressing gown that hung on the back of the bathroom door had faded. Each morning, Sarah would hold the frayed terry-towelling to her face as silent tears dripped from her chin. The smell grew fainter and fainter, until eventually it disappeared.

The tape was her salvation; it brought her mother back to her, night after night.

Until one evening when her father swept into her bedroom in an alcohol-fuelled rage, ejected the cassette and threw it against the wall with such force that it shattered into tiny pieces.

"For God's sake, will you give this bloody music a rest!" His voice shook the floorboards and Sarah cowered against the wall, eyes wide and scared, clutching her favourite teddy bear.

He dropped to his knees, pounded the floor with his fists. "I'm so sorry, so sorry, forgive me."

For a moment Sarah was rigid, afraid to move, until he'd looked up; his creased face streaming with tears. He held his arms open. "Please …" he said.

Sarah went to him. He embraced her so hard she struggled to

breathe. She could smell the sweet scent of whisky on his breath as she burrowed her head into his chest.

"You are so special to me, cariad," he said, as he rocked her in his arms, his voice distorted by emotion. "I never meant to scare you, please forgive me. But it's more than I can bear to hear her voice, night after night. I know you think it helps you, I feel your pain. It's natural and it's called grief. Do you understand what that means?"

Sarah shook her head as her thumb crept between her lips.

He sighed and pulled her hand from her mouth. "When we lose someone we love, we have to learn to adjust. We have to come to terms with the fact that life carries on as normal around us, even though inside we feel like dying too. We feel angry because Mummy should be here, with us, and she's not. So, we try to find something we can cling to, some memory that keeps the person alive to us. And in so doing, keeps the pain at bay." Her father ran a hand through his hair. "Duw … I miss her so much. I'm terrible at this kind of thing. But, do you see what I mean?"

"I think so. But that's Mummy's song."

He smiled and smoothed a hand across her hair. "It wasn't Mummy's song really. It was from a musical, you know, like *The Sound of Music* or *The Wizard of Oz*? It was called *Porgy and Bess* and was really old, made about 1935, I think. Nearly as old as me, and that's old, isn't it?" Sarah smiled and relaxed a little. "But your mother adored it, and adored that song even more. But when I hear it now, I think of you as a baby in her arms as she rocked you to sleep." He stopped and gulped, lowering his gaze to his lap, where he twisted his gold wedding ring round his finger. "And sometimes it hurts too much to hear it over and over, do you understand now?"

"I'm sorry if I hurt you, Daddy."

With a low moan, he pulled Sarah into his arms. "You didn't hurt me, cariad. Life, guilt and loneliness hurt me. You're all I have now, and I love you more than life itself. But you have to learn to let go of Mummy. We have to learn to live without her. We have to learn to grieve together. Can we try?"

Sarah nodded as tears slid down her cheeks. "But I miss Mummy so much."

"So do I, angel. But we can't bring her back just because we hear her voice. I will never stop you playing that tape. I promise I'll get a new copy made for you. But not every day, every night, over and over. It's not helping you … and it's not helping me."

"Okay. But promise we can talk about Mummy more, then I won't need to listen to her singing."

He nodded, his gaze watery. "You're such a wise child; you take after Sarah in so many ways. Not just that you grow to look more like her with each passing day." He sighed and stroked her cheek. "From now on, we will talk about her every single day. And every year on her birthday in May, we'll get out this tape and play it all day long. How does that sound?"

Sarah nestled her head into his chest, feeling the thud of his heartbeat as his arms wrapped around her.

'One of these mornings, you're gonna rise up singing,
You're gonna spread your wings as you take to the sky,
But till that morning, there's nothing can harm you,
With your daddy and mommy standing by.'

Sarah sniffed and wiped a hand across her face, before draining her wine glass. God, had that conversation really taken place over twenty years ago? She could remember it as if it was yesterday.

As the tape crackled and whined to an end, Sarah crossed the room, the scent of cigar smoke heavier as she passed her father's fire-side chair. With care, she lifted another of her mother's paintings – this one a winter's scene of Snowdonia – from the wall. Part of her wanted to hurry to get the safe open, ready to believe her father's torrent of warnings. The other part remembered similar alcohol-induced rants from the past, and she couldn't help but view the letter with a huge degree of scepticism. Probably one reason she'd held back from telling Dom.

She would have remembered the safe combination, even without her father's reminder. Her mother's birthday, the one day they were allowed to bring her back to life every year, usually fell around the Whitsun Bank Holiday. It had become a regular day trip out, usually to Snowdonia, Porthmadog or Caernarfon.

Sarah keyed the code into the digital panel, and watched the red numbers flash. The panel beeped and the metal door swung open.

It took ten minutes to unload the safe and pile the contents onto her father's desk. There was so much to go through it would take hours, days even, and she'd no idea what she was looking for. Among the contents were four complete manuscripts, parcelled up separately. There were articles and two books on something called *The Mabinogion* – which she remembered was something to do with Welsh medieval legends. It didn't surprise her that her father was interested in that kind of stuff – it's what he'd lectured on all his life – but what did puzzle her was why it had been locked inside the safe with all his personal paperwork.

On the top shelf of the safe, among jewellery boxes that held the last of her mother's jewels, was a black velvet bag half-full of what looked like gold sovereigns – eleven in total. And alongside the bag, another sealed white envelope with her name printed on the front in her father's neat script. Ripping the envelope open, she slipped out a single piece of paper; again her father's distinctive hand filled one side.

Sarah,

You have made it to step two. The phone number below will lead you to step three. Don't delay.

Please keep an open mind and trust everything you hear, however incredible it seems. And please, please, cariad, I beg of you to tell no one and take this next step alone. Secrecy is paramount,

Sarah, please keep yourself safe.
   Good luck, my precious angel.
   Dad x

Sarah read the letter through again, and her frown deepened. What on earth was her father playing at? Why couldn't he just leave a Will like a normal person? All this cloak and dagger business, death threats and whatnot. Was it linked to the identity of the mystery woman in Carter's office? The more she tried to figure it out, the more confused and angry she became. This was typical of her father. He'd loved playing games, and as a child, she'd adored the treasure hunts he spent hours organising for her and her friends. But this was ridiculous. And what about the *… secrecy is paramount … please keep yourself safe*. What was all that about for God's sake?

She shuffled through a few of the papers, looking for anything that might be 'Will-like.' Her eyes strayed again to the letter; the phone number was a local code. She reached out for the telephone, hand hovering over the receiver. Should she call now?

Sarah registered Dom's singing had moved to the kitchen and from the spicy smells drifting through the house, dinner was well under way. She should wait. And perhaps she ought to hold off telling Dom until she'd had chance to go through all the papers, make this top-secret phone call, and follow up this mystery woman.

Sarah collected the manuscripts and books together, crammed them back into the safe as quickly as possible, then paused. What exactly was she doing? What was stopping her from telling Dom? Was she really going to start mistrusting her own husband because of a few words written in a letter from a bitter, probably senile, old drunk? Just because her father hadn't liked or trusted Dom – and had made his views abundantly clear – it was no reason for her to start distrusting him too.

No, they'd talk after dinner. Dom would know what to do

next. She folded up the note and slipped it into the pocket of her jeans.

"Not hungry, babe?" Dom asked.

Sarah looked down at her plate and shook her head. "I'm sorry, but no, not really. It's lovely, thank you, but there's too much going on in my head."

She dropped her fork and pushed the plate across the table. Her appetite had disappeared, not aided by images of blood and glossy black feathers which seemed to haunt her every time she set foot in the kitchen. She forced a smile and nursed her third glass of Chardonnay as Dom tucked into her barely-touched portion of chicken stir-fry and rice.

"Do you want to talk about it then? You were going to tell me what happened at the solicitor's?" said Dom between mouthfuls. "Are we millionaires yet? Has the old bastard finally come up trumps?"

"That's my father you're talking about," Sarah snapped, anger flaring like a struck match. "Show a bit of respect. We only buried him yesterday."

Dom stopped chewing and held his hands up in surrender. "Joke, babe. No offence intended. It was you who made the comment first as I recall."

A flush of heat spread up her neck, and she distracted herself by staring up at the cobwebbed corners of the high-beamed ceiling, waiting for her heartbeat to tame. The steady drip of a leaky tap in the enamel sink, seemed to tick away like the timer of a bomb. Sarah was determined not to blow. Perhaps she had voiced something similar after their initial encounter with Adrian Carter, but that didn't give Dom the right to make insults. She covered her unease by draining her glass and pouring the remainder of the bottle.

"You're knocking back the vino tonight, aren't you?" said Dom, raising his eyebrows. "You've managed the whole bottle on your own."

Sarah slammed the bottle down on the table. "Why do you talk to me in that stupid, patronising tone?"

Dom sighed and pushed his plate away. "Here we go …"

"See! You're doing it again." Sarah took another gulp of wine and wiped her hand across my mouth. "Lighten up. It's just a glass of wine, not hurting anyone, is it? Not hurting you? I did ask if you wanted some. You're my husband, not my father." She paused, heart thumping, knowing the alcohol was taking control of her tongue, knowing it would be much better to shut up right now. "Oh, that's right, I don't have a father, do I? As you said, the old bastard's dead at last!"

"That's enough, babe. Chill out."

"Chill out? You bloody chill out and stop telling me what to do."

Dom sighed but stayed silent. He took the plates across to the sink. "So, what did the solicitor say?" he asked again, his back to her.

"Why'd you want to know?"

He looked over his shoulder. "What do you mean, *why do I want to know*? What sort of question is that?"

"A valid one from where I'm sat."

They stared at each other in silence; her father's letter burned inside her pocket. His words became more rational the more defensive she became.

Trust no one.

Dom frowned. Eventually, he turned off the tap and took his place back at the table. "I think we're on different wavelengths here. Something's clearly bothering you. Is it something I've done?"

Sarah shook her head, eyes fixed on the empty wine bottle.

"Okay, is it something I've not done?"

She looked up and ignored his half-smile. "You're doing it again."

"So, what the hell's the matter?" Dom's voice had an edge now, and Sarah could see the prominent veins in his neck. "Why are you turning against me? I don't understand …"

"What's to understand?" Something inside egged Sarah on, wanting to hurt him, wanting to lash out and push him over the edge. "My father is dead."

"So, why's that suddenly my fault? I mean … you've hardly given him the time of day in the past God knows how many years and now all of a sudden –"

"Don't you dare judge me!" Sarah clenched her fists. "You know nothing."

"I know enough."

"And what's that supposed to mean?"

"It means I don't know why you're defending him. I don't know how you can even say his name out loud without –"

"Don't!" Her eyes filled with hot tears. "Just don't."

"But it has to be said. If you didn't want me to react like this, then you should never have told me. I've seen you broken-hearted about the way he disowned you, and I'm sorry, but you can't expect me to be anything but furious." Dom paused. "He cut you off without a penny, as if you didn't exist, just because you wouldn't play along with his sick obsession. I don't know how you can honour his memory and simply forgive him."

"I didn't," she whispered. "I never will. But it wasn't like that … you wouldn't understand –"

"No, quite honestly, I don't want to understand. He pushed and pulled you back and forth on a whim all through your life. Either he wouldn't let you out of his sight, or he sent you away to boarding school 'cos he didn't want you in the house. What kind of upbringing is that for a kid? He was a drunk and a bully –"

"Dom!"

"Sarah, it's true. Dress it up how you like, but you can't hide the facts because they hurt. He attacked you, had you by your throat, on your sixteenth birthday - and told you that you were responsible for killing your own mother. What kind of sick bullshit is that? And even though he told you over and over he hated you and couldn't stand the sight of you - you still stuck by him, pandered to him."

"He was drunk. I told you. He was drunk and confused. He woke in the middle of the night after a bad dream." Sarah breathed deeply. "Look, it was a one off. And what choice did I have at sixteen? I had no money, no family. I had to forgive him, or at least pretend to. And most of the time it was okay. It was the drink –"

"Yeah, and if I had my time over, I'd have shoved his beloved bottle of Scotch up his arse." Dom took a long drink of lager and Sarah could see his hand shaking. "He knew my opinion of him, all right, that's why he never wanted me in his house. He could see what I thought of him. He was ashamed. Well, at least I hope he was, the sad old bastard." Dom brought his fist down on the table with a smash. "He was possessive, no … obsessed with you. If you hadn't got out when you did, he'd have groomed you into being a substitute wife. It's sick. I'm sorry, but he was sick. And I don't just mean the drink."

Sarah reached across and covered Dom's hand with her own, entwining her fingers through his and squeezing hard. "Please, Dom. I don't want to go through this again, don't drag up the past. Please don't make all the feelings surface after it's taken so long to bury them. He's dead. We can't change the past. I can't stay angry forever. What I have to do is sort out the future, our future, and I don't know where to start. I don't know what to do."

Dom lowered his voice, but he sounded strained. "So tell me, let me help …"

Sarah shook her head, feeling the dulled effects of the Chardonnay.

"Why?"

"Because I can't –"

"Why? Tell me."

"Because it's complicated."

Dom pulled his hand away and they sat in silence for what seemed like hours, but could only have been a minute. The merry-go-round was back, whirling and twirling in Sarah's brain. Where to start? What to say? Who to trust? Wills. Manuscripts. Treasure hunts. Beautiful women. Christ. What would Dom think of her father once he heard all this?

Finally, Dom stood, scraping his chair on the flagstone floor. His knuckles whitened as he gripped the back of the chair.

"I think I begin to get the picture," he said, his voice tight. "It's too complicated for someone as thick as me to understand. That's what you really mean, isn't it? Do you realise your old man has achieved from beyond the grave, what he never could when he was alive, no matter how hard he tried. He's turned you against me, hasn't he?"

Sarah shook her head again, feeling full to the brim with emotions. Her brain was muddled and thick with alcohol, and she couldn't seem to find the right words.

"No, it's not that –"

"Oh, yeah. Sure it is. Your old man never thought anything of me. Never thought I was good enough, intellectual enough, for the precious daughter he wanted all to himself. Even my money wasn't good enough because it was *new* money. And who knows, maybe he was right. I can imagine him looking down his nose at me. '*Only plays for Watford, just a Championship club. Can't even play in the Premier League.*'" Dominic's smile was full of scorn. "I know what he thought of professional footballers. I know what he thought of his daughter being the wife of one of them. Jesus Christ, he'd have had a heart attack if he'd ever known what a WAG was …"

"Enough!"

Sarah staggered to her feet and faced Dom, holding onto the kitchen unit for support. She couldn't take anymore; she had to get out before she exploded. She held up a hand to silence him.

"I think it would be better if you left in the morning. I'm likely to have to stay around here for a few days, maybe even a week. And I want to be on my own. Understood?"

On unsteady legs, Sarah stumbled across the kitchen, turning as she reached the door. Dominic sat back down at the table and held his head between his hands. He stared unseeing into the distance as if he too had a million thoughts overloading his brain. As she watched, he rubbed his chin, over and over – a sure sign of nerves. Her heart ached with a sudden need to hold him, to feel him and touch him, to kiss him. She shuddered and took one step back into the room.

She stopped herself, steadying her hand against the door frame. No, she wouldn't. Her pride wouldn't let her; he'd said too many hurtful things, opened too many old wounds. Besides, less said the better. She didn't want to lie to him more than she had to. The hurt in his gaze burned deeply inside her. With a loud sigh, she slammed the door behind her. They could both sleep on it, and enjoy making up in the morning.

* * *

A shrill buzzing noise broke through the dream.

Merry-go-round images merged and flashed, flashed and merged. Father's face, angry and distorted with rage. Dom's voice, calming and reasoning. Mother's gentle caress, soft lips on her forehead. *Summertime.* And in the distance the sing-song lilt of a child's voice calling out ... *Sarah ... Sarah ...*

What the hell was that noise?

Sarah opened her eyes to bright white light and flashes of pain.

"God!"

She sat up in bed and held her head in both hands.

It was her mobile. She grabbed it from the bedside table with a shaking hand, squinting at the 'anonymous number' on the display.

"H-hello?"

"Good Morning, Mrs Morton. It's Miles Harvey-Barnes here."

"Who?"

"We met briefly at your father's funeral … his literary agent."

"Oh, yeah …" Sarah dropped back against the pillows, ran her tongue around the inside of a sandpaper mouth. "I'm sorry, Mr Harvey-Barnes –"

"I was just wondering if you'd had time to look into your father's affairs. The publisher tells me they never received the signed copy of the contract we sent to your father, and it's important we get things moving. You know, strike while the iron's still hot, so to speak."

"I haven't given it a second thought to be honest with you."

"Oh, it's just that I thought you had an appointment with your father's solicitor yesterday? I presumed you would have discussed his estate?"

Sarah sat up straighter; her nerves hummed as her head continued to throb. Anger crept through the thickness of her hangover.

"Mr Harvey-Barnes, I have no recollection of telling you who I had a meeting with yesterday, and I am positive I would not have discussed the contents of such a meeting with you –"

"Mrs Morton, please –"

"Hear me out. Now, I may be in the wrong here, and you may be acting with all best intentions, but I'll be perfectly honest with you and say that at the moment, it doesn't feel that way. I have no idea how you got my mobile number, but I do have your details. I have heard what you have to say. And when … and if … I want to get in touch, I am quite capable of doing so. So, please do not contact me again. Do you understand?"

"O-of course, Mrs Morton. I apologise profusely if we've got off on the wrong foot. But we do have the matter of a legally binding contract to discuss –"

"Are you threatening me, Mr Harvey-Barnes?"

Silence.

Her chest tightened as she continued. "Besides, did you not just tell me the contract had never been signed?"

"Please, Mrs Morton, rest assured –"

"I'll be in touch, Mr Harvey-Barnes."

Sarah ended the call and threw the phone onto the bed. With a growl, she curled up and pulled the duvet over her head. How dare the arrogant little man keep pestering her. He'd left two voicemail messages yesterday. Someone must have passed on her phone number. And how on earth had he known about the appointment with Adrian Carter, unless he'd overheard a conversation at the funeral?

It was no good. Now she was awake – and annoyed – she needed the bathroom and painkillers in equal measure. She threw back the duvet, swung her legs out of bed, and slipped her feet into her sheepskin slippers. Shivering, she pulled on a dressing gown over her nightdress. The room was icy cold. The dusty beams of sunlight filtering through the half-opened curtains did little to improve the temperature. She'd have to take time to get her head around the antiquated central heating system, or get someone out to take a look at it.

As she crossed the room, Sarah noticed the tray on the windowsill, with croissants, orange juice and a mug of coffee.

Dominic. Bless him. Her heart leapt. Remorse settled in her stomach as she remembered last night's row. Her words had been cruel and needless. It was time to make up.

The floorboards creaked as she pulled open the bedroom door and made her way across the landing. She leaned over the banisters, listening for any tell-tale noises from below. The house hummed in a silence that was both eerie and total.

"Dominic?"

Nothing.

"Dom! You there?"

Sarah padded across to the front-facing window at the end of the long landing. Her heart hammered with every step as she recalled more details of their drunken argument, including the fact she'd ordered him to go home. Why did she always let her father get to her? And why always take it out on Dom?

A smile stretched across her face, and relief washed over her as she registered the BMW gleaming in weak sunlight. Thank God. The last thing she wanted was for Dom to leave her alone at Charter House. Thinking back, she was sure he'd mentioned something about going for a jog this morning. That was it. He hadn't left her – he'd never leave her.

Rubbing her temple to release the tension, she chastised herself for drinking too much. She hurried into the bathroom and turned on the shower, knowing she'd have to let it run for at least ten minutes before it got anywhere near hot.

While the tepid water continued to spurt and hiss from the lime-scaled shower head, Sarah padded back into the bedroom and recovered her jeans from the floor. Digging into the pocket, she found the note from her father's safe. She grabbed her mobile from the bed, and before she changed her mind, keyed in the digits on the piece of paper, remembering to add 141 to withhold her own number ... just in case.

She held her breath as the phone rang once, twice, three times.

"Hello?" A woman's voice, serious but young sounding.

"Oh, hi, erm, I'm sorry to bother you, this is probably going to sound pretty strange –"

"Sarah?"

The words died on her lips and the nervous smile disintegrated.

"Sarah Morton?"

Sarah nodded, then realised. "Sorry, yes. Who are you?"

"Isabel Griffiths. Your father's PA."

"My father had a PA?"

Sarah shook her head as if her ears were playing tricks, and at the same time, tried to identify the other woman's accent. American? South African? She was rubbish at accents.

Isabel laughed. "Okay, research assistant, whichever you prefer. He told me to expect your call. Sorry if I startled you."

"He told you I'd call?" said Sarah slowly. "I'm sorry, this is weird, but you do know my father is ..."

"I know he's passed away. We discussed things, you see, all eventualities, and I knew you'd find my number." The woman sighed. "We need to meet, Sarah, as soon as possible. Things will become much clearer then."

Sarah realised the gap meant she was expected to reply, but shock and confusion seemed to have rendered her incapable of even the most basic function.

Isabel continued. "I'm sure you're totally screwed by everything at the moment, and it's cool, I understand. But we have a lot of stuff to discuss. Can you meet me for coffee? No, in fact, if I give you my address, could you come round here? There's things you need to see."

Sarah decided it was probably best to just jump on-board the merry-go-round for now and see where it took her.

"Erm, yes, I suppose so. Where are you?"

"Staff quarters, Bangor Uni. Do you know where they are?"

Sarah remembered the tiny bed-sit cum study her father had kept at the university and had a vague idea of the direction. She guessed Isabel's flat was in the same road and promised to be there after lunch, staring long and hard at her mobile after the other woman hung up. Maybe the meeting would finally throw some light on matters. It might certainly solve the mystery of the woman in Carter's office. She grabbed some clean clothes from her suitcase and hurried into the steam-filled bathroom.

Sarah glanced at her watch for the umpteenth time, almost twenty past one and Dom still wasn't back. She paced the sitting room and hallway with a mixture of frustration and fear. By her calculations, Dom had to have been out over four hours, and that was way too long for a jog, even with his regimented fitness routine, and even if he was trying to burn off any remnants of last night's anger.

She'd tried calling his mobile, and heard an eerie response from the charger on the set of drawers in the bedroom. So, wherever he'd gone, he hadn't thought he'd need his phone, and that made sense if he was jogging out here in the middle of nowhere. But it didn't explain his absence getting on for five hours later.

Sarah's nerves began to get the better of her, and constant bumps and sighs from the old building didn't help. She remembered the oppressive feeling she'd experienced when they first arrived, not helped by the dead bird in the kitchen. But the voice, the vision, the sense of ... wrongness.

He'd most likely simply got lost in the labyrinth of lanes and couldn't find his way back to Charter House, but anything could have happened. She hooked the BMW keys from the telephone table, grabbed her mobile, and slammed the door behind her.

The day was still grey, but slivers of sunshine pierced the clouds in places, and there was no sign of rain. The wind continued to howl around the eaves, and the sycamores swayed in perfect symmetry. She filled her lungs with salty air, letting nature calm her.

Stepping out from the shadow of the house, Sarah heard the crunch of gravel. She half-turned expecting to see Dom appear around the corner of the garage, limping or winded or both. There was no one. But from the corner of her eye, she saw a movement behind one of the sycamores in the drive.

"Hello?"

Moving in front of the car, she had a clear view of the other side of the tree, and it was empty. She shook her head. Probably the wind. Or maybe a trick of the light or a lengthening shadow as weak sunlight dappled the leaves.

With a sigh, Sarah headed towards the driver's door, and once again a fleeting movement caused her to turn sharply. She was certain this time - someone standing by the dry-stone wall, beside the stile that led onto the cliff path.

"Hello?"

Nothing but the sound of the wind rustling the bare branches, and the rush of the ocean in the distance. She was positive she'd seen something, someone. Perhaps they'd climbed the stile and disappeared behind the hedgerow. It wouldn't hurt to take a look.

She reached the stile, and pulled herself up for a better view. The cliff path was deserted in both directions. There was no one in sight; it had to be her eyes playing tricks on her stressed brain.

Sarah stepped down and hurried back to the BMW, her boots crunching on the gravel. She jumped as the car alarm beeped, and for a second her heartbeat filled her ears. Oh, come on, Dom. Where are you? She had a mind to call 999 but if it was a case of a lost jogger, she'd look a bit of an idiot and probably get charged with wasting police time.

A noise halted her in her tracks. No, not a noise – a voice. A child's voice. A voice that seemed somehow familiar.

Sarah. Sarah. Sarah.

Sarah cocked her head, straining to hear above the persistent gusts of wind. She turned back towards the cliff and scanned the area again. Nothing but the sounds of the breeze and ocean, and the cry of a distant gull. Her pulse quickened. If she wasn't careful her imagination would run away with her sanity. Her nerves were frazzled, not aided by the lingering hangover.

Sarah. Sarah. Hurry, Sarah!

She sprinted towards the stile, clearing it in one fluid movement. This time she hadn't imagined it. This time she was certain she'd heard a child's voice calling her name.

Without a second thought, Sarah set off across the open field, squinting against the wind. As she reached the middle of the field, she could make out the form of a young girl in the distance, long hair blowing around her face. She had one arm raised, pointing out to sea.

Sarah started into a run. "It's okay. I'm coming!"

God, she hoped the girl could hear. There'd clearly been some kind of accident and she was in distress. Sliding on the muddy ground, she negotiated the worn track, staggering over loose rocks as she clambered down a sharp drop in the path. The girl hadn't moved. She stood as still as a statue, but from what Sarah could tell she didn't seem to be in any imminent danger. Her ashen face was etched with terror.

Sarah's breathing was ragged and she had a stitch in her side, but still she forced her legs to move faster. She took huge strides back up the other side of the steep slope, and reached the level section of the pathway where she'd first seen the girl.

The path was empty.

"Hello?"

Sarah came to a stop and panted, hands on hips. A roaring noise filled her ears, and she shook her head, unable to work out if it was the sound of the ocean or the rush of her own blood.

"Hello! Is anybody there?" She shouted louder this time.

With a burst of adrenaline, she rushed towards the cliff edge.

No … please don't say it was too late. Don't say she's fallen. God, don't let her have jumped!

Sarah slowed right down and inched forward on her hands and knees, as close to the edge as she dared on the thick, springy grass. Spray clung to her face as she bent forwards and looked down at the surging tide far below, crashing against the huge rocks at the base of the cliff.

Holding her hair out of her eyes, she focused on the foamy mass. At first she could make out nothing but shiny black rocks, green in places with seaweed, and the crashing white of the waves.

But then a flash of red caught her eye as a huge wave broke and receded. She shielded her eyes and squinted against the wind. Something red and black was wedged in a chasm between two rocks.

Suddenly, the form became clear. She could make out the distinctive shape. It was a person, in dark trousers and a red anorak, lying face down.

Clothes she recognised.

Sarah's scream, mingling with the cries of the circling gulls, carried away on the breeze.

She dropped to her knees and screamed again.

"Dom-i-nic!"

Chapter Six

Air whooshed from her lungs, leaving her gasping, head spinning. As she scrambled to her feet, the cliff edge spun near, looming in and out of focus. She looked down again, but couldn't – wouldn't – accept it was Dom.

All she could do was scream.

Repeatedly.

"Dominic!"

Sarah closed her eyes and tried to control her breathing, taking long mouthfuls of salty air. Plan, she needed a plan. She scanned the cliff edge. There was no way she could get down this sheer drop. But a little way to the right, she saw a path, cutting through thick yellow gorse bushes. As she found her balance, she heard a noise like a cat's wail. It came from her own lips. The wind whipped around her, and she battled with her hair, pushing it down into her collar to keep it out of her eyes. She stumbled along the cliff edge, her heels impeding every step, gorse and blackthorn bushes snatching at her clothes.

Stop. Think. What would Dom do? She squeezed her eyes tight. Help. She had to get help. She dug into her pocket for her mobile, and, fingers shaking, punched 999. She held the phone to her ear, planning her words carefully. Silence. Frowning, she looked at the screen. Call failed. Damn. The little signal bars were empty. For God's sake …

Sarah gazed down at the rocks below. From here the trail looked impossible. In places, the path disappeared into the sandstone bedrock, and in others had been washed away by years of bad weather that had turned the red clay into a waterfall during heavy rain. The track of the coursing water was still visible and slippery. But there was no other way.

She grabbed hold of the nearest bush, ignoring the flare of pain as sharp thorns bit into her palm. She lowered herself over the edge of the cliff and onto the path.

"I'm coming, Dom! It's okay. I'm coming."

Sarah knew she spoke more to steady her thumping heart than to reassure Dom; perhaps she spoke to persuade herself he could hear. But the words were carried away on the wind, no chance they would be heard against the roar of the waves. She shook her phone, still no signal, but in desperation she pressed redial. Silence. Call failed.

With a deep breath, she took her first steps, and, within seconds her boots began to slide. She picked up speed. Branches clawed at her hair like malevolent fingers, and her cardigan snagged on gorse thorns. She reached out and grabbed the first thing to hand, an overhanging bush, and halted the slide. Sarah reached a narrow ledge and paused. Pulling herself upright, she breathed deeply to fill her depleted lungs, and craned her neck over the ridge to see if Dom had moved. From here, she could see the curious angle of his head, his twisted limbs. A steady drip of crimson pooled beneath his left shoulder. She clung to the cliff face and retched. It was difficult to judge whether the tide was rising or falling, but the thought that Dom might drown, or his body washed out to sea, was enough to focus her. She checked her phone again. Heart pounding, she saw one tiny bar on the display as the signal wavered in and out. She pressed redial and said a silent prayer. A single beep. Call failed.

Tears burned as she looked down; the jagged rocks looked bigger and fiercer the closer she got to the bottom. There was nothing for it. She closed her eyes, gripped a handful of coarse grass, and lowered herself down. Her boots hit the sandy surface, shale sliding beneath her feet. She picked up speed, and, screaming, plummeted down towards the rocks below. Sarah grabbed furiously at anything and everything, branches snagged her clothes and thorns scratched her face and arms, her fingernails tearing against the rock face. Her mobile slid from her grip and disappeared into the foaming water below.

"Noooo!" Sarah yelled as she jolted to a stop on something solid. A thick coiled tree root halted her fall. The high heel of her left boot dug into the sandstone, and as her body lurched, her foot twisted, hot needles exploding through her. Pain burned in her lower leg as she wrapped her arms around the tree trunk and wedged her good knee against the gnarled timber.

It bent ... but thankfully held her weight.

Shooting stars of pain clouded her vision and she screamed her frustration to the heavens. How could she be so stupid? Why not just head back to the house, phone for help and wait – like any sane person. Goddamn it!

She looked upwards as tears ran down her face. The sky was turning charcoal grey; dark clouds spread across the horizon like a mountain range. Sarah recognised from her childhood the early warning signs of an impending storm. Almost on cue, heavy raindrops splashed on the rock around her. She had to do something ... and fast.

Ignoring the throbbing ache in her leg, Sarah twisted and grabbed hold of the nearest bush, testing its solidity. The root creaked and bent further as she shifted her weight. If she put too much stress on the old branches, and the bush wouldn't hold her weight, she'd plummet the final thirty feet onto the rocks. It was impossible to get off this cliff face alone. No matter how hard it was, she had to stay still, stay calm, and try to attract someone's attention.

"Help!"

The only reply was the answering echo of wind and ocean. What about the young girl? She'd almost forgotten about her in the unfolding drama. Was there a chance she'd already gone to fetch help? If not, where was she?

"Please … someone … help!" The wind carried the words out to sea. Sarah filled her lungs and screamed. "HELP!"

Her head slumped and she sobbed at her own stupidity. What use could she be now with a broken ankle? This was surely penance for her idiocy. But did Dom deserve to suffer too because of it? Sarah looked back to the heavens, raindrops stinging her face, and prayed.

God, I know I only turn to you when I need you, when I want something. But please, please help me. Help Dom. Please, don't let me die here. Please, don't let Dom die, don't let him be dead. Help me find the strength to get out of this.

The root cracked and Sarah lurched forward, squealing as she dropped another few inches. Her pulse pounded in her ears as the trunk bent even further – but held. Her damaged leg was trapped under the weight of her whole body, and she was sweating and dizzy, but she didn't dare move, couldn't move. She looked up, desperately searching the cliff face for something she could grab hold of; some way she could try to crawl and pull herself upwards.

"Hello … hello. Can you hear me … down there …?"

For a moment, Sarah could have sworn she was dreaming, or she'd passed out and was hallucinating. And now, she was sure she could hear a dog barking in the distance.

"Yes! Hello … Help. Help me!"

"Hello … stay there … I'm coming down …"

The voice trailed off as Sarah strained her eyes against the deepening gloom. She could make out a pale white face against the dark sky, peering at her over the grassy edge of the cliff.

"Don't try to get down!" she yelled. "Fetch help. It's too dangerous." She filled her lungs, screaming the words as loud as she could. "Don't come down. Just get help. Please!"

The face disappeared for a second, and then reappeared a little further to her left. She had a clearer sight of the person

– a young man, chubby faced, dark hair and glasses. He was carrying a rucksack and Sarah could hear the yap of a small dog somewhere nearby.

"Can you hear me? Don't come down – the path has collapsed! There are two of us. We're injured. Please, can you fetch help?"

"Stay there. I'll be as fast as I can. Come on, Jim."

The face disappeared and the barking ceased.

Sarah sobbed and looked to the sky. "Thank you, God."

* * *

His hands were shaking. Red couldn't remember the last time he'd experienced real fear. This suffocating sensation made his limbs as heavy as lead, and his brain feel like it had melted into a churning vacuum of mush.

Yeah, sure in his teens, he'd enjoyed that adrenaline rush of fake-fear; the kind you experienced on the highest, fastest rollercoaster ride. Or the time he'd pushed his first Corsa 1.2 up to 120mph and the chassis had shaken so much the windscreen cracked from corner to corner. That kind of scary stuff was great. Intense. Made you feel alive and breathing, reminded him of the thrill of good sex.

But he didn't like this kind of fear.

This fear was like a cold, creeping ache that started somewhere in your stomach and spread throughout your body until it felt like your fingers and toes were blocks of ice, ready to turn black and gangrenous. He half expected to see his fingers crumble to the floor in front of his eyes.

Now, he knew what real fear was.

How could it have gone so wrong? How could things get blown into a million tiny shards of shit in less than thirty seconds? And what was he thinking to have allowed himself to get involved in the first place. He'd had doubts from day one. But as always, he'd stopped thinking with his brain. He'd let the smell of money and the promise of fulfilled fantasies lead him astray.

And now look.

He rubbed his palms together to rid himself of the shivers. Even though the heating was on full-blast, the flat felt like the inside of a freezer. He doubted he'd ever be warm again – the second he recalled that piercing scream which had seemed to go on for hour upon hour – the icy-blood began shooting through his veins and the shakes started up again. He remembered the disturbed seabirds; how they'd risen squawking in protest from their resting places on the cliff. He'd almost wanted to beg them to do something – and how he'd wished he had the power of flight at that moment.

He still wasn't clear how it had happened. He'd tried hard to recall the build-up. The other man had rushed him, Red remembered that, clearly thinking he could overpower him, mumbling something about citizen's arrest and old man Williams's murder. And there'd been a struggle. Red might have landed one decent punch, and then recalled hitting the ground, hard, rolling in mud that clung to him from head to toe. He kicked out several times, then managed to get to his feet. He dragged Morton upright, shook him a little, yelled in his face, tried to get the other man to calm down. He'd never had any intention of hurting him. And then the next thing, feeling Morton lurch backwards, and the slippery waterproof jacket sliding, gracefully, through Red's fingers.

Like a slow-motion replay of a football game.

He laughed, a humourless sound, and picked up the vodka bottle, tipping it to his lips, eyes closed. Realising it was empty, he flung it aside with a growl. There was no chance of getting more. He couldn't ever imagine passing over his front door step again. How could he face people? Surely they'd know. Something about his expression or character would scream the word in their face. Murderer.

He was a murderer.

How odd that sounded. It wasn't as if he wasn't used to the odd scrape with the law, as a young kid he'd pushed the boundaries, right? But he'd never hit anyone; in truth he hated violence. Like his old man said, the mind was more powerful than the fist. He rubbed the bump in his nose and snorted, remembering his shock the first time his father had punched him, breaking his nose. Shame the old sod hadn't practised what he preached. No, he'd never been averse to the odd back-hander if he felt in the mood. But Red had always believed violence wasn't the answer to any of life's problems, and surely that was proved today.

He crossed into the kitchen and flicked on the kettle. Now his father was on his mind, he remembered another of his beliefs – that a cup of strong, sweet tea was good for shock. Red realised it was probably shock that held him tight in its grip. Maybe a hot drink would thaw his nerves a little and he could get his brain into gear. Decide what the hell he had to do next.

Alibi. The word flashed into his mind like a neon sign above a strip-joint. As far as he knew there was nothing to link him to Dominic Morton, and he'd been extra careful that no one had seen him near Charter House. But still … he had to have a cast-iron alibi, just in case the footballer's death was investigated as suspicious, and a tenuous link led police to his door.

And there was only one person for the job.

While the kettle boiled, he picked up the phone and pressed speed dial number four. The call was answered on the second ring.

"Hello."

Red cleared his throat. "It's me. We need to talk."

"Yes, we do, there's been developments. I've been waiting to hear from you …"

"Not now. If anyone asks the question, I've been with you all morning, right?"

A pause. "I don't get it. What –"

Red counted to ten. "I can't answer now. Let's meet in person. But I've been with you all day. Got it? Can you come round this evening, talk face to face? And bring alcohol – beer and vodka."

"Okay. You're not making much sense so what choice do I have? I hate it when you turn weird on me. You could at least –"

Red sighed and cut the call. He wasn't in the mood for niceties.

* * *

Danny looked down at the swirling water. Waves crashed against shiny rocks, breaking into white foam, then receding and returning, with a repetitive roar. Spray misted across his face, and, when he licked his lips, he could taste the ocean. There was something hypnotic, mesmeric even, about the attraction of water. He knew the suicide statistics around the North Wales coast ran into double figures each year. And standing here now, the greys and blues of ocean and sky merging, he believed he had an inkling of the kind of magnetism that could attract a troubled mind.

Even though he could relate to the phenomenon, he wasn't comfortable with it now. Although the initial 999 call had been logged an accident, or possible suicide, to him it just didn't fit. There was no note, no reason, no explanation. And more worryingly, he'd met the guy only days before and he'd seemed the least archetypal suicide victim Danny could imagine. Young, fit, healthy, rich, in the prime of his career with a beautiful wife and a whole life ahead of him. And even though he knew from his training suicide victims were often blind to their own selfishness, Danny couldn't accept Dom Morton would throw himself off the edge of a cliff, right after his father-in-law's funeral, when his wife needed him most.

And with the suspicions about Professor Williams's death still unresolved, Danny's stomach contracted when the report come through about an unexplained death on Anglesey, and he'd registered the victim's name. He had no choice but to request the case, making a trip out to the scene before darkness fell. He prayed it would end up as no more than a tragic accident, but at the moment Danny's gut instinct was turning somersaults.

"Sir."

Danny turned to see PC Conrad Hughes, the local Moelfre officer, approaching. His hand rested on the shoulder of a black-haired, bespectacled young man, whose round face was etched with worry, dried tears and snot stains.

"This is Martin," said PC Hughes. "You know, the young chap I told you about. Martin raised the alarm. I brought him up from the village, told him he'd nothing to worry about, but thought you might like a word?"

Danny nodded, reading the Constable's expression. He'd been warned Martin Cole was a nervous lad, with a mental age well below his years. Reclusive but harmless, PC Hughes' opinion. Danny nodded and held out his hand to shake the young man's.

"Good of you to come over, Martin. Do you want to tell me what happened here this morning?"

"I was walking, heading out toward the Point for a bit of fishing, me and Jim ..."

"Who's Jim?" asked Danny, pulling his notebook from his pocket.

"Jim is Martin's little Jack Russell," said PC Hughes. "They go everywhere together."

Martin nodded. "Jim likes fishing."

Danny smiled and tapped his notebook. "Right. So, you and Jim were following the cliff path?"

"Yeah. He knows this path like the back of his hand, he does, well ... his paw. Anyway, sniffing the gorse and that, you know. Or disappearing off down rabbit holes, he goes right over the edge sometimes, scares me half to death. Well, this morning, he did that. I reckon he must've heard something, see ... before I did. I went to the edge to call him back and that's when I heard it."

"What did you hear, Martin?"

"This voice. I knew it were a woman. Help, help, she was

calling. Someone, please help me. Help!"

Danny nodded. "So what did you do?"

"Well, Jim started to bark, so I put him on his lead, didn't want him going over the edge, see. Then I looked down, and couldn't see nothing at first, but I shouted out – and she shouted back, the woman, I mean. Jim was yapping like a fool, so I had to drag him back to be able to hear her."

"What did she say?"

"Said not to come down. Said there was two of them, but the path had give way. Not to come down but to go and get help."

"Could you see her?"

Martin hesitated, then shook his head.

"What could you see?" said Danny.

"I could see someone on the rocks, right at the bottom, lying sort of flat out on the seaweed. Looked like a fella, short hair, in a red coat."

"What did you do next?"

"I went along the cliff a bit, leaned over, you know on the longer grass, see if I could see the woman, but I couldn't cos the cliff edge juts out all along. I just called down to her to stay there and I'd get help."

"And you did?"

"Yeah, I ran across the fields, down to Dr Davies' bungalow. It was the quickest I could think to get to."

"Martin doesn't have a mobile," said PC Hughes. "I reckon his quick-thinking might have saved that young woman's life, don't you, detective? I've tried telling him so, but he's more worried he'll get into trouble for something."

"No, indeed," said Danny. "I'm sure you did everything to the book, young man."

Martin blushed and looked at his feet. "I heard the helicopter and saw the Coastguard come out. I heard the guy was already dead. I thought if I'd been faster –"

PC Hughes shook his head. "We've not got all the details yet, lad, but I'm pretty certain there was nothing you could've done different. You have to forget that now. There's one young lady who owes you her life. Who knows how long she could've held out down there."

Danny nodded. "Definitely. Have you any idea if the man and woman were together when they fell? The lady said the path collapsed, did she say if that was what happened to both of them?"

"I don't know. I mean, I guess so." He looked from Danny to Conrad. "That's what must have happened, isn't it? The path collapsed and he fell and she grabbed onto the cliff or some 'at. Is that what you mean?"

"Something like that," said Danny, offering an encouraging smile. "One final point, did you see anyone else this morning? Either here, or around Charter House, or while you were on your way to Dr Davies?"

Martin's bottom lip stuck out as he paused, deep in thought. After a few moments, he shook his head. "No. No one. I remembered thinking it was typical no one was around when I needed them to be around, you know?" He bit his lip, then added. "I might have heard someone calling out a bit earlier, but it was misty and the waves were loud. It could've been my ears playing up, or I suppose, it might have been the lady crying out for help." He paused, frowned, then rubbed his nose. "But then it wasn't really like her voice. It sounded more like a child."

Danny looked at PC Hughes who shook his head and shrugged.

Danny closed his notebook. "Well, that's a huge help, Martin, thank you for coming forward. I bet if you ask him nicely, PC Hughes will drop you home on his way. Thanks again."

Danny resumed his position on the cliff edge; the light was beginning to fade, pale grey to granite. Now the Coastguard had removed the body, and Sarah Morton had been airlifted to Bangor Hospital, there was nothing here on this stunning, windswept cliff that held any hint of the tragedy that unfolded earlier. Danny had asked SOCO to give the cliff path the once over as a matter of routine, but their search failed to reveal anything of importance, and the ground had been so churned up by rescuers' feet, it was unlikely to yield further clues. Next step was to interview Mrs Morton once she was up to it, and hope she could shed more light on her husband's death.

But there was one more person Danny felt compelled to call. He pulled his mobile from his pocket, and turned away from the wind, hunching his shoulders as he scrolled through his contacts and pressed call. The ringtone echoed for a minute and then clicked onto voicemail – "*This is DS Geraint Lewis. Sorry I can't take your call, please leave a message and I'll get back to you.*"

Danny took a deep breath. "Hello, mate, it's me. I've got some unfortunate news I think might interest you …"

November 1ˢᵗ 1859

These cliffs have become my home. I know each boulder, each crevice, each clump of yellow gorse and tuft of springy grass. Oh, I've tried to leave, many times, believe me. I set off with a determined step. Turning my back on the ocean, focusing on distant hills, I head inland. Each time I reach the crest of the cliff, join a well-trod path, and as excitement catches in my throat, buoyed by the thought that finally I will be free – I wake up and I'm back on my original spot, high on the cliff edge, high above the foaming waters and sharp black rocks where the poor, wretched Charter met her end.

I've witnessed many sides of human nature over the past days; the best and the worst have passed before me in the long, cold hours I have waited for my family to claim me. I've seen men risk their own lives, joined at the waist by ropes, wade into the stormy sea to drag people – alive and dead – from the churning waters. And I've seen others strip possessions from the dead, some still-warm, with no more grace than a butcher skinning hide from a cow. I've seen women whoop and holler, racing away with treasures held high above their heads, like the worst savages from the Outback. I've learned much beyond my years, and perhaps all too late. I've stamped my feet and screamed curses my mother would have been shocked to hear. But, of course, no one ever hears my cries.

My name is Angelina Stewart.

I am eleven years old.

And I am dead.

I know this is so. I know it but I won't accept it. I cannot grieve and I have no tears. This cannot be what death means. My family are good Christians, we believe in heaven and hell. We are taught of sins and damnation. But I am not a sinner, so why am I left to face this purgatory?

No. I slam a clenched fist into my palm. No. I will not give up believing that my mother is out there, somewhere, searching for me. And when she finds me, she'll take me home, she'll set me free.

I wait. I pace back and forth, from the very tip of the point back to the curve of stony beach only visible on the lowest tide. I cover this ground over and over, unable to escape a bond that attaches me to these cliffs like an invisible cord. But still no one comes.

One night I find a cave, unable to cope with another bleak, lonely night on the cliff edge. It is some poor comfort, but offers shelter from the biting wind and clinging rain. During the dark hours, when the noise of the ocean roars like a hundred angry spirits battling for release, I think of the Charter, submerged below an inky surface that glints and shines in the moonlight like diamonds.

Night was my favourite time on the Royal Charter. I'd spent much of the journey in the grip of terror. I had no faith in ships – and rightly so, in truth – even though my da told me everything would be fine. From the bowels of the ship, I listened to echoes of creaks, cracks and groans, and wondered that it didn't shake itself into a million timber pieces. I failed to see how this monstrosity of wood, pitch and nails – held together with a generous amount of hope - could carry us thousands of miles across so many oceans. Oceans that appeared, during the day at least, like monsters set on revenge; snapping and snarling dragons from the myths, trying to drag us down into their underworld.

But at night it was different, especially when the dragons

were calm and content to rock us to sleep. I'd sit tight between Mam and Da, wrapped in a coarse grey blanket. We'd settle up on deck, counting stars or imagining the world beneath us, far below the waves. Da told me stories of under-sea kingdoms, where mountains rose till their peaks almost scraped the bow of the ship; and canyons that ran to miles deep and swallowed whole cities in their wake. I don't know that I believed him; he always told a good tale, my da. But I liked the thought there was a secret world down there. It made the real world, up above, seem far less perilous.

Inside my cave, I curled into a ball, wrapped my cloak around my legs, and rested my head on my hands. He would come. Da would come. Or Mam would appear, crying and fretful in her grief. My family loved me; they would not abandon me to this place.

It was only a matter of time.

Chapter Seven

A high-pitched beeping noise woke her. Sarah yawned and stretched, eyes still closed, not quite ready to face the new day. She was relieved the dream was broken. She'd dreamt her father had taken Dominic fishing and tried to push him off the rocks. She chuckled as lucidity crept through her body. It had to be a dream. The last thing her father would ever do was spend any of his leisure time with Dom.

The beep sounded again, and she inhaled a strong aroma of disinfectant. The bed felt hard and uncomfortable, not her own luxury soft mattress. As the grogginess receded, she remembered her father's death, the funeral … Charter House. That made sense. Time to start the day; she had a mountain of things to organise, and she desperately wanted to get home. She sighed and opened her eyes.

Bright fluorescent lights shone down from above. A pale green blanket pulled tight across her legs. On her left, a curtain filled the space from floor to ceiling. An oblong window, with cream vertical blinds that shut out the darkness beyond, covered most of the wall opposite. She fought against confusion for several moments, flailing around like a non-swimmer thrown in at the deep end.

Where was she? What was the odd smell, odd noises …?

Hospital.

The answer dropped into her lap. At least that explained

the numbness and confusion. She lifted her hand to her scalp, fingers tracing the outline of an egg-shaped lump above her right eye. Looking down at her other hand, she saw nails that were bloodied and torn. Sarah frowned and concentrated on the rest of her body, aware of a dull ache from the top of her head down to her toes, accompanied by a sick feeling deep in her gut. Her left leg seemed particularly stiff and numb, and her ankle felt as if it were wrapped in hot, tight bandages. But what had happened? Had there been an accident? Why couldn't she remember?

Mind whirling, she fell back onto the pillows. Even that small amount of exertion left her weak and breathless. No point forcing it, time would heal, her memory would come back. She spotted a beaker on the cabinet next to the bed, and carefully lifted the plastic cup to her lips. The cool relief of the water was welcome against the dryness in her mouth.

As she slid the empty cup back onto the table, she noticed a small red button lying next to her pillow, marked 'Press for Assistance'. Sarah squeezed, and seconds later, a slim red-headed nurse pulled back the curtain.

"Evening, Sarah." She checked the watch pinned to the front of her navy blue uniform. "I'm Nurse Flynn, but you can call me Carol if you prefer."

Sarah nodded.

Nurse Flynn filled in a form on the clipboard at the foot of the bed. "Right, I can see you've had some water. Is there anything else you're needing? How're you feeling?"

"S-sore ... but okay. What happened?"

Nurse Flynn looked up as she clipped her pen into her pocket. "You don't remember?"

Sarah shook her head.

"You had a right nasty fall, mostly cuts and bruises, but you've a sprained ankle that we've strapped, you're to keep your weight off it for a day or two. You'll stay overnight just so we can keep an eye on you, but you should be home tomorrow. You had a lucky escape, lady." She came round to the side of the bed. "Let me just check your vitals, and I'll let Doctor know you're awake."

Nurse Flynn gripped Sarah's wrist, then shone a bright light into each eye, before pouring a fresh cup of water.

"I … I can't remember what happened …" Sarah said.

The nurse turned and smoothed the sheets. "You will. Give it time. It's just the painkillers, but they'll soon wear off. Try to relax for now."

"But who brought me in? What happened?"

Nurse Flynn paused and Sarah saw a flash of something – pain or sympathy – in her eyes.

The nurse smiled, "Ach, you were airlifted in by the RAF Search & Rescue. Do you not remember your helicopter ride? Right dramatic, I'd imagine."

"No …"

"Typical! If I'd had a chance of a trip with some of them hunks from RAF Valley I'd be sure to try and remember every detail! Real '*Top Gun*' types some of the men there, better looking than Tom Cruise, too. Ach, if only we'd had them over in Belfast in my day!" Nurse Flynn smiled and winked. "You're in Bangor Hospital." The nurse retreated and pulled open the curtain. "But details can wait, you need to relax and rest now. Just press the button if you need me. Are you hungry – can I get you some dinner?"

"No, thank you. I feel a bit sick. But I'd manage a cup of tea, if it's no trouble."

Nurse Flynn smiled and her green eyes shone. "Ah, I'm sure we can manage that."

The curtain rings clinked as the nurse disappeared, closing the drape behind her. Sarah relaxed back into the pillows and wriggled around to find a comfortable spot on the hard mattress. She rubbed the bump on her forehead and tried to concentrate on the accident. How she'd ended up – via a RAF Valley helicopter ride apparently – in Ysbyty Gwynedd in Bangor. The drugs were making everything fuzzy; she felt nauseous and disorientated, but her instincts told her something wasn't right. She didn't know what, couldn't put a finger on the cause of her discomfort – but something just wasn't *right*.

She gazed at the dark night outside the window; rain drops streamed down the pane, tracing intricate patterns between the slats of the blind. And against the orange glow of a nearby streetlamp, shadows waved to her as a lone tree danced in the wind.

The wind … something about the wind …
Howling … Crashing … Waves against the cliffs …
A young girl … Sarah … Sarah … Pointing out to sea …
Dominic …
"Dominic!"

Sarah watched as a curly-haired doctor, no older than thirty, slid a needle out of her arm. The grip of the panic attack left her weak and sweating. But the memories – when they finally came – had been real and horrifying. She'd screamed and screamed until she feared her lungs would burst.

"There," he said, as he dropped the used needle onto a tray held by Nurse Flynn. "That will calm your nerves a little, help you cope better."

Sarah stared at him, open-mouthed. "Cope … I can't cope without Dom. Where's my husband?"

Despite the drugs, she didn't miss the nervous glance that flashed between doctor and nurse.

Nurse Flynn sat on the edge of the bed and took her hand. "Sarah, try to stay calm until Dr McGregor's medicine starts to work. There's no need to be distressing yourself –"

"No need! Oh God, there's every need. Why won't anyone tell me what's happened to Dominic? Is he in hospital? Was he badly injured?"

Nurse Flynn dropped her gaze – and Sarah's stomach dropped with it. The nurse increased the grip on her hand as the doctor cleared his throat.

"I'm sorry," said Dr McGregor, switching his weight from one foot to another. "I'm afraid your husband didn't survive the fall. He'd been dead some time when the Coastguard reached you."

Sarah gasped; her free hand went to her throat. "Dead …"

"I'm so sorry –" said Nurse Flynn.

"No … no … no … I saw him on the rocks. I saw him down there and was trying to get to him when I slipped –"

She broke off as the doctor shook his head.

It was the nurse who spoke first. "We don't have all the details, Sarah. Your husband wasn't brought onto this ward, but I heard from the nurses in Accident & Emergency that the RAF guys did all they could to resuscitate him, but he'd been gone some time. I'm so sorry."

"Gone. What do you mean … gone? He can't *go* anywhere. He can't be dead. Do you hear me … he can't be dead. I won't let him be dead!"

Dr McGregor spoke in a hushed voice to the nurse, and with a swish of the curtain, he disappeared.

Nurse Flynn pulled tissues out of a box, and passed them across. "He's gone to fetch Dr Davies. Your GP, isn't he? He's been waiting for you to wake. It will be good to talk to your own doctor. But you have to try to stay calm, Sarah. I know how difficult this is for you. But there's reasons you need to keep calm –"

"Reasons?" Sarah said, her voice full of scorn. "I don't have a reason to live at the moment, let alone a reason to stay calm. My husband is dead. My father is dead. I've nothing to live for –"

"Oh, but you do, my dear." Nurse Flynn's eyes were bright as she stood. "But it's not my place … I've said too much. Dr Davies will be in to speak to you shortly."

With that the nurse parted the curtains and left the room.

Sarah leaned back and took long deep gulps; her eyes were gritty and her nose blocked. A constant drumming echoed inside her head as voices faded and blurred around her. Tears poured in a steady stream down her cheeks. Dom's face filled her mind. A face she'd never see again. No! She couldn't bear it, she couldn't think it, she wouldn't let it be true.

The child!

With a flash, Sarah remembered the girl standing on the edge of the cliff pointing. The doctors must be wrong! Dominic couldn't have been dead a long time. The girl had looked terrified. She must have seen him fall. Perhaps, she'd been the one to raise the alarm? But then Sarah had another memory … a young man's face, a yappy dog …

The curtain parted and Dr Davies appeared. "Oh, Sarah, my dear. I'm so sorry. What a terrible, terrible thing to have happened. So soon after losing your father, too."

Sarah nodded as the doctor pulled a chair up alongside the bed. In the quarter of a century Dr Davies had been her family GP, he'd hardly changed at all. Still with a preference for brightly coloured shirts and the same gold-rimmed specs, he oozed warmth and security. Sarah wanted to wrap her arms around him and dissolve into his embrace. She opened her mouth to reply but a sob broke out from deep inside her, followed by a storm of tears she thought would never end. Dr Davies took her into his arms.

When she finally pulled away, leaving a damp stain on the doctor's shoulder, she became aware of another man, hovering awkwardly at the bottom of her bed. As she blew her nose and wiped her eyes, she recognised the thick-set detective she'd met at Charter House. She nodded at the unspoken question in his eyes and waited for him to retrieve a chair from the alcove beside the window.

DS Buchanan cleared his throat. "I was shocked to hear about your husband's death, Mrs Morton. I'm sorry for your loss. Are you up to talking about what happened?"

Sarah sat up straight, and tried to control her emotions, allowing the warm buzz of drugs to numb her pain.

"I just remembered … a young guy. I was calling for help and he appeared at the top of the cliff."

Dr Davies nodded. "Yes, that's Martin Cole. He was out walking his dog and heard your cries. You're lucky he was in that neck of the woods, I doubt you'd have survived long out there at this time of year."

"And the girl? What happened to the young girl?"

Dr Davies frowned and glanced across to the detective. "Don't know anything about a young girl. Only Martin. He raced back to the village, knocked at my door, and Lizzie called 999 while I drove us back to Charter House." He paused and Sarah saw pain etched on his face. "Nothing I could do though, I'm afraid. No way I could've got down that cliff face at my time of life. So, we tried to keep you talking until the coastguard arrived …"

"I don't remember any of this," Sarah said, with a shake of her head.

"You wouldn't. You were drifting in and out of consciousness; hypothermia was beginning to set in."

Sarah frowned. "But there was a young girl. Definitely. I followed her along the cliff path. She must've seen Dominic fall. I heard her shouting my name. She must have known who I was …"

She trailed off as Buchanan shook his head. "I doubt that's possible."

"How'd you mean?"

"According to the doctors in A&E, Dominic had been dead about six hours by the time the body was recovered. That was about two-thirty pm. There's no way the young girl you saw could have seen him fall. What time did you find the …er … Mr Morton?"

"It must have been around half one. He wasn't in the house when I got up, but I assumed he'd gone for a run or something. I'd slept in late and went looking for him to give me a lift into town."

"And you saw this girl while you were searching for him?"

"Yes … well … no. I heard her calling my name when I got to Dom's car. I saw her on the cliff path, and when I got to the place she was standing, I looked down … thinking she'd fallen … and saw –"Sarah broke off as fresh tears rolled down her face. "I can't believe it. To think he was probably already dead, or lying there dying … helpless … and I just carried on as normal."

Dr Davies leaned forward. "Now … now. There's no use for that talk. You've no idea what he might have been doing out there; it's a pretty remote spot?"

Sarah shook her head. "None at all. Jogging maybe. Walking. We … we'd had a bit of a row the night before. I thought he might have gone to walk it off. It's something he did."

She broke off with a sob, remembering how they'd last parted company. What was it her mother liked to say? *Never go to bed on an argument.* How Sarah wished she'd listened to that advice. Now, she'd no chance to say sorry … even though she was. She remembered with a jolt her father's letter, his warnings. She shivered and stared up at the detective.

"I wonder if this was an accident. Will there be an investigation?"

It was Dr Davies who answered. "What do you mean, not an accident?"

"What if Dom didn't fall? What if he was pushed?"

"Why would you think that?"

Sarah's heart began to race and she glanced at the detective for support. "Well, it's a bit of a coincidence, don't you think? First my father, now Dom. What if my father *was* killed? He was scared, you know that, detective. He even warned me about my own safety. Of course, I didn't take any notice. But what if he was right? What if someone murdered him? Then it would make sense that someone might have done the same to Dom –"

Dr Davies leaned forward. "Now, shush, Sarah, dear. Goodness, calm down, don't get carried away. We've no proof there was anything suspicious in your father's death, and until the police have investigated, there's little point jumping to conclusions –"

"So you will investigate now, detective? You have to!"

"Of course there will be a full enquiry, Mrs Morton," said Buchanan. "But we have to wait for the post mortem results to establish cause of death. I'd already taken a statement from Dr Davies about your father's death, before any of this happened."

"And?" Sarah swung her head towards the doctor.

"And I agreed to re-examine the cause of death, which I have, and I've found nothing irregular in the death certificate. I'm not at all convinced in these wild accusations of your father's."

"No? Not even now Dom is dead too? Well, I am. I am now. I have to find out what really happened to Dom. I have to. I can't let someone kill my husband and get away with it." Sarah's voice thickened and she slumped back against her pillow. "Oh, dear, dear, God ... is this really happening to me?"

Dr Davies patted her hand. "Try to stay positive. I'm sure Dominic wouldn't want you making yourself ill. You have to try and put these thoughts to the back of your head, Sarah, you have other things to concentrate on, things you have to look forward to ..."

"Look forward to," she said, her voice thick and nasal as she spoke through a fresh wave of tears. "I wish I was dead!"

Dr Davies gripped her shoulders in both hands, looking directly into her eyes. "Don't say such things." He studied Sarah for several seconds, until her cheeks burned. Then he shook his head. "You don't know, do you?" he asked.

"What?"

Another glance towards the other man. "No, obvious you don't ..."

"What are you talking about, Doctor? What else has happened?"

Dr Davies continued to stare and took hold of her hand again. "The doctors did all manner of routine tests when you were brought in." He paused and gave a gentle smile. "And they made a discovery. You're pregnant, Sarah, about seven weeks. I know it's a mixed blessing – but it's still a blessing. And from the tests, the foetus appears unharmed by the fall. You just need to take it easy for a while and try to relax. It's a proper miracle, Sarah!"

* * *

Danny stood in the main reception and consulted the abundance of signs, each, it seemed, designed to confuse and infuriate. Many boasted words he could barely pronounce. Angiography. Nephrology. Hydronephrosis. Urology.

Finally, he found the one he needed. Pathology.

Minutes later, he knocked on the door of the office of Dr Mohammed Patel. It was opened by a young man with shiny black hair and thick-rimmed spectacles.

"Ah, Detective Buchanan." He held out a hand and glanced at his watch. "I was beginning to think you'd got lost."

"Funny you should say that."

Dr Patel showed a set of small, even white teeth. "Ah, yes, it is a maze out there. I am having been here twelve months already, but still I carry a little map with me at all times." He patted the breast pocket of the long white coat. "You wish to speak about the post mortem I have just completed? Dominic Morton. I am typing up the report at the moment actually."

He gestured to a seat and slid behind a corner desk. "I have to admit I am surprised you are involved … and so eager. I was led to believe this was an accidental death, and nothing I've found indicates differently."

"And what have you found?"

The pathologist adjusted his glasses as he turned to consult his computer screen. "Well, quite simply multiple injuries consistent with a fall from a high place. Similar to injuries I have before seen in mountaineering accidents where zero body protection was worn."

"Signs of a struggle? Defensive wounds?"

"None. Nothing at all to lead me to suspect suspicious circumstances."

"I saw blood at the scene, down on the rocks ..."

"Yes, there were lacerations to the skull. I suspect he landed on his feet, crashed onto the right side of his body, with his head taking full impact against the rocks. There were a total of twenty-one fractures, abrasions and bruises on the body. Both legs and right arm were broken, as were fractures to the skull, neck and jaw bone. The chest cavity was full of blood, most of the ribs were broken, and there was extensive internal bleeding in several parts of his body as well as under the skin. Oh, and there was serious damage to the protective ribcage layer that covered the heart." The doctor paused, looked up from his notes. "So, in short. A horrific death, yes. But a suspicious one, no."

"I see."

Danny had hoped for something. He'd hardly been able to bear the grief in Sarah Morton's eyes. And the puzzled, disbelieving, heart-breaking expression on her face when she'd learned she was pregnant ... well. Danny pushed the image away. It would take him a long time to forget that look. If he hadn't felt a connection with Sarah Morton before, a reason to help her as much as he possibly could – he certainly felt it now. He wanted to find something to back up his own instincts that neither of these deaths were the result of natural causes. But perhaps this was better. Perhaps if all medical evidence pointed to Dominic Morton's death being nothing more than a tragic accident – then that would be the best result for this poor woman who'd had the very worst life experiences thrown at her all in one go.

"Another possibility, Doctor. Can you rule out suicide?"

The pathologist looked up and frowned. "I did consider it in the course of my examination. But in the absence of any other contributory evidence, I cannot draw a conclusion. There were traces of dirt and particles of fabric under the nails, which I have sent off for further tests. But I put this down to scrabbling for purchase as he fell. And in general suicide victims do not tend to try to save themselves."

Danny nodded, chewed for a moment on his bottom lip. "But

from your findings, or as I understand it at least, you cannot totally rule out suspicious circumstances? I mean, okay there may not be signs of a struggle, but you can't know he wasn't pushed, can you?"

Danny sensed the pathologist's reluctance; Dr Patel didn't answer immediately. Eventually with a small nod, he replied. "No, I cannot be one hundred percent certain. I can only repeat there are no post mortem injuries consistent with anything other than a fall and that is what I shall report to the coroner for the inquest. I understand that may not be what you want to hear."

"It's not a matter of what I want to hear, Dr Patel. It's just a matter of doing my job properly. And from what you've told me, we don't have conclusive proof it was an accident. That's enough reason for me to continue my enquires." Danny got to his feet and pushed back his chair. "I suppose I'm relying on good old-fashioned cop's instinct, and I'm pretty certain in my own mind I'm right. It's now just a matter of proving it."

* * *

"I want to see my husband's body," Sarah repeated, folding her hands in her lap, where beams of syrupy sunlight played across the pale green blanket. The morning had dawned bright and blustery, no trace of the previous day's storm. A new start, the first day of the rest of her life, it may be, but Sarah hadn't managed a minute's sleep, counting the seconds until the doctor arrived to discharge her. She was desperate to get out of the oppressive confines of the hospital, but first she had to see Dominic. Until she did, she knew her brain wouldn't accept he was really dead. She could barely say the word, let alone believe it. And as for the pregnancy ... she slid her hands up to cup her flat stomach. No, she couldn't handle that either, right now. One step at a time. *Inch by inch is a cinch. Yard by yard is incredibly hard.* Another of her mother's mottos.

Dr McGregor's smile dripped from his lips. "I'm sorry, I'm

not sure I can make that decision –"

"Fine. Then point me in the direction of the person who can. I'm not going home until I've seen him." She gave a tight smile. "Please."

"Mrs Morton, in your condition, I'm not sure any excess stress is recommended."

"Then we agree, surely. Not being allowed to see my husband is causing me a good deal of anxiety."

The doctor's shoulders slumped, and he slipped between the curtains, muttering as he left, "I'll see what I can do."

"Thank you," Sarah called to the fluttering material.

With a sigh, she dropped back onto the pillows. She was mentally and physically drained. But during the long, dark hours she had made plans. She had to get back to her father's safe. She had to reschedule the meeting with his PA, forgotten in the trauma. Somewhere she would find answers; including how and why she had been orphaned and widowed within weeks.

The curtain rings rattled, and she looked up, expecting to meet Dr McGregor's frown, instead she found herself staring at Luke Evans's troubled face. Immediately, her resolve crumpled, and fresh tears sprang into her eyes.

"Luke. What are you doing here?"

"I came as soon as I heard. The ferry docked this morning at seven, and I got home to a mountain of voicemails. I rang the hospital and they said you were due to be discharged at lunchtime. I thought you might need a lift home."

Sarah sniffed back tears, realising she hadn't even planned her journey home. She'd been so focussed on getting to see Dominic one last time that everything else faded into insignificance.

"I can't believe what's happened," Luke continued. "I just can't believe it. It's like a horror story. I'm so sorry."

Sarah's hand trailed across her stomach, and she nodded, not trusting herself to respond.

"I heard he fell. Do you know what happened?"

Sarah shook her head. "No. They've talked about accidents.

Suicide, even ..."

"Suicide?"

"It's rubbish. Dom would never take his own life. I love him. I know him." She paused, fighting another wave of emotion. "I knew him."

The silence hovered above them, like a blanket of unspoken words. Sarah groped for the box of tissues that was her constant ally at the moment. Luke paced across to the window, flicking the blinds aside to glance out at the blue sky.

"Are you free to go home yet?" he said, moments later as he settled in the chair left by the detective the previous evening. "If not, I'll wait until you are. You're not going back to Charter House alone." He paused, reddened. "That is, I suppose you're going back there?"

Sarah tried to formulate her thoughts. She had to make plans. But what seemed so starkly clear in the middle of the night, now seemed like a jumbled, hopeless mess.

She cleared her throat. "I suppose I'll have to. I've still got so much to sort out – telling his family and the Club for a start. I've asked to see Dom's body before I leave. The doctor has just left ... gone to make arrangements, I hope."

"Do you think that's wise? Are you ready?"

"If I don't, Luke, then I can't accept he's dead. It's the only way." Sarah slid a hand across the blanket, touched his fingers. "But will you wait for me? Please."

Luke smiled; a genuine, heartfelt smile. "Always."

Sarah leaned on the walking stick and moved slowly towards the trolley, trembling at the human form she knew was the cold cadaver of her husband. One bruised arm lay alongside his body, fingers curled as if beckoning to her. How had it come to this? She looked down, tears blurring, and stroked the grey flesh, tracing fingertips along his jaw, brushing the roughness of stubble she once bemoaned. He hadn't shaved before he'd left that morning. What a ridiculous thought – as if it mattered now or would ever matter again. If she could have Dom back for just one day, she wouldn't give a damn about his stubbly chin; he could grow a full beard if he wanted. His eyes were closed, grey lids covering sparking irises that once pulled her into his soul. His face was waxy, cold, like a mannequin, dull bruises and grazes peppered the skin. But the small smile on his lips made him at least look at peace. Sarah was glad there was no sign of pain, no hint of distress.

Gripping his hand, she twined her fingers between his, and leaned towards him. Remembering how he'd loved the feel of her hair on his face, how she'd sit astride him, bending in for a kiss with a curtain of hair creating their own private world.

Sarah bent, touched her lips against his cold mouth.

For the last time in this world.

"I am so sorry, my love. I'm sure my heart will break. But I will find strength. For our child. And I will find out who did this to you. I promise. I love you, baby."

Chapter Eight

The lock stuck for a moment, aged tumblers grated, then with a snap, turned, and the heavy door swung inwards. Red paused on the step, breathing in a last dose of crisp salty air. A pheasant screeched in the nearby woods, unsettling him for a moment. Straightening his spine, he stepped forward onto an old piece of cocoa matting and absorbed the feel of the place. The air was cold and damp, laced with cigar smoke, pine and polish. A distant aroma of herbs and cooking came from the kitchen, but as his steps carried him deeper into the house, all was silent.

His phone call to the hospital had been polite and brief; the nurse provided the required information - it would be at least lunchtime before Sarah was released. So, it was now or never. As soon as it was light enough to manage without a torch, he'd jumped into the car and headed to Point Lynas.

The safe was in the study, that much he knew for certain. He'd done his homework, like the best boy scout; it was always best to be prepared.

A blast of ice cold wind met him head on as he made his way along the panelled hallway, stopping him momentarily. He paused, alert, breath escaping in white clouds. Silence. There must be a door open somewhere. It was typical of old Owen to be too mean to invest in a decent central heating system. In fact, the whole house was in serious need of renovation. It was like stepping into a time warp, and he didn't envy Sarah the job of dragging the old place into the new century.

He reached the study – third on the right – and eased the door open with his foot. He didn't expect intruder alarms or CCTV but it was better to be prepared. He adjusted the balaclava under his chin, and stepped into the room. The odour of cigar smoke was stronger here, ingrained into furniture and carpets. The walls were lined with bookcases, but the artexed ceiling was yellowed by years of chain-smoking. A shiver of apprehension and excitement ran through him. He was close to the answers. He was certain. He pulled off his glove and dug a slip of paper out of his coat pocket. Be prepared. Dib, dib, dob, dob.

An ugly landscape painting protected the door of the safe, but it took less than ten seconds for him to realise the code was wrong. He tapped it in again, slowly this time, taking care with each digit. Just a single bleep. In frustration, he yanked off his other glove, and tried again, making sure his fingers connected with one digit at a time. Another bleep, a red light flashed, and BLOCKED came up on the small display panel.

"Shit!"

He looked round the room, trying to quell the rising sense of panic. No point getting frustrated at the first hurdle. Think. Owen changed the code. Why? Or maybe it was Sarah. Either way, wasn't it possible they'd make a note of it somewhere? His gaze rested on the oak desk. Remembering to pull his gloves back on first, he rifled through the loose paperwork, flicked through a tatty leather-bound address book, and checked every envelope in the letter slots. Bills and general correspondence, nothing of note. Diary. That's what he needed. Two of the upper drawers were locked; he tugged several times without result. Damn. Surely that was the most likely place to keep anything of importance.

Dropping to his knees he peered into the gap above each drawer; a simple lever lock, nothing overly complicated. He spotted an engraved silver letter opener next to the post rack.

He grabbed the knife and inserted it into the gap; making connection with the lever, he manipulated the blade back and forth, listening out for the tell-tale click.

Crash!

The study door flew open, smashing against the wall. Another blast of cold air enveloped him. At the same time, in the marble fireplace, a tall blue vase holding wax sunflowers toppled and smashed against the grate.

Red jumped, the letter-opener jerked and pierced the glove on his left hand, slicing open the tender skin between his thumb and forefinger. He clambered to his feet as the letter-opener hit the carpet with a thud. His heart hammered as he moved towards the door. This bloody old place had more weird winds and gusts than the London Underground.

"Shit. Shit. Shit."

He looked around, shaking his hand as the wound began to sting. He tried to ignore it, not wanting to remove his glove and inspect the damage until he was away from Charter House. He glanced at the mess in the fireplace. Would Sarah know the vase was missing if he swept it up and removed it? He couldn't take the risk. No, best make it look like a break-in and then get the hell out of there; he could come back once he had the new code. He hurried to the far end of the room, opened the French window, and selected the largest rock he could find. He threw it against the window pane nearest the lock, and then trampled back inside, overturning chairs, yanking open drawers, and generally disrupting the room as much as possible.

A bang halted him in his tracks, one arm raised, with a Royal Doulton figurine in his fist, ready to lob it against the drinks' table. It had come from upstairs, right above him in one of the back bedrooms. It sounded like something heavy had toppled over. What the hell was it? Or maybe who? That was a consideration that had passed him by. Surely no one else was staying here? He crept across to the door, and opened it an inch, straining his ear against the gap. There was something up there, definitely something making a noise. He'd assume it was the old guy's cat, Percy, if he didn't know better.

He smiled at his own wit, and gave one last cursory glance around the room. Yes, he'd done a convincing job of creating a crime scene. Give Bill and Ben, the good cop, bad cop pairing, something else to investigate. And, it wouldn't hurt to check out the old guy's bedroom while he was here. Another good place to find a diary, and he might put his hands on something else of interest. Plus he could settle his concerns if there was anyone else in the house at the same time.

As he reached the bottom of the stairs, he heard a voice, low and hushed – like someone whispering on the telephone. Shit … someone ringing the police already? He had to put a stop to this before everything spiralled out of control.

He bounded up the stairs, three at a time, and slammed open the first door he came to. A freezing cold bathroom, with a dripping shower, crumpled towels and assorted toiletries. He yanked back the shower curtain, just to be sure, and then crossed the landing. The whispers were louder now. He breathed hard as he pulled the next door open. A plume of dust rose from the floor as a sheet slipped from an ancient rocking horse. An old, disused nursery, now only storage space and clearly empty.

He paused on the landing, trying to pick up the direction of the noise. He was half convinced it was a trick of the old building, or maybe ancient pipework hissing away.

There was little point creeping around; only the dead would have failed to hear him crashing up the stairs.

"Hello. Who's there? Who is it? I'm here to help."

He waited, hands on hips. Realising he was holding his breath, he exhaled, plumes of white vapour surrounded him.

"I know you're there. Come out and talk. I'm a friend of Sarah's."

Sarah … Sarah … Sarah.

"Yeah, that's right. I'm Sarah's friend. Who are you? Where are you?"

He looked upwards, seeing a loft opening in the high ceiling. But on closer inspection, cobwebs hugged every corner of the hatch; clearly it hadn't been opened in a long time.

A groan echoed around him, and with a clunking noise followed by a loud hiss, steam began to pour from the open bathroom door. He stood, rooted to the spot, heart racing. What in God's name was going on? If this was someone's idea of a joke, they were going to discover his lack of a sense of humour pretty damn soon. He approached the bathroom. It was still empty. But yes, the shower was working full blast, soaking the grey shower curtain, and in turn pooling onto the linoleum beside the bath.

Red stepped across the puddle and leaned over the bath to turn off the tap. As he did so, the bathroom door slammed behind him. An uplift of steam surrounded him, and for a moment he was disorientated, spinning full circle, arms outstretched, reaching for the door. On the point of screaming, his hands connected with the towel rail on the back of the door, and he yanked it open, leaping back onto the landing, dragging in lungful's of cold air.

Sarah … Sarah … Sarah.

That voice again. Above him, all around him. Whatever or whoever it was. He was seriously beginning not to care; he just wanted to get the hell out of the place. He backed down the stairs, gripping hold of the bannister. As he stepped off the bottom stair, another loud rattling noise made him jump. It came again, three sharp knocks. He pressed himself flat against the panelled walls and slid into the kitchen, heading towards the back door as fast as he could.

Knock, knock, knock.

Red pulled open the kitchen door and stepped out onto the patio. It was empty. The path round the back of the house, past the garage, onto the cliff field was also empty. Thank God. It was only as he began to sprint across the field, heading towards the lane on the far side of the woods, he realised the noise could have been someone at the front door. He shook his head. No matter. He'd no desire to stick around and find out. He was not a religious man, nor did he pander to any beliefs concerning paranormal activity – but he was coming round to thinking there was something in Charter House that badly didn't want him on its patch.

And although it was easy to think, out here, crunching over frost-covered leaves that it had all been a figment of his nervy imagination – deep down he knew it hadn't been. Yeah, there was a good chance he'd look back on the incident and laugh, but for the first time in his life, he was willing to believe in ghosts – that old Owen Williams was keeping an eye on his beloved Charter House even from beyond the grave.

* * *

Danny looked up as the door to the CID office creaked open. His stomach sank into his boots as his superior stepped into the room, face glowing like he'd spent too much time in front of a fire, and eyes trained directly on him. Shite. Danny crumpled his coffee cup and lobbed it into the bin.

"DS Buchanan, my office."

Danny followed; legs heavy as lead. "Sir?" He closed the door behind him.

"Simple enough question. I'd like a simple enough answer. Why are you intent on undermining my authority in this division? And why do you constantly ignore direct orders?"

Danny frowned, selecting his words with care. "I'm sorry, I wasn't aware that's what I was doing, sir. If so, I apologise. Are you referring to anything in particular?"

"Oh, no doubt I could come up with a list as long as my arm, but in particular I'm wondering why you are spending your time on-duty, investigating two deaths, both of which appear to be unsuspicious, while the work I asked you to complete by the end of yesterday's shift has not been touched."

Danny crossed his fingers behind his back. "Sir, I'm still

following up several lines of enquiry on the deception case. I'm waiting to interview potential witnesses –"

"Waiting for what? Hmm? Christmas? Another robbery? The entire population of elderly residents of Bangor to die so the problem no longer exists? This is a serious crime, detective. So far five elderly people have been robbed in their own homes. So far none of them have been harmed … but what if next time something goes wrong, and this con-artist turns nasty? What would you have me tell the citizens of Bangor when they complain it should have been stopped sooner? That the DS I put in charge of the investigation had better things to do and other things on his mind!"

Spittle rained down on Thompson's bronze name plaque as the silence lengthened.

Danny thought it probably best just to take it.

"I'm sorry, sir. I thought DC Mayou was proceeding with the house-to-house enquires. I should have checked –"

"No. You should not have checked. You should not have allocated the job to another officer in the first place. It is not your place to choose what you will and will not do. You are not DI. I gave you the job of following up the previous victims, not DC Mayou. Had he not informed me what he was working on, then I would have been none the wiser. Not how I run my department, DS Buchanan, do you understand?"

Danny nodded. He understood. Now it made perfect sense. Glyn Mayou covering his own back, that much was obvious. Mayou was a lazy bastard, over-weight, under-worked and approaching early retirement like a randy dog near a bitch on heat. He'd never made it above acting DS – and that lasted less than a month – and never would. It was too much trouble for him to get off his fat arse and leave his computer screen most of the time, unless it was to head in the direction of the nearest pub. He wasn't Danny's type of a bloke, and the only out-of-work conversation they'd ever had revolved around a time-share apartment in Malaga and how his fiftieth birthday – and early retirement – in two years' time couldn't come fast enough. Danny had no time for men who didn't want to do the job; the force would be better off without them in his opinion.

So, it was no surprise at all to Danny that Mayou landed him in this latest bucket of hot water. Now it meant if he wanted to go any further with Sarah Morton's line of enquiry, he'd have to be a lot more discreet or do it in his own time. Great.

"Sir, I apologise again for over-stepping the mark. I made a bad judgement call. I thought the two deaths being linked might prove to be important. I discussed it with DS Lewis and he suggested I follow up the second death. I'll get back onto the deception case this afternoon. I never intended to diminish your authority, sir."

Thompson looked down and the frown faded a little. "Apology accepted. I run a tight ship, Buchanan. If you don't like my decisions then you have every right to come to me and discuss it, but what you do not do is ignore or over-rule me."

"Yes, sir."

"I don't have the man hours to waste on non-existent crimes. We have real crimes to solve. I want a full report on the deception investigation on my desk by close of play tomorrow. You may liaise with DC Mayou if necessary. Right, get on with it."

Danny exited at speed, and forced himself not to slam the door behind him. Oh, don't worry, Detective Inspector, he thought – he had every intention of liaising with Glyn Mayou. And he was *very* good at liaison.

* * *

The blare of a horn, followed by the jarring impact of the car crossing a cattle grid, woke Sarah with a grunt.

"Idiot!" yelled Luke. He gave another angry blast on the horn as he pulled the car off the verge and back onto the driveway of Charter House. "Did you see the speed that moron pulled out? Nearly took the front end off us!"

Sarah pushed herself up in the seat and turned, seeing nothing more than a flash of red out of the corner of her eye. "Sorry, I think I'd nodded off. Did you see who it was?"

Luke nodded. "Bloody Craig Davies ... he'll kill himself in that sports car ... or kill someone else. He drives round these lanes like Michael Schumacher at Monaco."

"Dr Davies' son?"

"Yeah, bloody show off. If you thought he was arrogant at school, you should meet him today. He's got a proper playboy reputation. Drives a Porsche, owns a speed boat and a yacht, and wears women on his arm like designer accessories. Runs a dive school and surfing place in Rhosneigr. He's bad news. I'd give him a piece of my mind given half a chance." Luke slapped the wheel in frustration as he parked his Jeep alongside the silver BMW.

Sarah's gaze was drawn to Dominic's car and she shuddered. Just the first of many obstacles she would have to face. But not now, not yet. One step at a time. Inch by inch ...

"Wonder what he was doing here?" Luke applied the handbrake with force.

The appearance of Craig Davies had clearly rattled Luke; it was the angriest she'd ever seen him.

Sarah shrugged. "No idea. I've not spoken to him in years."

A scowl masked Luke's features. "He has his fingers in all sorts of pies. Still has a lot to do with my brother, actually."

"David? Really?"

Luke nodded. "Yeah, sees more of him than I do. Not that I'm bothered. I just don't like the thought of him hanging around here, pestering you. People like Craig Davies prey on the weak and vulnerable." Spots of colour rose in Luke's cheeks. "Not that you're weak, Sarah. Not at all. That wasn't what I meant ..."

Sarah stopped Luke's stuttered apology with a raised hand. "I know what you mean, I appreciate your concern. But you don't have to worry about Davies. I'm surrounded by his sort back in London. They don't impress me much. I can handle him, whatever it is he wants."

Luke pushed open his door with a smile. "I can believe that. Come on, let's get you indoors."

Sarah leaned on Luke's arm as they headed towards the front door. She kept her eyes fixed forward, consciously ignoring Dom's car. All she wanted to do was sleep, or try to, and spend some time alone before the reality of the situation took over. She had to start making phone calls and facing the task of funerals and such-like. None of it felt real. It was like a movie, or a bad dream. God, she'd give anything to be able to wake up.

Luke paused beside her as she fished her keys from her bag. "Are you sure you'll be okay here, Sarah? I'm happy to stay on for a while if you want me to."

"I'm fine … well, no, I'm not. But you know what I mean. I just want to get into bed, hide under the duvet, and be on my own."

Luke nodded. "I understand. But you call if you need anything. Anything at all. Promise?"

"I promise. And thank you, Luke. For everything."

"That's what friends are for. Here." He took the bunch of keys and selected the one she indicated, sliding it into the lock and easing open the door. "Let me at least have a look round, check everything's okay, and then I'll leave you in peace."

Sarah nodded and dropped her bag over the bannister. Her eyes fixed on Dom's trainers, still laced, lying discarded under the stairs. His tracksuit top hung on a lone coat hook. She reached out, drawn to it like a moth to a brightly-lit window on a dark night. She needed comfort, to feel a tiny part of him. Her mind raced back to that frayed terry towelling robe on the back of the bathroom door, and a sob escaped her throat as she grabbed the silky material and held it to her chest.

"The bastard!"

Luke's voice shattered her thoughts.

"What? What is it?"

She grasped her walking stick and hobbled along the hall,

meeting Luke as he came out of her father's study.

"He's trashed the place. The bloody bastard. I've a good mind to go after him, he can't have got far. I always knew he was a no good piece of shit. I'm going to call the police."

Sarah grabbed hold of Luke's wrist. "No, wait. Show me."

Luke moved aside and Sarah stepped into the room. Her eyes went straight to the safe. Her mother's painting was pushed aside, but the safe appeared to be closed. She hurried across, balancing against the desk for support, pulse throbbing in her head. She twisted the handle. Locked. Thank God. It was a good job she'd changed the code from her mother's birthday to Dom's. Not that she'd had any kind of premonition, just a niggling fear that someone else might know the original code. And it looked as if she'd been right. But who would do this? Craig Davies? Really? But why?

She surveyed the room. Almost every drawer was open, papers discarded and thrown haphazardly across the floor. Chairs were overturned, cushions unzipped. Whoever it was had been searching for something, and Sarah had no doubt that something was amongst the contents of the safe. She heard Luke on the phone back in the hallway, presumably to the police. A lump of white stone she recognised from her mother's favourite rockery sat in pride of place in the centre of the threadbare maroon rug. She followed the trail of glass back to the French window, easing the door closed with her foot, remembering detective programmes she'd seen on television where white-suited men brushed powder across glass to hunt for fingerprints. Did that kind of thing happen in real life?

Luke appeared in the doorway. "Don't touch anything. They're sending someone out straight away."

Sarah nodded, easing aside blue shards of porcelain that had once stood tall and proud in the fire grate. She'd always hated the vase and the plastic sunflowers it contained, but it had been her father's favourite; a family heirloom all the way from Australia, he'd said. And now it was scattered into a million pieces across the floor.

A hand on her shoulder stilled her racing thoughts. "Are you okay?"

"I'm not sure, Luke. I'm not sure how much more I can take."

"Come on. Let's get you out of here, leave the police to do their job. Why don't you go and have a lie down and I'll bring some tea up later."

She opened her mouth to object, but Luke silenced her with a shake of his head.

"I'm going nowhere. Not now. At least not until the police have been and I've secured that window. Go and relax, Sarah, you look exhausted. You can leave everything to me."

Sarah nodded, biting down on her lip to stop another wave of tears. She detested feeling so helpless and needy. But Luke was right. If she didn't lie down, she'd fall down. It was like all the energy had been sucked out of her body. It took all her remaining strength to drag herself up the stairs, and even with Luke's arm around her waist, she felt as weak as a new-born lamb.

At the top of the stairs, she turned and hugged him. "What would I do without you?"

Luke smiled. "You don't have to worry about that right now. Go on. Rest."

* * *

Danny punched the air as he dropped the telephone onto its base. He yanked his jacket from the back of his chair, and flashed a look of distaste in Glyn Mayou's direction as he passed the other man's cluttered desk.

"Got a call?" asked Mayou, looking up from a bulging sandwich. "Want me to tag along?"

Danny paused, anger warming his neck. Nothing usually got in the way of Mayou's tea breaks. Maybe the silent treatment was getting through.

Danny turned with a bright smile. "No thanks, Glyn. I'd rather pull my own toenails out. Thanks all the same."

He slammed the office door and stood outside Rhodri Thompson's, counting to ten before knocking.

"Come."

Danny pushed the door open as he pulled on his jacket. "Sir, just had a call from a uniformed officer who has attended a 999 call at a property out at Point Lynas. A confirmed case of burglary and malicious damage."

"And?" Thompson's eyebrows rose.

"The house in question belongs to Sarah Morton. The wife and daughter of the two men who died recently. The case DS Lewis had been involved in. I'd like permission to attend the scene, sir. I'm sure you'll agree the deaths are beginning to look both connected and suspicious. Are you happy for me to go now, sir?"

Thompson pursed his lips and frowned. "Do you have the crime reference number?" he asked, turning to his computer screen.

Danny held out a piece of paper, which Thompson took his time typing out. He scanned his screen for several moments, before turning to Danny with a sigh and a nod.

"Thank you, sir."

Danny couldn't quite manage to hide the smile of triumph as he backed out of the room.

"We might have hit the jackpot actually."

Ted Reid, head of the SOCO unit, pulled off his face mask and stepped into the hallway. He held up a clear plastic finds bag.

Danny peered at the contents. A thin silver blade with a beautiful carved handle, ivory, perhaps, or bone. A smudge of red pooled in the bottom left hand corner.

"That blood?"

Reid nodded. "Yup. Can't be sure it's human of course, but it stands a fair chance. Looks like he was using the letter opener to try and access the desk drawers. He might have been disturbed, but anyway, he got injured somehow. Fingers crossed we should be able to trace him within hours if he's on file."

"Good work." Danny handed back the bag. "Anything else?"

"Some fingerprints on the safe, but smudged and could easily be the owner's. Everything is clean. Too clean. I'm pretty sure he wore gloves."

"A professional job?"

Reid pulled the mask over his head. "Possibly. Although I've got some reservations about the entry point. Here, I'll show you."

Danny followed, stepping with care over discarded books and papers, and trying not to grind broken glass into the wooden floor. They stopped in front of the French windows. Danny vaguely remembered them on his previous visit. The day they'd cleared the dead bird from the kitchen. He'd tried the doors and they'd been securely locked.

Ted Reid picked up a lump of stone. "This appears to have been used to smash the window. It was over there on the rug. No dabs."

"And?"

"Well, why smash the window?"

Danny frowned, not at once realising where the question was leading. "Well, to gain access to the key. Oh …"

Reid crossed his arms and nodded. "No key."

"Perhaps he removed it?"

Reid shook his head. "Unless he took it with him. That's the only possibility. The room's been thoroughly searched and there's no key here. I took the liberty of getting the young chap who called in the crime to find out about the key, and apparently there's only one key that's known about and that's on Mrs Morton's key ring. And it's still there."

"But there must be another key in existence?"

"Maybe so. But it's never left in the door, so she says. Her father was a stickler for security, she reckons it's the last thing he'd ever do."

Danny looked round the room, taking in the exposed wall safe. "Did he get into there?"

"No."

"But that was the target?"

"It would appear so."

"And who's the young guy? Is he still here?"

Reid nodded as he fastened the catch on his briefcase. "In the kitchen giving a statement to young Robbins. He's a good lad, Robbins, make good CID one day."

"We could do with some new blood," said Danny. "Anything else you can tell me?"

"Nope. I don't think he came in through the garden. I think that's a set up."

"No other entrance has been forced?"

Ted shook his head.

"So, he had a key?"

Ted smiled. "That's your job to find out, I'm afraid. I'm off to get some DNA from this sample and hopefully find a match. Let's see who can solve the crime first, shall we? Loser buys a round?"

Danny grinned and slapped the other man's retreating back. "You're on."

A loud voice came from the other side of the kitchen door.

"I don't know why you're not just arresting him? It's bloody obvious, isn't it?"

The voice fell silent as Danny pushed open the door. PC Robbins looked up from his note taking, cheeks blazing.

"What's obvious, sir?" said Danny, removing his ID card and placing it on the table in front of the dark-haired man. "DS Buchanan, CID."

The man glanced at the card and handed it to Danny. "Detective, I've been explaining to the officer, we saw who did this."

"You saw the robbery take place?" Danny pulled out the stool opposite and straddled the wooden seat. "Sorry, sir, I didn't catch your name?"

"Evans. Luke Evans. No, we didn't see it actually happen, but we saw him making a getaway. Nearly crashed into us as a matter of fact."

"Him would be?"

"A Craig Davies, sir," replied PC Robbins, glancing at his notebook. "Mr Evans was bringing Mrs Morton home from hospital at approximately mid-day –"

"And Davies pulled out of the drive like a maniac just as we got here. Minutes later we find that mess in there. He's total scum. It doesn't take Einstein, does it?"

Danny observed the man's scowl and tight jaw. "Well, I'm not Einstein. But I agree we should speak to this Mr Davies. Any ideas where we find him?"

The young man visibly relaxed. "Thank you. Finally, someone taking me seriously. I don't know his address but he runs a tacky dive school called *Deep Dayz* in Rhosneigr, over on the other side of the island. Anyone in the village will point it out to you. He's bloody well known around these parts, mostly for all the wrong reasons."

Danny ignored the latter statement and got to his feet. "And you've given a statement to PC Robbins?"

"Yes."

"Fine. And Mrs Morton?"

"I've just checked and she's resting. But she can't tell you anymore than I, detective. I went into the study first. Is it okay if I organise a repair to secure the window now before it gets dark?"

"Of course. Please carry on."

Danny watched the man head back into the study. One uptight fella, and his assertions about this Davies character felt almost too personal. Danny wanted to speak to Sarah Morton. But perhaps now wasn't the time; she certainly didn't need any more stress than absolutely necessary. He'd let her rest. And if the DNA matched with yer man Davies, he might even have the crime solved before she woke.

Chapter Nine

**'Pleasure Tours & Fishing Charters.
All aboard the Sea Goddess II.'**

The sign hung on a rusted chain and rattled in the wind as if about to crash to the ground at any moment. Underneath was a life-size model of a ruddy-faced fisherman, dressed in a yellow sou'wester, holding in one weather-beaten hand a huge cod, and in the other a red arrow pointing down to a small quay. Sarah shook her head, remembering teenage days spent on this jetty; little changed in Moelfre in a lifetime, let alone a decade.

Huw Parry, more affectionately known as Huw the Boat, was probably the one person on the whole of Anglesey who knew as much about the Royal Charter as her father. An ex-fisherman, he now ran pleasure trips around Puffin Island, and fishing charters across the bay. She and Luke had loved helping out with pleasure tours in the summer holidays. Huw was a strong advocate of leaving the wreck as a memorial to the dead, and Sarah remembered him joining forces with her father to shout objections at a meeting at Moelfre Town Hall not long after her mother died.

She peered through the steamy windscreen of her father's

Jaguar, out across the choppy blue water and sweep of golden sand. She hadn't been able to face the BMW. Not yet. A half-empty Pepsi bottle stared back at her through the car window, and the thought of losing forever a little part of Dom's DNA prevented her from opening the door. Besides it was a manual, and driving her father's automatic had been enough of a challenge with a dodgy ankle.

She rubbed her eyes, tired and gritty with lack of sleep, and thought back to the detective, Buchanan. There was something about the man that attracted her. Not in a sexual way, God no. That part of her life, her body, she could never imagine functioning again. But a connection, some kind of empathy enveloped her whenever she was in the man's presence. It was hard to explain. Almost like an unspoken understanding, but about what, they'd never discussed and she couldn't begin to guess.

Buchanan hadn't brought good news. Craig Davies had been questioned and released. The DNA found in her father's study wasn't on file; neither did it match that of Davies. Apparently, he'd simply travelled across the island to Charter House to pass on his condolences at her recent bad luck. Right.

"But I hardly knew the guy," Sarah kept repeating.

"I know ... and I understand your frustration." DS Buchanan shrugged. "But we can't hold him without suspicion, and we've no grounds to charge him. He's got a stonking alibi for the morning of your husband's death, and there's nothing at all to link him to your father."

"So we're back to square one?" Sarah swallowed to repel the sting of tears.

"For the time being, I'm afraid so, yes. We've also nothing to link the break-in to either death. Nothing was taken, after all. It could have been an opportunist theft, there's a lot about at the moment." Buchanan looked down, but Sarah had already seen the lack of conviction in his eyes. "Some low-life heard what had happened, perhaps thought he'd try his luck while the place was empty. It makes sense."

Sarah shook her head. "Not to me. I don't believe in coincidences. Never have."

That train of thought had led her here, to the quay in Moelfre, listening to Huw's infectious laughter from inside the small Portakabin on the dockside below. Sarah climbed out of the car, and carefully negotiated the wooden steps down to the jetty, picking her way through great frothy piles of green nylon nets and towering stacks of lobster pots. She knocked on the door. Fingers crossed he would remember her. Had she changed very much in the past ten years?

"Well, well, I'll be darned if it isn't Sarah Williams. How are you, del? Heard you were back at Charter. Terrible sorry 'bout your da. Heard about the accident too, aye. Treacherous them rocks out at Lynas. Tragic. Come you in. I've a cuppa on the boil."

Huw turned down his radio programme, and, taking her stick, helped her into a rickety wooden deckchair. Minutes later, he handed across a cup of charcoal-coloured tea in a chipped yellow mug that looked like it hadn't seen washing-up liquid for years. With a grunt, he dropped onto a low bench and took a loud slurp. The tea tasted a million times better than it looked, strong and sweet, and Sarah felt warm and safe for the first moment since she'd seen Dom's body on the rocks.

Huw the Boat hadn't aged at all. But then, he had looked at least eighty for as long as she could remember. He wore the same dark blue overalls, and his complexion was still nut brown where it wasn't covered by a bushy white beard. As kids, they'd always affectionately called him 'Captain Birdseye' – and the twinkle she remembered remained in his watery blue gaze.

Several cups of tea later, after discussing a potted biography of the past ten years of her life, Sarah managed to turn the conversation onto her topic.

"Aye, my family been involved in The Charter from the day she sank in one way or another," said Huw, his eyes bright with pride. "My great grandpa tried to help, in the rescue, like, but could do no more than pull bodies from the water for days, so he told. Terrible, terrible, tragedy." He paused and shook his head, a solemn expression on his face. "I don't think no one knows for sure how many lives were lost, all records went down with the ship, so they reckon. The currents round Anglesey can be so strong once a body goes in, no knowing where it'll resurface. Lots end up Blackpool way, coast of Cumbria even. My father remembered his dad's tales, shocking they were; said it haunted him till day he died, seeing so many women and children perish in front of his eyes and not a thing he could do about it. Guess that's why I've always felt the need to protect the old wreck, for the ol' man's sake." He paused while appearing to collect his thoughts, and looked up with a tired smile.

"I think my father felt the same," she said. "I know he did."

"I'd not seen your da for a good few years, but I did hear he was asking a lot of questions 'bout the Charter, recent. Always was poking 'is nose in around the library and church, or writing off to Lloyds – the register of shipping – for somethin' or other. My thinkin' is he'd found somethin' in them records, dunno what, mind. He was an awkward bugger at times – God rest his soul – couldn't work him out if I'm honest. Never knew when you'd got old Owen. Not that I should be speaking ill of the dead, like." Huw pulled the navy knitted cap off his head and lowered his gaze.

Sarah touched his arm and slid her empty mug onto the desk. "It's okay. I know what my father was like. I'm more interested to learn what I can about The Charter. Have any new discoveries had been made recently?"

"Gold you mean – treasure?" He grinned a toothless smile. "Not that I know of, del. Always tourists around in the summer months, rich folk, thinking they be the ones to find the Australian gold. Turn up in fancy dinghies, or their posh yachts, and dive for a couple o' tides. Then get bored, go home."

"Someone said my father might have found out some new information about the wreck. I know what local gossip is like round here."

"No, bach. If I'd heard, I'd tell you. Last bad storm was '88 or '89, some coins was washed up over on Lligwy Bay. Was rumours then some diver had found gold, caused a bit of a fuss. Said he'd seen bullion buried deep in the sea bed, but his oxygen ran out before he could free it. Load of salvage firms turned out from Liverpool, went all frantic for couple of months, but I never heard they found much. Was round bout the time there was talk of lifting the old girl – but we put a stop to that. Me and your dad. Back then folk round here listened to Owen Williams.

"I remember seeing Owen on the local TV news, the BBC. Angry as hell he was, nearly got himself into a fight with some bloke run a diving firm in Liverpool. Had a right good laugh about that we did, me and the boys."

Sarah remembered the incident well. The live broadcast had made her father even more vocal than normal; his booming voice and angry face filled the television screen, making Sarah shudder from the safety of their living room. The interviewer, clearly embarrassed, cut short the report when her father and the diver almost came to blows. No wonder, when her father called the man no better than a 'common thief'. She recalled her father's words; the feeling as raw today. Flashes of similar humiliation, dating back through her adolescence, caused her to break out in a cold sweat.

"Last I heard was some metal detector bloke found a couple of coins over in Red Wharf 'bout four, five years back. Think your father was involved in some memorial at Llanallgo round the same time; some relatives came over from Australia and there was them media types sniffing round the place. But no, I've heard nothing, nor seen nothing, out of ordinary. What's troubling you, del?"

"I found some of my father's papers. Seems he'd taken to writing a lot about the wreck, and I wondered why the sudden interest." Heat spread into Sarah's cheeks at the semi-truth.

"Your da … he'd grown bit odd in his old age. Bit reclusive, like. We rarely seen him down in Moelfre, only seemed to mix with them hoity-toity University types. Wish I could be more help, del."

"It's okay, Huw. It's good to see you anyway. Good to see a friendly face."

Huw gave a stern look. "If you want my advice you'll steer clear of anything to do with the Royal Charter. Let the dead rest in peace, always been my motto. There's been enough fighting in this village over the years. Enough grudges held and lies told to last a lifetime, aye. I don't want to be saying too much, but let the past stay there. That'd be my advice, Sarah, del. You'd be wise to be takin' it."

Later that night, Huw's words came back as Sarah twisted back in forth in bed, becoming increasingly sweaty and frustrated as sleep refused to find her. Why leave well alone? Had it really been a threat to keep her nose out? She'd never been one to obey orders. She would find out what her father had discovered. What did she know about the wreck of a ship over a hundred years ago – she wasn't even sure of the exact date – that could possibly link it to a modern day double-murder? Nothing.

Sarah thought back to the times her father had attempted to get her interested in local history, and in particular the story of the Royal Charter. His overzealous bullying had resulted in her detesting all things historical, but she could never have told him so. Perhaps that's why she'd rebelled and studied geography as a teen, knowing it would infuriate his snobbishness. She could remember with clarity his frustration, and subsequent anger, when she failed to be bitten by the same historical bug that resulted in him dedicating his life to its cause.

She glanced at the bedside clock – 3:30. She threw back the duvet and balanced on the edge of the mattress, trying to find her slippers in the darkness. Her eyes were drawn to the far side of the bed and a gulf of anguish ripped through her, leaving behind the sick feeling she was becoming accustomed to. Her mind was so pre-occupied, she expected a human form there, could hardly accept the empty space. She'd thought keeping her mind busy might help cure the insomnia, but the idea worked against her. She was now so switched on, there was no way she could unwind enough to sleep. Since her conversation with Huw Parry, there were too many questions, and she had to start finding the answers.

She wrapped herself in her dressing gown, shivering in the frosty air, and settled in front of the dressing table. The night was inky black; heavy clouds blocked out any sign of moonlight, and storm-force winds whipped the sycamores into a frenzy. Rain rattled against window panes and old roof timbers creaked mournfully.

In the distance, the sound of the tide battering the cliffs at Point Lynas rumbled like an angry beast, and once more her thoughts were dragged back to the wreck. Had it been a night like tonight? Rough seas and high tides? She'd heard many tales of piracy all around the Anglesey coast, even local legends about 'wreckers' who made a living out of guiding lost vessels onto the rocks and looting the cargo.

Sarah pictured the scene. She'd witnessed many wild storms, seen fishing boats tossed like toy yachts on ten-foot waves and watched canoes get hooked on a riptide current and dragged miles out to sea. She'd been raised all her life to respect the ocean and immense power of Mother Nature, and she could well imagine the sounds and smells associated with that night – the heavy, salty, sulphur-like smell of the raging sea; the roar of the waves as they crashed against the high cliffs; the feel of spray and foam soaking to the skin with a dense, clinging, coldness. Could the passengers see the coastline or their rescuers? Would it have been possible to swim to shore? How many lost their lives? How many survived?

She wanted to know, needed to. The hunt for answers became an ache in the pit of her stomach. She dragged her bag from the floor and powered up her laptop, waiting while the network searched, and then accessed Google. She typed Royal Charter and clicked search, and within seconds was presented with over 800,000 links.

She grabbed a notebook and pen, and clicked on the first website.

Hours later, she looked up from the screen, stretched her aching back and rotated her stiff neck. The first hint of a winter's dawn reached across the sky. The clouds were thinner now and the rain had passed, but the wind still battered the sea-facing side of the old house.

Sarah flicked through thirty or more pages of notes, and realised, for the first time, why her father had been so captivated by the story of the Royal Charter. She was shocked by the loss of life involved. Not the handful she'd imagined; there were definitely over four hundred dead or missing presumed dead. Some of the sites were purely factual, but others documented the night of the storm with such pinpoint accuracy and eye-witness testimony, she could almost envisage herself there, on-board the floundering vessel.

Sarah had run a search on her father's name, and felt a belated surge of pride, when she'd found his name listed on more than a hundred websites, including the notorious BBC interview from 1988. She ripped the pages from her notebook, deciding she needed to make a quick guide summary of the hundreds of haphazard notes. She opened her journal, turned to the next blank page, and began to write.

THE ROYAL CHARTER

'*The Royal Charter was a steam clipper built at the Sandycroft Ironworks on the River Dee, launched in 1857. She was a new type of ship, a 2719 ton steel-hulled vessel, built in the same way as the existing clipper ships, but with auxiliary 200 horse-power steam engines which could be used in the absence of suitable winds.*

The ship was used on the route from Liverpool to Australia, mainly as a passenger vessel able to hold up to 600 passengers and crew, although there was room for some cargo. She was considered a very fast ship for the time, able to make passage to Australia in under 60 days.

The ship left Hobson's Bay, Victoria on 26 August 1859 bound for Liverpool, equipped with her full complement of officers and crew, commanded by Captain Thomas Taylor. She carried a total of 371 passengers and 112 crew and company employees. Many of the passengers were gold miners, returning home to the UK after becoming rich at diggings in Australia. Many were carrying large sums of gold around their persons, and there was also a large consignment carried as cargo.

According to records, a fast passage was made around Cape Horn even though they had passed uncomfortably near icebergs; the passengers all commended Captain Taylor's handling of the ship.

However, as the ship reached the north-western tip of Anglesey on 25 October, the barometer was dropping and it was claimed later by some passengers, though not confirmed, that the Captain was advised to put into Holyhead harbour for shelter. He refused and decided to continue on to Liverpool. His decision became the ship's downfall.'

Sarah broke off to find the notes she'd made from an account written in the local parish records. She rubbed her wrist and stretched aching fingers, but she was still driven to complete the task. Finding the relevant notes, she began again.

'Off Point Lynas the Royal Charter tried to pick up the Liverpool pilot, but the wind had now risen to force 10 on the Beaufort scale and the rapidly rising sea made this impossible. As night fell the wind rose to force 12 (hurricane force) in what became known locally as the 'Royal Charter gale'. As the wind rose its direction changed from E to NE and then NNE, driving the ship towards the east coast of Anglesey. At 11pm she anchored, but at 1.30am on the 26 October, both anchors snapped in quick succession. Despite *cutting the masts to reduce the drag of the wind, she was driven inshore with the steam engines unable to make headway against the gale. The ship initially grounded on a sandbank, but in the early morning of the 26th the rising tide drove her into the rocks at Point Lynas, where she was battered by huge waves whipped up by winds of over 100mph, and she quickly broke up.'*

Turning the pages, she searched for an eyewitness report from one of the rescuers, known after the event as the Moelfre Twenty Eight. Through the efforts of the local men, who formed a human chain into the sea, a total of forty-one passengers and crew were rescued, all men, with no women or children saved. This site reported over four hundred and fifty victims. Sarah rubbed goose-bumped arms.

'We seen the wreck at day break, meself, Thomas Hughes, and Mesech Williams were watching from the cliffs, but there was nothing we could do save stand and watch the tempestuous sea and the helpless wreck. Every moment we expected to see the waves burying in their depths the wrecking vessel, and we could scarcely believe it when we seen a man let himself down from the decks by a rope and into the midst of the breakers.

We learned later his name was Joseph Rogers (a Maltese able seaman) who'd volunteered to swim with a hawser to shore, and who, though three times driven back by the hissing floods, nobly persevered, and succeeded in making fast the rope to the rock below us.'

The bravery it would have taken to jump into the sea that night. The conditions must have made his task virtually impossible. Sarah scan-read the list of names of the local men that made up the Moelfre Twenty Eight, recognising many that still had families in the area: Thomas Roberts, Owen Hughes, Lewis Francis, John Parry, Evan Williams.

Williams!

Why had that never occurred to her before? Mesech Williams had already been mentioned. There was also a Robert Williams, a Joseph Williams and a William Williams.

Sarah tried to stop herself jumping to conclusions. Yes, there was a slight chance one of these men was her ancestor, but Williams was a common name in Wales. And she was sure she'd heard her father tell people over the years, his family were not Moelfre born and bred. But it was certainly one possibility that made sense. Perhaps one of her relatives was one of the men involved in the rescue of the Royal Charter.

Somehow, that didn't seem right, although she couldn't put her finger on the reason why. She made a mental note to ask Grandma Ruth what she knew about her father's family. Several generations of her maternal family were from Anglesey. Sarah knew she was certainly Welsh, so was her father and paternal grandfather, Richard Williams, but prior to that she had no idea.

She wondered why she'd never asked more questions, and why, thinking back, her father always remained secretive about their family ancestry. It seemed odd; he was so outspoken on every other topic, and yet stoically private about his family.

Perhaps the reason had something to do with an article she found from a local newspaper, The North Wales Gazette, in 1861.

'Following the wrecking of the steam clipper, the Royal Charter, a large quantity of gold was said to have been thrown up on the coasts near Moelfre, with some families becoming rich overnight. Some of the Moelfre Twenty Eight were said to have become instantly wealthy, with many outsiders now questioning their motives at the time. Were they the heroes they pertained to be? The gold bullion cargo was insured for £322,000, but the total value of the gold on the ship was reportedly much higher as many of the passengers had considerable sums in gold, either on their bodies or deposited in the ship's strong room.'

She turned back to the notes taken from the parish records.

'*The bodies of the victims of the shipwreck as they were recovered from the sea were brought up the hill from the village to Llanallgo Church which became the mortuary. The Rector, Reverend Stephen Roose Hughes, took on the job of identifying the dead, and carefully recorded the physical details of each body, its clothing, the contents of the pockets and any detail which might enable an identification of the body to be made. Each body was carefully looked after and the stream of relatives which soon started to descend on the village came one by one to the Rector to search for their loved ones. In some cases bodies had to be exhumed for identification. Records show that within twelve months, Reverend Hughes had written 1075 letters of reply to those which had been written to him inquiring after missing family.*

Of those who perished 140 lie in the graveyard at Llanallgo, 64 are buried in Llaneugrad, 45 in Penrhosllugwy. Others lie in the graveyards of the parishes on the beaches of which they were washed up. These are Llanddyfan, Llanwenllwyfo, Llanfairmathafarneithaf, Llanbedrgoch, Llanddona and Amlwch.'

She'd also found a newspaper cutting from 1862 about the Rector.

'*The strain of the sinking of the Royal Charter led to the early death of Reverend Stephen Roose Hughes of Llanallgo Church, who passed away on February 4th, 1862. He gave his life to the dead of the Royal Charter wreck.*'

And as part of the piece, a story detailed how Charles Dickens immortalised the life of Stephen Hughes, and the story of the shipwreck, in his book, The Uncommercial Traveller. Apparently, Dickens visited the scene, talked to the Rector, and was so moved, he chose to make it part of his next book.

Dickens gave a vivid illustration in one passage:

'So tremendous had the force of the sea been when it broke the ship, that it had beaten one great ingot of gold, deep into a strong and heavy piece of her solid iron-work: in which also several loose sovereigns that the ingot had swept in before it, had been found, as firmly embedded as though the iron had been liquid when they were forced there.'

Sarah recoiled at the mention of gold sovereigns, remembering the contents of the safe. Were they from the Royal Charter?

She dropped her pen and rubbed her eyes. Finally, she felt ready to sleep.

Yes, she'd raised new questions, but at least she'd found answers to some old ones. And tomorrow – later today – she would start to go through the contents of the safe with a clear head and far more knowledge.

She'd made a start by assembling all the pieces of the jigsaw. Family ancestry, missing treasure, local rumour. Her next job was to sort out all the straight-edged pieces, and start to build the framework. The physical pain of Dom's absence again cut through her – he'd have been as excited as a child to have been involved.

With a sigh, Sarah dragged her exhausted body back into bed, pulled the duvet over her head and drifted, finally, into a sleep full of dreams of ghostly people, crashing waves, and gold ingots.

Chapter Ten

Danny yawned and pushed open the curtains to reveal a bright blustery morning. He was surprised; rain had lashed down and wind rattled the window frames most of the previous night. Another thing about North Wales that reminded him of home; the speed the weather could change. Home. He tried not to think of his mam and sister too much. Or Dinah. Tried not to let the loneliness bite too deep. He knew he had to make a decision soon about Christmas, and already knew he'd probably take the coward's way out and declare he'd been forced to work over the festive period.

He closed his eyes for a moment, resting his forehead against the cool window pane. He didn't like to appear like a big soft Jessie, and he'd never tell another single soul, but something about the view from his window at this quaint little B&B took his breath away and turned him maudlin.

Bangor Pier jutted out below, like an accusing finger pointing the way across the dark narrow channel of the Menai Straits. The far bank, which led eventually off to the right to the colourful town of Beaumaris, was a high wall of tree-lined slopes edging down to narrow strips of shingle beach. To his right, an expanse of blue shining water led the eye to the craggy pale rocks of the Great Orme, off Llandudno. And to top it all, if he opened the window and leaned out, he could see the beginning of the majestic range of mountains that led, somewhere out of his view, to Snowdonia. King of them all. Or was it Queen?

His finger itched as it connected with the packet of Marlboro in the pocket of his cardigan. Despite the strict No Smoking laws, he'd succumbed a couple of times, wedged face-first out into the chilly November air to ensure not one swirl of smoke blew back into the room. Mrs Howard-Jones was a doll. But even dolls could be dangerous when rules were broken.

Today was his day off. He should be making plans to take a trip out. Down the coast perhaps as far as Conwy or Llandudno. Or inland. Have a look around Llanberis or maybe take the train up to the summit of Snowdon. There were a hundred things on his list of stuff he wanted to do. But somehow he couldn't seem to settle to any of them.

Truth was, Sarah Morton troubled him more than he'd admit, more than was professional. There was an intimacy between them he was pretty certain they both felt, created that day in the hospital when she discovered she was pregnant. He'd never seen such raw emotion in anyone before, and even though in his usual cack-handed way he'd failed to offer any useful sympathy, he had understood. He'd seen her only a few days previously with her husband, and recognised her complete reliance on his strength. So, it was a surprise to Danny that she seemed to have recovered at break-neck speed and was acting like some super-hero-avenging-angel. It was an act. Danny was certain of it. Sometime or another she would crack, do something stupid, and he wanted to be there to put a stop to it.

She appeared not to have considered her own life might be in danger. Two deaths so far. A killer who was no doubt getting increasingly frustrated. But by what? Or whom? And Sarah Morton was holding back, another thing he felt sure about. But how could he convince her to trust him – a dodgy-looking Irish copper – at a time when she probably found it impossible to trust anyone in the world?

He glanced at his watch. Almost nine. Perfect. He'd take breakfast and then stroll down to Bangor University. The History

Department. Or whatever fancy name it went under nowadays. Someone must know Professor Owen Williams, could maybe point him in the right direction to explain why the elderly academic feared for his life. He pulled off his baggy cardigan - a much-loved reminder of his first Christmas with Dinah - tugged on his jacket and locked the room behind him.

Sightseeing could wait for another day.

* * *

"Come in, bach, come in. Oh, it's lovely to see you. Here, let me help you."

Grandma Ruth ushered Sarah into the small front room of her bungalow. Sarah towered over the tiny woman as they embraced. Gran was at least a foot shorter than her five foot nine inches, and it came as a shock how much old age and arthritis had shrunk the thin frame of the elegant woman Sarah remembered from her childhood.

Sarah looked round the tiny room. She noted a couple of her mother's watercolours on the facing wall: one of Melin Llynnon, a working windmill on Anglesey, and another of a salmon-coloured sunset across Holyhead Mountain. Sarah had always disliked this bungalow. It wasn't so much the dimensions she couldn't cope with, it was the fact that every corner was jam packed with clutter. She doubted her Grandma had thrown anything away in all her eighty-four years. Add to that her love for stuffed toys, Royal Doulton, and general oddments that to Sarah would fall under the category 'tat', and there was hardly room to breathe let alone swing the proverbial cat.

"It's okay. I'm fine. I'm just more awkward than usual with this ankle," Sarah said, as she leaned her stick against the gas fire and removed an over-sized panda from the huge chintz armchair, biting back a squeal as she almost disappeared into the padded seat. She'd forgotten about the killer chair; it got her every time.

"Now, I've got the kettle on, and I've made a ham salad and that nice cherry Madeira cake you love, for lunch …"

"Gran! You didn't have to go to any trouble," Sarah said, pulling herself out of the confines of the chair with both hands.

"It's nice to have someone to go to the trouble for."

Sarah leaned across to the sofa and clasped her gran's fingers between her own; the skin was as smooth and delicate as a calfskin glove, but thick purple veins lined her swollen hands.

"And it's nice to have someone who cares," said Sarah. "I just don't want you going to any trouble for me. But that's not to say I'm not starving!"

Gran smiled and squeezed her hand with a faint grip. "I'm sure you're not looking after yourself, are you young lady? And with eating for two as well …"

"I'm fine, honest. But I have an idea I'd like to put to you."

Gran paused, her hand on the back of the sofa. "How are you now, really, Sarah, bach? Are you okay?"

The pale blue gaze was full of concern, and Sarah remembered the high emotion when she'd broken the news of her pregnancy during a tearful phone call from hospital. Gran was the only person in the world she'd found it easy to tell, and her common sense approach made the decision to raise the child alone feel like the only choice Sarah could make.

"No," Sarah said, looking away as tears sprang up in her eyes. "But I will be. I promise."

"You have no choice, I'm afraid. You've the child to think about. So many of my friends went through the same in the war years. As many fatherless families back then as there are today, but for totally different reasons. Families were *proper* families back then, and they rallied, you know? The whole street would support a widow. I was lucky, I know that."

"At least I have you."

Gran gave a gentle smile and patted Sarah's cheek. "Always."

Half an hour later, they were both cramped around the fold-up kitchen table; this room was even smaller than the lounge. Sarah had eaten more than she thought possible, but the food tasted so good that once she started she couldn't seem to stop. A jolt of guilt ran through her as she realised how she'd neglected herself since Dom's death. She'd not eaten a proper meal since returning to Charter House, and could only hope the baby hadn't suffered because of it.

"God, I'm full." She winced as she leaned back and undid the button on her jeans.

"You won't be fitting into those very much longer, young lady," her gran said with a look of disapproval at the tight faded denims.

"I know. I'm sure I'm getting a bulge already. Or perhaps that's the three slices of Madeira cake showing."

Gran chuckled. "It's good to see you eat, bach. You need to keep your strength up. It's a shame you can't get meals-on-wheels, like I do!"

Sarah drained the last of the strong tea from a rose-patterned china cup. "Well, that's where my suggestion comes in actually. I've been thinking about this a lot, and I have a proposal to offer you."

"Really?" Pure white eyebrows disappeared beneath a coiffured hairline of the same colour.

Sarah drew in a shaky breath. "I've decided I'm going to stay up here, for the time being, at least until the baby's born. I need peace and calm, and there's no reason with my career why I can't work from home. I couldn't bear to sell the house at the moment." Sarah paused, remembering the presence she felt there. The voice she'd heard calling her name. "And I think it seems stupid for you to pay rent here while I'm rattling around that old place on my own, so I wondered how you'd feel about moving into Charter House with me?"

"Are you sure? I mean, I'd love to have you near, love to have you and my great grandchild to look after, but what about your life down in London? What about your friends?"

"I don't have anyone I would truly miss, more acquaintances and colleagues than real friends. And it's only four hours on the train. Besides, I'd have to move out of the penthouse. We're on the ninth floor, which would be no good with a baby. As long as I can arrange something with my work, then I'm totally prepared."

"But what if it doesn't work out for you? It's a different pace of life up here than you've been used to for the past ten years. Are you sure you've thought this through, bach?"

"Absolutely. I've decided to put the London apartment up for rent, and if it doesn't work out then I always have that to fall back on if I want to return." She paused again, visualising the loft apartment, with high ceilings and one complete wall of glass, overlooking the Thames and Canary Wharf beyond. It had been Dom's choice more than hers; he'd fallen in love at first sight. "But I doubt I will. Too many memories …"

Grandma's hand found hers on the table top, and squeezed. "I understand." She paused and her eyes followed the walls. "I always thought I'd see my years out here. I've grown fond of the little place. Mind you, the friends and neighbours I was close to have long since moved … or died."

"So, what do you think? Could you live at Charter House?"

"I don't honestly know. It's nothing to do with you, bach, either. That place holds lots of memories for me." Her eyes were bright with tears. "Your father never liked me, you know? Even when your mother and he were at their happiest, he couldn't stand the sight of me. Worried I saw the real him, he was. He came to hate me. And I him."

Sarah shook her head. "He never said a bad word about you –"

"He didn't have to. He knew how I felt about him. Oh, and I'm sure the feeling was mutual – one of the reasons we avoided each other as much as possible for the past twenty years."

Sarah sat back in her chair, shocked. "I knew you didn't get on, but I never thought –"

"I accepted him because your mother begged me too. Believe me … it's amazing what a mother will do for her child."

Sarah let the silence lie heavy between them. It was her gran who broke it; she spoke slowly as if choosing her words with care.

"Your father was a difficult man. I know I don't have to tell you that, Sarah." Her pale gaze met hers and Sarah nodded. "I'd go so far as to call him a bully. They'd call him a control freak these days, I suppose. He was too old, too strict, too set in his ways, but she fell for him, didn't she? Loved him. Wouldn't listen to me. Ah, but him! Him I could never forgive."

Sarah could see she was struggling to keep her temper.

"I could have forgiven him for his arrogance, and the way he looked down on me, if he'd treated my daughter well. But he never did. He controlled her, totally dominated her. She had no life: no career, no independence, no real friends or a life away from him, other than her choir and her painting. And she put up with it because she loved him … no, she idolised him. It wasn't natural, the hold he had over her, and it angered me. She was an intelligent woman, wanted to be an archaeologist, you know, which was how she met Owen. But he put a stop to it all with his sergeant major ways. Just like he tried to control you and stop you having a life of your own. You did right moving away when you did; he'd have drained the life from you if you'd stayed on Anglesey."

Sarah's cheeks burned. She'd never disclosed her real reason for leaving to her grandmother, but it looked as if she'd been wise enough to work it out in her own mind anyway. But it was better to let it go now. Her father was dead. What was the point in raking up more pain for either of them?

"I hated him for losing both of you … both my Sarahs."

Sarah recalled similar words in her father's letter.

"If she'd never met him, my Sarah would still be here today."

"What?" Sarah pulled back and met the cold stare.

"He killed her as true as if he'd plunged a knife into her heart."

Her grandmother began to cry.

"Aw, that's enough," Sarah whispered. "You'll make yourself ill. Please, don't."

Gran straightened her back and wiped her eyes. "I've lived with this for twenty years, bach, losing your own child makes you strong. Having you back is like a breath of fresh air. There's so much of Sarah in you; your eyes and smile, even your voice and your laugh brings her back to me."

Sarah hugged her, feeling the sharp jut of shoulder blades, and found herself overwhelmed with a rush of affection.

"Your father is dead now, God rest his soul. You can't live with ghosts, Sarah. You can't live with ghosts ..." Gran paused and blew her nose. "So, could I live in his house, with him and his rules?" She shook her head. "No. But it's your house now, your rules."

"I will make it my house. Make it brighter, fresher. Make it a place I want to raise my child."

"Then I'd be delighted, bach. If you want me, I'd be delighted."

"Oh, Gran!" Sarah pulled her back into her arms. "There's something else I wanted to ask you about - Father. I've not yet seen his Will, but he left a letter and some bits and pieces in the safe for me. It's all a bit of a mystery. What can you tell me about my father's family?"

"A letter, you say. Typical. Well, I'm sorry. But Owen Williams was never one to do anything simple. If there was a scene to be played, he knew how to play it. If there was fuss to be made, you could be sure he'd be in the middle of it. Trust him not to leave a Will, and be done with it, like any other normal folk." She pursed her lips and shook her head.

"So, did they come from Anglesey? I've only ever heard him talk about my grandparents, Richard and Miriam, but they both died before I was born. Thing is ..."

Sarah paused, weighing up her options. She wanted to be honest with her gran, but her father's words of warning rattled round in her head. She couldn't risk panicking her, with stories about Dom's death and the break-in.

"Something tells me this has a lot to do with that damn shipwreck."

Sarah looked up, open-mouthed. "How did you know?"

"Obvious to me. It was all Owen ever cared about, wasn't it? Obsessed he was. More so in recent years, so I heard, like it took his whole life over."

"So I gather. I got talking to Huw the Boat yesterday, he'd heard the same. But Father left some information about the Royal Charter, and I've researched it on the Internet. I knew very little, other than he was something of an expert. But I found out quite interesting stuff, including the names of some of the local men who helped with the rescue. Huw said his ancestors, the Parrys, were involved. And there were two or three Williams among them, and it got me thinking one of them might have been a relation. That would make sense …"

"There is a connection, but you've got it the wrong way round."

"What do you mean?" She frowned. "Wrong way round?"

"Your father was a descendant of the Royal Charter. Years ago, he loved to boast how his great-great grandfather, Charles, built the house on the cliffs, reputedly with Charter gold. But he wasn't a descendant of the rescuers; he was a descendant of the rescued."

"How'd you mean?"

"Your other grandmother, Miriam Stewart, was the granddaughter of Charles Stewart, one of the few who were rescued from the ship. He survived, along with his young son, John – Miriam's father."

"My family were Australian?"

"Welsh originally. Charles's father went out there during the gold rush."

"I see."

"And if you want to complicate things even more, some

of *my* family were among the Moelfre twenty-eight, as well as your Grandpa Hughes's. It's always the way in these small communities. But if you ask me, the Royal Charter has brought nothing but trouble to this town."

"Why?" Sarah paused, remembering Huw's similar omen.

"Too much infighting. Stupid, really. Families round here know how to hold grudges that last for generations. That's why Owen felt he never fitted in. None of the Stewarts ever did, though when Miriam married Richard Williams things settled down a bit. His family were well to do. His father was Mayor of Llangefni at one time." She rubbed her eyes and yawned.

"Gran, are you ok?"

"Just tired. I get like this in the afternoon."

Sarah jumped up from her chair. "I'm sorry. I've put you through the mill today. Go and have a nap and I'll get cleared up here. And how about I send Luke round tomorrow to pick you up, and you can come stay at Charter House for the weekend. See how it feels before you make a permanent decision. Okay?"

Her gran nodded as Sarah helped her from her chair, and squeezed up against the wall as she made her way into the lounge. She paused at the kitchen door, and her voice was little more than a whisper.

"Just be careful, bach. That ship has ruined an awful lot of lives. Don't let it ruin yours too."

She closed the door on her final word. Sarah stared at the empty space for some time, head spinning with thoughts, images and the shock of old revelations.

Too late, Gran. I have a feeling it already has.

* * *

"You do know this is a complete and utter waste of time?"

Red slammed the drawer of the filing cabinet with enough force for it to rock on its base, once, twice. With a frown, he spun to face the door. "Well, I don't hear you coming up with any better ideas, Einstein."

"I told you. It has to be at Charter House."

"And I told you it's not. He's changed the safe combination. Short of demolishing the bloody place and ripping the safe from the wall, what more do you suggest? I can't believe he wouldn't have kept a copy. And if he did, surely this is the place."

"But he was hardly ever here. Why would he risk leaving something so important in an unlocked office in a part of the university anyone could access?"

"Staff quarters, not anyone."

"Anyone who knows the key code. And you know how paranoid the old guy was … no, this is a waste of time and effort."

Red yanked open another drawer and pulled out a pile of bulging folders. "Well, then humour me. I went along with your stupid bloody idea of visiting London and look where that got us. Exactly bloody nowhere. The bloke's not even in the country."

"Well, excuse me for not knowing his agenda. They worked closely together, it still makes more sense to me that he'd have a copy, than Williams would leave one here. The old fella was paranoid and had clammed up tight – no thanks to you and your heavy-handed tactics."

"Look!" Red clenched his fists and took a step forward. "If you're just going to stand there and whine, why don't you just piss off? Go and follow one of your own leads if you're so convinced about them. But seriously, I mean it; you need to get the fuck out of my face before I lose my patience."

Red turned away, breathing deep and hard, counting from one to ten and back again.

The door slammed, and he was grateful to have the office to himself. Part of him agreed, even if he wouldn't admit it, this was probably another wild goose chase, and he was becoming more and more frustrated with each passing day. It surely wouldn't be long before Sarah recovered from the death of her husband and started her own investigations. She must have read the letter by now, had to be making connections. How long before she looked elsewhere for assistance? And then how long before the puzzle was solved?

He threw the folders back into the drawer and kicked it shut. The most frustrating thing was he'd got to the point where he wasn't even sure what he was searching for. Safe combination. Treasure map. Last Will and testament. Confession from a dying man. Who knew? But there had to be something to link all the pieces together; the old guy might have been paranoid but he wasn't a genius. He must have confided in someone. It was just a matter of finding out whom.

He propped his hands on his hips and looked round the room. The desk and bookcase had yielded exactly nothing, same with the haphazard pile of papers on a corner unit, and now the filing cabinet too. He'd even checked waste bins and potted Aspidistras. He slid aside another of the ugly amateur paintings old Owen seemed to be a fan of, running his fingers along the back of the dusty frame. His gut instinct was that the answer had to be at Charter House. But how to go about getting what they needed was another matter … it looked like it might be time to change tactics and go through Sarah Morton rather than around her. He'd been desperate to avoid involving her. But his options were becoming more and more limited. Time even more so.

He made sure he left the room exactly as they'd found it, and switched off the light, checking the corridor was empty before leaving the room. He consulted the small hand-drawn map as he reached the lift. The other professor's office was on the opposite side of the staff quarters, across the courtyard, but not far. He may as well check it out now he was here, especially as his right-hand man had deserted him in a usual trademark huff.

Red took the lift to the ground floor, giving the map a discreet look as he crossed the reception area, then looked around, familiarising himself with his surroundings. He stumbled, breath catching in his throat, as he recognised the shaven-headed guy perched on the visitors' chairs, attention taken by the notice board beside him. The man removed a leaflet from a dispenser and began to flick through the contents. Shit and bugger, what was *he* doing here? The fat cop from the good cop, bad cop pair he'd seen at Charter House. Surely he'd not made the connection so far; surely they weren't so close behind? Red exhaled and slid his hands into his pockets. Just walk, keep moving. Look natural, relaxed, invisible. Head for the main entrance and just … keep … walking.

As Red reached the glass door, he started as a loud voice called out.

"Hey. Hey, there. Sir?"

Red paused, hand shaking pressed flat against the glass. A strong Irish voice, followed by footsteps.

"Sir?"

The voice was getting closer. Fuck. Oh sweet fuck it. Red set a smile and turned.

The Irish man was right behind him, examining a piece of paper. "Sorry, you dropped this, I think."

He held it out to Red. It was the map of the campus, highlighting the staff offices and professor's quarters. Red reached out and grabbed it with more violence than he'd intended. The other man took a step back in surprise.

Red let out a high laugh. "That's the third time today I've dropped it. No wonder I spend my days wandering aimlessly round these corridors. Thank you so much, my friend, I'm grateful."

Red studied the scuffed tan loafers, deciding it better not to meet the cop's gaze. He'd no desire to find out if it were true that a good copper could always read a guilty expression. Before either man could speak again, a tannoy sounded above their heads.

"Could Detective Buchanan please make his way to Dr Salmon's office. Thank you."

"Ah. Best go." The bulky man reversed. Red watched the shoes disappear.

"Thanks again." Red raised a hand as a parting gesture.

"No worries."

Red made it out of the door, down the steps, across the car park and all the way to the bus stop before he paused for breath or dared to look back. The tiny hairs on the back of his neck were erect, and his palms were oozing sweat. He'd felt sure if he'd turned, he'd have seen Detective Buchanan staring back at him from the other side of the glass.

Once inside the security of the bus shelter, he dug his phone from his pocket, and thumbed through to 'Messages.'

If you're still in there. Get the hell out. Cops.

He pressed send.

Chapter Eleven

"I fear I'm going to be very little help at all, detective. I've only been director here for the past eleven months. But of course, ask away, please, ask away."

Danny sighed and crossed his legs. Another dead end. He could feel it before he opened his mouth. Why could nothing ever be simple? Dr Rosemary Salmon was a buxom woman in her late fifties, with silver hair precariously scraped into some kind of top-knot, and tiny spectacles that had a habit of sliding down her nose every time she spoke. A delightful aroma of rose-scented talcum powder, or such, seemed to surround her like an aura. She screamed academia and instantly Danny was out of his comfort zone. The fact that she barely seemed to know Owen Williams did not improve his mood.

"When you say Director … you're Director of what exactly? Excuse my ignorance, but I'm not up to speed with university life, I'm afraid."

Dr Salmon waved the comment away. "Of course. I'm Director of the Centre for Medieval Studies, which is part of the University of Wales. We were established in 2005, as a breakaway from the history department, with the aim of drawing on expertise in the area of medieval studies from across university departments and fostering collaboration and scholarly exchange at Bangor and further afield. Our activities focus on initiatives that help create a stimulating intellectual environment for staff, students, and members of the community interested in the broader area of medieval studies." She broke off, and blushed in a rather girlish manner. "Excuse me. The curse of corporate speak. One never quite realises when the line has been crossed."

Danny cleared his throat and refocused; aware he'd been on the point of drifting off into another dimension.

"And Professor Williams still worked for the Centre?"

"He was an Emeritus Professor under our general classification. We cover many different aspects you see. Welsh history, Anglo-Norman, even Music studies." She paused again, made a zipping motion across her lips. "Anyway, yes, Owen held a part-time position and he was mainly called up for conferences, debates, that kind of thing. He did tutor a small group of archaeology students who were involved with him in the AAT –"

Danny pulled his notebook from his inside pocket. "AAT?"

"The Anglesey Archaeology Trust. Professor Williams was one of the founders. They are a group of enthusiastic amateurs who look after sites of interest on Anglesey. Here … they won a grant and an award just last year actually."

Dr Salmon took down a framed photograph from the shelf behind her desk. Danny recognised her, Owen Williams, and a group of about fifteen students. Another distinguished looking man held a glass vase aloft, centre stage, face alive and laughing.

"Who's this gentleman?" Danny asked, tapping the glass.

"Ah, that's Hugh. Hugh Gillingham. Another of our professors. He took over as Chairman of the Trust when Owen stood down. They manage the AAT between them, and a jolly good job they make of it too. *Wisdom is supreme; therefore get wisdom. Though it cost all you have, get understanding.*"

Danny looked up. "Sorry?"

Dr Salmon blushed and repositioned her specs with a fuchsia-coloured fingernail. "Apologies. You must think us academics are all a bunch of barmpots, and we do ourselves no favours." She smiled. "That was the motto of the AAT. Owen chose it, I believe."

"Would it be possible to have a word with Professor Gillingham?"

"He's out of the country, I'm afraid. Let me check when he's back." She turned to her computer and the screen filled with a spreadsheet of names, colours, dates. "Not until the 15th. He's back into work on the 19th. But I could drop him an email if that helped?"

"No. It's fine. I'll take his details and contact him at a later date if need be. So, can you remember the last time you saw Professor Williams?"

She adjusted her glasses again. "I think it was at the start of term on open day. We chatted briefly. He seemed on good form. Seemed quite bright actually, saw him chatting for quite some time with Hugh. I had a feeling it was something to do with the AAT but I'm not sure why. Otherwise, he was pencilled in for a couple of debates in December. It's a quiet time of year, start of term, you know. Students are settling in, timetables getting organised. Owen's work would kick in towards Christmas. That is, I mean, had he not passed away. Such a loss. He had a fascinating academic brain. He could reel off dates like telephone numbers. Always a tragedy I think when such a gifted individual dies, another little piece of history is gone. If you know what I mean."

Danny knew exactly what she meant. Any loss of talent was a tragedy, whatever the age or creed.

Dr Salmon gave a high-pitched cough. "I have to admit to being somewhat curious. I was under the impression Owen's death was a simple heart attack, at least that was what I heard. And I saw his family, albeit briefly, at his funeral. There was no hint of ... how is it referred to ... suspicious circumstances?"

"We're not altogether sure whether there are any suspicious circumstances or not at the moment. That is the point of the investigation. That and the fact that Professor Williams's son-in-law died within days of the funeral."

"No! Really? I spoke to him, a footballer as I recall. Owen's poor daughter must be devastated."

Danny shook his head and got to his feet. They were past the point of gaining any useful information and edging into gossip and intrigue which was something he couldn't be party to. He pulled out his business card and handed it across the desk.

"If you think of anything else that might shed light on Professor Williams's life or know anyone who might have information, would you be so good as to pass on my details. As I said, we're just trying to build a profile at the moment. Tick boxes, you know how it is."

Dr Salmon took the card and nodded. "Of course. And will you please pass on my condolences to Owen's daughter. Tell her she's in our thoughts here at the University. Her father was a good man, remembered fondly by all the staff and students. I truly hope that there is nothing malevolent in either death, Detective. Truly."

"One final thing, I wonder did Professor Williams still keep an office here?"

"Yes, he did. And I don't believe it's been emptied yet. It was on my list of things to do, contact his next of kin about his personal belongings. I'm jolly glad I kept putting it off now."

"Could you show me? I mean, you've no objection if I have a look round?"

"Of course not. This way."

Owen's room had the same smell of cigar smoke, polish, pine and dust as Danny recalled the first time he went to Charter House. Books, too. Old paper had a particular smell. The office was compact, book-lined …and looked every inch what it was. None of the desk drawers were locked, but not one yielded anything of interest. Danny noted that some of the books had been moved recently – narrow footprints scraped through the layer of dust, but otherwise nothing seemed disturbed.

There was a watercolour on the wall, hanging slightly off-centre, similar to the ones that hung in Charter House. This one a dark scene of angry seas crashing against jagged rocks. The sea is a beast of a thousand faces. One of his father's lines. Danny had never forgotten that. From warm and welcoming to deadly and hostile. Danny straightened it, squinting to read the tiny signature. S … something. He bent lower. No, it was just a squiggle.

Ten minutes later, Danny exited the corridor out into the fresh air. He looked up at the turreted red-bricked buildings around the courtyard, more like a fortress or a palace than a learning establishment. These types of places, and its people, felt foreign to him, but he'd be lying if he said he couldn't see the attraction.

Something had kept Professor Williams interested right into old age, and Danny couldn't help wondering if this dedication could have more sinister roots. He might be grasping at straws, but if he put his mind to it he could think of a dozen or more reasons why someone might want rid of an old professor who wouldn't let go. At least it wouldn't hurt to look into the workings of this AAT and see where that took him, and he'd like a chat with this Gillingham bloke. Lewis was back in town tonight for a couple of days R & R away from his drug undercover work. It would be good to catch up over a few pints and bounce ideas. The further he dug, the further away he seemed to get from any sign of malpractice, and there was no way he could let Thompson win on this. No way at all.

* * *

Later that evening as the wind shrieked its fury around the eaves of the old house, Sarah settled at her father's desk and spread out the contents of the safe. The conversation with her gran had finally given her the strength to complete the task, and she wanted to get it out of the way before the journey down to Watford. The Club had been fantastic about handling the press but Sarah still dreaded the funeral. Dom's body had finally been released and a private service was to be held the following Monday in the churchyard of the village where his family lived. She shook the thought away for another few days.

Again, the sense of unease took over as Sarah ran her fingers across the carved mahogany that edged the cushioned writing area on her father's desk. She sighed and sat up straight. Such a lot had happened since she'd last sat in this chair. She remembered her reluctance to tell Dom about the safe contents. If only she'd refused to let her father's words wind her up, there was a chance they wouldn't have argued that night. And perhaps Dom wouldn't have rushed out the next morning without waking her. She recalled the breakfast tray he'd left on the windowsill. It could all be her fault Dominic died …

Sarah picked up the letter she'd collected from Adrian Carter's office. She ran her thumbnail along the seal but stopped herself re-reading the words; she could remember them pretty much verbatim. There was no need to get upset again by her father's words. As far as she was concerned, it was far too little, far too late. She fingered the small silver key and decided the next plan had to be finding the lock it fitted. Sarah was sure there was nothing in the house it would open, and it was too small to be a safe key. It looked more like one that opened a gym locker. Her father said it would become clear, but nothing so far had thrown any light on it.

Sarah put the key to one side, and picked up the bag of gold coins. These had to be some of the cargo off the Royal Charter. She nodded as she turned a coin over in her palm and read 'Sydney Mint. Australia. One Sovereign.' On the other side there was the profile of Queen Victoria and the date 1857. Sarah rubbed the shiny surface, imagining the journey this small coin had travelled. She opened her mother's jewellery box, lifted out the top layer, and dropped the coins into the space beneath.

She slid the heavy hardback books, *The Mabinogion*, across the desk and thumbed through the yellowed pages and lines of ancient Welsh, examining the elaborate gold-leaf titles. *The White Book of Rhydderch*, and *Red Book of Hergest*. She'd heard her father mention *The Mabinogion* and knew from her schooldays it was a collection of Welsh stories and legends. He'd lectured and specialised in the subject at Bangor. She wondered if these books were in the safe because of their value. Perhaps they were originals or famous copies. But what connection could they possibly have with the Royal Charter?

With a grunt, she lifted the heavy volumes and shook them. Nothing fell from between the pages. She slid them to one side and pulled the bundles of files towards her, flicking through four bulging folders, earmarked and tattered around the edges. These were obviously manuscripts of her father's books. The oldest-looking were written longhand; she studied pages covered in her father's distinctive, elaborate handwriting. The newest, a shiny red file, was neatly typed, and she wondered how many hours it had taken her father, with his proud lack of keyboard skills, to type the hundreds of pages.

As she mulled, the phone on the desk let out a high-pitched trill and flashing lights. Sarah started, took a deep breath, and lifted the receiver. "H-hello?"

"Hey. At last I've got you at home. Is that Sarah?"

"Em, yes. Who is this please?"

"Oh, yeah. Hi, it's Craig Davies." His voice was bouncy, with something like the hint of a US accent. He'd clearly been watching too many Hollywood blockbusters as Sarah knew he was Anglesey born and bred. "Not sure you remember me from school? We have met, I'm –"

"Doctor Davies's son. I know who you are."

"Cool. I've been trying to catch up with you since you've been back in town."

"Well, I've had quite a lot on my plate."

"Yes, of course." He gave a nervous cough. "I'm sorry to hear about your husband. You've had a bad run, for sure."

"Thank you. Erm …it's getting late, I'm assuming there's a

reason for your call?" Something about the Californian twang irritated her intensely; she was in no rush to prolong an inane conversation with him.

"Oh, yeah, sure. Well, like I said, I've been hoping to run into you –"

"Actually, you very nearly did, pulling out of our drive last week."

He paused. "Oh, that was you?"

"Sure was." Sarah bit her lip, realising she'd mimicked his accent.

"Oh, well, apologies, I thought it was only Evans in the car. But hey, I spoke to the police so that misunderstanding's all cleared up now. We're cool, right?"

Sarah ignored the question. "So, you wanted to run into me …?"

"Oh, em, sure. Right, well, I thought it would be cool to catch up some time. Not sure if you know, I'm co-owner of a new seafood restaurant in Trearddur Bay?" Sarah remained silent. "Well, I wondered if I could offer you a meal there? On the house, of course. Only downside would be the company, uh, you know … me!"

Anger uncoiled inside her; Sarah couldn't believe what she was hearing. Was he having a laugh at her expense? A few days ago he was a suspect in her father's murder and now he was offering her a date?

"Thanks for the offer, Craig, but I'm sure you can appreciate I'm not really in the right frame of mind for dating at the moment."

"Oh God, no, Sarah. That wasn't what I meant at all. Jeez, how could you think such a thing?"

"Okay, so why would I want to go for a meal with you? Gratis or otherwise?"

"No … free, not gratis. You know, on the house, like. Drinks included."

Sarah bit back a smart comment. "Why?"

"I have a spot of business I'd like to discuss with you." He broke off, but she could sense more in his voice, and waited. "Well, to be honest, like, I did have a business deal going with your dad, before he popped – er passed away."

Hairs on the back of her neck bristled. Another guy with business dealings with her father? *Jeez.* Had he turned into Donald Trump in her absence?

"What kind of business deal?"

"Well, I have fingers in lots of pies." He sniggered, and she remembered Luke saying almost the exact same words. "I deal in the import and export business and I've a friend heavily involved with first edition books. I had a conversation with your dad a couple of months ago, and he led me to believe he might have a few old Welsh books he wanted to get shut of. Cut his losses, you know. They're pretty obscure, not really popular nowadays, but I said I'd have a chat with my mate and see if I could do your dad a favour."

"That's good of you."

"Well, I'm that kinda guy!"

For sure.

"And what did your friend say?"

"He wasn't all that keen. Anything written in Welsh has a pretty small market as you can imagine." Again, Sarah chewed on her bottom lip and kept silent. "But he said he'd be willing to take a look at them, as a favour for me, like. Have you seen any old Welsh hardback books knocking around?" His tone was light, but it failed to hide the excitement in the question.

"Nope."

"Oh?"

"Sorry."

"You sure?"

"Erm, I think so. I mean, I've not emptied my father's study yet, but I can't remember seeing anything."

"They're big, thick volumes. Look like bibles with spring catches and really colourful covers."

"You sound like an expert …"

"Me? God, no." He forced a laugh. "Just looking at the picture on the email my mate sent. I'm clueless about these kinds of books, not my scene at all."

Sarah cleared her throat and adopted a casual tone. "Like I say, I'm sorry I can't help you. But if you want to give me your friend's name and number, if I do come across anything then I can give him a call. What kind of money are we talking?"

"I think he'd want to see them first. Check authenticity and condition, you know. Can't be too careful in this game. But I'll leave you my mobile, call me direct, any time, if you find them. They're both a version of a book called The Mab … Mabinogion, or something like. Never heard of it myself, have you?"

She knew Craig was lying. He'd gone to secondary school on the island and was a regular Welsh speaker; he'd know a hell of a lot more about Welsh legend than she did.

But sensing the emphasis on the question, she replied quickly. "No, but I don't speak Welsh, I'm afraid."

"Really? You should be ashamed. Good Welsh gal, like you."

"So, you have no idea on value? Didn't your friend mention it in the email?"

"Um, hang on, I'll look. Oh yeah, depending on condition, between £50 and £150 for the pair. Not to be sniffed at really, for a couple of tatty old books."

"Blimey, yeah." Sarah hoped the tone sounded genuine, while making a note to run a quick Internet search herself later. "For that kind of money, you can be sure I'll be having a good sort through my father's study."

"Cool." The sigh of relief was audible. "And dinner?"

"Another time, I think." Sarah faked a loud yawn. "Well, excuse me but I was just on my way to bed. Thanks again. Speak soon."

"Okay. You be good, now. Night y'all."

Sarah cringed as she balanced the phone back on its base. If she never had to speak to Craig Davies – or his no doubt imaginary friend – again it would suit her down to the ground. But it raised more than a few questions about the books in the safe. If her father had been thinking of selling them, she could well imagine him going to Christie's or some other reputable auctioneer. What she couldn't imagine him doing was picking up the phone and calling a cretin like Davies. So, how exactly had he come to know about her father's books?

With a sigh, Sarah shut off the desk lamp and made her way into the darkened hallway, pausing to double-check she'd secured the safe. She lingered at the bottom of the stairs with one hand on the light switch. Long shadows crept across the wooden floor, and she realised dusty beams of light were reflecting through the frosted glass around the front door, directly across from the infra-red security light above the garage. She frowned. Who or what had activated the sensor?

With a gentle tread, she made her way across to the front door; turning the deadbolt with care, she inched open the door. Yellow light flooded the driveway, but as she scanned from one side to the other, saw it was clearly empty. Her heart began to pick up speed. It could be something as simple as a moth or a faulty sensor, but her nerves tingled again with the sense of '*something*'. It was the same feeling she'd had on that first night back at Charter House.

She pulled the door open wide, grabbed an umbrella from the hallstand and stepped out onto the stone step. A flash of grey caught her eye, just the slightest of movement in front of the sycamore at the start of the drive. Probably a rabbit, they seemed to be overrun with them this year. Chastising herself for her jumpiness, she made her way down the front steps, breathing in the salty night air.

Crunch.

Sarah stopped dead. She'd not yet reached the gravel surface of the driveway, yet she'd distinctly heard the sound of a foot tread on the chippings. She swung her head from left to right, but there was nothing. The storm had passed, not a breath of wind moved the branches of the trees. Everything was still and quiet.

She jumped as the security light clicked and plunged the drive into darkness. It was a new moon, so the blackness was total; it took seconds, minutes for her eyes to adjust and she blinked rapidly. She shivered as goose bumps covered her arms. She didn't like this, didn't want to be out here on her own in the dark. Who knew who was wandering about in this day and age? She pushed away an image of Craig Davies that popped into her head. Why was she getting spooked?

Sarah ducked back into the hallway, slammed the door, engaged the deadbolt, and pulled across the heavy iron bolt for good measure. She took deep, rapid breaths and thought about calling 999. But say what? A rabbit activated the security light and she was a wuss scared of living alone. Forget that idea, besides … she had to start getting used to it.

Heading upstairs, Sarah hurried her bedtime routine, and within fifteen minutes was curled up under the duvet trying to concentrate on her latest read. Anything that stopped her obsessing on the cold, empty space beside her was more than welcome.

As if on cue, her eyelids began to droop, and the book slid to the floor. She reached over to turn out the bedside lamp and allowed the impending darkness to carry her into a welcome sleep.

Bang!

The sound of something like a gunshot echoed through the air, yet before I could react, icy cold water submerged me, covering my mouth … nose … eyes. A roaring pressure filled my skull and when I opened my mouth to scream, salt water drove into my lungs with such force my throat felt torn and on fire.

Blind to everything except a muddy brown swirling mass that engulfed and surrounded me. The underwater currents were so powerful, holding me under, dragging me deeper. I could feel my strength fading, yet suddenly the sea released me and I broke through the surface, gulping mouthfuls of cold, stinging air.

'Help me!' I screamed; my voice whipped away by the wind.

Distant, distorted voices shrieked around me; I waved my arms above my head to get their attention. Someone, something was pulling me down again, down, deeper back into the raging whirlpool. I held my breath as water engulfed me for a second time, and kicked out at the hands clasped around my ankles, dragging me ever lower. I fought with the thick woollen shawl tangled around my legs, fingers slipping as I struggled to undo the heavy belt around my waist.

Ma! Pa! John!

Why did no one come? Terrified, I pushed upwards toward the silvery light. Something about the twinkling reflection beckoned me, calmed me, as my body continued to thrash against its confines.

The pain inside my head and lungs roared its wrath, but I was powerless to stop it.

I closed my eyes and prayed to the blessed Jesus Christ our Saviour.

'Lord, save me. Please, help me. I don't want to die'.

My ears popped from the intense pressure, and at the exact same moment the pain stopped.

Stopped dead.

Not a gradual fading, just a single blessed release.

I looked at the white light, smiled, and mouthed a silent thank you to my Saviour, my Lord, who'd come to save me.

I closed my eyes, and let the gentle swell carry me towards the brightness.

Bang!

With a squeal, Sarah kicked off the duvet, wrapped tight around her. Her ankle hummed with pain and her cotton nightdress clung like a second skin as sweat trickled down her spine. She thrashed around in the bed for several seconds, before her heartbeat began to slow.

All around her was still, familiar, and she let out a heavy sigh.

A dream. Just a goddamn dream. But so real. So, so vivid.

She lay there, letting the chill air caress her skin. She took deep breaths and pulled her hair back into a ponytail on top of her head, away from the dampness of her skin. Her body shook, not from cold, but fear. She could remember every terrifying detail of the dream, could feel the water filling her lungs and life ebbing away.

Drowning her.

Sarah felt as if she'd just lived someone's death.

Dominic's?

A sob escaped and she pressed her knuckles against her lips to stop the torrent of wild thoughts that rose like a tsunami from the bottom of her stomach. *Please, God, no.* She wasn't strong enough to be haunted by scenes of Dom's final moments. Please let it be nothing more than a coincidence, a bad dream never to be repeated.

Sarah closed her eyes, slowed her breathing, trying to calm herself with rational thoughts. It couldn't be Dominic; that was absurd. Plus, deep down that didn't fit. It hadn't felt like a strong, fit man fighting for his life. It had felt like … like …

Bang!

She shot upright and grabbed her throat, choking away a scream. The realisation that something, a noise, had pulled her out of the dream with force. It had been a welcome release, but now the sounds were ominous, threatening. Memories of the security light incident, the dead crow and dark shadows jumbled around in her brain like moths flapping around a light bulb, scared of being burned but unable to avoid its magnetism.

The rational part of her brain finally took charge, recognising the sound, probably a window banging in the wind. The catches were ancient and weak; she was always refastening them. She pulled herself out of bed, and tested her ankle as she wrapped her dressing gown around her waist. Hadn't the wind already dropped before she'd come to bed? Perhaps it had picked up again with the following high tide. The micro-climates around this coast were so unpredictable.

Memories of the dream clung like a bad odour as she made her way slowly downstairs. She shook her head, determined to clear the jumbled images, and strained her ears to determine the source of the banging.

Another sound. Sarah stopped at the top of the stairs. A rustling noise and the creak of a floorboard. A beam of light flickered between the banisters, across her lower legs, a flash of white against pale skin, before plunging back into darkness.

The study.

She sidestepped the remaining stairs, missing the bottom rung with the squeaky tread. Her fingers sought out the walking stick from the hallstand, and she gripped it like a baseball bat as she turned at the bottom of the stairs and crept along the length of the hallway. Muffled bumps echoed through the old house. Whoever it was, they weren't making a whole lot of effort to keep quiet. That either meant they didn't know anyone was in the house … or they didn't care.

Crack!

A flare of white light.

An explosion of pain in the back of her head.

And blackness swallowed her.

Chapter Twelve

Danny took a long pull of larger, and slammed the empty glass on the table with a contented sigh. He glanced at his companion's glass, still two-thirds full, and felt a flicker of embarrassment.

"My shout. You ready for another?" Danny said, wiping his lips with the back of his hand.

"You're like a bloody goldfish, you are," said Lewis taking another sip of his pint. "And I've never met an Irish-man who didn't like Guinness before."

"Half-Irish, remember. Blame my Scottish dad. But I like the proper black stuff, to be sure. But this stuff you get over here …" Danny wrinkled his nose. "Well, it could put a man off for life, if you know what I mean."

"I doubt it would put you off …"

An explosion of noise filled the small room as the door opened, and a pile of football supporters emptied into the bar. 'Bangor City' – it said on their woolly hats. A gust of cold wind followed them across the room as the noise level trebled. Danny shivered, fastened his top button.

He glanced at the bartender, smile in place, ready to serve. "Will you be getting that down your neck before I get stuck behind that lot?"

Lewis scowled and swallowed the rest of his pint in one go. "Happy?" he said, holding the glass aloft.

"Ecstatic." Danny pushed back his chair. "And you can cast your eye across those notes while I'm getting them in, can't you? Get yourself up to speed."

"I'm still amazed Thompson went for it. Must be your half-Irish charm."

Danny grinned and made it across the small snug of The Antelope before the rest of the football crowd arrived. He'd have to slow down a little; Lewis obviously wasn't a big drinker, and Danny had no desire to live up to every Irish prejudice. Not that he was anywhere near as bad as some he knew, even in his own family. He'd seen too much of what damage alcohol could do to risk ever becoming dependent on what his own ma called the *evil of drink*. In fact that evil had been the biggest influence in his decision to join the Gardaí at such a young age.

Danny balanced the two pints together and weaved his way through the expanding crowd of fans. Spirits were high, most likely a home win. It made for a good atmosphere – a good craic as they'd say back home. Danny was looking forward to finishing his day off – even though he'd spent most of it working – with a few more pints and a nice Madras at the most excellent curry house he'd discovered near the station.

He frowned as he saw Lewis on his feet, gesturing to him with a frown.

"What?" Danny asked, still gripping the lagers.

"Just had a message from control, Bob Perkins, you know, my mate. A call's come in from Charter House. Sarah Morton has been rushed to hospital."

"No." Danny bent his knees and slid the glasses onto the table. A rush of hot lager burned the back of his throat. "Is she okay?"

"Alive at least."

"What happened?"

"Head injuries. That's all I know. We'd better make a move, she's at Ysbyty Gwynedd. Are you okay to drive?"

"Yeah. That was my first. Shit." He gave a last longing look at the golden beer, glimmering in the colourful fruit machine light.

"This is getting out of hand."

"Too right. Let me talk to her, if she's up to it, okay? If you think she's clamming up on you, let me have a go. We need to tell her about …" He nodded to the brown envelope on the table. "But let's play that by ear, right?"

"Sure. Shite, I hope she is up to talking. She's been through enough …"

Danny gathered up the papers and followed Lewis towards the door, pausing with his hand on the shoulder of a white haired supporter. "Help yourself, pal," he said into the man's ear, motioning towards the vacated table. "We've been called away. Fill your boots."

The man gave a wide smile and thumbs up. Danny pulled up the collar of his jacket as he stepped out into the cold night air. Sarah's face was fixed in his mind. Dear Christ, let her be okay. Her and the baby.

* * *

The gentle sway of an incoming tide on a shingle beach. Somewhere close. The taste of sea salt on her lips; the acrid scent of seaweed on the breeze. Her eyes were closed and, when she lifted her head, warm rays of dancing sunlight played across her face.

Where am I?

Sarah … Sarah … it's safe now. Wake up. Sarah …

A child's voice called her name. Close by, yet far away. Sarah frowned and struggled for clarity like a drowning man trying to reach air.

Where am I? Who are you?

The voice came again, fading now. *Sarah … it's okay … Sarah …*

"Sarah?"

She jumped. This voice was different, louder, nearer.

She forced open her eyes; a blurred, sandy-coloured form

hovered in front of her face. Like someone under water, coming closer and closer to the surface; an image shimmering and fading. Her eyelids began to droop.

"Sarah!"

The image refocused. The edges formed into a face with deep creases across its forehead and concern in the clear gaze.

"L … Luke?" She ran her tongue over cracked lips. "Where am I? C-can I have some w-water?"

Luke looked away. "Em, I'm not sure. Hang on, I'll fetch someone."

He disappeared and Sarah craned her neck to look around her surroundings. She let out a low moan and her head slumped back into the pillow. A hot flare of pain erupted like a struck match, and she lifted a hand to feel a sticky plaster pad across the back of her head.

She recognised the white walls, the small window, the green curtains.

A blue uniform appeared beside her; she recognised that too.

"Hello, Carol."

"Well, I don't know if you're just one accident-prone lady or you're liking us so much you can't stay away!" She smiled and her long red ponytail bobbed as she poured a glass of water from a plastic jug and lifted Sarah with a hand in the centre of her back. Sarah took long, grateful mouthfuls of the cooling liquid, and then dropped back onto her pillow, more gingerly this time.

"Are you in pain?" asked Nurse Flynn.

She nodded. "A little."

"Okay, I'll ask the doctor about upping your pain relief. We've had to be careful what we give you … for obvious reasons."

Sarah saw her flash a worried glance across the room, and turned to see Luke hovering in the open doorway.

"Why?" Sarah frowned, trying to make sense of things. "What happened –?"

She broke off and her mouth formed a silent 'O'. Her hand instinctively went to her stomach, fingers twisting in the thin cotton of the hospital gown.

Her breath came in short, sharp bursts. "What … please … tell me …?"

The nurse gripped her left hand. "Your baby is fine. We're monitoring everything as we speak. But the heartbeat's strong and there seems nothing to worry about."

Sarah relaxed back onto the bed. "Thank God. Thank you, God."

Nurse Flynn smiled. "Well, he or she is one tough little cookie –"

"It's a girl," Sarah said.

The nurse frowned. "Oh, I didn't know you knew the sex already. Isn't it a bit early for your scan?"

"I haven't had a scan. But it's a girl. I don't know how I know. And in fact, I didn't know I knew until I said it. But it's a girl, I'm sure of it."

"Well, she's determined to make an appearance that's for sure. She's survived enough traumas while still inside your womb to last her a lifetime."

Sarah touched the plaster again. "What happened?"

"You had a fall, so I've been told. You were brought in early this morning, and I didn't come on shift till two pm. But you were unconscious for some time, and the A&E doctor sedated you while tests were carried out. He was worried about swelling of the brain if there was a skull fracture, but the results have come back fine, there's no fracture, just a compound compression and bruising. Nothing too serious, you should be out in a couple of days."

"Thank you."

"Ach, you've nothing to be thanking me for. It's my job. I just want you to promise me you'll be more careful." Sarah nodded. "If you want to be thanking anyone, you should be thanking this young man here. He saved your life by all accounts. If he'd not found you when he did, well, who's to know what would've happened."

Sarah turned and smiled at Luke, who still stood just inside the doorway as if unsure whether to come in or wait outside. She gestured for him to sit beside her, and smiled as Nurse Flynn fussed around the room, before pausing at the door.

"One last thing, there's a couple of strapping detectives waiting to see you when you're awake proper. One of them said to tell you he's a friend of Morse?"

Sarah smiled. *Lewis.* "Give me five minutes, and send them in please."

Nurse Flynn nodded. "Half an hour and then I'm clearing everyone out, you need your rest."

She closed the door behind her and Sarah turned to Luke.

His eyes were deep pools of pain. "Why didn't you tell me you were pregnant? Why don't you trust me?"

"I do."

He shook his head. "No you don't. You can't do."

"I found out last time I was in hospital. I've told no one, other than Gran. I've been so confused; I just couldn't decide what to do."

"You could have told me. You have to trust me. Promise me."

"I'm sorry. I promise." Her shoulders slumped and hot tears stung her eyes. She bit down on her bottom lip and looked out at the cloudy grey sky, where seagulls rode the thermals, soaring high and low. She'd give anything to be able to spread her wings and fly right now. Fly away from this whole terrible ordeal.

Luke sighed and changed the subject. "I've just rung Grandma Ruth to let her know you're awake."

"God, I'd forgotten about Gran. Where is she?"

"Still at her bungalow."

"She was supposed to move in today. I can't risk it now, will you tell her, explain what's happened. But don't scare her either." Sarah squeezed the bridge of her nose. "Shit what a mess this all is. You will speak to her, tell her I'm fine?"

"Of course."

"So … so what happened?"

"I got worried when I couldn't get hold of you. I'd been calling all morning to tie up arrangements about collecting your gran, and to see if you wanted shopping while I was in town. You didn't answer your mobile, so I drove up to Charter House. I saw your car was there, but couldn't make you hear. When I looked through the letter box, I saw your walking stick and I could just make out your foot on the hall floor. I'm afraid I've had to break another one of the small window panes in the back door, but I'll see it's replaced."

Sarah frowned. "Everything's really fuzzy …"

A sharp rap at the door broke her concentration. Detective Lewis popped his head round and smiled. "Okay to join the party now?"

Sarah nodded and returned a weak smile. "Only if you've brought your own bottle. Pull up a chair."

She watched as Lewis entered the small room, closely followed by his partner, Buchanan. Their eyes met for a moment and Sarah nodded, reading his question. She was fine and the baby was fine, that's what he wanted to know. The room suddenly seemed over-crowded. Buchanan took a seat near the door and Lewis settled himself beside the bed. His hair was the untidy blond cut she remembered, and he still had an uncared-for air around him. His jacket was creased to within an inch of its life, the top button missing from his grey shirt, and his tie struggled to hold the collar in place.

"Been in the wars again, Mrs Morton?" he said.

"Sarah … and yeah, it would appear so. Luke was just talking me through what happened. Detective Lewis, this is Luke …"

Lewis held up a hand. "We've already met. Luke was good enough to give us a statement while we were waiting for you to wake up. So, what happened?"

She frowned. "I'm trying to remember."

"It looked as if you'd fallen down the stairs," said Luke. "Doctor said you've had a nasty whack on the back of the head.

And I found one of your slippers half way up the stairs, like you'd tripped and fallen on the way down."

Grey swirling memories crowded her brain, pushing and shoving for dominance like lambs at feeding time.

A young girl calling me, beckoning me. The roar of waves crashing against rocks. Inky black water pulling me down. A loud gunshot in the air.

"I heard someone –" She broke off, forced her mind to rewind. *Waking from a dream, hearing noises, creaking floorboards, torch light …*

"What?" asked Lewis.

"I heard someone. There was someone in the house. I woke and heard a noise. I went downstairs and I could hear someone in my father's study."

Sarah saw a worried look flash between the two men. Luke gave a shrug and a barely perceptible shake of his head.

"Yes, I did! Why are you looking at me like that?"

"Like what?" A nervous blush appeared in Luke's cheeks.

"Like I'm some kind of idiot. I know what I heard. I know what I saw!"

"Okay," said Lewis, his voice calm and soothing. "Okay, we believe you. Try not to get upset. What exactly did you see?"

"Well … I … um."

Come on, think, Sarah. What exactly had she seen? Nothing.

"Talk me through what you remember," said Lewis.

"It's still really fuzzy. My head hurts and it feels like I'm under water." She tried to shake her head, but the pain reignited in the back of her skull. She grimaced and rubbed her temple. "I remember talking to Craig Davies on the phone –"

"What did he want?" snapped Luke.

"I – uh. Nothing, he just wanted to see how I was."

Luke smiled but it was full of scorn. "Unlikely. He's like a bird of prey, hovering over a motorway, waiting to swoop on the road kill. I've warned you about him, Sarah. I told you, detective –"

"Sir, we questioned Mr Davies at length."

Sarah nodded. "And like I asked him to call? Get over yourself, Luke. He asked me out on a date, if you must know. And I gave him short shift. Happy now?"

A heavy silence descended over the room; Lewis cleared his throat awkwardly. Sarah's cheeks burned; it wasn't like her to snap. But she was sick of everyone thinking they owned her and could tell her what to do. Who the hell did Luke think he was? She met Buchanan's gaze, over Luke's left shoulder, and exhaled, trying to let go of the anger.

Lewis spoke. "So, after the phone call, something woke you, you said?"

Sarah gave Luke one last glance. "Yes. A noise. I'd been dreaming, and I woke and lay there. And then a bang. I got up and went downstairs. Oh! Yes, I remember a flashlight and noises like drawers being opened, papers being thrown around." She turned to face Luke. "Have a look! My father's study. Someone was in there, I heard them. They were wrecking the place again, searching for something."

"I've already checked the study," said Luke quietly. "I checked the whole house while I was waiting for the ambulance. There's no sign of any forced entry this time, nothing's disturbed. Obviously I can't be one hundred percent certain nothing's been stolen – but it doesn't look like a crime scene."

Sarah shook her head and turned to Lewis. "But there was someone there. It must be a mistake. Get someone to check, and take fingerprints. There must be something. I heard them ..."

"Sarah, please try not to upset yourself. Are you sure you weren't just having a bad dream, a nightmare, or perhaps even sleep walking and tripped on the stairs?"

She thumped the bed with a fist. "No! Why won't anyone believe me? I'm pregnant, not retarded!" She took quick, deep breaths. What more could she do to make people believe her? Even Buchanan was looking at the floor as if determined not to express an opinion. This wasn't fair. She was beginning to feel like a hysterical, grieving widow. She closed her mouth with a snap as she realised if she didn't calm down there was a chance she might start to come across as one.

"All I can say is it looked like you'd fallen when I got there," said Luke, his voice low. "I'm not trying to make you look bad. I'm just telling it like it is. You were kind of crumpled at the bottom of the stairs. I was scared to move you in case of neck injuries. And as I said you had a slipper on one foot, and the other was half way up the stairs. Your walking stick was alongside you –"

"Yes!" Sarah interrupted, punching the air. "You see, you see. I don't take my walking stick upstairs. I leave it in the hall stand which is on the other side of the front door to the staircase." She turned to Lewis to explain. Luke nodded. "So, if I had my walking stick next to me, I must have already got to the bottom of the stairs and crossed the hall to pick it up." She looked from one to the other, to Buchanan and back again. Her chest tightened as she waited for their reply, any reply. "I'm right, aren't I?"

Lewis nodded. "Yes, if that's true. Then yes, you couldn't have fallen. Unless you were on your way back upstairs with the stick –"

"No way." She shook her head. "I remember picking it up. I heard noises and picked up the first thing that came to hand to use as a weapon." The words came quicker and quicker as the memories started to creep back. "I grabbed my stick, and crept along the hall. And then someone hit me, from behind."

"But you were definitely at the bottom of the stairs," said Luke.

"Then someone moved me, arranged it to look like a fall. The more I think of it, the more I'm sure there were two people. Someone in the study and someone who hit me. Easier to cover their tracks if there were two people working together. That's possible, isn't it?"

Lewis shrugged and nodded. "Anything's possible. But why no sign of a burglary this time? Luke's adamant he's checked the whole house. Besides, what were they looking for?"

Sarah swallowed hard. Gold, books, manuscripts, ancient

maps, you name it. But she wasn't ready to talk about that, not yet, especially not now when they obviously considered she was living in fantasy land. She wanted proof. When she had that, then she'd tell them everything. Buchanan would understand why she'd had to do it alone, even if no one else did. She shrugged and reached for the plastic glass and took another sip of water.

"I suppose it's possible they cleared up after themselves, isn't it?" asked Luke. He ran a hand through his hair. "I mean, if they went to the trouble of making an assault look like an accident, then it wouldn't be that hard to cover up a robbery. I mean, I've only been in the study a few times. Who's to say stuff hasn't been moved? All I can be sure of is everything looked neat and tidy, and I found no forced entry, totally different from last time. That could just mean they're professionals who panicked when they realised someone was in the house, and did a good cover up job."

Lewis nodded and steepled long thin fingers beneath his chin. He remained silent and contemplated Luke's words.

"So, does that mean you believe me then?" Sarah asked.

Finally, Lewis sat forward and planted his elbows on his knees, so his pale face was almost level with hers. She could smell the tangy scent of familiar cologne, Jean-Paul Gaultier, one of Dom's favourites.

Lewis nodded. "Yes, I believe you. There's another reason I believe you, too." He paused, flashed a look at Buchanan. "I don't want to upset you, you have more than enough on your plate, but DS Buchanan has issued an exhumation order this afternoon. We want to do further tests on your father's body."

Sarah gasped and put a hand across her mouth. Luke dragged in a long intake of breath beside her.

"Why?" she croaked.

"We've finally heard back from Dr Davies, and it seems he's not happy with the death certificate after all. There wasn't enough there to give a natural causes death in his opinion. There'd been a cock-up with the patient records, apparently. And the only reason the death certificate was issued without a post mortem was because someone told the locum doctor your father strongly disapproved and didn't want 'cutting open.'"

"I don't know what he thought in later years, but he wanted a full investigation into his death, and to me that means a post mortem first and foremost. Who told the locum that?"

Lewis shook his head. "He can't remember. Got a bit stroppy when DS Buchanan interviewed him, actually. Didn't like his professional ethics questioned, so he said. Lucky we didn't bang him up for the night to cool down and ponder his ethics."

Sarah smiled, despite herself. "Do I need to agree or sign anything?"

"I've got the papers here, if you're sure you feel up to it."

She nodded and took the pen and paper from Buchanan as he approached the bottom of the bed, and signed where indicated. "I hate the idea of it. But it has to be done. I let my father down. Better late than never we find the truth. How long will it take?"

"A few days." Buchanan bent forward and collected the papers. "You just relax and get well, you hear. I'm classing this attack on you as attempted murder, and until we run tests on your father's body, I've persuaded the coroner to delay the inquest and keep an open verdict on Mr Morton's death. They may not be linked, but I'm not willing to make any mistakes."

Lewis untangled his long legs and stretched his back as he stood. "As soon as we have any results, we'll let you know. You've got our number if you need us. I don't want to scare you, but I'd suggest you try to keep alert and not spend too much time alone." He flashed a glance at Luke. "But just get some rest, look after that baby, and I'll be in touch, okay?"

Sarah nodded as Nurse Flynn appeared. "Okay, guys. Time's up. Lady needs her beauty sleep."

As the detectives trooped out of the room, Luke leaned across and kissed her cheek. His lips left a warm glow on her skin; she lifted a hand and ran her fingers over the spot.

"Look after yourself, Sarah. I'll come visit tomorrow, okay?"

Her eyes were heavy, and she stifled a yawn. "Sure. I'm sorry I got stroppy. Thank you, Luke. For saving my life."

"Don't be daft. See you tomorrow."

* * *

Red tightened his grip on his mobile, feeling the urge to squeeze the life out of something. Or someone. What a complete bloody shambles.

It answered on the third ring.

"Where are you?" Red growled.

"At work. Why?"

"You took off a bit sharpish last night. Thanks for the support."

A loud sigh. "Make your mind up, partner. Go our separate ways you said if anything went wrong. Take two cars, you said, don't wait for each other. Those were your rules. And who am I to break them."

"Cut the crap. You did a runner."

"Whatever."

"I had to move her, try to make it look like an accident. Not a whole load of fun being there on my own."

"Aw, diddums. Was you scared of the darky-warky?"

Red swallowed down a whole dictionary of expletives. It was a good job there was distance between them at that moment. God knows why he'd ever let himself get sucked into this whole charade. But yes, he shivered as he thought back to the previous night, he had felt unnerved. Dragging Sarah over to the stairs, listening to the creaks and moans of the old house – all with that sickly, panicked feeling running riot inside. He'd not forgotten his last visit; the awful voice he thought he'd heard, and the faulty hot water system. He hated that bloody place with a passion. Almost as much as it seemed to hate him.

He took a long breath, kept his voice level. "You really think you want to be discussing rule-breaking?"

"I saved your skin."

"You pretty much put yourself in the frame for attempted murder. It's you who should be thanking me."

The laugh was high and scornful. "Ah, you make me smile. You really think I'm worried about that? Like you're in any position to be running off to the police. Purlease."

"We had a deal. Not to hurt her, just to scare her."

"She was six steps behind you, you idiot. If I hadn't stopped her in her tracks you'd be collecting your belongings in a plastic bag this morning. Some gratitude. It's nice to know where your priorities lie."

Red swapped the phone to his other ear. "Meaning?"

"It's clear you've got it bad for Mrs Morton. Ulterior motives or what?"

"Bollocks."

"Hmmmm."

"Cut it out. You went too far and you know it. You could have killed her."

"Well, that would have been one obstacle out of the way I suppose."

Red felt his cheeks tingle. "Don't you even care?"

"About what? About the fact we're still following your pathetic orders and getting exactly nowhere. Yes I care a lot. I've had enough. One week or we do it my way."

"No!"

"Yes."

"Well, because I care, I've rung the hospital. She's okay, no thanks to you."

"I'm so pleased. Not as pleased as you though."

Red swallowed, ignored the jibe. "We should see what happens; give it a few days once she's discharged. This will unsettle her; make her more reliant on those around her."

"It had better make her into a gullible idiot who'd fall for anything; otherwise I'll start playing by my rules. And unlike you, I really don't care who gets hurt. I'm not sticking around this backwater much longer. Understand?"

Red scowled, unsure how the balance of power had slipped out of his grasp again. He always came away feeling like a loser who should try harder; a plate spinner who was a failure at his act.

"Understand? One week."

The line went dead. Red threw his phone across the room, watching as it bounced off the back of the sofa and disappeared. One week. Yes, he wanted it all to be over. And he might have a few shocks in store for his partner-in-crime by then too.

December 1st 1859

I open my eyes and groan. If I were not already dead, this cold would surely kill me. Another day. I don't think I can bear another day. My limbs ache and coldness gnaws at my insides, my blood flowing like iced water. It seems to have been windy forever, roaring in my ears and tearing at my clothes. And, as if to add to my woes, the past days have brought sleet storms. The noise is maddening. There is never peace, never quiet. I yearn for a time of silence, of shelter. Of safety.

I unwrap my shawl, kick my legs free and stretch until my back clicks, reluctant to face a new day but knowing I must. Stiff and sore, I shuffle towards the cave entrance, hoping, as I do each morning that this is but a nightmare. But no, my reality remains. I'm glad to see that although the wind continues to buffet and tug at the gorse, the weather is dry, the sky clear, and to the east a buttery light spreads across the ocean as the sun struggles above the horizon. Despite the leaden feeling inside, this sunrise pleases me. It serves to remind me there will be better days, and I should not give in to the dark images of swirling grey water that choke and blind me.

No. This is a new day and new optimism. I stretch my arms and stop mid-yawn. A noise. No, no. A voice. Voices. More than one. Oh, my Lord! People. I can hear people.

I scramble to my feet and rush out onto the plateau. In between streaming gold rays of sunshine, a small group marches along the path above the cave entrance, in single-file and sombre like a funeral procession. In the midst of the crowd, a young woman catches my eye – face reddened with tears and torment – and for a moment I recognise that look and almost feel I know her.

"Good day, madam." I call to them and wave my arms above my head, jumping up and down. "Please, sir ... down here!"

A heady giddiness fills me as I begin to make plans, and a nervous laugh escapes me. At last I shall be rescued, at last I shall return to my family. Oh, Ma. Dear, dear Ma, soon we'll be together again. I run along the plateau, right to the edge where the cliff face crumbles into the ocean. I shout until my throat burns, refusing to let them pass without acknowledgement.

"Sir! Please. Can you help me? Can you find my father? The Stewart family. Sir!"

A blow makes me stagger, so strong it is physical. I watch the empty faces, heads stooped against the pressing wind but the expressions remain blank. They don't hear me, but ... of course they don't. In my excitement, my curse slipped my mind, and the raw truth hits me afresh.

But lest I should forget.

My name is Angelina Stewart.

I am eleven years old.

And I am dead.

I watch the people pass. I am as invisible to them as the air they breathe. But I am curious. Who are they and why are they here?

I recognise a minister, his tall hat and dog collar mark him out from the crowd. Two elderly gentlemen follow his steps, one supporting the young woman, dressed head to toe in black. Her face, partly hidden beneath a layer of delicate lace, is etched with grief. She holds a kerchief to her mouth and appears to mumble incoherently. At the rear, four younger men, well-dressed and distinguished, follow at some distance, talking among themselves. The minister leads the way; arm aloft as if leading his flock into church. They are heading out to the Point. I snap to attention; I must follow.

Scrambling over springy grass, I soon catch up and join them on the path. Of the four people at the rear, a man carrying a silver-tipped cane, with the gait of a gentleman, thick dark curls protruding from his hat, is by far the most vocal. Even as he talks in a whispered hiss, the nasal tones of his voice carry back to me as I match their steps, my own feet far more sure-footed on the narrow, uneven track, than they in their polished shoes.

The man holds the cane high, pausing to face his companions. "I must be honest with you gentlemen, I fail to see what he thinks is to be gained, dragging us all the way out here in this God-forsaken weather, not to mention this mud. Good God, man, does he not think we have seen rocks before? Or an angry ocean or a high cliff? What difference will any of this make to the inquest?"

The man who replies has a deeper voice and is a good deal taller than his companions; he carries himself with a straight back and light step. "He is thinking of both the survivors and the relatives of the deceased. He seeks solace for those who have travelled many miles to visit this spot. We should commend him on his hard work and dedication, not question his actions. Reverend Roose Hughes has done our Parish proud."

"Reverend Roose Hughes will see himself in an early grave if he does not ask for help," replies the first man. "I hear he examines each body personally, stripping and searching every corpse. St Gallgo's Church is still a mortuary, furniture stripped bare to make room for the dead. Now, no man here can agree that is normal behaviour by a man of the cloth."

The comment is met by nods and grunts of agreement from the silent parties.

"I disagree, Mr Astley, sir," the taller gentleman presses. "I'd say that is quite normal for a man who cares for his flock. Reverend Roose Hughes is determined that as many bodies are identified as possible, and he has taken it on himself to notify as many living relations back in Australia as he can. And for the others, he is determined they shall receive a good Christian burial. Commendable, I say, and I am astounded you do not all agree."

"And while he goes about his business, parishioners are denied the use of their church and forced to worship elsewhere. You think this right and proper, sir?"

"I think it right and proper as our Christian duty to accept whatever we must under such terrible circumstances. And I believe that the Reverend should have the backing and respect of every single individual of his congregation. I am surprised at you, Astley. Now, let us get on, listen to the Reverend's prayers and then get back to the Church school and close the inquest without delay."

I shadow the small group; the pathway bends and twists as we climb to the highest part of the cliffs. An inquest. I have heard that word before. It is an investigation, by these men who must be officials, to work out what brought The Royal Charter to such an untimely end. No doubt, someone shall pay; someone will be found at fault and have to answer to the law. And I know there would be question of cargo. I understand enough about the rules of the ocean. But what interests me is the talk of survivors. My family will be among them, I am certain. This is why I must wait here. If this Reverend Roose Hughes is taking it on himself to bring people to this spot to grieve or show respect, then it will not be long before I am reconciled with Ma and Pa and John. Happiness spreads through me like a warm breeze, just the thought I will see my family again is all I need.

I hug myself and although aware of the solemnity of the occasion, I can barely stop myself rejoicing. I step forward and join the small gathering on the very edge of the high cliff, clasping my hands to my breast in the same way as the young woman, mirroring her grief and wishing to fit in with the living. The officials remove their hats, and together, heads bowed, hands clasped, we stare down at the churning water as Reverend Roose Hughes leads us in prayer. Dead and alive alike.

"Dear Lord, we return this day to a spot of such equal beauty and tragedy to celebrate the passing into your care of the Smith family. Father: Phillip. Children: Pip, Joseph, and Emily. Taken into your arms when the Royal Charter perished. Please guide them on their journey and keep them safe from harm. We also ask, Lord, you give support at this time to their sole survivor, Estella Smith, loving wife and mother who grieves for her loss and begs you give her strength and compassion. Lead her forward and show her the way of your light, dear Lord. Amen."

Reverend Roose Hughes embraces the young woman who surely is Estella Smith; her sobs rise so even the gusts of squalling wind and rumble of waves cannot mask her heartbreak.

"Please let us join voices in the Lord's Prayer," he says.

Even the curly-haired official removes a glove and wipes a tear from his eye. I look down, tears choking, unable to bear such raw grief.

I had made the decision to reject God – during these lonely days the decision seemed an easy one. But now, the message is clear. I must stay strong, for I know now they will come. So, I *will* pray.

"Our Father, which art in heaven. Hallowed be thy name ..."

Chapter Thirteen

Sarah stood at the edge of the high cliff, looking out across the shimmering blue ocean - so different from the last time she'd stood in that spot. Pale winter sunlight reflected off the sea, gulls swooped and dived, and a single-file procession of brightly-coloured canoeists hugged the coastline away to her right. The air was the fresh, invigorating cold of a winter's morning that she loved. Frost had crunched beneath her feet as she'd made her way from Charter House to the cliff top, gripping the wreath of roses and carnations she'd brought back with her from Watford.

Dominic's funeral was something she needed to erase from her mind as quickly as possible. Watching the heavy velvet curtains jerkily come together as the casket disappeared from view was almost more than she could bear, and without Luke's supportive arm across her shoulders, Sarah was sure she would have collapsed. The hiccupping sobs of Dominic's mother and sister forced her out of the crematorium, unable to face anyone else's grief. The last echoing notes of 'The Lord is my Shepherd' had barely faded, and she was already dragging Luke across the car park, vision blurred by tears. The sooner she could leave Watford behind … the better. She'd planned to tell Dom's family about the baby, but the moment had felt so wrong.

Sarah took deep breaths and shook her head, trying to ignore flashes of panic that still lingered. Concentrating on the task in hand, she bent and laid the wreath in the long grass, smoothing down waxy leaves so the white flowers were visible. Tears blurred as she read the words on the card.

'Dom. So you never think for one hour, one minute, or one second you're not in my heart. ILYSM. Sarah xxxxx'

Finally she stood, rubbed her arms, and looked over the drop, down to the shiny black boulders where Dom met his death. The sea lapped and swayed against the jagged crevices; the swell pulling long tendrils of seaweed lazily through the water.

Officially, the reason for Dom's fall remained inconclusive. But Sarah knew. She may not know the face behind the hand that pushed him, and may not fully know the reason why. Yet. But she knew Dom's death was no tragic accident.

She'd stood at this exact spot before.

In both life and dreams.

She'd stood here as a child, no more than five or six. Her mother's hands gripping her shoulders as they settled in the coarse grass as near to the edge as allowed – sketch pad balanced across her mother's knees. It was a hot spring morning, and Sarah marvelled at the abundance of colour. Her mother seduced her with her knowledge of Latin as she reeled off the name of each plant, and transferred the images onto canvas in a few effortless strokes. Sarah remembered how she'd squeal with delight and point out each plant time and again, just to hear the foreign-sounding words.

The Latin was long forgotten, but the plant names still sprung to her lips. The bright yellow gorse bushes, the pink nodding heads of sea clover, the perfect white sea aster, and deep green sandwort, had spread out beneath them like a magical artist's palette. The ruddy tones of the sandstone cliff seemed to kiss the azure mixture of sea and sky.

Sarah recalled how she'd cried at its beauty, its peacefulness – the sheer magnificence of nature. Her mother wiped away the tears, and laughed along with her. Hushing and hugging, they'd rolled in the long grass, breathing in the heady scents on the breeze. Her mother's golden hair glinted in the sun as she'd picked out a stray blade of grass. Her blue eyes twinkled, and Sarah had never seen her laugh so much, love so much. She'd kissed the flushed cheek and thanked her being such a magic Mummy, and later they'd held hands as they'd made their way home through fields of swaying crimson poppies.

Sarah's heart ached as she realised how much beauty she'd been introduced to through her mother's passions. And she never tired of it, even now. She studied the cliff face, so different in mid-winter than in her memories of mid-May. The gorse bushes looked brown and tired; the sandstone was slippery and wet with no colourful plants in its nooks and crevices. But the blue sea met the clear sky so effortlessly; the sight still gave her goose bumps.

In her dreams, she'd also stood here.

Sarah closed her eyes and remembered the howling wind and stinging rain on her face; the sound of the raging sea as it battered the cliffs and rocks below. The day Dom died, the young girl, long hair tangling around her face as she pointed out to sea. Sarah remembered the feeling of dread she'd carried as she raced across the field towards the figure, hearing her own name called from unknown lips. The feeling someone was close by every time she woke from the same dream.

But who was she?

Sarah opened her eyes and searched the ocean, looking for inspiration, an answer. Did she believe in ghosts? Was that the question she was consciously avoiding? She declared herself open-minded in the face of cynics. In private, she'd always questioned if they did exist, why her own mother never came back when her beliefs on the subject had been so strong.

Sarah laid a hand across her stomach and smiled. But then perhaps miracles did happen. There were greater powers out there than she would ever understand.

"Thank you."

Her own voice made her jump. She hadn't planned on saying

it aloud. She waited for a reply but could only hear the distant cry of seagulls, swooping behind a small fishing boat on the horizon.

Perhaps, she did have help from beyond the grave. She'd thought it might be Dom, but that never felt right. It seemed important to find out the identity of the young girl.

"Who are you?"

Sarah waited, hands on hips. Silence filled the frosty air.

"I will find you. I promise."

Silence engulfed her like a security blanket, and Sarah closed her eyes, breathing in the moment.

"Sarah?"

She gasped and jumped, swinging round to face a tall, elegant woman dressed in jeans and a black fur jacket.

"Yes. Who are you?"

"Isabel. Isabel Griffiths? We spoke a while back …"

Sarah nodded and shook the outstretched hand.

"I'm sorry to turn up like this, uninvited," Isabel continued. "But you didn't show up for our meeting and I didn't know what else to do. I knew roughly where your father lived, so I took a gamble and headed out here. It took an absolute age to find the place."

"I called a dozen times," said Sarah. "Left messages. There was an accident, I couldn't make our meeting. But I tried to let you know."

Isabel blushed and dug a shiny pink mobile from her shoulder bag. "New phone. Left mine on a train somewhere between Bangor and Chester. Sorry. I never thought. Are you okay now?"

Sarah frowned. "Okay?"

"You said there'd been an accident …"

"Oh. It wasn't me. Well, in a way it was … but …" Sarah waved the comment away. "No matter. It was good of you to come all the way out here. Come on, let's go back to the house and warm up. Coffee?"

"Lovely. Thank you. I tried the front door. And then happened to see you out here." Isabel held her face up, closing her eyes against the sun. "It's a stunning spot. No wonder Professor Williams loved it so much. He talked about Charter House all the time. I feel like I know the old place."

Sarah took a good look at the research assistant. The landscape wasn't the only stunning thing around here. Sarah could almost hear Dom's appreciative wolf-whistle. Long blonde hair, clear complexion, and a figure a supermodel would pay good money for. The skinny jeans and knee-high boots accentuated the length of her legs. Sarah felt instantly fat and dumpy, and had to concentrate on not waddling as they crossed the open field back in the direction of Charter House.

A short while later, both women sat either side of the kitchen table, warming their hands on steaming mugs of coffee.

Isabel looked around with a dreamy expression. "I just adore this old building. So much character. I'd love to own a place one day. Some hope!"

Sarah took a sip of coffee. "I'm just the opposite. I've always preferred new places. All mod cons, you know. It's probably being brought up here."

"Your father talked about you a lot."

Sarah stopped, put her mug back down. "He did?"

Isabel took a sip and nodded. "Always. You're a travel writer, right?"

"Yeah."

"He was one proud Daddy."

Sarah smiled, warmth tingling her frozen cheeks. "He was never one to show much emotion."

"It's a male trait. He was proud of you, but I'm guessing he probably never said so."

Sarah shook her head, clearing her throat as she felt the urgent press of tears. "You have a lovely accent," she said, needing to change the direction of the conversation. "American?"

"Canadian. Right near Toronto."

"So why Wales? Why Bangor?"

"I came over here on a study exchange, and you know how it goes. Met a guy, fell in love, got pregnant, settled down."

"You have a child?"

"Yes, a little boy. Thomas. Do you have children?"

Sarah shook her head. No. Dom had so wanted a family, but she'd decided to wait, concentrating on her career. Now, she wished she'd made a different decision, given Dom what he desired before it was too late.

Isabel drained her coffee. "It wasn't the fairy-tale ending. We split when Thomas was only two. He's five now. But he's settled and I love my job, so why leave? I feel I have more roots here than I have back home. There was only me and my mom. I might go back one day, but not yet."

The room fell silent, and aware of a distinct change of atmosphere, Sarah got up and cleared the mugs into the sink before turning back to Isabel.

"When we spoke you mentioned there was some urgency for us to meet?"

Isabel nodded. "We should start at the beginning ..."

"I think I should tell you something first, just so you know the full story. The accident. It was my husband. Dominic. He was killed a couple of days after my father's funeral."

Isabel sat back in her chair as if she'd been slapped. Her face drained of colour. "No? Really? Oh my God."

"I found his body at the bottom of a cliff – just where we met today actually. It was the first time I'd been back there ..." Sarah blinked hard. "Well, I fell trying to get down to him, sprained my ankle and ended up in hospital. And found out at the same time I'm pregnant. So ... now you know everything. That's why I didn't get in touch again."

"Oh God." Isabel ran a hand across her forehead. "I'm so very sorry. How are you coping?"

"I'm not sure that I am. I have friends, my gran. But it doesn't feel real. I just go through the motions every day, you know?"

Isabel nodded.

"And I've had all these unfounded suspicions about my father's death, then Dom's. But I couldn't tell anyone anything because all I had was this rambling letter." Sarah took a deep breath. "I've struggled to get anyone to take my suspicions seriously, but now it might be starting to pay off; the police have agreed to an exhumation of my father's body for further tests."

"Really?"

"It's the only way they can prove he was murdered as no post mortem was carried out. It's all so terrible. But I hold onto the thought that if it means someone will be brought to justice for his murder – and I believe Dom's – then it will be worth it in the end."

Isabel was a sickly grey colour and began to bite her bottom lip.

"Are you okay?" said Sarah.

She gave a weak smile. "I hate things like that. It's such a shock."

"I know. But that's why it's so important to find out what you meant …"

"Sure. I understand now." Isabel cleared her throat. "I met your father – or Professor Williams as he was to me then – while studying English and Medieval History. I was twenty one, on a foreign exchange course, and attended archaeology lectures your father ran. I was bowled over by his passion and commitment to his work. After I became pregnant, I think he took pity on me, and I did bits and bobs of research for him. Eventually I became his research assistant, and later his PA, I guess you'd call it. I typed out his manuscripts for him, sent his work out to publishers, booked his diary. You name it. He called me his 'Girl Friday.'"

"I noticed some of his later manuscripts were computer-typed and wondered how he'd managed. He'd only recently discovered computers and the joys of the Internet."

"When things started to get more serious with regards to the Royal Charter discoveries, your father needed to confide in someone. I think he considered it safer to bring me on board and we pooled our resources. To begin with I thought he was being overly paranoid, but now, I don't know."

"But what exactly had he discovered?"

Isabel frowned. "You don't know?"

Sarah shook her head.

"No, I guess that makes sense, he wouldn't have risked leaving any details with you and potentially putting you at risk ..."

"Sorry ... what? I'm totally confused. What had he discovered?"

"The gold, Sarah. The missing gold from the wreck of the Royal Charter!"

* * *

A sharp tapping noise intruded into Danny's thoughts. He'd been engrossed in witness statements, trying to find some connection between the elderly victims of the recent scam involving utility company representatives. And just when he felt sure he could put his finger on the link, it slithered away from his grasp.

The noise again. Three sharp raps. He looked up, rubbing his eyes and blinking. The room had settled into an uneasy silence; all heads turned to the front of the room where a sweaty-faced Thompson waited for their attention. Danny bit back a groan. Now what? Their eyes met for a fraction of a second, and Danny felt sure he saw a flicker of warmth. No. He had to have imagined it. Thompson turned his back and wrote a single word on the white board.

Brodifacoum.

Thompson turned. "Right. Any of you heard of this?"

Silence and a good deal of head shaking.

"Well, then you all have a lot of work to be getting on with." Thompson snapped the lid back onto the marker pen and balanced his weight on the edge of the nearest desk. "Regarding Danny's potential case ..."

Danny jumped at the mention of his name and sat up straighter.

"One Professor Owen Williams. Following the exhumation of the body, post-mortem toxicology test results were on my desk when I got in this morning. I thought you might want to ' know."

A jolt of electricity shot through Danny's body. "Was he murdered?"

Thompson let the question hang in the air for long seconds. "There was a high dose of a toxin called brodifacoum found in his body. According to the pathologist it's an anticoagulant, used to treat heart conditions or thrombosis, embolisms, that kind of thing. And from what I've learned it's very effective if used safely. If administered unnecessarily or in high dosages it can cause death pretty quickly, one to two weeks after ingestion of a lethal dose, or within a month of prolonged abuse. The drug induces internal bleeding, which is usually fatal." Thompson pointed his pen at Danny. "I'd suggest your first point of call is to check with the victim's GP and establish there's nothing on his medical records."

Danny shook his head. "There isn't. I know those records by heart."

Thompson paused, licked his lips. "If that's the case then clearly you have a murder enquiry on your hands."

DC Mayou looked up from his computer screen, quoting aloud. "Years ago the drug brodifacoum would have been known as warfarin, this is just a more advanced derivative ..."

Danny whistled. "Rat poison?"

Mayou nodded. "A modern day equivalent."

"Shite." Danny exhaled, quickly glancing at Thompson. "Sorry, sir."

"I think you need to make this case your priority, Buchanan," said Thompson. "Your instincts were right, and until DS Lewis returns full time at the end of the week, I'd like you to head up the enquiry. This is going to be a difficult task. The victim has been dead for nearly a month; you've lost all the usual leads and tactics. I'd suggest motive is the key. Talk to everyone and anyone who knew Professor Williams, draw up a complete diary of his life if you can. Talk to the locals, listen to local gossip, get them to trust you. And do it fast …"

Danny scribbled down notes before looking up. "And what about the second murder?"

Thompson frowned. "The son-in-law?"

"Yes. There's a connection. He didn't jump and it was no accident. He was pushed. I'm positive."

Thompson got to his feet. "Then find me evidence, DS Buchanan, and you have a double murder enquiry on your hands. Good luck."

Chapter Fourteen

"Gold? What gold?" Sarah swallowed, trying to keep her concentration. "I don't know anything about any missing gold?"

"Really?" Isabel raised her eyebrows. "I thought you were raised in Moelfre?"

"I was. But I mean … this ship went down hundreds of years ago, how can the gold still be missing after all this time? Do you mean the gold coins I found in Father's safe?"

Isabel shook her head and sighed. She reached down and lifted a bulging yellow satchel onto her lap. "I bought some of your father's files. I think it might help explain things."

Sarah watched as Isabel unloaded bundles of paperwork, secured with pieces of string, very much in the style of her father. She thought back to the research on the Internet. All roads seemed to lead back to that shipwreck. What was it Grandma Ruth had said?

'… be careful, sweetheart. That ship has ruined a lot of lives. Don't let it ruin yours, too.'

And Huw the Boat, his parting words.

'Let the dead rest in peace, always been my motto. There's been enough fighting in this village over the years. Enough grudges held and lies told to last a lifetime.'

Did they both know more than they were letting on? And hadn't she read somewhere about rumours of people stripping gold from dead bodies washed up on the beaches? Weren't there tales of local families becoming inexplicably rich over night? But that could have no connection on her father's death surely. That was 1859 not 2011.

Isabel looked up. "Your father got increasingly paranoid about leaving anything at Charter House after the first couple of break-ins. Consequently, I ended up taking it back to my flat rather than leaving it at the office. Now I have a whole filing cabinet's worth."

Sarah shook her head in amazement. It dawned on her now. Despite everyone saying the Royal Charter had taken over her father's life in recent years, she'd found little or no mention of it at Charter House. Why had the thought never occurred to her before? Everything she'd learned was from research on the Internet, yet if he'd written books on the subject, and researched the hard way, it made sense he would have reams of paperwork.

"I have done some research, so I know the basics," Sarah said as Isabel flicked through the papers. "Plus I spoke to my maternal grandma, and she filled me in that my other Gran, Miriam, was the granddaughter of one of the survivors of the sinking –"

"Charles Stewart." Isabel nodded; her blonde hair swaying as she spoke. "He survived as did his son, John – Miriam's father. His wife and daughter, I think her name was Angelina, were lost at sea – presumed dead. And it was this loss that seemed to trigger Charles Stewart's obsession with the wreck." She flicked through what looked like photocopies of old newspaper articles, then tapped one sheet of paper with a French-manicured nail. "Do you know the value of the cargo the Charter was carrying? Over £300,000 at the time. Converted today that would be over £25 million!"

Sarah took a sharp intake of breath. "Wow!"

Isabel smiled. "I know, remarkable! That's on inflation index alone, not even considering the increase in the value of the gold." She blinked wide blue eyes and shook her head. "Anyway, as I say, Charles Stewart was consumed by grief. He believed he'd caused his family's deaths by assuming women and children would be rescued first; so he strapped gold ingots to his daughter and filled his wife's pockets with gold coins. Unfortunately, the ship broke up before any of the very basic lifeboats could be launched. Because of the excess weight, as soon as the women hit the water they went straight to the bottom."

Sarah shuddered. Vivid images, nightmarish flashbacks, filled her mind.

Icy water submerged me … nothing but a muddy brown swirling mass …underwater currents so strong, like hands dragging me lower …pain inside my head and chest roared … I closed my eyes and prayed … prayed … prayed …

"Sarah?"

She jumped. "Y-yes?"

Isabel leaned forward, her elbows propped on the table, half rising from her seat. "Are you okay? You looked as if you were about to faint."

"I … er … no, I mean, yes. I'm fine. I'm fine."

What else could she say?

"You sure?"

Sarah nodded. "I'll just get a glass of water."

On shaky legs, she crossed the room, aware of Isabel's eyes on her, and gripped the tap as cold water splashed into the sink. She filled a glass, letting it overflow as her heart raced and fluttered. The start of a headache pounded against her temples and she let the water run over her wrists for several moments. Her forehead was hot and clammy and a wave of nausea pressed just above her stomach. She stared out of the window with dull eyes, the beauty of the gardens for once lost to her.

Surely not morning sickness starting now? No. This had nothing to do with her pregnancy. This only happened when she talked about the shipwreck. This feeling of suffocating, no … not suffocation, drowning. This horrible image of dying right before her own eyes. She'd thought it was Dominic. But last time it had felt too weak, too vulnerable.

Was it a child, fighting to live … and failing?

Was it Angelina?

"Sarah?" A hand touched her shoulder. "What is it?"

She shook her head, voice catching in her throat. "I don't know. Honestly. I don't know."

Isabel tugged her shoulder with gentle insistence. "Then come and sit down. We should talk about it. It's what your father would want. I know he wanted us to share this experience. We were the only people he trusted. Come on. Tell me."

Isabel led Sarah back to her chair, and settled opposite with an expectant expression.

"I've been having bad dreams," said Sarah.

"That's hardly surprising with what you've been through ..."

"No, you see, that's just it. I thought it was all down to Dominic's death, grief over my father, or whatever. But I don't think it's connected. It's something to do with the shipwreck, I'm sure of it. When you described the death of Charles Stewart's daughter –"

"Angelina …"

"I've been there. I've seen her drowning. I've felt her fight for her life … and I've felt that life drain from her."

Isabel frowned. "I don't understand. How'd you mean?"

"In my dreams … I've lived that girl's death."

A tense silence filled the room. Sarah could see the concentration on Isabel's face, but she could also read the doubt in her eyes. And she didn't blame her. Tables turned, and she'd be suggesting the need for medical help about now.

"There's some connection between the girl and Charter House," Sarah said. "I'm sure of it. Other things have happened too."

"Like what?"

She told Isabel about the events on the day Dom died, with the image of the girl leading her to the cliff top. About the eerie feeling she couldn't shake on the day of her father's funeral; the bizarre effect the dead crow had on her. She explained about the voice that woke her on the night of the break-in – how someone attacked her and left her for dead.

Isabel's eyes opened wider as the words tumbled from Sarah's lips. She had to tell someone, had to get it out of her system. And more importantly, as she heard the words, the fears, the ideas, voiced aloud for the first time, Sarah realised she didn't really care what anyone else thought anymore.

Because she believed.

"Do you think I'm mad?" Sarah asked when the words finally ran dry.

Isabel shook her head, just the slightest of movements, then made eye contact. "No, Sarah. I think you're being haunted."

Haunted.

The word sounded so foreign that a laugh popped from between Sarah's lips. "I'd never thought of her as a ghost. Not until today," she admitted. "But I think you're right. She has tried to help me, guide me, ever since I've been back at Charter House. But why?"

Isabel picked up the papers again. "That's what we have to find out."

"But you believe me?"

"Absolutely. I have no reason not to. I strongly believe in reincarnation, that we never really die, that we just move on. So, I have to accept the paranormal – my mom had really strong beliefs and I was raised to understand our souls never die and tormented souls never rest. I don't have all the answers. But yes, Sarah, absolutely, I believe you."

"Good." Sarah let out a long breath. "So, let's carry on where we left off shall we? Let's put this jigsaw together, and along the way perhaps we'll find the answer to whatever is troubling Angelina too."

* * *

Red pushed open the bar door and breathed in the smell of the open fire. He loved this place. The Douglas Inn had nothing fancy about it – neither the ale nor the food were top quality, and the weather was rarely clear enough to see across the Irish Sea to view its namesake – but it held a familiar feel for Red that took him back to happier times. He ordered his usual pint and settled in his usual seat, closest to the window.

Today, the spot afforded him a stunning glimpse of the ocean, which, despite a distant mist, sparkled like polished sapphires. He wasn't one to get soft over pretty views and the like, but something about this particular corner of this particular nondescript pub settled his soul like nothing else. He took a sip of real ale, wiped his top lip, and settled back against the worn leather seat, listening to the crackle of logs in the hearth.

Minutes later, he heard chair legs scraping across tiled floor. He opened one eye. "What kept you?"

"Some of us hold down a full-time job and can't spend most of the day in the boozer."

"Spare me the amateur dramatics. You want a pint?"

"No. I have a life."

Red staged a mock yawn. "Don't let me keep you."

"They've made an appointment for tomorrow morning."

"They?" Red's pulse quickened. "Both of them?"

"Yeah."

"So, she has the other key?"

"I dunno. But why else?"

"How quickly can you let me know what happens tomorrow?"

"I could lose my job you know, I could get struck off …"

"And I don't give a fuck."

"I have no idea why the hell I put up with your –"

"Spare me. How soon?"

A deep sigh. "Within the hour, depending how it goes. He trusts me. And he won't be able to keep it to himself."

"Good." Red settled back, closed his eyes again; a satisfied smile on his lips. "See you then."

The chair scraped again, sharper this time, and a cool draught signified he had the bar to himself once more. Finally, things were going his way. And two fingers to the 'my way or highway approach.'

No one threatened him, no one. He'd have the last laugh. Always.

* * *

"Right, where were we?" said Sarah, putting two fresh mugs of coffee on the kitchen table and retaking her seat opposite Isabel.

"Charles Stewart's guilt ... well, more than guilt ... it ended in madness. We found records that John eventually had his father sent to a sanatorium in Snowdonia, near Llanberis. According to his hospital referral records – 'for his own safety as well as that of others.' All later records were lost when the sanatorium was destroyed in a fire, but it's presumed he ended his life there and John Stewart took over Charter House."

"What a shame."

Isabel nodded. "But what we do know about Charles Stewart was he never gave up trying to find the lost gold. I suppose he thought if he could rescue the gold, then the death of his wife and child wouldn't have been completely in vain. John wrote in a diary extract his father spent days standing in one spot on the cliffs at Point Lynas staring out to sea, searching the waters for any sign of life, refusing to believe his family was dead. Tragic. But in the days and weeks after the sinking, gold coins in their hundreds were washed up on many of the surrounding beaches, not to mention bodies with gold still attached. It seems Charles and John spent many days collecting gold, and within weeks had enough to buy a plot of land on the exact spot on the cliffs at Point Lynas ... so Charles could continue his vigil."

"I heard the same – that Charter House was built with Charter gold."

"I have the original records here. The house was built by a

local firm from Amlwch and finished within the year. But it was never a happy home, not until Charles Stewart was sent away. Your grandmother told many tales of her childhood, full of her grandfather's fury and alcoholism. He must have lived a tormented life. He hated everyone, even his surviving family."

Isabel tucked the building documents back into a file. "Now, much of the next section is conjecture. We have no proof, but your father was sure he was correct. There were a couple of local families in Moelfre who decided to invest in some diving equipment, very rudimentary stuff at the time as you can imagine. But there were plans for a large salvage operation firm to come in from Liverpool and scour the seabed to recover the gold. Of course, this caused uproar among the locals, some of whom were still housing a few of the survivors.

These families invested in the diving gear, they already had boats, and set about recovering the gold. According to parish records, a meeting was held in the spring of 1860, when Charles Stewart virtually begged to be allowed to join the salvage expedition. He even offered to fund it with gold he'd already collected. But the locals refused point blank. He was a foreigner. Not welcome and not wanted, and the locals believed if they could squeeze him out, he would sell up and go home to Australia. But they didn't realise Charles could never do that – he would never go home without his wife and daughter."

Isabel shook her head and paused for breath, face flushed. Her enthusiasm and excitement touched Sarah. In Isabel, her father surely found everything he'd sought in his own daughter.

"And so," said Isabel. "This started a feud that went on for generations. And I believe exists still today."

"I never knew. Everything my father said, I thought it was all in his imagination. How could people hate someone so much just because they had a different accent and came from a different part of the world? I mean, the man was half mad with grief; did none of these people understand the word *compassion*?"

Anger writhed inside her; memories of her father's funeral

still festered away like an open sore. The looks and whispers she'd taken as dislike for her, could well be far more deep-seated than she could ever have imagined.

"Well, that was part of it. But the locals had a far stronger reason for detesting the Stewart family."

Sarah frowned. "What?"

"They believed Charles Stewart stole the gold they invested time and money in recovering from the wreck."

"No … really?"

"And your father spent the best part of his life trying to prove or disprove this theory."

"And did he?" The words were little more than a whisper.

Isabel smiled. "Oh, yes. He sure did."

"And …"

"He not only found out that Charles Stewart did steal the gold. He also found out how he did it and where he hid it."

"No way," Sarah whispered.

Isabel nodded. "I haven't seen the gold. I don't even have all the pieces to put the puzzle together completely. But I know your father has seen it, touched it. And he told me he believes the value will be a substantial amount, maybe even several million pounds."

"So, why didn't my father do something about it? Why not come clean, sell it, give it away or whatever the hell he liked. I don't know the relevant law, but there would be treasure trove or salvage rights or something, wouldn't there? So no matter what the snooty families of Moelfre thought or didn't think is of no consequence. Legally, they surely could do nothing?"

"Legally, you're probably right. But who said anything about legal? To start with you must realise Charles Stewart didn't leave a detailed treasure map with a big arrow pointing 'gold is here.'"

"What did he do then?"

"First, let me tell you what your father discovered. When the Moelfre families set about the salvage operation, obviously Charles Stewart had the perfect spot for monitoring their progress. He spied on them. We found hospital records showing he had to be treated for shotgun wounds to both legs, and substantial stomach injuries, in the summer of 1860. We can have no definite answer, but rumour among the locals was that he was shot at by some of the families coming in close to the rocks on boats, while the gold was being loaded onto others. They must have seen Charles watching from the cliffs, and to stop him finding out where the gold was taken, they peppered him with bullets. He survived, but it was a close call. Can you imagine his anger, his need for revenge, once he'd recovered from his injuries?"

"But if they'd just given him back what was his, or the equivalent amount, then none of it would have happened, would it?"

Isabel shrugged. "We have no way of knowing. Remember, he was far from sane. Perhaps he was unreasonable; there are varying reports of his actions. Some, notably from the parish priest at the time, said all Charles Stewart really wanted was to search and recover the bodies of his loved ones. Other written extracts from parish meetings say he was like a man possessed who believed the whole cargo was by rights to be divided equally among the forty or so survivors."

"He may have had a point," said Sarah.

"Perhaps, but that was never going to happen, was it?"

"So, while he was injured, did they salvage most of the gold?"

"Yes, they were successful in removing about half apparently. And now for the really grisly part. Not long after Charles Stewart returned home to Charter House from hospital in Bangor, a son of one of the main families involved, Emyr Parry, went missing and his body was never found. Lots of rumours, and counter-rumours, started up that Charles kidnapped the boy and tortured him to death, after first forcing him to reveal the hiding place of the gold. There's much speculation whether this is true or not. Some believe the young man simply ran away from home because he was a simpleton and mistreated, and his family fabricated the whole story to cover up child abuse or neglect. I don't think it's even clear whether Emyr knew where the gold was stored or not. But what is fact, is that before the families were able to divide it or sell the gold on – it disappeared from the unknown hiding place they'd carefully chosen – disappeared for good."

"And what happened to Charles Stewart?"

"My belief, and that of your father, is he was hounded into madness. He became obsessed with defending his family, his home. He survived numerous attacks on his life, and obviously what police protection existed back then wouldn't have been a jot of help to this Australian family no one wanted there in the first place."

"So, that drove him mad?"

Isabel nodded.

"But had he got the gold?"

Isabel smiled. "That is the sixty-four thousand – or maybe the sixty-four million dollar question."

Sarah could barely speak. "And what's the answer?"

"Well, your father believed he had. Had always believed it to be so. But if Charles did have it, he certainly never sold it. How could he? The missing gold was his ticket to life. In his final years before madness claimed him, he began to put the pieces together of an elaborate puzzle. A plan he believed only members of his own family would be able to crack. His son had disowned him by this point, so I think he turned his back on John. But perhaps he hoped someday, one of his descendants might care enough to start asking questions, start reading books, start solving clues."

Isabel paused and took a deep breath. "And that person was your father, Sarah. He solved the clues and discovered the gold. Can you believe that? And I think he has left enough pieces of the puzzle equally divided between the two of us to solve this thing and recover the gold."

Sarah stared at Isabel. Her heart banged away in her chest and she realised she was holding her breath. She exhaled and tried to assemble her jumbled thoughts into some kind of rational order, wishing, not for the first time, for Dom's guiding presence.

"So, why didn't my father just come clean? Like I said, what stopped him?" A wave of revelation washed through her head, clearing her vision. Sarah looked up and Isabel nodded. "The death threats? The attempts on his life? Someone knew, someone found out, didn't they?"

"Early on your father made the mistake of rewriting his Will to include this new fortune. He lodged it with his solicitor in Holyhead. There was a breach of security, a break-in according to the firm, and your father's will was among the items stolen. Owen doubted their word; he always believed it was an inside job. Some relative of the Charter families who worked there had stolen it, and the firm were covering. But once word was out Owen Williams knew where the missing gold was, can you imagine how it ruined his life?"

Sarah nodded. Yes, of course she could. But why hadn't he turned to her?

Isabel seemed to read her expression. "Owen would never have involved you, Sarah. He wouldn't have wanted to put you in any danger. He loved you too much to do that."

"But he involved you?"

"I was expendable." She paused, shrugged. "I wasn't family."

"Why didn't he go to the police, then? Make them listen to him?" She trailed off, already knowing the answer; hadn't he attempted to do just that?

"Oh, he tried. Believe me, but I think he tried too hard. In the end the police were so sick of him, I'd bet they were glad when he died. I wouldn't be surprised if they had something to do with rushing through the death certificate and not pushing for a post mortem. But don't quote me on that. Your father was an angry man in later years, and when he got angry everyone knew about it."

Sarah allowed herself a weak smile. Isabel certainly got to

know her father well over the past six or seven years. But the police hadn't been responsible. She'd seen the guilt in the eyes of DS Lewis on that first visit. Her father's death had made it clear they'd got it wrong and that decision could also have cost Dom his life.

"Did you hear about the first break-in?" said Isabel. "Your father nearly committed murder himself."

"What?"

"He interrupted a burglary one night. He confronted a masked man in his study and smashed him over the head with a candlestick. Unfortunately – or perhaps fortunately for Owen – he didn't land a killer blow. The burglar got up and punched Owen, knocked him out cold."

Sarah ran a hand across her face. "I can't believe I had no idea about any of this."

"You can't change the past, Sarah. You have to focus on the future. And I believe you can solve this mystery once and for all. Not to mention find the Charter gold."

Sarah bunched her hands into fists. "The most important thing for me right now is to find out who killed Dominic and my father. Anything else will just be the icing on the cake."

"And you'll let me help you?" said Isabel.

Sarah reached across the table and squeezed the other woman's hand. "Of course. I wouldn't know where to start without you. What do we do next? Do you know?"

Isabel shook her head. "I don't have specific instructions, but I think we should start with the solicitor."

"Adrian Carter? He seemed less than useful."

"No. Smithsons in Holyhead."

Sarah frowned. "They are the family solicitors, going back years but I heard my father had a dispute and I thought you said –"

Isabel smiled. "Your father was a very clever man. He believed in that old adage about eggs and baskets. He wanted to ensure the pieces of the jigsaw were spread far and wide to ensure no one ever had any chance of completing the puzzle."

"So what's at Smithsons?" asked Sarah.

"I think there may be a new Will and I think the details could be in a security box your father held there." Isabel picked up her bag, removed a black wallet and took out a small silver key. "He left me this but was very clear that the box needed two keys."

Sarah dug into her jacket pocket and removed her purse; rummaging between the loose change she retrieved her identical key. "Snap!"

Isabel nodded. "Yes, I thought as much. I think these are keys for the deposit box. When Owen gave me this, I always thought you would have the sister key."

"So, we should make an appointment to see this solicitor as soon as."

"Already sorted. We meet Mr Berwyn Pugh at eleven tomorrow."

Sarah raised her eyebrows and gave a low whistle. "You don't waste time, do you?"

"Girl Friday, remember?" Isabel paused. "Have you given any thought to possible suspects?"

Sarah drained her coffee. "After Dom died, I thought of little else. But as I've not been around for so many years, I really have no idea."

"Perhaps we should make a list," said Isabel, pulling a notebook from her satchel. "I live and die by making lists. I think I have some kind of OCD. I blame my mom, she's just the same."

"Well, my first suspect would be the totally creepy Miles Harvey-Barnes –"

"Oh, he was Owen's agent."

Sarah stared, open-mouthed. "You mean he really was? He was genuine? I'm afraid I've been rather rude to him since the funeral."

Isabel nodded. "Oh, yes. I've met him a few times. He's a pompous little man. But his company got an excellent deal with a good-sized publisher. I think Owen signed to them, just the week before he died."

"Yes, that's what Harvey-Barnes says. But he also says they've never received the signed contract back in the post. Quite honestly, I don't know whether or not to believe him. There are certainly no contracts lying around at Charter House. So if it's not there, where else could it be?"

Isabel shrugged. "We'd spoken mainly by email in the few weeks before he died; he'd become withdrawn, even more difficult, and I have to admit there was a distance opening up between us. All I know was he was excited he'd finally got a deal, and he'd negotiated a decent-sized advance."

"So, could they still publish, without a contract, I mean?"

"I don't know. But the work belongs to your father, and is protected by law - so if you inherit the copyright, I wouldn't think so."

"So, he's just a pushy little prat then, rather than anything sinister?"

Isabel smiled. "Nice phrasing, but yes I think so. But then again he has got beady eyes and half-moon specs. Never trust anyone with half-moon specs."

"I'll remember that," Sarah said, with a smile. "My other suspect would be Craig Davies. He rang me a week or so ago with some cock and bull story about my father selling him some old books."

"*The Mabinogion*?" asked Isabel. "Yes, I remember Owen was completely fascinated by them."

"I'd like to know how Davies knew so much. It doesn't feel right."

Isabel frowned. "But if Davies knew about the gold, why would he be so interested in a couple of old books? They may be valuable, but not in the same league as the treasure."

Treasure. A modern-day treasure hunt, with clues and maps in the style of Indiana Jones. But unfortunately, this adventure had taken a much more sinister turn, with the deaths of at least two people.

"You may be right," Sarah said. "But for me he stays at the top of the suspect list. The books could be a cover, I don't know. But I do know he's been hanging around Charter House, and I wouldn't trust him as far as I could throw him."

"Okay. Who else?"

Sarah shrugged and tapped the table, trying to conjure a name. "I read a name on the Internet when I researched the Royal Charter. Sidney Winters. It reminded me of a row my father got into years ago. Winters ran a salvage firm in Liverpool, and he secured rights to dive on the wreck. I'd forgotten all about it until recently, but it was a big thing at the time."

"Winters?" Isabel frowned. "I don't recognise the name."

"No, you wouldn't, it was a long time ago. I was sixteen, it was the summer after I'd finished my GCSEs and I was back in Moelfre. I remember working in the garden one day, tending the vegetable patch. We heard this loud explosion, like a bomb going off somewhere. It shook the ground. It turned out Winters' firm had used explosives to blow apart a section of the hull of the wreck, to try and find gold in the cargo holds."

Isabel raised her eyebrows. "I never knew anything about this."

"Oh, it caused all sorts of uproar locally. We had newspaper journalists and TV reporters knocking on the door, night and day. Eventually, the locals got an injunction against Winters and he was forced to abandon the project. My father was the ringleader. He was incensed by Winters' arrogance, and some heated words were said by both sides. Years later, my father confided that Winters had issued death threats. He'd warned my father in an anonymous letter of 'underworld contacts' in Liverpool that would see my father 'in a box'. He only had to say the world and my father was a dead man."

"No!"

Sarah nodded. "I didn't know how serious it got until years later."

"So, you think Winters might have carried out his threat all these years later?"

"I know that seems unlikely, a vendetta lasting more than a dozen years, but it's not impossible." Sarah frowned as she tried to recall more information. A sudden thought struck her and she banged the table making Isabel jump. "What if Winters heard rumour my father had located the missing gold and came back looking for revenge?"

"It's possible. He'll go on the list. I think we should tell the police at the very least, and ask them to look into Sidney Winters."

"I'll try to contact DS Buchanan. I need to find out if they have the results of the exhumation." Sarah ran a hand through her hair. "So, that's about all I can offer. How about you? Any thoughts on suspects?"

Isabel shook her head and tapped her pen against the edge of the table. "I've given this a fair bit of thought. When I heard about Owen's death, my instinct was to jump in with both feet, but Owen had been really strict. He warned me if anything happened, I might be in danger too, which I totally get. But by doing nothing, I've missed the chance of discovering any clues the police overlooked."

"How about friends or associates he may have confided in in recent years?"

Isabel screwed up her face in concentration. "Owen lived a very private life. He always considered himself an outsider and rarely mixed with the villagers. But I don't have to tell you that." She paused and smiled. "He liked Luke Evans and the policeman, Conrad. He'd befriended a young man that helped him with odd jobs and gardening, but other than that he kept himself very much to himself."

Sarah nodded, remembering the voice at the top of the cliff the night Dom died, and the round-faced youth from her father's wake. "Martin. I forget his last name. He raised the alarm when I fell down the cliff."

"He's a bit slow. I don't think he ever says a lot and I wouldn't say they were close, certainly not someone Owen would confide in. The only other possibility I can think of …"

"Yes?"

"Well, he was close to one of the other history professors, Dr Gillingham; they were both on the board of this archaeology trust. He might have confided in him, I suppose. Trouble is, Dr Gillingham is in America, has been for some months on a study tour, and I don't know when he's due back."

"Could you find out?"

"I can try. Someone will know." Isabel glanced at the list. "So, we have a start. Let's see how it goes at Smithsons tomorrow before we make any more decisions."

Sarah glanced at her watch. "Look at the time. Luke will be here any minute with Grandma Ruth in tow."

Isabel shuffled the papers back into her satchel. "Right. I'll make a move."

"Oh, don't worry, no rush. I don't think my friends and family trust me here alone. I'd asked my gran if she wanted to come and stay a while back, but I put her off after the break-in, you know just in case she got involved. But apparently she's taken things into her own hands – packed her suitcases and arranged a lift so she told me on the phone this morning." Sarah got to her feet. "I'd better go and make the bed up and get her room ready."

Sarah walked round the table and held out a hand. "Thank you. I feel better already having you onside."

Isabel smiled and took a step forward, reaching out to pull Sarah into her embrace. "We'll get to the bottom of this. I owe it to your father. And I know revenge is what you have in mind, but I reckon Owen has done his best to set you up for life."

Sarah returned the hug then pulled away, keeping hold of Isabel's hand as they walked along the hallway. At the door the women embraced again.

"See you in the morning," said Sarah. "Take care."

She watched as the white Fiat did a three-point turn and

headed down the drive, waving, with a smile, until Isabel disappeared from view.

Chapter Fifteen

Danny took a long sip of espresso, forcing himself not to wince at the bitter taste. Christ, he'd never make a yuppie – or a student – nowadays. You couldn't beat a steaming mug of Ovaltine in his opinion, just like his mam used to make with boiling milk and four sugars. But that was never on offer at these trendy café-bars, and he was doing his utmost to train his taste buds. Around him, the shop bustled with life: rapid chatter, the rattle of cutlery and chink of china, the aroma of strong coffee mixed with freshly-baked bread which would, under normal circumstances, make him salivate. But, having polished off a huge plate of bacon, sausage and eggs, with four extra rounds of crusty bread, toasted on one side just how he liked, he could barely fasten his jeans let alone think about lunch.

He wasn't looking forward to this meeting, and he'd been glad when Sarah said she had an appointment in Holyhead and would meet him in town to save him the journey down the labyrinth of narrow lanes to Charter House. There was always a fine line between questioning and accusation. Trouble was, difficult questions had to be asked. Danny couldn't shake the feeling Sarah Morton was holding out on him – and today was the day he had to find out why.

He glanced at his watch, then out of the window. Holyhead was like many port towns he knew, by-passed by the hordes of tourists that headed for the docks, and yet to benefit from the huge cash injection needed to revive its flagging economy. A new marina and the first mushrooming of trendy harbour-side apartments were the first hints of things to come. In the town itself, too many shops were boarded up; the others predominately a mix of charity and pound shops. There was a general air of abandonment about the place as people quietly went around their business – a blur of coloured umbrellas hurrying between shops.

Danny rubbed sweaty palms against his trousers as he picked out individual faces in the crowd, hoping to catch a glimpse of blonde hair or the pale denim jacket he'd often seen her wear.

"Detective?"

He jumped and the front legs of his chair hit the ground with a thump. He turned as Sarah stamped water from suede boots.

"Hey, take a seat."

"How are you?" she asked as she slid into the vacant chair.

"Fine. You? How's that ankle?"

"Better. Just stiff and a bit sore in a morning."

"And the … er …" Danny's gaze travelled south.

Sarah smiled and patted her tummy. "She's doing fine."

"She?"

Sarah shrugged. "I appear to know the sex. Don't ask me how. Add it to the general weirdness."

Danny gave an awkward smile, then jumped to his feet. "Shite. I mean … damn. I have no social skills, so you have to excuse me. Can I get you a drink?"

"Pot of tea would be lovely. I'm not a fan of the coffee in these places."

Danny grinned as he joined the queue, returning with a tray containing a large teapot, milk jug and two cups all in a bright banana colour.

"Shall I be mother?" said Sarah as he settled into his chair. "Let me guess. Milk and two sugars?"

"Three," said Danny, feeling his cheeks tingle with warmth.

"I'm every Irish stereotype you know all rolled into one."

Sarah smiled, transforming her face into that of a teenager, poured the tea and took a long drink, warming her hands around the cup. Danny thought it was a damn shame she didn't smile more often.

"Is this about the exhumation?" she asked as the silence began to grow awkward. Danny hadn't known where to start and was grateful she'd taken the initiative.

"Partly." He blew on his tea. "You were right, we were wrong. There was a toxin in your father's body that, if administered unnecessarily over quite a long period, could easily kill him."

"What drug?"

"I doubt you'd have heard of it. Brodifacoum."

Sarah shook her head and sipped her tea. The silence lengthened. Danny watched the trickle of raindrops meander down the window pane like silent tears. He knew the bent head, turned posture, meant Sarah was battling her own tears.

Eventually she plucked a tissue from her pocket and blew her nose. "At least we know."

Danny nodded.

"Did he suffer?"

"I shouldn't think so."

"But this drug, what did it do? How did he –"

"Sarah … I doubt there's anything to be gained, is there. Really?"

She looked up, tear-filled eyes tugged at his soul. "I need to know."

Danny sighed, clasped his hands together under the table and leaned forward. Christ, he hated his job at times.

"The drug causes internal bleeding that can cause embolisms, strokes, that kind of thing. I doubt very much whether your father would have been aware anything was wrong right up to the very end."

"You can't know that."

Danny looked down, swallowed. He wouldn't lie to her.

Better to say nothing.

She sighed. "So … murder."

"Yeah."

"And Dom. How does this change things?"

"It can't change things, not really. But my boss has agreed to let me run this as a double-murder investigation. He agrees there could be a connection. It's a start."

"So you have to start over afresh? Like as if this was a new crime?"

Danny nodded. "I have been digging behind the scenes. I spoke to people at the University." He paused. "I think what we have to concentrate on is motive. This was premeditated – quite clearly someone wanted your father dead. We find out the why and it should lead us to the who."

Sarah looked down, picking at a rogue thread on a loose button on her cuff. After a few moments she gave up on the cotton and fiddled with the strap on her bag. Reading body language wasn't his greatest skill, but this was a woman carrying considerable weight on her shoulders. Trouble was, she was also a pregnant widow who was more than likely at the end of her tether.

Danny swallowed the last of his tea. "If there's anything you know that could indicate what this motive, this missing link, might be, now is the time to tell me."

Sarah looked up with a frown. "What do you mean?"

Danny shifted in his seat. "I've had a feeling for a while now you're holding back on me. And you might well have your reasons, but if you know anything, anything at all, you can trust me."

"You seem to have a short memory, detective. As I recall, the first time we met at Charter House, it was me who found the whole idea of murder and death threats ludicrous. It was you who put all these notions into my head and then appeared to reject them."

"Not at all, Sarah. That's not how it was –"

"But you didn't believe me about Dom. And you didn't want to believe my father might have been hounded to his death ..." Her voice and colour rose; her breathing became faster.

"Okay, but then from dismissing the whole notion of your father's death being anything other than natural, you were suddenly eager to make us consider the option of murder. Why?"

"I'd hardly say eager was the right word ..."

"And now you're avoiding the question."

They glared at each other for a moment as the atmosphere thickened.

"Sarah, what changed? That's all I want to know."

"Other than my husband dying?" Sarah paused, shook her head, took a long breath. "You can't think this has anything to do with me, can you? I'm not a suspect surely."

Danny shook his head. "Of course not ..."

"Then why do you think I know more than I'm telling you?"

He shrugged. "You seem worried, burdened. I can understand it must be difficult to trust anyone at the moment but I need your help."

She opened her mouth, then closed it with a tiny shake of her head. "I've just lost my husband. My father. My life. Damn right I feel burdened."

Sarah pushed back her chair, grabbed her bag, and rushed out of the door before Danny could follow. She was instantly swallowed into the crowd. He sank back into his seat and slapped the table in frustration. Exactly what he hadn't wanted to happen. But despite his softly-softly approach, Sarah had reared up far too easily for his liking. Would it be classed as sexist to wonder if there was something more than pregnancy hormones behind her behaviour?

* * *

Berwyn Pugh was a silver-haired man of about sixty with thick bushy eyebrows of the same metallic colour that seemed to have a life of their own. Sarah remembered him vaguely from her childhood; a life-long servant of her family who she'd thought had fallen from favour. But perhaps that had all been a smoke screen and part of her father's elaborate plan.

Mr Pugh greeted her warmly, with no sign of hostility, and settled Isabel and herself in his office with a silver tray containing a china tea service. It was like being back in Edwardian times, even down to the young girl who delivered the tea, who had almost curtsied as she backed out of the door. Sarah could imagine her father fitting in very well here and loving the ambience.

After the normal preliminaries had been handled, Mr Pugh pulled a bulging file towards him across his desk and propped his glasses on his nose.

"Well, I always knew this day must come … I don't know the full details but I understand your father made some quite unusual requests. There is a Will which he lodged here and although I know it's not necessary, I must ask for identification before I can disclose any further details."

"We've both brought our passports," said Sarah, rooting in her handbag as Isabel did the same. "We assumed we'd need them to be allowed access to the safety deposit box."

Mr Pugh cleared his throat. "Er … deposit box?"

"We hold keys, we assume whatever my father lodged with you was in a box that may be in Isabel's name."

"No. I'm afraid not. We don't offer that kind of service."

Isabel returned Sarah's puzzled frown. Increasingly, Sarah felt out of her depth, confused and frustrated by her father's actions. She knew her run-in with the policeman earlier hadn't helped. She'd liked him, felt some sort of empathy, but then it seemed he'd been playing her along and all the time had her down as a suspect. Although … even as she pushed the thought to the back of her mind, she realised the unfairness of it. She had rather jumped down his throat. There were surely procedures he had to follow, and he'd looked uncomfortable enough. Damn. Blame her hormones.

Sarah forced her thoughts back to the present as Mr Pugh pressed a button on his desk. The young assistant reappeared and took away the passports for copying.

Mr Pugh consulted his file, then focused on her with an embarrassed expression. "I'm afraid there is also a request here for a password?"

Sarah gave him a blank look. It was Isabel who answered. "*The Mabinogion.*"

Mr Pugh adjusted his glasses and smiled. "Thank you."

He slid out another thick envelope, similar to the one she remembered from Carter's office.

"This is your father's last Will and Testament. Obviously, you are free to take this away and absorb it in your own time, but in simple terms everything is left to you, Sarah. Charter House included. There are several small benefactors, including yourself, Miss Griffiths, but the bulk of his estate passes to his daughter."

Sarah took the document with a shaky hand. Was this it? Surely this wasn't the end of their search. It told them nothing, and failed to explain the mystery keys.

"There's one more thing your father asked me to pass onto you." Mr Pugh reached inside the file. "I'm happy to carry out his wishes of course, but, before you ask, I have no idea of its meaning."

He moved the file aside and laid a small black book on his desk.

"A bible?" Isabel leaned across from her chair.

"Yes." Mr Pugh shuffled papers back into the file. "His own bible from Llanallgo Church according to the inscription."

Sarah picked it up and flicked open the front cover, taking care with the delicate object, which was already peeling and torn along the spine.

"No. This was my mother's."

"Really?" said Mr Pugh. "Sorry, I assumed …"

"I remember it used to be on the chest of drawers beside her bed." Sarah ran her finger across the faded inscription and breathed in the musty smell of its pages, remembering how her mother had introduced her to the sanctity of the bible in an attempt to explain the story of Jesus. "I'd forgotten all about it."

Sarah squeezed her eyes shut as if that could stop the swell of tears that tickled the back of her nose.

Isabel touched her arm softly. "But why leave it here?"

"I've no idea." Sarah shook her head, sniffing as she pulled tissues from her pocket. "Surely Father said something when he left it?"

"Not a word. Other than it should be passed onto you on the occasion of the reading of the Will. I wish I could help you more, I really do."

"And the keys he left," said Isabel, pulling a key ring from her bag and selecting the shiny silver key. "We have one each. If it's not here, do you have any ideas?"

"May I?" Mr Pugh held out a hand and Isabel passed the bunch to him.

He examined it for less than a second. "I'd guess it's a bank safety deposit box. If you know your father's bank, I suggest you contact the manager and take it from there."

Sarah shook her head. "I don't, we never discussed anything like that."

Mr Pugh tapped the Will. "Well, as you're named co-executor, you will have to make it your business to find out anyway, my dear, sooner rather than later. Have a good hunt around. If your father has a desk, he will surely have a drawer or a file of personal paperwork. Look for cheque books, bank statements, deposit books. Once you have that information, start making phone calls. If you need any further help, you only have to pick up the phone."

Mr Pugh paused, tapping his pen against the blotter on his desk. "I don't know what was troubling your father in recent times, Sarah, and that bothers me. I feel it was a matter of trust.

I'd known Owen for over forty years and yet recently it was like I'd become a stranger. There was an issue of a break-in here; some files were interfered with, including your father's, that is true. But his reaction to it was … well, not what I'd call normal. I suppose what I'm trying to get to, Sarah dear, is that I thought a lot of your family, and while I don't want details as to what kind of legacy Owen left you, just take care not to get too wrapped up in possible conspiracy theories. Your father had a definite tendency towards paranoia in recent years, and I'm trying to be as tactful as I can. Follow your own instincts, Sarah, that's all I'm saying. Don't believe every word your father says to be the truth."

Sarah nodded as she got to her feet. "I've heard similar things already, Mr Pugh. Lots of people seem to be warning me to take my father's fears with a pinch of salt. And I may have been inclined to believe them, but now I know he was murdered, you'll understand I'm a little more inclined to trust his judgement. Maybe if more people had believed him he might still be alive."

Sarah reached out and scooped the Will and bible up with one hand. They slid towards her, across the polished surface, and before she could adjust her position, the bible tumbled to the floor, open pages splayed as it hit the carpet. As Sarah bent to recover it, a slip of cream-coloured paper floated to the ground. She recognised the distinctive brand of paper, and could already see looped letters on one side.

Isabel reached down and collected the paper, opening it to its full A5 size.

"What is it?" said Sarah.

"Looks like quotes." Isabel handed the paper across. "Bible quotes. Maybe he was just making notes and left the paper in there by mistake?"

Sarah studied her father's distinctive hand.

Wisdom is supreme; therefore get wisdom. Though it cost all you have, get understanding.

May integrity and uprightness protect me, because my hope is in you.

Ask and it will be given to you; seek and you will find; knock and the door will be opened to you.

She turned the page over, the reverse was blank. "No. This doesn't feel like a mistake. It was deliberate, I'm pretty certain. But what does it mean?"

"Ask and it will be given …" muttered Isabel. "You know all of these quotes seem very fitting."

"How'd you mean?"

"Well, look, the first one. It basically says get wisdom. Surely that's what we are doing? Following whatever this puzzle is your father has set us. The second speaks of uprightness and his hope being in you. That's the whole point of our quest –"

"Yes, I see. And the last line goes onto say we will find what we're looking for. It's like all the quotations are a personal message from my father to me."

Isabel nodded. "So if it's a clue, what are we missing?"

Sarah shook her head. "I've no idea."

Mr Pugh held out his hand and read the quotations. "Well, I'm not a particularly religious man, but I think they are all quite famous biblical quotes. From memory, that last one is Matthew. Chapter seven, verse seven. The famous seek and ye shall find line."

Outside, on the main street, overlooking the busy harbour, where a ferry was currently disgorging its multi-coloured cargo, Sarah and Isabel sheltered in a shop doorway. The temperature had dropped noticeably, and the rain had turned to sleet.

"I'm going to give my gran a quick call, back at the house, see if she can find a cheque book or bank statements in Father's desk. If it's a bank in Holyhead it will save another journey. Do you want to hang on or do you need to make a move?"

"No, I'm cool. I told you I'm in for the long haul. Come on … make that call!"

"Gran, you are the business. Do you know that?" said Sarah a few minutes later as she jotted down the details her grandmother relayed across the phone.

"I found a cheque book, bach. Hardly like cracking the Da Vinci Code."

Sarah laughed. "You're amazing."

"If you say so, bach. I always did like a good crime novel. Now, I've cleaned out every cupboard in the kitchen and dumped two bin liners full of out of date food. And I've got a casserole in the oven, so what time can I expect you home?"

"Gran! You're not there as chief cook and bottle washer." Sarah's stomach growled as she imagined thick gravy and tender stewing steak and dumplings. "But it does sound delicious. But don't you dare get doing too much."

"I won't. The place needs a good going over. Besides, I prefer to keep busy. This old place … well, it's full of creaks and groans. You notice it more when you're here alone. What time are you back?"

Sarah heard the edge in her grandmother's voice, and she could sympathise. "Couple of hours max. I want to pay a visit to his bank. I'll see you soon. Can't wait for the casserole."

"I'll see you later, bach. Young Luke has been on the phone, he's coming round this afternoon to make a start on chopping the weeds around the back of the house. I didn't think you'd mind. I'll make extra for dinner."

Sarah said goodbye and hung up the call, realising she'd barely given Luke a thought the past few days, so much was going on in her head.

"Problem?" asked Isabel hopping from one foot to another as she squeezed under the shop canopy, flakes of sleet clung to her hair and dripped onto her shoulders.

Sarah shook her head. "Nope. All good."

"The bank's in town?"

"Just on the right at the top of the hill. Come on, let's get out of this weather, and see what they have to say."

The badge said Marilyn Sommersby. Marilyn had to be the youngest, most attractive bank manager in existence. With long highlighted extensions, a teak spray tan, and the tightest blue trouser suit ever designed, she looked more like an under-cover glamour model on a job swap. Every male eye in the bank followed the sashaying ass as the three women crossed from the Customer Services desk to Marilyn's bijou partitioned office. Sarah tried to hide her lingering limp and straighten her spine against any hint of pregnancy posture.

Marilyn indicated to the two purple padded chairs as she pulled the computer keypad towards her.

"I opened your father's security box myself for him, just over a year ago. I'm so sorry to hear that he's passed away. He was one of our longest-standing customers. A lovely man." Marilyn spoken with a heavy Liverpudlian accent that also seemed more suited to the glamour model tag. "Let me just access his details. Could I ask if you have ID with you? Or the authorisation letter?"

"We have passports and we both have a key. I don't have any letter though."

"No, that's fine. As long as the ID matches with the authorised persons on here. You'll need the eight-digit access code of course though."

Sarah looked at Isabel. "Do you know it?"

"Not a clue. Owen never mentioned a code. Just the key."

"Do you keep a note of the code on file?" asked Sarah, feeling a tight hot ball lodge itself in her stomach. Surely not so near and yet so far.

Marilyn shook the mane of blonde curls. "No, we don't set the code and we never ask for it. We advise not to use birthdays or any numbers associated with account numbers or sort codes.

I'm sorry, I can't help, you really need that code."

"Can't you override it? Or use a master code?" said Sarah, biting down on her bottom lip so not to explode.

"No, I'm sorry. There's no way we can access the box without the code."

Isabel tugged Sarah's sleeve. "I was thinking on the way over. I had a mini-brainwave. You know the solicitor mentioned that bible quote was Matthew 7:7? Well, I wondered what chapters and verses the other quotes were. I mean, it might not be relevant, but we're following a carefully laid trail, and if this is the next step, it could be connected."

Sarah nodded. "You could be right. It feels like something my father would think up. Yes, I really think that's an idea." She turned to face the bank manager, who sat with her smile firmly in place, but wore a bemused expression. "I know this is a terrible cheek but do you think we could borrow a computer to access the internet before we try to open the security box? We have an idea how to find this code we need."

"Of course." Marilyn twisted the monitor one hundred and eighty degrees and slid the mouse and keypad toward Sarah. "I'll give you some privacy. Yell when you're done."

"Yell when you're done," mimicked Isabel as the door closed with a click. "She sounds like Cilla Black and looks like she makes porn movies for a living."

Sarah held a hand in front of her mouth to hide her laughter. "Shush, she'll hear you. She doesn't exactly fit the ambience here, but as long as she's good at her job."

Isabel typed rapidly into the computer while Sarah held the paper aloft. Five minutes later and the job was complete.

Quote number one : Proverbs 4 : 1
Quote number two : Psalm 25 : 21
Quote number three : Matthew 7 : 7

"So if we're right we have our code," said Isabel. "4-1-25-21-7-7. Owen must have spent months, even years, planning this. Everything is so bloody precise, down to the last detail."

"Well, let's not get too excited, it may not work. Let's go get Marilyn."

A labyrinth of damp grey corridors sloped down into the foundations of the bank as the women headed towards the vaults, led by Marilyn and her assistant, Ben. Apparently two staff keys were needed, and Ben would wait in the adjoining room while the box was opened. Keys rattled, doors clanged, and Sarah fought back a nervous giggle as she imagined herself living through the opening credits of *Porridge*, one her father's favourite old TV comedies. Finally, a heavy door opened into a dim room, and Marilyn ushered them inside to be faced by sparse furnishing consisting of two chairs, a table and a conveyor belt mechanism. Marilyn gave a smiley wave and disappeared, and the door slammed with an echoing clang.

"What's going on?" Sarah whispered.

"According to Ben, we just wait. The box will appear. And when we're ready to leave, we simply push the button next to the door. No one can say it's not secure enough, I suppose."

Sarah's heart fluttered and her palms began to itch as surveillance cameras whirred into life from every corner of the room. "Do you remember the numbers?"

"Yes …"

A grinding, rattling noise interrupted Isabel and the room began to vibrate. A partition in the far wall opened and a silver box, about the size of a large biscuit tin, slid through on rollers and began to make its way jerkily across the room. The conveyor belt whirred into life and the whole room hummed with the sound of mechanical equipment in operation. The small silver tin looked so innocuous as it jerked to a halt in front of them, dwarfed by such large machinery, that for several seconds they both sat immobile.

"Do we just take it?" whispered Isabel, voicing Sarah's own thoughts.

Sarah feared the whole thing would start up again of its own volition the minute she touched the box, and drag her kicking and screaming into the bowels of the earth.

"I assume so. Shall I do the honours?"

Isabel bit her lip and nodded. Sarah slid from the stool, lifted the box, and placed it on the table.

"It's much lighter than I thought," she said as she rummaged in her pocket to retrieve the key. "Is it key or code first?"

"Key, I think. Here let me." Isabel slid her key into the upper lock and it turned smoothly. Sarah did the same and a square panel sprung open, displaying a small numeric keypad beneath.

Sarah gestured. "You do it, my hands are shaking."

She watched as Isabel keyed in the first four numbers, keeping the fingers of her left hand tightly crossed behind her back. The keypad stayed silent, which she hoped was a good sign. Isabel leaned across and keyed the final digits slowly … 2 – 1 – 7 – 7.

Something beeped and the lid of the box slid open, smooth and silent, like a magician revealing his trick to an open-mouthed audience. The space inside looked empty.

Isabel obviously thought the same. "No way … there's nothing there!"

Sarah stepped forward and plunged her hand into the cool space. She searched with her fingertips and finally touched paper at the furthest corner; she removed a large white envelope.

"What? That's it?" said Isabel.

Sarah tore open the envelope. Two sheets of paper fell onto the table, and as she separated them, she again recognised her father's handwriting.

You have reached my next clue successfully, and I hope safely, my dearest Sarah. I am so proud you have trusted me thus far and believe you now have Isabel by your side, please trust her totally. There is only one man who can help you from here on in, he knows of my plans, but not the true reasons why. Tell him as little as you need, but use his knowledge as much as you can. His name is

Professor Hugh Gillingham. He can be contacted on the number below or via Bangor University.

Your loving dad, Owen x x

(Remember, ' Wisdom is supreme; therefore get wisdom. Though it cost all you have, get understanding'.)

Isabel gasped as she read the note over Sarah's shoulder. "Professor Gillingham. So, he is involved. And that quote again, what does that mean?"

Sarah shook her head. "Did you find out when Gillingham is back at the Uni?"

Isabel smiled. "I think our luck's in today. I made enquires in his department and he's back in the country but not back at work for another week. It shouldn't be too hard for me to find his home address from the staff records. I say we go and pay him a visit as soon as possible."

"Absolutely. And then there's this."

Sarah held the second sheet of paper towards the light, scowling as she read the lines of meaningless words.

"It's Welsh. My native tongue, but to my father's intense disappointment, I can't speak more than a few dozen words. That's probably why he's recommended we get in touch with this Professor Gillingham."

"Okay, so I need to head back to Bangor and run a trace on Professor Gillingham. What say we meet at my flat in the morning and pay him a visit first thing?"

"Sounds like a plan, partner."

Sarah treble-checked the box was empty and let the lid fall back into place with a loud click. Another task ticked off, another full side of the jigsaw complete. But now they were working on the sky, the top part, all blue and little to identify the pieces. Sarah had a feeling they'd just seen through the easy part and the hardest was yet to come.

Chapter Sixteen

Red picked up his mobile phone and checked the display for the millionth time. Nothing. What was the delay? He couldn't make plans until he knew what they'd discovered today. He had his suspicions, of course, but Owen Williams was a wily old sod who never played the hand you reckoned on. Probably why he'd got along so well with the old guy before … not that it mattered now. You had to move on.

He drained the last of his pint and headed to the bar. He wasn't so comfortable here as the Douglas, but he knew this had been Owen's watering hole of choice. He wanted to be somewhere close, ready for whatever. Speed was important now, more so as he didn't know exactly how many people he was up against. Increasingly, he had the feeling he was working alone. But that was okay, things happened for a reason, his old man had always been one to say that. It will come out right. Red hoped to God that was right. He'd virtually put his whole life on hold on the whim of one drunken binge.

He paid for his pint and headed over to the fruit machine, slipping a two pound coin in the slot and watching the colours roll, until with a click and a jerk they landed on three plump red cherries. Money rattled into the tray; he dug his hand in and retrieved two pound coins. He pressed the button again, hypnotised for a moment by the pings and squeaks of the machine. Minutes later, money lost, he returned to his seat, scowling when he saw the table was no longer unoccupied. His frown deepened when he recognised the greasy black hair and freckled complexion.

He was about to move to another table, when the young lad turned, and fixed him with pale irises that sent a chill through Red's blood.

"Afternoon," Red said, straddling a brown leather stool. "How's it going, lad?"

Martin licked his lips, thick tongue moving back and forth as if winding himself up to reply.

"You not drinking?" said Red when the silence lengthened.

"No. Here for my dinner."

"Right." Red took a swallow of lager. "So, how you doing? Still working on the cottage? I've not been out that way in a while."

Martin nodded but still didn't speak.

"Anyway you want to watch how you go in this weather." Red gestured to the window where an angry army of sleet rattled the pane. "You'll catch your death walking in this."

The lad continued to lick his lips; the movements wet and slug-like. Red shifted in his chair. This wasn't his idea of a fun afternoon; could the day get any worse? He knew Martin Cole vaguely, more by reputation than association. The poor young lad who'd lost his folks in a house fire. Backward, some said. In shock, said others. Either way, on this evidence young Martin wasn't the full picnic.

"Have you chosen from the menu? The early-bird, is it? I'll go and fetch one over, might have a look myself, come to think. Only so much curry a fellow can handle."

He was half-standing when the boy spoke.

"I seen you."

Red swallowed and sat. "What's that?"

"I seen you. Charter House. Lots of times."

"I doubt that, lad."

Martin continued, persistent and urgent. "Yes. Times when you wasn't supposed to be there. I seen you. Watching."

Red forced a smile and took a sip of lager, mind racing. He wiped his lips and shook his head. "I don't think so, Mart. Told you, mistaken identity. It's not my neck of the woods."

Martin shook his head, gaze fixed. "I seen you there."

Red leaned forward, lowered his voice. "You want to be careful what rumours you go round spreading, lad. You understand?"

Martin shook his head. "Lots of times."

"And so why were you there then?" Red hissed, leaning in close to the other man's ear. "Lots of times, eh? What does that make you then? A bleedin' peeping Tom?"

The dark head pulled away slightly as the boy stiffened.

Red smiled. Piece of cake.

The door opened, a gust of icy air carried in a handful of snowflakes. The stranger, hunch-backed and leaning heavily on a stick, stamped his feet, leaving puddles on the lino, then carried in through to the snug next door. Snowflakes dotted his flat cap and shoulders like confetti. He cast a rheumy eye over their table as he passed and touched his cap in greeting. Red saluted with a tight smile and glanced at the window; it was coming down in buckets now. Proper snow. Unusual on the island. All part of the weird day.

"I've had the police on the phone, see."

Red jumped, not expecting more from his companion.

"Aye?" said Red.

Martin clasped chubby fingers together in his lap. "A detective. From Bangor. I've got to give a statement. It's important."

Red sat up straight, groped for the cigarette packet in his coat, then remembered and crossed his arms.

"Okay. That's not a biggie, nothing to worry about. Is that what's bothering you?"

Martin nodded, licked his lips. "I can't lie. I could go to prison and I can't leave Jim."

"I understand. Look, I can help you." Red turned, glanced around the empty lounge. "Tell you what, I'll fetch the menu and treat you to a bit of food. And we can talk about it, okay? Make sure we get our stories straight. What you say?"

Martin stared straight ahead. "I can't lie."

"Absolutely. We'll sort it. Give me five and I'll be back and you can choose the food."

Red clasped an arm across the lad's shoulders squeezing the old, blue anorak between his fingers as he got to his feet. Heart thumping, he strode into the coolness of the foyer and kicked open the door to the men's toilets. The room was empty. With a growl, he thumped the towel dispenser, stepping back as the front sprung open and green paper towels littered the tiled floor, clinging to wet patches. He punched the machine again. And again. Not stopping until there was a bloom of red streaks across the metal casing. He ran his hand under the cold tap, staring with empty eyes into the mirror, brain working overtime.

Finally, he breathed out, straightened his collar, sucked his knuckles and fixed a smile. His mobile buzzed and he dragged it from his pocket, switching it off without even registering the display. Priorities had changed, he couldn't allow himself distractions.

Back at the bar, he slid his right hand into his pocket and gestured to the landlady with his left. "Someone's made a hell of a mess of the gents, love. Best you take a look in case someone does themselves an injury." He smiled and shrugged. "And I'll have a couple of those menus. Cheers."

* * *

Sarah waved goodbye to Isabel and watched as the little white Fiat reversed out of its space in the small shoppers' car park, and pulled onto the main road. She glanced up as thicker flakes of snow swirled down onto the windscreen, settling for a moment before the wipers swept them aside in one deft arc. She needed to get home; it was a forty-five minute journey from Holyhead out to Charter House, even in good conditions. But there was something eating away at her she had to get out of the way first.

She tried, at times like this, when her emotions seemed to snap away at reasonable behaviour like an angry terrier, to imagine what Dom would do. What would he say? How would he react if he were here to advise her? And she was almost positive at that moment, he'd be telling her straight it was her responsibility to apologise.

She scrolled through her contact list, and selected the number for Danny Buchanan. The call answered on the first ring.

"Mrs Morton?"

"Hello, detective. It's still Sarah."

He paused. "I'm sorry. I seem to have put my size elevens right in there –"

"No. I've rung to apologise. I made a mountain out of nothing. This whole few weeks, well ... it's taken its toll on me. I have regrets, you know? Not being here for my father at the end. Arguing with Dom before he died." She breathed hard. "There's a ton of things I'd change if I could – but you did nothing wrong. Just hit a nerve, you know."

"Totally. I get it. But it's not a problem. I have the tact of a tractor."

Sarah smiled, swapped the phone to her left hand, and rubbed a patch of the window clear of condensation. The snow was falling heavier; already the car park was covered in a soft sparkling carpet. Through the fog, she could barely see across to the other side of the road.

"Anyway, I need to head home before the weather sets in. Did you make it back to Bangor okay?"

"Fine. I've been making calls all afternoon."

"How's it going?"

Danny sighed. "In a word – slowly. I've now interviewed both doctors, the undertaker, the pharmacist, and pretty much everyone in the village who had contact with your father in the last few months. No one saw anything, or knew anything out of the ordinary, which is pretty much par for the course with these things. All seemed above board with the doc's son, Craig Davies.

Doubtless he's a bit of a rogue, but I don't see him as a murderer. He was as scared as a deer caught in headlights when I hauled him into the station; shook and stuttered his way through the interview, but everything he said stands up. No, I don't think he's our killer." The detective gave a loud tut. "So, I fear I'm right back where I started."

Sarah bit her lip, frowned. "I might have some news soon. I'm not sure. But I want to assure you as soon as I'm positive there's a connection with the case, I will tell you. And I do trust you."

"Now, that sounds intriguing. Are you sure I can't help now?"

"No. Not yet. Sorry to be mysterious."

Danny cleared his throat. "Okay. I can't force you to tell me. But I'm going to get a few extra patrols around Charter House. I don't like the thought of you out there alone while someone clearly has an agenda. Whatever that may be. I'm not trying to spook you, I'm sure there's no real threat, but until we catch whoever is behind this. Well …"

Sarah flushed, thinking of her grandmother there alone. Had Luke arrived yet? Why hadn't she considered there might be danger? Two people had been killed so far. What was the matter with her? Where was her judgement nowadays?

"Thank you, detective. I really appreciate it."

"It's Danny. And it's no problem."

Sarah felt a warm glow inside. Talking to him, with that soft Irish accent, made her feel safe. It brought back memories of the security she felt in Dom's presence.

She started the engine. "Well, I have to go. Thanks again … Danny."

The roads were snow covered, but gritted, and slush swept against the tyres. Sarah let the car tick over for a moment at the traffic lights on the station bridge, deciding whether to go the long route, via the A55 down to Menai Bridge, and then back round the island to Moelfre. Or whether to risk the most direct route, via Valley and Cemaes, and the coast road. In the end, a passing grit-lorry persuaded her to take the coast road, and keeping in a high gear, and sticking at around thirty miles per hour, she was soon approaching the steep hill at City Dulas, not far from the turn off to Charter House. The wipers kept up a steady thunk-thunk as the BMW negotiated the conditions with relative ease.

For most of the journey, she'd followed the tail lights of a Land Rover at a distance, figuring if he could get through, then so could the BMW. Darkness was beginning to fall, urging her onward. Sudden flashes of orange illuminated the white world, and Sarah jumped as another road maintenance lorry passed in the opposite direction; a hailstorm of grit pounding the bonnet and windscreen. Dom's face flashed into her mind. He'd hated snow ploughs with a passion, and was more likely to turn down a side street and go miles out of his way than pass a 'gritter'. Sarah could almost hear the echo of his curses in the empty car.

"Sorry, babe," she whispered to the stuffy interior.

Snow was a rare event on Anglesey. The micro-climate, winds, and the salty sea air, usually meant storms held onto the snow until they reached the high peaks of Snowdonia a few miles further inland. But today the conditions had come together to ensure the island got its fair share. She could imagine small children squealing their delight at the rare event. What irony that she should get stuck in a once-in-a-decade snow storm.

Another mile on, when the Land Rover turned into a farm, she was left to contend with the conditions alone, and Sarah dropped her speed down to twenty as the car slid out of a bend. Passing Llanallgo Church on her right, she said a silent prayer to both her parents, trying hard not to think of them lying in the frozen churchyard. She could just make out the shadow of the church spire through the storm and indicated left into the winding lane that led to Charter House.

She was the first to drive along the lane since the snow fall, and in her rear-view mirror, she could see pink-tinted tyre tracks through virgin snow. The surface crunched under the tyres, and, recognising the bump of packed ice, Sarah used her gears to slow to a crawl. She gripped the steering wheel, and mouthed the 'steer into the skid' line over and over to herself as she battled to hold the BMW in the centre of the narrow lane. What to do if she met an oncoming vehicle, she had no idea.

It took an age to reach the crossroads, two miles from the main road. As she reached the intersection, she eased the steering wheel to the right, mumbling a prayer. She dropped her speed right down, and pulled out onto the lane.

A child stood in the middle of the road.

Sarah screamed and stamped down on the brake pedal. With a jolt like an electric shock, the car ricocheted out of control, steering wheel spinning uselessly through her fingers. She closed her eyes as two distinct bumps shuddered beneath the wheels. Front and back. The white world twisted and bucked outside the window as the car seemed to spin for an eternity. Sarah forced herself to catch hold of the steering wheel, while at the same time searching for the child. She'd hit her. Christ. There was no way she could have missed her.

Her stomach lurched and she gave a yell as the BMW began to skid backwards. She tugged the wheel to the left, but the car continued to slide, like a graceful ice skater crossing the rink in an elegant arc. In panic, she stamped down on the brake again but this only speeded up the movement. With a sickening crunch, and the tinkle of breaking glass, the back end hit an invisible embankment. The car tilted and the left-hand rear wheel dropped into a ditch with a shuddering jolt.

"Shit!" Sarah slammed both palms against the steering wheel. "Shit. Shit. Shit."

She snapped off her seatbelt and opened the door. Howling wind snatched her breath away as she hung onto the side of the car, searching the immediate area. Nothing but churned-up rivers of snow where the tyres had struggled to grip. Sarah dropped to her knees, scanning beneath the car, praying there was no broken body. She staggered into the middle of the lane and pushed through the wind, almost making it back to the crossroads, checking the ditches on both sides of the road. But there was nothing. No blood stains, no dirty snow, not even any footsteps other than her own. How could that be? She'd most definitely seen a young teenage girl, long hair streaming across her face, staring straight into the car. Sarah remembered the eyes, wide with horror, pale skin, pinched with cold, and a long dark coat or shawl. She couldn't have just disappeared, could she? This was ridiculous. Sarah considered making a 999 call just in case. But what point if there was no body. It was like she'd just disappeared into thin air …

… like a ghost.

Sarah pulled open the car door and clambered into the driver's seat, slamming and locking the door behind her. Out of the gale, in the relative silence of the interior, she forced herself to think. Not a ghost, surely not a ghost. This figure hadn't floated into her vision, all white and ethereal. She'd been real and solid. *There.* Those sickening bumps were testimony to the fact. Sarah spun round in her seat, squinting against the curtain of snow; sure she must have missed the injured girl, perhaps flung far aside and already covered with snow. She breathed fast and deep, eyes watering from the cold, and despite her best intentions, she was back on the cliff the day Dom died. She'd thought she recognised the face through the darting flakes, assuming it was someone she knew from the village. But no, now she knew. It was the same girl she'd seen on the cliff the day Dom fell.

Sarah shook her head as melting snow dripped steadily from her hair onto her jeans. She had to move, get the car back to Charter House and have it checked out when the weather improved. With a shaking hand, she turned the ignition key, selected first gear, and released the clutch. The engine whined and screamed, rear wheels spinning uselessly as they did their best to grip in the icy mud. A forward surge of movement, but the smell of burning clutch made her release the pressure on the accelerator. The ditch was too deep. The car slid backwards, and she heard another crunch as the back bumper impacted again.

Sarah knew it was no good making any further attempt to drive the car out; she'd only end up doing more damage. Imagining the fury in Dom's face was enough to persuade her to turn off the ignition and head out into the storm. She needed someone to tow her out of the ditch, and remembered the Land Rover that turned off back on the main road. It wasn't ideal, but it was maybe a half hour walk at most. If she rang the breakdown services from here, in this weather, she'd be waiting hours. With a sigh, she pulled her waterproof over her head, wishing she'd thought of it earlier, grabbed her handbag, and pushed open the door.

The blizzard hit her full in the face, icy wind swept flurries of snow, like evil needles into her eyes, and shrieked its fury through the overhead trees, bending them almost double. She pulled both toggles together under her chin so the lace tightened on the hood, allowing her just a small visor shaped opening in front of her eyes. Remembering her sunglasses, she pulled the door back open, slipping them onto her nose and securing the hood.

With a moan, Sarah looked at the car and bit back tears. The angle it had settled was so severe, it was immediately clear there was no way she could ever drive it out of the ditch. The rear light and bumper were both badly damaged, and fresh soil spoilt the whiteness where the underside had dug a deep furrow along the ground. She shook her head; there was no point getting emotional. Sarah had never developed the bond both her father and Dom had with their cars, but the BMW meant much more to her since Dom's death.

She turned back into the wind, keeping her chin tucked into her collar, and bent her back against its force. Her eyes studied every inch of the road; a part of her wanted to find the girl, curled up and in shock. At least it would provide an explanation, because what was the alternative? She paused and straightened her aching back, propping one hand on her hip as she drew in mouthfuls of stinging cold air. The exertion was like trying to walk under water, or through the soft sand of a desert. The thickening flakes made visibility almost zero, and without any kind of flashlight, Sarah suddenly feared what would happen if a vehicle approached. Short of jumping into the ditch, she could see no way the driver would either see her or miss her, and images of that girl's face as she disappeared below the level of the bonnet continued to haunt her.

She began to realise just what a bad error of judgement she had made, and cursed her impetuousness. She'd made exactly the same wrong choices on the cliff the day Dom fell. The last time she'd seen the ghost, she reminded herself. Was there a connection? There was no way she'd be able to reach the farm; it was a good three miles away, and in these conditions it would take hours. She scrambled into a gateway and pulled open her handbag. As she slid her hand into the side pocket, and her fingers met fresh air, she gave a choked yell. She'd slipped her phone into the recess on the door handle after ending the call to Danny, thinking it was easy access if anyone called.

With a growl of frustration, she trudged back out into the centre of the lane and continued onwards. There was no point returning to the BMW – knowing her luck there'd be no signal, which wasn't unusual out here. No, she had to push on. Besides, she should alert the emergency services; she couldn't just dismiss the fact there could be an injured child out here. She could always say she'd made a mistake, perhaps hit a badger instead. She bit back a sob and pushed forward, desperate for the nightmare to be over.

As she reached the crossroads, Sarah saw a small cottage. It appeared out of the fury of the storm like an oasis in the Sahara. She remembered Luke pointing out the cottage. It belonged to Martin, the young man who had done odd-jobs for her father

Drifted snow piled up around the gate, but there were fresh footsteps on the path. The gate squeaked as she closed it behind her and she squeezed between overgrown hedgerows. The house was in darkness, and her initial buzz of excitement dissolved away as she knocked the front door.

Silence.

Sarah took off her glove and rapped harder on the frosted window. Muffled yapping started up somewhere inside. She'd heard that bark before.

Sarah clenched her fist and thumped harder.

The door swung inwards beneath her hand.

"Hello?" Her voice was carried away with the roar of the wind. She tried again, leaning into the darkness of the hall. "Hello!"

No reply. The persistent yap, and a rhythmic creak from some part of the roof. But apart from that, silence.

"Is anybody there? Martin? It's Sarah Morton. My car's got stuck in the snow."

Sarah stepped into the hall out of the boom of the wind. "Hello? Is anyone here?"

Her heart began to beat faster as she edged along the hall, slipping her glasses into her pocket. She noticed a pale orange glow illuminating the open doorway at the far end, and beyond that, an old-fashioned sink unit and snowy window. The burning smell was stronger as she entered the kitchen, and a thin cloud of black smoke wisped its way to the ceiling. A blackened kettle sat on the electric hob, illuminating the gloom with a glow reminiscent of an electric fire. She hurried across to the cooker, noting a table laid out with two mugs and spoons. Burning paint fumes were so thick she could taste them; she tugged her scarf up over her nose and turned off the hotplate. As she carried the kettle across to the sink, she noted half of the base had already burnt through into a hole. It was amazing the whole lot hadn't exploded in flames.

A creeping sense of unease ran through her veins as she turned on the tap and pushed open the window. Sarah had heard talk of Martin Cole being something of a simple soul, but what could have happened to make him leave the house in the middle of preparing tea? And from the cups, he'd had company, or was expecting it. So, where had he disappeared to? And where was the persistent yapping dog?

She headed back into the hall, shielding her eyes as she flicked on the light switch. The gloom was replaced with a harsh yellow glare from a bare bulb hanging in the middle of the ceiling. She pushed each door in turn – a broom cupboard, combined dining room and lounge, and a small bathroom – all empty.

Sarah stood at the bottom of the stairs and stared up into the blackness.

"Hello? Is anyone up there?"

The yapping increased, louder now, and more persistent.

Who or what she expected to answer, she had no idea. Every fibre of her being screamed at her to get the hell out of there, but some sense of righteousness persuaded her to stay and investigate.

Before she could change her mind and run back into the blizzard, Sarah hurried up the narrow stairway. Both doors on the small landing were closed.

She pushed open the door nearest the end of the stairs. A blur of white leapt out. Sarah squealed and scrambled backwards, smacking her head against the wall before registering the tiny paws clawing at her jeans.

"Whoa!" Sarah bent and grabbed hold of the small terrier. "Hey! Good boy! Calm down. What's your name?" She grabbed hold of the collar and held the wriggling body fast in her arms. "Right, well, Jim. Why are you locked in there? Where's your master?"

A smooth pink tongue ran across the back of her hand, as Jim answered in a series of high pitched squeaks. His big brown eyes gazed into hers, and Sarah could swear she saw a mixture of fear and confusion. He wriggled in her arms, legs pumping against her stomach. Conscious of the baby, she lowered the dog to the floor, and he took off bounding forward, not down the stairs as she expected, but back into the bedroom. He stopped at the door and turned. His claws pattered on the linoleum and he gave a couple of sharp barks.

"You want me to follow?" said Sarah. Jim spun in a circle and began to pant. "I'll take that as a yes."

The door squeaked as she pushed it open; the room behind was dark and eerily silent.

Sarah ran her hands along the wall to her right as Jim rubbed against her ankles. Her fingertips found the switch and a weak glow of a single lamp brightened the room.

There was a shape on the single bed beneath the window; a human form, curled sideways beneath a faded blue duvet, facing away from her.

"Martin? It's Sarah Morton. Are you okay?"

No movement. No response. She approached the bed slowly as Jim continued to dart back and forth, urging her onwards.

"Martin. Are you ill? Should I call a doctor…"

As she reached the foot of the bed, it was clear a doctor would be no help to Martin Cole. His eyes were closed but there was no way anyone could fool themselves he was sleeping. His lips were drawn back to expose vomit-stained teeth and an enlarged purple tongue hung from his mouth. A pool of vomit covered the pillow beneath his head, and his skin had a grey, mottled look she'd never seen on a human being before, more like out-of-date sausages.

"No!"

Sarah took another step forward, her brain unable to accept what it was seeing. She had to be sure. This couldn't be happening again. It couldn't. It just couldn't.

She reached out, shook his shoulder. "Martin?"

Silence.

She dragged in a deep breath, slid two fingers into the crook of his neck, and, remembering her first-aid training, pushed on the pulse point.

Nothing.

Icy fingers clawed at her hair, ripping the clothes from her back, and thick snowflakes swirled like a swarm of maddened bees around her head as Sarah stumbled out of the cottage. She plunged further into the night, whirling in a disorientated circle, arms outstretched like a madwoman.

Dead ... oh my God ... dead ...

Freezing bullets stung her face, blinding her; the protection of her makeshift mask forgotten in her desperation to get as far away from the cottage – *the corpse* – as she could. She had to put distance between them. She had to get away. She raced into the blackness, wanting the night to swallow her whole and deliver her safely out the other side. She screamed, over and over, but no one answered the cry as she staggered along the narrow lane. The tracks of her tears mixed with her running nose, and Sarah struggled to breathe as she slipped and stumbled across the icy ground.

Dead ... his face ... so bloated and ... oh God, his tongue ...

She heard a distant bark as she came to a crossroads. Was she nearing a house? Sarah stopped, hands on her knees as her lungs screamed for air, and pain ripped through her ribcage. She choked and gagged, spat snow and phlegm into the gutter. She blew her nose into her glove, and took long gulps of the freezing air, anything to still the thudding which banged in her ears.

"Dear God! Which way?" Sarah screamed to the heavens. "Oh, Dom. Please. Help me. Dom, where are you?"

There had to be a house somewhere near. Instinct told her that she was heading inland, following the direction of the wind. Surely she had to hit the main road before long. There had to be an end to this nightmare. Someone would take her in, offer her shelter, call the emergency services. It would be okay. This was 2011 for Christ's sake; people didn't die in snow storms ...

Martin Cole is lying there. You left him. Dead ...

That's enough! Keep moving. Turn left, head back towards Moelfre.

Sarah squinted against the swirling whiteout; her ears strained against the roar of the wind. Surely she should be able to make out the church spire if she'd made it to the main road?

Nothing. Just the silhouettes of dark hedgerows either side of her, and bare fingers of tree branches above.

She straightened and pushed forward, covering another mile or more. Or less?

She had no concept of distances, directions. Just a vague idea she had to end up somewhere, anywhere.

Without warning she began to shake. Her legs trembled and she took more deep breaths. She was burning up. She pulled off her scarf and unzipped her coat. What was the matter with her? She dropped to the ground, and with a sob dragged herself along on her hands and knees. Her legs wouldn't work; it was like they'd just given up.

She was so tired now. She could barely move. All she wanted to do was sleep.

Sleep. What a wonderful idea. If she could just lie down and get her breath back, then she could start again. The snowflakes were so soft, so gentle, like the luxury of a crisp, clean pillow. So white. Somewhere to rest, just for a moment or so.

Her body slipped sideways, eyes already half-closed. She curled into a ball and blinked against a sudden light. The darkness was illuminated with vivid flashes of white. She'd never seen anything more surreal. More beautiful. Where there was blackness, now there was white. Pure, crystal, virgin white. It was stunning. Truly stunning.

Sarah wiped her nose and smiled. She lifted both arms. Was this an angel? Really? Her guardian angel, just like in the song?

She closed her eyes as she staggered to her feet.

Take me. Please.

"Dominic!"

A loud blaring noise pierced the calmness. Shattered the peace.

Sarah fell onto her knees.

Silence.

Blackness.

Chapter Seventeen

The gentle sway and pull of the ocean fills my ears. Fine spray from breaking waves covers me like a gossamer veil. Dominic grips my hand in his, our fingers laced, and together we walk the length of the curved beach. Cool sand slips between my toes and tepid water laps at my ankles as we follow the high tide mark.

Sarah.

I turn to Dom, his back is to me but I can see he's not spoken. His gaze is drawn to the far horizon, where the palest blue sky meets the deepest blue ocean. A sweet aroma tickles my nostrils, a heady mix of honeysuckle and the salty fragrance of sea air.

Sarah.

The voice calls my name again. I stop and turn, shielding my eyes against the glare of the sun, and scan the empty beach. I tug at Dom's hand, eager to see if he can hear the girl's voice too, or if my imagination is playing tricks on me. His grip on my hand remains vice-like; his arm solid and muscular, tug as I might he refuses to turn.

Sarah. Trust no one. Tell no one.

'Who are you?' I call, raising my voice so it echoes off the surrounding cliffs. 'Who … who … who …… are … are … are …… you … you … you?'

Movement beside me, Dom turning, his face obscured by the glare of bright sunlight.

'Can you hear the girl's voice, Dom? She's trying to tell me something, but I don't understand. Can you hear her calling my name?'

Dom shakes his head and bends towards me. Feeling the warmth of the sun's rays on my face, I lift my chin to accept his kiss. Closing my eyes for the merest of seconds, I relax into his strong embrace.

When I open them a rotted corpse hovers before me; its lips stretched back in a hideous grin. Long wispy strands of hair matted around its face, tendrils of dark green seaweed tangled in the locks and plastered across its forehead. The skin is slimy, green, peeling away from bone in places, revealing sinew and muscle beneath. Clear blue eyes gaze at me from beneath half-decomposed lids.

I am transfixed by the gaze. As the eyes blink once, twice, I fight back nausea, trying to read the message I somehow know they are trying to convey.

And the smell … sweet and sickly, like concentrated honeysuckle. I close my eyes and gag, hold my hand over my mouth, and when the feeling of sickness passes, I open my mouth and scream as long and loud as my lungs will allow.

Sarah … Sarah …

"Sarah!"

She woke with a jump, heart pounding, covered in sweat.

The distorted image came into focus as she rubbed her eyes. "Luke?"

She recognised the bedroom, and the unmistakeable groans of the roof timbers at Charter House. She relaxed back against the pillows. She was safe. It was a dream, nothing more. She closed her eyes and stretched, recalling the horrible images of the nightmare, vomit-stained teeth and dark eyes, staring in horror, through the snow storm. She wrinkled her nose. No, that wasn't right. There'd been a beach, blinding sunlight and warm seas. Dom's arm, strong and muscular. She shivered. What was the matter with her?

Hearing the rattle of a teaspoon, she opened her eyes, remembering Luke somewhere in the melee of thoughts. He held out a cup of steaming liquid.

"Here. I've been waiting for you to wake. Your gran's had the kettle on the boil for the past two hours."

"Is she okay? Gran?"

"Fine. We're all fine. Nothing to worry about."

Sarah frowned as she sipped sweet tea. Something about boiling kettles. The smell of burning. Something about a swirling snow storm. Dark eyes. Screams.

The cup hit the saucer with a clunk. "God." She met Luke's eye and he took the cup from her. "Oh, God."

He leaned over and slid the china onto the bedside table. Sarah looked down, recognising her tartan pyjamas. How had she got here? What the hell happened?

"Calm down. It's okay," said Luke. "Everything's fine."

"How can it be fine? How can …"

She shoved the duvet away, fingers burrowing, tugging the cord of her pyjama bottoms, finding the bulge. Relief. She looked up at Luke, eyes already swimming with tears.

"Don't you remember? Doctor Davies came?" Luke smiled. "Baby is fine."

"Really?" Sarah gulped. "Promise?"

"I couldn't lie to you, Sarah. Ever. You must know that."

Sarah lay back, waiting for the tears to pass, her pulse to slow. "How much do you know? The boy … Martin Cole …"

"It's been dealt with."

"He's dead."

"Hush. Yes, it's all sorted. I'll get the car moved in the morning."

"I don't understand. How can I not remember anything?"

"Shock. Hypothermia. You're lucky to be alive, Sarah." His voice caught. "God knows what you were thinking walking off in that weather."

Images flashed through her head like a television in a

dark room.

There was a knock on the door and Luke crossed the room. Sarah couldn't see who was on the other side, just a low rumble of voices. The room was lit by one small bedside lamp, and shadows encroached from every corner. The window was dark; it had to be the middle of the night.

Luke closed the door, balanced on the edge of the bed. "The police are downstairs. They need to take a statement, but Dr Davies made it clear you needed rest. Are you well enough?"

Sarah pushed herself upright and rubbed her eyes. "Who is it?"

"Sergeant Hughes has been here all night and the Irish detective chap has just arrived."

Sarah relaxed a little. Danny. It would be okay now.

"Sure. I have to speak to them. I suppose I'd best get it over with. Although the thought of going through it all again …"

Luke squeezed her hand. "You know, you've had a hell of a lucky escape. Sergeant Hughes said you'd walked a good few miles onto the main road, almost to Llanallgo Church. If the taxi driver hadn't spotted you … well, who knows what might have happened …"

Sarah clenched her fists until fingernails dug into her palms. "I can't remember very much after I left the house. Just that I had to get the hell out of there. The rest is a blur."

"Dr Davies said you were delirious and showing signs of hypothermia. It's no wonder it's a blur. When I heard what had happened … well … it makes you realise what a person means to you, doesn't it?"

As their eyes met, and held for a moment, Sarah saw a flash of pain. A desire buried like the depths of an iceberg, only the very tip ever on view. She shook her head, puzzled, unable to find the right words. His shoulders slumped, he looked away, and when he turned Luke was back in the room. Gentle, helpful, adorable … Luke.

Sarah felt heat rise in her cheeks, but words kept their distance.

Luke smiled, a sad smile of acceptance and headed for the door, pulling it shut behind him without another word.

Sarah closed her eyes. Please, not now. She was still Mrs Morton, would always be, even if her husband was on the other side of an invisible divide. How could she explain this pain inside that made the thought of another man in her life repulsive? How could she make that sound sensitive – the last thing she'd ever want do is hurt Luke. He was everything to her at the moment. But not that. Not now. Not ever.

Sarah slumped back against her pillow, aware of the sound of muffled voices downstairs, followed by a recognisable yap. *Jim!* In all the upset and rush to get away from the cottage, she'd abandoned the poor dog. Her last memory was of him shivering on the door step as if torn between staying with his master and following her out into the storm. She'd left before he'd made his mind up.

A few moments later, there was a knock at the door and Danny entered; his eyes were dark and tired, his clothes more creased than normal. He looked for a chair, and seeing none, held onto the iron bedstead and studied her intently.

"Hey."

"Hey."

"We have to stop meeting like this." Danny smiled, but it was forced. "How're you feeling?"

"Okay, physically. I just can't get it out of my head. His face, you know, the smell ..."

Danny dropped his gaze, nodded. He knew. She could see in his eyes he'd seen exactly what she'd seen. Sarah shook her head to clear the image.

"Are you up to talking about it?"

"If I have to. It's not something I'll forget in a hurry."

Danny nodded. "We'll get a statement later, but as I hear it, you went to the cottage because your car skidded into a ditch. You weren't expected?"

Sarah hesitated. The girl in the snow storm. The same girl

on the cliff when Dom died. The same girl who inhabited her dreams. Angelina. She was the reason Sarah turned up at Martin Cole's cottage. She was meant to find the corpse – but how could she ever explain that?

She shook her head. "No, I'd never been to the cottage before. I hoped to call the breakdown service or get a lift home."

Sarah drew her legs up under the duvet and patted the bed. Danny paused for a moment, then perched himself as far away as possible, back pressed against the wrought iron. Sarah sensed his awkwardness. But they concentrated on ignoring the intimacy and continued the conversation.

"Did you know the deceased?"

"No. Well … I knew of him. I understand he used to help out around here … you know, gardening, odd jobs, and the like – but not since I've been back. Although … thing is I thought someone had been tidying up the old vegetable patch recently. I thought it might have been Martin. At least, I couldn't think who else it could be." Sarah frowned and shook her head. "But the last time I spoke to him was at my father's wake. Then the day I fell down the cliff, the day Dom … died … it was Martin who heard me calling for help. He fetched Dr Davies."

"Did you see anyone in or around the cottage while you were there?"

Sarah shook her head. "Not a soul. There were footsteps in the snow, I remember that." There was more yapping from below. "I abandoned poor little Jim. Is he okay?"

"Well, he didn't abandon you. Taxi driver said the dog was sat beside you, shivering in the road. Wouldn't leave your side. Sorry, we had to bring him here, none of the kennels were open –"

"Can I keep him?" The words sprung from her lips before she had chance to stop them.

Danny's frown melted into a smile. "Not sure he'd leave your side anyway, taken a right shine to you, he has."

"Jim led me to the body."

"Really? Can you go through what happened? I know it won't be easy but it's got to be done. Even in cases of suicide there are procedures –"

"Suicide?"

"We found a note. In the bedroom."

"No, that can't be right. You see, he'd made tea, left the kettle on the stove. I turned it off, put it in the sink. You know, it was almost like someone left the kettle on the stove on purpose. I mean, why would Martin do that if it were suicide? And what kind of person makes tea and then in a flash decides mid-meal to kill themselves?"

"Not always logic in people's actions. Especially people desperate enough to take their own lives."

Sarah met his steady gaze, trying to work out how to convince Danny of the evil she knew existed without mentioning the ghost girl who led her there.

"I don't believe Martin Cole took his own life. I can't explain why, I hardly knew him. But it just doesn't feel right."

"Well, we have evidence, and it's pretty conclusive – empty paracetamol bottle, empty whisky bottle and a suicide note. It seems a pretty cut-and-dried suicide to me."

"What did the note say? Did it give any reason?"

Danny slid his gaze away again. Something about his expression made Sarah's stomach swirl.

"Danny?"

With a small nod, he slid a plastic bag containing a single sheet of paper from his inside pocket, and handed it over in silence. The writing was large and childlike, letters carefully formed and written so heavily the paper was almost torn through in places.

I'm sorry. I can't live with myself and what I've done any longer.

I killed Professor Williams. I can't explain the resons.

I've wanted to confess for so long, but this seems easier, a cowards way.

I guess I am a coward.
I'm not scared of dying. I will be with Mam and Dad again.
I'm sorry. Martin Cole.

Sarah drew in a long gulp of breath and looked up into deep brown eyes that were clearly judging her reaction.

"H-he killed my father. Is that true?"

"That's what he says there."

"But … but … it makes no sense."

"Why? Young man, not too bright, can't live with the guilt. Some would say it makes perfect sense."

Sarah caught something in his tone. "But not you?"

Danny remained silent.

"Besides," she added, "he doesn't say anything about how he killed my father? How he got the poison, or why he murdered him? Where's the motive? I'm no detective but there always has to be a motive, doesn't there? You said so. No, it's wrong. It's all wrong."

"Well, I have to admit I was shocked when I read the note. We have to wait for the post mortem of course, but there it is in black and white, a signed confession."

Sarah ran her fingers over the letters. "Suicide notes can be faked, forced. Why were you shocked? You don't believe it either. Do you? I can see it in your face."

"It's not so much not believing – it's more not understanding. I mean, yes, we have the evidence and the note."

Sarah followed Danny's gaze, drawn to the strip of blackness, peering between the velvet curtains like an omnipresent eye. Outside, snowflakes still fluttered against the glass. The night was silent now, the wind bated, just the rush of the ocean in the distance.

He sighed and continued. "I've been talking to Conrad Hughes, he knew the lad well. He's pretty cut up, so I've sent him home. Conrad was in charge of the investigation when the lad's parents died, and took the lad under his wing. I like Hughes, he's one of the old-school, reliable, you know, trustworthy, and he reckons the Cole lad was a gentle giant. Loved nature, animals, that kind of thing – always fund-raising for the RSPCA. Treated Jim like a baby. Conrad reckons he couldn't kill a mouse, let alone a human being. Especially not when he'd survived the trauma of seeing his own parents burn to death in a house fire."

"Exactly. Does Sergeant Hughes have any ideas?"

Danny shook his head. "Not a thing. Said he'd not seen so much of Martin recently, thought he might've got himself a girlfriend. But it was very hush-hush. Conrad thought she might be married."

"That doesn't make him a killer."

"No, unless perhaps he was provoked, made to do it, only thing I can think. Conrad reckons his worst fault was being easily led. Poor kid. He struggled to make friends, and was apt to get involved with the wrong sort now and then. Was a bit of trouble couple of years back, when he got mixed up with some small-time local druggies and they used him as a runner."

Danny rubbed his palms together and added. "And then my main problem – as you mentioned – is motive. Why? Why would a simple lad, without an enemy in the world, want to kill your father? What emotion drove him? He wasn't interested in money, fair to say we can discount love. So what? Revenge? No … it makes no sense."

Sarah opened her mouth, then closed it with a snap.

When she looked up, Danny was reading her face as intently as a novel.

"So, is now the time to tell me what the hell's going on?"

Sarah looked away, mind racing, tears threatening.

Danny leaned forward, one hand brushed her thigh; he pulled back and sat up straight. "Look. I don't know what more I can do to make you open up to me. But people are dying, Sarah. There's a killer out there. And even if you think you know nothing of relevance, it's up to me to make that decision. Please don't make me pull rank."

Sarah coloured and tried to keep her voice level. "It's not about relevance. It's about trust. I'm doing my best, okay? I've lost everyone in the world. I have no idea who to trust. You don't know how it feels –"

"I know exactly how it feels." Danny stood up quickly, moved to the window, pushed the heavy drapes aside. Still staring out into the darkness with his back to her, he said. "You're not the only person to have lost someone you loved most in the world, Sarah."

Silence wound around the room, wrapping them tight in its embrace.

Danny's voice was thick when he spoke again. "But that doesn't give you the right to withhold evidence that potentially could lead to a killer. You see that, don't you?"

He turned.

Sarah nodded.

"Tell me," he whispered.

She gestured for him to sit again and told him everything – from the day of her father's funeral until the moment she walked in on Martin Cole's corpse.

Everything except Angelina Stewart.

* * *

Red checked his watch. Another ten minutes. He adjusted the dial to maximum resistance, medium speed, and upped his pace. He grabbed his towel from the front of the treadmill and wiped his forehead. His face, bobbing, red and shiny, stared back at him. Mirrors in gyms were a mystery to him. Who wanted to see themselves looking like shit during a workout? There was some serious narcissistic behaviour going on if someone felt the need to examine and appreciate their body mid-workout. Not even body-builders were that vain, surely?

He closed his eyes and let the sound of Radiohead carry him away. He'd spent almost three hours in the gym. A spontaneous spinning class had got him well pumped. Followed by twenty minutes fixed weights, twenty minutes free weights, and his muscles were on fire. But still he wasn't done. Cardio next. Thirty minutes on the rower. Twenty on the cross-trainer. Now a gentle jog and finish off on the bike. Fair to say, there was some excess energy that needed sorting.

He knew he should be feeling bad. In fact, he was quite worried about why he felt exactly the opposite. He wondered how he'd fare if he ever took one of those psychotic tests? Which side of the line would he fall? But there was something in that old adage that practice made perfect. It had been so easy. Hardest bit had been getting the kid pissed. He'd been virtually teetotal. But at least that meant one bottle of Bells had done the job. That and a cheap packet of paracetamol from the local petrol station. Getting him to write the note while semi-comatose had been tricky, but a challenge.

He smiled and upped his speed. He was feeling pretty good about things, pretty pleased with his achievements.

Radiohead absorbed him until he came to the end of his run, and he moved to a quieter corner of the gym and straddled the power bike. The local news dominated the bank of screens above his head; the Cardiff studio seemed pre-occupied by weather reports and pictures of frozen-looking reporters standing in snowy streets. Quite what they thought it added to the experience for the viewer, he had no idea. Surely people could open their own front door and see much the same thing. It was this kind of drivel that had made him smash his own television set years earlier and he'd never owned one since. It made him too angry. But if the country's obsession with the weather stopped an unimportant little death in the backwaters of Anglesey hitting the news, he was all in favour of as many weather forecasts as possible.

He kept his eyes on the silent television as he sensed someone climb onto the bike beside him. As the final bars of 'Creep' faded, he pulled off his headphones and took a long pull of water.

"I don't like taking orders from you." The voice was low and angry. "What am I doing here?"

Red stole a look. "Riding an exercise bike. Badly."

"This is so not the time for jokes."

"No? I'm actually in the mood for a good laugh." Red slowed his speed and dabbed the back of his neck with his towel. "Murder usually puts me in a good mood."

"What?"

"Keep pedalling. Keep smiling."

"And you better start talking."

Red heard the whir of the pedals start up again. He took his time. He liked being in charge. The balance of power had been slipping away from him in recent weeks. It was good to have it back. He was no one's fool. And no one yet had successfully double-crossed him. Hopefully the conversation that took place over the next ten minutes would ensure no one ever would.

Red leaned forward, increased his calorie count on the display, and used the opportunity to check who was in the vicinity. It was clear.

"There's nothing to worry about," he said. "There was a problem. I've fixed it."

"What kind of problem? You've no right to do anything without checking with me first. You know what you're like, you go too far. I'm not risking my own neck to cover for you."

"You're a fine one to talk about impulsive behaviour."

"Don't avoid the subject. What's happened?" The voice dropped to a whisper. "Murder?"

"I had to eliminate a problem. That's all you need to know. Someone saw too much, and unfortunately that someone had a conscience and was going to talk to the police. I had to step in and stop him. No need for you to get involved. I just thought you might want to know."

"Why?"

"Because you've lost your little pet."

"Sorry?"

Red tried to hide his grin. "Martin."

"No."

"Sorry."

"Why?"

"Told you. He saw me at Charter House. Had to stop him talking."

"But why kill him? It was your mess."

"No. Yours too. He'd seen you with Sarah. And simple as he was, he knew he'd seen you there with old Owen too. Oh, he was ready to blab all over the shop."

"Another death though. More blood on our hands. No … your hands."

"Oh, no. You're in this as much as me. Owen's death was your baby. So, never try to pull that one on me, you hear? I've got enough evidence to see you put away for life and don't forget it." Red adjusted his voice from threatening to airy. "Besides, you might want to thank me. I've done you a favour too."

"Ha. I very much doubt that, you selfish, manipulative bastard."

"Tut. Tut. There's really no need for that. Your little pet was good enough to write a lovely suicide note before he went to join his folks on the other side."

"What do you mean? I never know when to trust you."

Red pedalled harder. "You should *never* trust me. I wouldn't. No, poor Martin had to clear his conscience and admit to the murder of Professor Williams. It was the guilt, you see, that forced him to take the overdose and make little Jim an orphan." Red snorted. "So, if the police do get anything from the exhumation, they've now got their man too. What a very nice parting gesture, I thought. You should say a nice thank you to Mart when you say your prayers tonight. Don't forget now."

Red smiled and winked as a leggy red-head squeezed between the bikes. Her eyes met his for a second too long and Red squirmed. She'd got a cracking pair of tits and a sparkly pink jewel hanging from the bared belly button. Clinging black Lycra showed every inch of her ass as she bent to tie her laces. Red adjusted his seating position. Murder. It had a lot to answer for.

"You are one sick bastard, you know."

"Ha." Red jumped off the bike, watching the red-head retreat towards the stairs. "I'm one clever bastard, that's what I am, and you know it. I've sorted this mess. You just make sure you're more careful and don't pull anymore stunts unless I'm involved. Understand? I've got no morals; that must be obvious. You cross me, you're next on my elimination list, you get that? Stick to your role and report back to me daily. If not, I'll come looking for you. Anything about that you don't understand?"

He waited.

"No."

"Good." He snapped the towel at the bike. "Enjoy your workout."

He strode towards the exit. If he hurried he might catch up with the red-head on the stairs, persuade her to meet him in the steam room. There was still some pent-up energy that needed to be spent.

Chapter Eighteen

Sarah's breath fogged the window pane as she gazed out at the new day. The first of December and it couldn't feel less like Christmas. The scene, however, was pure Christmas card fodder. A crisp, calm, jaw-dropping morning. So fresh, vivid and alive. The sky was a pale blue canvas, and the whole earth felt brighter and cleaner, illuminated by blankets of white that covered the island far into the distance.

Something pulled her out into the snow. Some long-buried childhood need to squeeze her feet into cold wellies and kick through snow drifts, to feel frozen fingers inside sodden mittens, lobbing snowballs.

Minutes later, she closed the front door with care, so as not to wake Grandma Ruth, and followed an excited Jim out into the white world. She pulled her hat down around her ears and wrapped her scarf tight, smiling as the young dog skidded to a stop in a deep drift. He gave a puzzled look and backed away with a bark, then sniffed the snow, before cocking a leg, and racing off down the drive. It may have been his first sight of snow but it obviously met with his approval.

Jim raced in ever-increasing circles as they crossed the field towards the cliff edge, kicking up clouds of powdery snow and barking in delight. Sarah's pace was slow, and she stopped a few times to catch her breath. She began to sweat, and pulled off her hat and shook her hair free.

Eventually they reached her destination. She was drawn back to this spot. She stopped near the cliff edge and looked down at the boiling waters, where white-topped waves broke across shiny boulders. She clipped on Jim's lead and knelt to brush snow from the flowers.

"Happy December, angel. You always adored Christmas." She choked back a sob. "God, I miss you so much, it's like a constant ache. I wish you were here, more than anything. I miss talking to you, relying on you. I miss touching you, feeling your warmth beside me. This is so hard. You'd know exactly what to do next, what words to say to calm me down. I don't know how I can carry on without you. And this is only the beginning. I love you so much, Dom."

Sarah waited for a reply, straining her ears. So desperate to hear Dom's voice again, she found herself hoping that, if this spot were conducive to spirits, he might choose to visit too.

Nothing.

Just the rush of the tide, and the cry of a circling gull, dipping and gliding, scanning the ocean for food.

Tears blurred as she stood and brushed snow from her knees. She pulled out a handful of tissues and blew her nose, tugging Jim's lead, keeping him back from the edge. Although the pain burned hotter, somehow she felt closer to Dom here. She knew she'd never visit the grave his parents had chosen in Watford Crematorium. This was her spot. Their spot. This was where she would come to grieve. And she'd bring their daughter back here so they could talk to Dom without anyone judging.

Sarah held her head back, feeling the sting of the wind on her cheeks as watery sunshine warmed her face. Flicking hair from her eyes, she recalled the first sighting of Angelina, standing on this very spot, looking out to sea. Isabel said she was being haunted, and after the experience the night before in the snow storm, she was ready to concede that it must be the truth. She couldn't wait to talk to Isabel about the child appearing in the storm, as if determined to get her into Martin Cole's cottage. It was killing her to keep it bottled up inside, but the thought of telling Danny was impossible.

"Sarah!"

A figure approached, blurred in the sunlit whiteness; from the gait it was a man – and definitely not ethereal. Was it Danny? He was due back today to meet Isabel and discuss their plan to visit Professor Gillingham. No more going it alone.

Sarah blew a final kiss in the direction of the flowers, surprised to feel a rush of guilt burn her cheeks, and headed back across the field. The man was standing beside the stile, and gave a wave of acknowledgement, which she returned. She closed the distance and squinted. This time she recognised the crossed arm stance, the Barbour jacket and cap.

Luke.

Something inside her stomach dropped; a heavy weight that caused her to groan aloud. Since the awkward silence the night before, Luke had kept his distance. But they were adults, they could handle this. Besides, on her current list of problems, Luke's feelings weren't exactly a priority.

Jim arrived at Luke's feet minutes before her, and he was on his knees, fussing over the excited terrier when she arrived at the stile.

"Morning," said Sarah. "You're up and about early."

"Been feeding the animals, had to use the tractor. I came to warn you, some of the lanes are barely passible if you're thinking of going out. Not so much the snow, proper solid black ice underneath, it is." Luke kept his eyes on Jim. "Thought I'd try to move the BMW while I'm out. I've got Trev with his Massey to give me hand. Came over for the keys, is all."

Sarah heard the apologetic note in his voice. "Walk me back to the house and I'll get them for you. Thanks for your help, Luke. I'll pay whatever it costs you to get it out of the ditch and tow it into town."

"Don't be daft." Luke brushed snow from his gloves and held out a hand as Sarah negotiated the ice-covered stile.

"No, I mean it."

Sarah squeezed Luke's fingers through her glove, and felt him pull away sharply the minute she was on safe ground.

"How you feeling today?" Luke asked as they crossed the drive. "Did you sleep?"

She shook her head. "No. I'm exhausted, but I'll try and stay awake as long as possible and hope I'm too tired for nightmares when I do go to sleep. God, I can't believe what's happening to me. Maybe I should bury myself under the duvet and hibernate."

"Well, I'll be out of your hair soon as I've got the keys."

Sarah stopped short, grabbed hold of his sleeve. "Luke ... don't."

He looked down at her, face red with cold. "Don't ... what?"

"You know. Please. Don't abandon me. I can't give you anything else, right now, but please don't think I can live without you. Don't turn your back on me, I'm sorry if I've hurt you ..."

Luke stepped forward and pulled Sarah into his arms. She recoiled for a second, then dissolved into his embrace, remembering the feeling of being held, feeling safe. She breathed in the smell of soap and aftershave and held him tighter.

When they broke apart, Luke brushed a lock of hair from across her face.

"Better?" he asked. "Don't think you haven't got me. Never. I'm here for you, as long as you want me. Need me. It's enough for me that you know how I feel. And I'm sorry if it's made things difficult. I'll try to put it right. I'm sorry –"

Sarah held up a hand. "Enough. No apologies. Let's go indoors and have a coffee."

"I'd like to get off if you don't mind. Trev's waiting at the bottom of the drive."

"Well, when you come back then. Luke, I don't deserve you and I don't know how to thank you. I'll get the keys, two secs."

Minutes later, Sarah gave Luke a brief hug and watched as he sprinted along the drive, agile in the icy conditions. She heard the toot of a horn, the rumble of a tractor's diesel engine, and

Gillian E. Hamer

then the world fell back into the kind of silence only heavy snowfall can produce.

Fresh from a shower and still towelling her hair, Sarah pushed open the kitchen door half an hour later; the smell of frying bacon reached her nostrils, and her stomach growled.

"Morning, bach. How are you?" Grandma Ruth turned from the stove and gestured for her to sit.

"Better. But I feel like a hotel guest, whereas you're the visitor. I should be looking after you."

Her gran waved the comment away. "Oh, now, you've had a hell of a shock. Here, drink this." She slid a steaming mug across the table. "Sweet tea, good for the shock according to my mother. You were out early, bach. Luke came round looking for you."

Sarah sipped the scalding brew. "I saw him. I went for a walk in the snow. I love it, always have, and we get it so rarely nowadays. Little Jim had a whale of a time, racing round like something possessed."

Gran nodded to the makeshift bed of pillows next to the washing machine. "Little Jim is a greedy lad. He's polished off three sausages and scrambled egg for his breakfast. We'll need to buy dog food today, or as soon as we can get to the village. I don't mind sausage but draw the line at best sirloin for his tea."

Sarah smiled and watched Jim turn his attention from Gran to her, and back again, ears pricked, ready to pounce into action.

"Yeah, and a bed, and some toys or something. Bless him."

Sarah tucked into the Full English with gusto, mopping up yellow yolk with thick slices of crusty bread. Perhaps the best thing about being pregnant was the ability to enjoy food without the guilt of calorie consumption. Yesterday, she'd doubted she'd ever have an appetite again, and perhaps the smell of burning would take some time to clear from her memory, but here she was tucking into spicy sausages like it was her last meal.

A loud knock at the kitchen door made Sarah jump. Thinking it was Luke, she called out to enter without looking

279

up from her plate.

"That was fast. Don't stand on ceremony, come and get stuck in. How bad's the damage?"

"Sorry?"

Sarah stopped chewing, swallowed, and looked up. Danny stood on the door mat, pulling off gloves and stamping snow from his boots, while trying to calm a hysterical Jim. He tugged off his coat, hung it on the back of the door, and held his hands out above the nearest radiator.

"Sorry, I thought you were Luke." Sarah hurriedly wiped egg yolk from her chin. "How were the roads?"

"Awful. I've just seen Luke attaching chains to the back of your Beemer," he said. "Christ, what a journey. Had to use the Police Land Rover, no way my car would've got through. Anglesey is in lock-down. Not so bad on the mainland, think the mountains shelter us a bit."

Gran looked up from the sink. "Fancy a bacon sandwich, bach? You look done in."

"Go on, you've twisted my arm. What's the harm of two decent breakfasts in this weather, eh?"

He winked and Grandma Ruth giggled like a teenager and spread more bacon in the frying pan.

"Are you two mates?" said Sarah. "Something I missed?"

"Me and your gran bonded last night. We share similar concerns. Most involving you."

Sarah's cheeks tingled and she stared into Danny's eyes willing him not to say more in front of her grandmother. She wanted to protect her gran as much as possible, there was no point worrying her for nothing. He nodded as if understanding and changed the topic.

"So, have you called Isabel?"

"Yes. Gave her a brief resume and told her you were coming out to fetch me. All being well I said we'd be with her lunchtime."

"There you go, young man."

Gran slid a plate of sandwiches and a mug of tea in front of

Danny. His eyes lit up like a child on Christmas morning.

"Splendid." He opened the bottle of red sauce and proceeded to cover each sandwich in turn.

Gran smiled. "Going up for a bath, dear. Leave you young ones to it. See you in a bit."

As the door closed, Danny put down his cup. "You look rough. You sleep at all?"

Sarah shook her head. "Too scared of the nightmares."

"And you're sure you want to go ahead with this? You could let me handle it –"

"No. I have to do this. For my father. For myself." Sarah saw his worried face. "I'll be careful. Besides, I have you now, what can possibly go wrong?"

Danny looked down; his neck bloomed in colour.

Sarah covered the silence by pouring herself more tea. "I keep thinking back to last night. How I just left the place. I can't believe I did that now. I just ran. As far and as fast as I could. I didn't even have the presence of mind to find a phone. I mean, what if I'd been wrong and he wasn't even dead? What kind of coward does that make me?"

Danny swallowed and shook his head. "There's no point beating yourself up. Why the hell should you feel guilty? You didn't kill him. You panicked, that's all, it's not a crime."

"Here, now, in the cold light of day I can agree with you. But last night was awful. I've not wanted to think about it too much, but I guess we have to. Do you think if Martin's death isn't suicide that it's somehow linked to my father's?"

Danny chewed for a moment and held a slice of bacon out to Jim.

"I can't discount it but I've no evidence to prove it. No DNA at the crime scene so far and obviously different cause of death. It could be a coincidence – but it would have to be a huge one." He took a gulp of tea. "I've been awake all night too, finding out about this shipwreck, the salvage teams, details of these family feuds. I'm not having a go, but you've quadrupled my suspect list overnight."

"I'm sorry. I was only trying to do the right thing for everyone. I felt I had to respect my father's wishes."

"It's okay, I'm over it. But I do want to consider motive. In terms of Martin's death first and foremost – why kill him? If this is all an elaborate treasure hunt with a pot of gold at the end – what's Martin Cole got to do with it? If he knew something important, surely he was more use alive to anyone, than dead?"

Sarah dropped back in her chair. "I don't know. All I do know is I want this to be over so I can move on with my life. And you can't begin to know how much of a relief it is to have you on side, really."

Danny pushed his plate away and tossed the last morsel to Jim. "You should have done it a whole lot sooner. Trust me and you'll be fine. I won't let anything happen to you, Sarah."

Without realising what she was doing, Sarah reached across the table and touched the back of Danny's hand. He flinched, looked up, but didn't pull away. They sat in comfortable silence while Jim chomped on the last of the bacon.

The kitchen door opened with a bang; a gust of wind blew snow across the flagstone tiles. Luke stamped into the kitchen, shrugging off his coat as he entered.

"Damn, that was hard work. More careful we tried to be, deeper a hole we dug. Anyhow, I don't think there's actually too much damage –"

He broke off, choking on his words as he took in the scene. His eyes focused on the table. He dropped his coat, and took a step backwards, muttering,

"Sorry, like. Didn't know I was disturbing ..."

Danny pulled his hand away and Sarah got to her feet.

"You're not disturbing anything. You managed okay?"

"Aye. Here's your keys. I've reversed her in next to the garage, she'll be okay to tow into town with the Landy when the road's clear. She's not leaking oil and I can't see too much damage underneath, suspension feels okay. But I'd get on to your insurance and get it sorted."

Sarah took the keys, turning to switch on the kettle. "Cheers, Luke. That's one less thing to worry about. Right, what can I get you? Full English?" She turned to see him zipping up his coat. "Where you going? Thought you were staying for breakfast?"

"No, change of plan. Dewi at Llanerch wants me to help him out; moving some of the pregnant ewes inside, now the snow's come. Bad forecast for the rest of the week, so he says. Said I'd give him hand –"

"Well, at least stay for a cuppa to warm yourself up –"

"No. It's okay, thanks. I'll give you a call tomorrow, see if you need anything. Take care now."

"Luke …" Sarah trailed off, not sure what to say.

He turned at the door and she saw embarrassment and pain in his eyes. What could she say, here, in front of Danny? Nothing. Nothing that wouldn't hurt him more and only make the situation worse for everyone.

She dropped her gaze. "Thank you. Thank you so much."

Luke nodded, and without a word, slammed the door behind him.

"Damn."

"Awkward?" Danny asked.

"Very. But not the time or place. I'll speak to him."

"I didn't realise –"

"There's nothing going on. Seriously. All I want to do is end this nightmare. Find out who killed my father. And Dom. Poor Martin Cole too. I can't handle anything more than that right now. I'm grieving and I'm a mess, and a pregnant mess at that." She breathed out and met Danny's gaze. "Will you help me?"

"Do I need to answer that question?"

* * *

Sarah concentrated on the hiss of slush against the tyres as Isabel manoeuvred the Fiat with confidence through the slushy streets of Bangor. Danny had taken some persuading, letting them visit Professor Gillingham alone, but finally concurred. His presence would make the situation difficult. Besides, a university professor was unlikely to be much of a danger.

Sarah glanced at the printout on the dashboard. "Have you got the address?"

"Number twenty-eight, Ffordd Moel-y-don. I have found it on the A to Z. I think it's somewhere behind the main university buildings, near the pier."

"It's good of Professor Gillingham to meet us at his home."

"Yeah, it is. He's not back at lectures for two weeks. When I explained the urgency, he was happy to see us."

Isabel indicated and turned left into the narrow side street that led down to Bangor Pier. Minutes later, she pulled on the handbrake and stopped the car on the hill, looking across the expanse of deep blue water. It flowed from their left in tight, swirling eddies from the confines of the Menai Straits then, here in front of them, exploded into the wilds of the Irish Sea, like champagne from a bottle. The wooded cliffs of Anglesey on the far bank were a fitting backdrop; the snow-covered trees a wonderful sight. In the distance, she could make out the multi-coloured houses of the quaint town of Beaumaris, and beyond that the jutting point of Penmon lighthouse and Puffin Island.

"Beautiful," sighed Isabel, echoing Sarah's thoughts. "Owen loved the Menai Straits. He gave me a small oil painting for my birthday a few years ago of Church Island with the Menai Bridge in the background."

"Oh, that was my mother's. I mean, she painted it. I hadn't thought of it in years, but it used to hang in his study. It was her hobby, painting and sketching, and she got quite good. She loved the ocean; she did sketches all over Anglesey. That's how I remember spending my summer holidays – lying face up to the sun on a picnic blanket while mother painted beside me. I'm glad I still have my memories of her."

"How lovely."

Sarah sighed, feeling the familiar tug of emotion. "Yes, she had quite a talent; she sold a couple of pieces to a gallery in Beaumaris. She said she felt real peace on the Straits that she never felt anywhere else."

"Do you want to have the painting? I mean, I do love it, but I don't mind."

"Of course not. It's yours. Enjoy it. It's what my mother would have wanted."

"Owen never said who painted it or there was such an attachment."

"He wouldn't. That was my father all over. He didn't care much for what he would have called 'sentimental clap-trap'. I'm glad you love the painting – you must keep it."

"Thank you. I'll treasure it even more now."

Professor Gillingham was nothing like Sarah's archetypal idea of a medieval history professor – more like her image of the latest James Bond actor. His dark brown hair, cut in the latest scruffy style, tanned features, designer jeans and expensive black shirt, looked out of place amongst the towering shelves of hardback books and antique mahogany furniture.

She didn't miss the sideways glances from beneath thick dark eyelashes as Isabel shook her blonde hair free from her hat and removed her jacket to reveal a tight cream jumper and black jeans. Was it her imagination or was Isabel's spine a little straighter than normal; her breasts a tad more prominent? Sarah wrapped her long black coat across her stomach, pushed deeper into her chair, and tried to ignore the professor's obvious approval. Gut instinct told her he probably shared Bond's success with the ladies too.

Sarah looked down at the business card they'd been given on arrival.

Dr Hugh Gillingham – Early medieval archaeology of Wales and Ireland, specialising in sculpture and the church.

The conversation had been polite and perfunctory up to now.

Isabel had taken the lead, making small talk about her days at Bangor Uni., and students and lecturers they both knew. Dr Gillingham had talked non-stop for the past ten minutes with obvious pride, about the aims and achievements of the Centre for Medieval Studies.

Sarah nodded and smiled when it seemed necessary, but she was itching, literally, to get down to the important matter of her father's note. Finally, Isabel managed to steer the conversation in the right direction.

"Yes, Sarah has had a lot to contend with in the past few months," she said. "Owen's death set off a series of events that led us to your door."

"Really?" Dr Gillingham raised his eyebrows.

"Yes, my husband died shortly after my father," Sarah said. "We think the deaths may be connected."

He frowned. "But I heard Owen died of a heart attack. Are you saying you think his death was suspicious?"

"There's an on-going police investigation," said Isabel.

Dr Gillingham slowly shook his head. "This is all news to me. I was in Florida at the time, on a medieval research college tour, or I assure you I would have been at the funeral. Even though I'd only grown close to Owen since we set up the centre in 2005, we'd been colleagues for the past twelve years. I had no idea his death was anything other than natural causes, none at all."

Sarah inched forward. "My father never discussed any fears he had with you? Never mentioned his life may have been in danger?"

Dr Gillingham's eyebrows shot up again. "Danger? Good God, no. Not an inkling. But if I'm honest your father had become somewhat reclusive over recent years, I'm not sure he would have confided in me."

Sarah nodded; it wasn't the first time she'd heard a similar remark.

"But I mean, what exactly are you saying?" asked Dr Gillingham. "That he was murdered?"

"Yes. There has been an exhumation and post mortem. It would appear he was poisoned."

"Exhumation? Poisoned? Oh, but that's just ridiculous. Why?"

Isabel flashed a look, and Sarah opened her handbag.

"We were hoping you may be able to tell us, doctor? Or at least shed some light on the matter," said Sarah, removing the letter.

"Me? Why?" Dr Gillingham looked genuinely confused, and searched their faces in turn.

"Because of this note my father left."

The professor read the short passage; his lips moved slightly. Sarah saw the flash of recognition, deepening into a frown, as he came to his own name.

"My dear, I know nothing about this. It's all very bizarre."

He spun his leather chair away from the desk, and strode across to the window, looking out across the snowy lawns, before turning towards them.

"I'm sorry, Sarah. I have not the remotest idea what your father is referring to. I would love to tell you he left me a letter or a package, or we'd made some kind of secret pact, and in the event of his death I was to divulge it to you. But surely that only happens in movies? It has certainly never happened to me. And to be honest I'm not too sure what you're trying to imply. Am I in danger of incriminating myself?"

"Not at all. I'm simply trying to establish the truth. If you'd asked me six months ago, I would probably have agreed with you. But truth is often stranger than fiction, as I've discovered. I'm not accusing you of anything. I quite believe you don't know what part you play in all of this, but I'm equally convinced you do have a part to play. If my father's organisational skills up to now are anything to go by, then you must be involved whether you know it or not."

Isabel touched Sarah's arm, and slid forward in her chair. "What Sarah means, Dr Gillingham, is Owen left a series of clues. Ones she and I were asked to follow. They have brought us to your door. If you would be willing to talk to us, we feel sure there will be something Owen was certain only you would know. We're simply asking if you will help us."

The professor walked back to his desk, picked up the note and re-read it as he dropped back into his chair.

"I wish I could help, my dear. I really do. I'm sorry if I was a little sharp. I think it was such a shock, and I must make it clear to you I have played no part in any of this. If there is a police investigation, as you say, then I must be assured you believe I'm not withholding any information. It appeared to be the inference, and it is not the case."

"Dr Gillingham, I apologise," said Sarah. "I'm so emotionally involved, too eager I suppose, perhaps my tone was accusatory. That wasn't the intention. As Isabel put it so much more eloquently than I, we are here to ask for your help. Nothing more."

The professor studied her for several minutes, slender fingers tapped the desk in front of him. Sarah's face burned under his scrutiny, but she held his gaze for as long as she dared, hoping he could see the truth there, even if her words had let her down.

Finally, he sighed, allowing himself to relax back in his chair. "Please, call me Hugh. Dr Gillingham makes me sound like a decrepit old fart." He smiled at Sarah's expression. "And, my dear, of course I will help you in any way I can. But I fear I have no idea how."

"Would it be okay if we asked a few questions? Isabel has made a list. Would you have any objections if we made notes?"

With a wave of his hand, he nodded. "No objections. But that quote. It is biblical. Do you know the significance?"

"Yes. Proverbs 4 : 1. It led us to one of Father's clues."

"Really? It is also the motto of The Anglesey Archaeology Trust."

"The what?"

"Oh, I assumed you would know of it. I'm Chairman of the

Trust. The AAT is basically a group of amateurs who look after the sites of archaeological interest on the island, or at least ones that aren't in private ownership or managed by the National Trust or CADW. I took over the position from your father three years ago. We're a voluntary organisation subsidised by government funding and public donations, and we use the quote from the Book of Proverbs in our marketing and membership literature. I thought it unusual your father should include it in this note. I'm trying to see a connection – but at the moment alas I can't."

Isabel said, "Yes, I've heard Owen talk about the Trust. Perhaps the connection will become clear in due course."

"We think the reason my father gave your name may be connected to this ... which may be the final clue." Sarah slid the Welsh verse across the desk, and watched with a feeling of dread at the puzzled expression on Dr Gillingham's face. "We were hoping you may be able to translate for us?" she added, optimistically.

"It's Welsh," he replied.

"Yes, but from my very scant knowledge, I thought it may perhaps be some kind of old Welsh, and we guessed you were the expert –"

Dr Gillingham shook his head. "I'm sorry, my dear. The only word I recognise here is Charter. I don't speak a word of Welsh and I've never been tempted to try, medieval or otherwise."

Beside her, Isabel gasped.

Sarah said, "But I thought ... at least we hoped ... I mean, why did my father include your details in with this transcript, if he knew you wouldn't be able to read it?"

Dr Gillingham shrugged. "No idea. This gets more and more bizarre. Owen knew I didn't speak the language; he chastised my ineptitude on a regular basis. So, whatever part I am to play in his grand scheme, I can assure you it wasn't the role of translator. Luckily, I have some very talented colleagues who handle that side of things for me. In fact ... I may have an idea. We need to get this translated, correct? So would you trust me to ask one of my colleagues to help out? I can email her now and scan the document over. What do you think?"

Sarah looked to Isabel who shrugged. "We have no choice, do we?"

"Okay, but there must be complete confidentiality. Can you send it now?"

"Of course. Give me five minutes. Please help yourself to more coffee."

Dr Gillingham slid the paper into the scanner, tapped away at his keyboard, then sat back with a satisfied smile. "There, done. Now, we must be patient and wait for the reply."

"Can I ask how well you knew my father?"

Dr Gillingham took a sip of coffee and wiped his lips. "He took me under his wing when I first arrived here, somewhat wet behind the ears and a tad snobbish. Graduated from Cambridge you see, and this was all a little bit too *Welsh* for me to begin with."

He smiled at what Sarah could imagine were colourful memories, recalling her father's patriotic pride.

"But your father soon put me right, about quite a few things actually. I was in awe of his passion and dedication. He got me involved in the AAT, and then last year I returned the favour, and put him in touch with a literary agent. Fellow who'd published my last non-fiction book on medieval sculpture, and got me a jolly good deal. I knew your father had written three or four books, and had another in the pipeline about his ancestral lineage and the wreck of the Royal Charter. So, when the agent showed interest, I ferried your father over to Manchester to meet him, and later to sign on the dotted line and the like. Funny little chap, but a cracking agent, really knew his stuff, goes by the name of –"

"Miles Harvey-Barnes?"

"Ah, you know Miles?"

"We've met."

"Ah."

Miles Harvey-Barnes was another of the problems she'd allowed to simmer on the back burner; one she would have to address pretty soon if they were to see her father's work in print. Despite her reservations, it seemed clear from Isabel's prior knowledge, and now Hugh Gillingham's recommendation, Harvey-Barnes was the genuine article, and not the money-grabbing vulture she'd suspected. If she was wrong, she was happy to admit it. Didn't mean she had to like the guy.

A beep echoed around the room. Dr Gillingham turned back to his monitor and his eyes widened in relief.

"What is it?" asked Sarah, edging forward. "Has she translated it?"

Dr Gillingham nodded. "She has. Perfection. She's just added a note that some of the phrases have not got a perfect literal translation, so she has used the nearest available word. Here, let me print a copy."

Two minutes later, Sarah held the printed translation in her hand, and compared the two verses.

Y datrys y pos y Charter,
Mae 'n cymeryd deall a calon a sgil ....
'gael hyd i'n cliwiau yn cyddio oddimewm,
mae rhaid ymchwylio 'r hanes
O'r cromlechau hynafol
I olygfa clir y Rhyfeiniad,
O'r Paganau 'n ddifn odan y ddeuar
A'r gamau'r Belgaidd newydd,
Y diwedd fydd eich dechrau,
Ac ella y dechrau fydd y diwedd
Ceuwch eich meddylwin i'r presenol
Y Mabinogion fydd eich cyfaill.

And beneath, the English equivalent.

To solve this Charter puzzle,
Takes wit and heart and skill,
To find the clues concealed within,
You must search history at will.
From Neolithic circles,
to Roman's vantage view,
From Pagan's deep below the ground,
to Belgian steps, built new.
The end will be your starting point,
The start may be your end,
Close your mind to the modern day,
Let The Mabinogion be your friend.

Isabel spoke first. "Does it mean anything to you, professor? What are these Neolithic circles, Belgian steps and what not?"

Dr Gillingham stared at the computer screen in silence. After several moments he began to nod, and what Sarah hoped was a spark of inspiration lit his eyes.

"You know, my dear, I rather think I may have an idea." He turned to one side. "I have an Ordnance Survey map of Anglesey somewhere, just give me a moment …"

He slid a battered OS map out of a desk drawer and studied it for several minutes with a frown. Sarah's heart did cartwheels as the realisation hit her that they may at last have begun to slot the important, middle pieces of the jigsaw puzzle into place. The pieces that made up the actual core, and maybe, just maybe would soon distinguish the bigger picture. It felt right.

"Well, my dear," said Dr Gillingham, "I rather think we may be onto something here. And I think I know why your father entrusted me with this task. But I can't fill in all the blanks. Could I ask a couple of questions?"

"There are issues of confidentiality, Dr Gillingham," said Isabel.

"My dear, I understand your point, but if I am to assist any further, I think it is pertinent I should know a little more about the quest in which I find myself an unwilling participant."

While Sarah understood Isabel's reason for caution, her over-riding view was not to antagonize the one person who may possibly hold the only key to solving the riddle. Dr Gillingham really was their only hope.

"Doctor, Isabel and I have to be careful. There have been two attempts made on my life, possibly more. And only this week another suspicious death that may be linked." She monitored the professor's reaction, one of open-mouthed disbelief, and nodded. "Yes, it is true. More than an issue of trust, I think we are both aware there's always the chance that by telling you too much, we may also be putting your life in danger. Like I said, truth is often stranger, and a lot scarier, than fiction."

Dr Gillingham took in the information. "Okay. Yes, I understand. This is possibly a lot more serious than I first imagined. But the good news is I think I can help you. Answer me one thing. Is this some kind of treasure hunt? I mean, are you led to believe there may be a pot of *gold* at the end of the proverbial rainbow?"

Isabel stirred, and Sarah's expression evidently gave away the answer, as Dr Gillingham pressed on without waiting for a reply.

"Ah, that makes sense. For I think what we have here, my dear," he tapped the original Welsh verse, "is your father's version of a treasure map. And what we have here," he gestured to his computer screen, "are all the clues to solve it. And the good news is your father knew every clue would require my expert knowledge. Each point in this verse ties up with archaeological sites the AAT have excavated in the past five years."

"Really?" Sarah said with a sigh. "You know what all of these places are?"

Dr Gillingham nodded. "Yes. I do. Here. Look." He tapped the map. "Neolithic circles. These have to be the hut circles we've been working on recently. They're here on Holyhead Mountain. Also on the mountain, but right on the summit, is the Roman

Fort. We worked there in 2010. The year before we had a dig at Bryn Celli Ddu, down here, near Llanddaniel Fab. And previously, we excavated an area of the Belgian Promenade at Menai Bridge."

They examined the map for several moments, trying to see where the clues may lead.

The professor sat back down. "You see, Owen knew I would be the only one who would know all these places. But why?"

"What about the rest of the clue?" Isabel picked up the translation. "Are we overlooking something?"

Sarah looked over her shoulder. "The end will be your starting point. The start may be your end ..."

"Ah." Professor Gillingham drummed his fingers on the edge of his desk. "The start is the end. The start is the Neolithic hut circles, right? They're the first clue?"

Sarah nodded, her pulse racing. "Why?"

"I was thinking that Owen must have buried something at these sites. But if the start is the end, perhaps he means only at the first. And then it came to me, we had a ceremony. It was your father's idea. And he put a collection of university artifacts together and buried them in the main hut circle. You know, one of these time capsules that are all the rage."

"That sounds like a perfect place to hide a clue," said Isabel.

Dr Gillingham got to his feet. "Then ladies, without further ado. Are you ready to begin?"

"Now?" said Sarah.

"We have another few hours of daylight left. And I've got a 4X4. So why not? If what you say is true, time is of the essence. I'll get my things."

The professor turned off his computer and left the room.

Sarah slid the paperwork into her bag, and glanced at Isabel. "Is that okay with you?"

Isabel checked her watch. "One quick call to the child minder and I'm yours." She looked round. "Do you think the prof would mind if I hunted down the loo?"

Sarah smiled. "I shouldn't think so."

Isabel left and she heard the mutter of voices outside the door. Not for the first time, she ached for Dom. Decisions had never been her strong point. She knew Danny wouldn't like them taking off like this, but this was an opportunity she couldn't miss – the possible final piece of the jigsaw. Besides what harm could it do? A university professor and her father's right hand woman - if she couldn't trust them, who could she trust?

"Right," said Dr Gillingham, minutes later, popping his head round the door. "Are we ready?"

Sarah got to her feet. "Where are we going?"

"We are going, my dear, to find ourselves some Neolithic circles."

December 25th 1859

There has been snow fall overnight. Just a whisper of white magic. I have never seen snow before, and despite how much I have come to detest this strange, foreign cold, I cannot stop myself running out onto the field, falling to my hands and knees and scooping tiny piles of icy crystals, until my hands are frozen and my skirts soaked.

The peal of bells from the nearby church rolls across the fields towards me, and I hear singing in the distance. It carries on the wind and lifts my spirits. I recognise the melody. A Christmas carol. *The First Noel.* One of my favourites. I close my eyes, lost in memories of Christmases past, of sunshine and picnics and beaches. Here, it is a different kind of Yuletide. I imagine a bunch of jolly carol singers, making their way from house to house along frost-covered lanes and frozen ditches, shivering on doorsteps under bunches of milky mistletoe.

I, too, had once loved to sing, and the words come back easily.

"… in fields as they lay, keeping their sheep. On a cold winter's night that was so deep."

I open my eyes. Another voice has joined mine; a rich bass to complement my high soprano. A voice I would recognise anywhere!

In seconds, I am on my feet, racing away from the field towards the cliff edge, where I see the figure of a man, on his knees, hands clasped in prayer. Before him, a beautiful Christmas wreath, all silky green leaves and bright red berries, shines out from a white canvas.

The man's voice, rich and clear, pulls me towards him like an invisible rope.

"Noel. Noel. Noel. Noel ..."

I open my mouth and join him on the final line as loudly as my lungs will allow.

"Born is the King of Israel!"

The man stops, clutches his chest, and turns.

My heart thuds like a blacksmith's hammer.

I am frozen like a statue on the path.

He hears me. He hears me!

I rush towards him, arms outstretched. "Father!"

But his eyes are dark dead pools, swimming with tears. He turns his back on me and stares out to sea. His shoulders slump and I know he is sobbing. I cannot approach; cannot cross the boundary of my embarrassment. This is not my father. This is a shell of a man I once knew, broken and aged and mad with grief.

I drop to my knees. The last vestiges of hope drain from me. This is not how it was supposed to be. I knew they would come to find me, but I'd expected joy not sorrow, laughter not tears. And I expected most of all, my dear mother to be here. Her absence is more pain than I have ever had to bear, it tells me all I need to know.

She is dead. And this life, this purgatory, is all I am left with now.

Father is talking, mumbling and rocking back and forth, as the peal of bells reaches its crescendo.

I step nearer to hear his words, aching to be able to reach out and touch him.

"Merry Christmas, my angel. Merry Christmas, dear wife." His voices catches and he reaches into his pocket, retrieves a handkerchief and blows his nose. "I am a wreck without you both. I am but a ghost myself, walking and breathing, yes, but still a ghost. Wherever you are, you hold my heart, both of you. And I will never leave you. Never leave this spot."

He scrambles to his feet, rubs his knees. "I have come back to Lynas. And here I shall make my home. Here on this spot, where I can look for you every day. And you will come. I know you will. I feel you will. Bless you both, my poor lost angels."

Another man approaches, footsteps crunching across the frozen ground. It is the Reverend who came before, the same sad, yet hopeful, expression on his face as he stands beside my father and extends an arm across his shoulders.

"Merry Christmas, Charles. We missed you at the service. You cannot stay out here, man, you'll freeze. Come back with me now, come back to the vicarage. Mrs Roose Hughes has laid on the most fantastic spread and she will not take no for an answer."

"I can't leave, Reverend. I can't let go. Not till I know. There's no bodies, see. What if they're out there somewhere, waiting for me? How could I live with myself if I abandoned them again?"

"They wouldn't think that, Charles. They are with God now. He will protect them until you can be together again."

I want to scream that it isn't so, that I am here. That no-one protects me and I need my father more than ever.

Father looks across the ocean. "I have made plans, Reverend. Plans with the evil gold. I shall buy this land, build a home, and John and I shall spend our days here. At least here I feel close to the family I have lost."

He bows his head as tears claim him again.

The Reverend helps my father back onto the pathway. We stand, not six feet apart, face to face. I think to scream and shout and stamp my feet, but it would be pointless, I know that now. I reach out a hand towards his face, but it is no more than smoke.

Instead, I open my mouth and I sing my favourite verse, high and true and sweet.

"Noel. Noel. Noel. Noel … Born is the King of Israel."

The men stop. Father turns, eyes searching, back and forth.

"Did you hear that, Reverend?"

Reverend Roose Hughes looks around. He shivers. "Hear what?"

Father pauses, curls of white breath whirl away from him.

He shakes his head. "Nothing. It was nothing."

Chapter Nineteen

The snow-covered acres surrounding Charter House sparkled in the misty winter sunshine; a touch of pink coloured the fields, matching the first hint of dusk in the sky. Dotted across the ground, tendrils of steam rose where the sun had warmed the soil beneath, drifting like spirits weaving their way up to the clouds. He didn't feel it often, but on days like this, Red could see the benefit of living in such an out of the way place; spectacular scenery and wild, windswept walks were an everyday occurrence for him, whilst some paid thousands for the privilege.

His car bumped along the driveway, hitting potholes hidden beneath the slush. He concentrated on the road. His timing was vital, too important to risk error by daydreaming. When opportunities were gifted, even at short notice, he believed in taking full advantage.

He drove towards the garage, taking care to keep the tyres inside already-impacted tracks. He parked at the side of the house, out of view of the front door, and in five strides – again, avoiding virgin snow – he mounted the steps and gave three sharp raps on the brass-plated lion's head knocker. Hideous. But old Owen all over. He stamped his feet on the cocoa mat and glanced at his watch.

No point getting frustrated, softly softly catchee monkey. Another of his father's gems.

After three minutes, he knocked again. The yap of a small dog started up in the distance. He had a cold rush of recognition …

The door opened slowly; a small, anxious face, surrounded by a halo of cotton wool hair, appeared in the gap.

Bending to make eye contact, he gave his widest smile and flashed his gym membership card.

"Hello there, Mrs Hughes? Or should I say Grandma Ruth?"

Her face did an odd thing; it both frowned more, yet seemed to relax at the same time.

She peered at the card. "Yes."

"How are you?" he asked, slipping his wallet back into his coat.

Her voice was cautious as she studied him with care. "Do I know you?"

"I'm Detective Constable Matt Jones. I'm a colleague of DS Buchanan. He's asked me to nip out and check you were okay while I was in the area."

He spoke slow and loud as if he had little practice in the art of conversing with the elderly. In truth, he'd had too damn much.

Her eyebrows rose but the door stayed in place. "I see."

"You know DC Buchanan?" he asked, unsure she'd picked up the name the first time round.

"Not really. I've met him though. Nice chap, isn't he -?"

Red flashed another smile. Perhaps not so senile after all.

"Well, he wanted me to check you were okay."

"So you said, bach, and I'm fine. Pass on my thanks to the detective, won't you." She stared harder, pale eyes reading every inch. "*Do* I know you?" she repeated.

Red shook his head, purposely ignoring the question. "Is there anything you need while I'm here?" he asked in a loud voice, a shiver of apprehension inching its way down his spine.

"No, thank you, dearie." She smiled. "All's fine. I'm in the middle of preparing dinner though, so if that's all …"

The door began to close.

Fuck.

He jammed a foot in the gap. The door stopped, shuddered. The lion rattled. He gave it a solid push. The old woman staggered, caught hold of the frame, one hand going to her throat as panic washed over her face.

"What are you doing?" The words were a squeak. "Who are you?"

"Well now, that's not exactly neighbourly, is it?" He smiled and stepped into the hall, easing the door closed with his foot. As the woman backed away, beginning to tremble, he made a big deal of pulling on a pair of black gloves he took from his pocket. "And I suppose a cup of tea is out of the question?"

The woman stood her ground, fists clenched at her side. "Get out now."

Red grinned. "Oh, feisty. I love it. But I don't like taking orders, see – much prefer giving 'em. Understand? I need a favour. So, listen very carefully and no one will get hurt."

"I'm not alone here, you know." There was a distinct wobble in the old woman's voice despite the fury on her face. "I'll call for help, I will. You've got ten seconds, you hear, or –"

Red began to clap. "Bravo. Quite the actress. Unfortunately I know different, so let's not be silly. Like I say, all I need is a favour from you. You can either come quietly, without any fuss. Or …" Red pulled a roll of thick plastic tape from his inside pocket. "… we can do it the hard way. And I really don't mind either."

Mrs Hughes took another step back. "Don't hurt me."

Her resolve was broken. It was a done deal.

"Of course not. I can be the perfect gentleman."

He took a step forward and held out his arm; the old woman yelled and flinched from him.

"Don't be silly. Take my arm. We're going for a little ride."

"I don't want to. My granddaughter will be back any minute; she'll be worried to death. There's police coming and going here, do you know? They'll be hell of a trouble. Just tell me what this is all about and I'm sure we can sort it out, eh."

He ignored her and lifted a long navy-blue coat from a hook in the alcove beneath the stairs.

He held it out. "Yours?"

She nodded.

"Good. Pop it on, then, and we can be on our way."

"No."

Red shook his head slowly, mimicking regret. "Don't make me do this the hard way. Please."

Mrs Hughes groaned but consented to slide her arms into the coat. She stopped and peered at him, leaning in closer. "Are you sure I don't know you?"

Red turned away. "Positive. Now, there's nothing left on in the kitchen is there? I don't mind the dinner spoiled, but we don't want to burn the old place down, do we?"

She shook her head, still frowning.

"Good. Now, I'm going to keep this tape in my pocket, but if you do anything stupid I'll use it. Ankles, wrists, mouth, the lot. Do you understand?"

Eyes wide, she nodded but stayed silent as if fear had stolen her voice.

Red pulled the front door open. "Right then. Nice and quiet, now. Careful as you go and hold onto me, it's proper slippy outside. And we wouldn't want you having an accident, now would we?"

The threat was implicit and clearly understood. The old lady paused to button up her coat and followed him down the icy steps without another word.

Minutes later, as they reached his car, he heard the sound of sobs. Shock kicking in, no doubt, but he couldn't help that. He opened the rear door, checked the child locks were on, and helped her inside. Hiding a smile, he slammed it shut and looked up at the old house. Dark windows glared down, judgemental, yet complicit in his crime. If they were his only witnesses, he had nothing to fear.

It really was too easy. Like a lamb to the slaughter.

* * *

"How beautiful is this?" said Isabel as they climbed out of Dr Gillingham's Lexus forty or so minutes later. They were parked in a car park near South Stack lighthouse on the side of Holyhead Mountain. The Irish Sea was spread out before them, a rolling carpet of sparkling sapphires, and behind them sunlight lit up the snow-speckled yellow gorse bushes that covered the side of the mountain.

"I've been up here years ago, with Father," said Sarah, pulling on her gloves and lifting her face to breathe in the smell of the ocean. "Listen to those gulls. We visited a bird sanctuary round here, then went down to South Stack and watched the ferries crossing to Dublin. But I don't know anything about Neolithic circles."

Dr Gillingham locked the car and joined them. "All okay, ladies? Hell of a spot, isn't it? Must admit it's the first time I've been up here in this weather, rather glad the snow's thawing. Not that it ever lasts too long this near the coast. The sea salt carries in the spray and acts as a natural de-icer. Still …" he coughed as if embarrassed he might be showing a hint of nerdiness, "glad the roads were clear, though the mountain is still covered."

"I was just saying I've been here years ago, to a bird sanctuary with my father –"

"Yes, that's Ellin's Tower." Dr Gillingham pointed towards the cliff edge and a white square-shaped tower in the distance. "It's a RSPB visitor centre now, quite a big deal for the hordes of twitchers it attracts, gets rammed in the summer. These cliffs are famous for the variety of seabirds. I think the biggest attractions are some rare choughs, but there are puffins, peregrines, guillemot and razorbills. Noisy buggers, aren't they?" He smiled. "It is a special spot, and in the summer this heathland becomes a riot of colour. I've even spotted the odd basking adder in the gorse, so watch your step."

"So, why have you brought us here?" Sarah asked, raising her voice above the cry of a circling black gull, which seemed to be eyeing them up in the hope of an easy meal.

"Ah, my dear. If you'd care to follow me. I can show you your Neolithic circles."

He gave a dramatic bow, and urged them to follow, swinging a small rucksack over his shoulder.

Sarah took Isabel's arm as they followed, picking a route through flooded pot-holes and rust-coloured slush, before crossing a narrow lane.

Dr Gillingham pulled open a gate, and they followed a cinder track through thick gorse bushes and out into an open clearing. Sarah paused to catch her breath, not sure if it was the icy air or constant buzz of anticipation that made her breathless. Hands on hips, she turned to look at the view. The sea and sky merged into an endless vista of blue, and the surrounding snow-covered fields dazzled. On the far horizon, one of the Irish ferries appeared, heading for Holyhead harbour. And towards the mainland, the hills that ran the length of the Llyn Peninsular rose out of the sea like the Loch Ness monster.

Sarah experienced a physical jolt; the kind that hits solid in the chest. She realised she was smiling. It was the first time she'd felt genuine pleasure since Dom died, and it helped to clear her mind of the lingering visions of Martin Cole's corpse. She hugged herself and wished, for the first time in her life, that she'd inherited her mother's artistic genes. How wonderful it would be to have the talent to bring something so beautiful to life on canvas. A heaven-sent blessing, her mother said, and now Sarah understood her passion.

But that alone didn't make her an artist. So, she slipped her mobile phone from her pocket and snapped a few photographs. In all her years travelling the world, and writing about its secrets and beauty, she'd never seen anything that moved her so profoundly. And to think it was on the doorstep of her birthplace. She had no doubt there was a moral lesson somewhere in there; one her father would have enjoyed hammering home. Perhaps that was one of his aims, from beyond the grave?

Dr Gillingham waited beside a large wooden notice board. "Takes your breath away, doesn't it? Everyone felt the same when they were working up here a couple of summers ago. These bumps and lumps you see before you, dotted among the gorse and heather, are Neolithic roundhouses. Otherwise known as Neolithic circles. We excavated four newly-discovered buildings just on the far side of that wall. This has to be your father's clue."

Sarah nodded as they studied the information board.

"This map is out of date, the new finds aren't on here," he added. "But this little green sticker represents where he buried the time capsule. According to this it should be in a wall recess in the biggest of the huts we excavated."

"So, you think Father has buried something in the time capsule?"

"Possibly with it, as I'm sure it was sealed … but it has to be connected. Owen got very excited about the idea - very demanding against quite a lot of opposition. The purists said it was a clash of cultures, that it contaminated the authenticity of the site. Have to admit, I was inclined to agree at the time. But Owen was adamant and funded it himself. It's only today, I realise he had ulterior motives."

Dr Gillingham strode along between the circles and the girls followed.

"How old are these roundhouses?" asked Isabel. "Excuse my total ignorance but how far back is Neolithic?"

Dr Gillingham's eyes sparkled, and for the first time Sarah saw passion for his subject. "The proper name is the Ty Mawr hut group. It's a village or small farming community. So far we have eight complete farmsteads, with twenty roundhouses and a further twenty outbuildings or food stores. Earliest occupation of the site is believed to date back to around 2000BC and lasted over several millennia – we've found Middle Stone Age, Neolithic, early Bronze Age to Iron Age - and even Roman -

artefacts on site."

He paused for the information to sink in, then continued, "The first known excavations were carried out in the 1860s and then nothing until the next recorded digs in the 1970s. The structures are amazingly detailed. These dry stone foundations are all that remain, but it would have also consisted of a timber framed building, supporting a turfed or thatched roof. The more we discover, the more we realise how advanced they were. Some of the stones have been carved into basins, and there's evidence in all these open fields in front of us that they were involved in rudimentary ploughing as well as raising livestock. And we discovered tonnes of limpet and periwinkle shells, so it's clear they were involved in forms of fishing too."

"They certainly picked a superb spot," Sarah said, stepping through what was clearly an entrance passage, down into the virgin snow of its interior.

"Absolutely. Shielded from the winds that came off the Irish Sea, just as it is today, and in a prominent enough position to see any invaders to arriving on the shores. Plus they had access to hunting, in the woods inland, and plenty of fish in the sea below. And the view. I'd hope they appreciated it just as much back then …"

Dr Gillingham looked out to sea, and Sarah followed his gaze across the ocean to the peaks of Snowdonia in the distance. None of them seemed to want to disturb the silence, and the special aura they all seemed to feel, standing in someone's home of thousands of years ago. Sarah felt a flicker of the emotion and passion her father must have felt when he discovered a new archaeological site and began to learn about its people. Perhaps she could finally appreciate what it was that drove him.

"Ladies, let's not forget our real purpose here today. Follow me. According to the map, your father's time capsule should be somewhere in the base of this stone wall."

Sarah and Isabel stood, a shivering audience, as Dr Gillingham entered the next circle and began to dismantle the bottom layer of an alcove in the wall. A few moments later he uncovered a small cavity, and removed his glove, sliding his hand into the gap. With a smile of satisfaction, he withdrew a silver canister. Isabel breathed deeply at Sarah's side, and her face broke into a wide smile as Dr Gillingham rose and brushed snow from his knees.

He held out the unusual object. "There you go, Sarah. I believe that must be for you. The original biscuit tin I remember is still in there, soldered and sealed, with this tube balanced on the top."

Sarah fingered the icy cold metal. "Should I open it here?"

"I wouldn't," said Isabel, "just in case. Let's take it back to my place. Danny can meet us there. I'm only five minutes from the police station and I'm sure he'll want to catch up. What do you say?"

Part of her couldn't wait to see what was hidden inside that tiny tube, but Sarah knew Isabel was right, they had to be cautious, and Danny would want to be involved. Sarah had made a promise to him only the day before and she didn't want to go back on her word.

"I think you're right. But thank you, Dr Gillingham. Thank you so much."

Isabel's flat was much larger than Sarah imagined from the outside. The Victorian townhouse had been converted into spacious flats with high ceilings and wonderful traditional sash windows. Isabel had scooped some firewood into the hearth and struck a match as soon as they entered, and the room was warming up rapidly. Isabel was in the kitchen making a much-needed cup of tea, when Sarah heard the intercom buzz. Muffled voices and then the sound of Danny's voice coming up the stairs. She smiled as she continued to examine the wall of photographs, all of Isabel's son, Thomas. Photos of them on the beach, in the woods, riding a small pony. Dozens of treasured memories.

Thomas was the most gorgeous-looking child, with blond

hair that curled into his neck, and wide grey eyes that made him look wiser than his years. His eyes followed her across the room, and as she settled back on the sofa, she was drawn again to his gaze. It was quite uncanny. There was something there ... almost like she recognised him but that didn't seem right either. It was a déjà vu reaction. As if they'd met before ... perhaps in another life. Smiling, she shook the thought away; she was spending too much time with the spirits; that was her problem.

"So ..." Danny's voice broke into her memories. "More adventures, so I hear?"

"Don't start, nothing reckless."

"So you say. Ringing me from half way up a mountain with some strange professor. Hardly sounds like a normal afternoon to me. Safe? I don't trust a word of it."

"It's true. Wait for Isabel and we'll tell you all about it."

Sarah smiled as Danny sat in the chair beside the fireplace. His face gleamed in the reflection of the flames as he held out his hands to the fire. There it was again, that warm blanket that enveloped her.

"How's your afternoon been?" she said.

"Ach, spent it banging my head up the wall, just the usual, you know?" Danny rolled his eyes. "I did manage to track down that salvage firm in Liverpool. Winters. Spoke to the old man, Sidney Winters - says he hasn't seen or spoken to your father in years and seemed genuine enough. Hadn't heard of any plans for more dives on the wreck either. Another dead end."

He sighed and scratched his chin. "And I got the post mortem results back on Martin Cole. There was no warfarin in his system, just the drugs and drink that killed him. So, that doesn't help a lot. And last but not least, my boss is asking all sorts of awkward questions, like why I'm ignoring an apparent confession and an opportunity to close down the case." Danny sighed and shook his head. "But other than that, you know, it's been a fine day."

Sarah touched her handbag, lying beside her. "Well, let's hope I can help."

Isabel pushed open the door with her hip, balancing a loaded tea tray. Danny stood and helped her, lowering the tray onto the coffee table. Isabel flopped onto the sofa.

"Sorry to be an age, just checking up on Tommy."

"Everything okay?"

"Yeah. My friend's going to keep Thomas at hers and I'll pick him up in the morning. Right. Tea and cake, help yourselves."

While Isabel poured, Sarah filled Danny in on the details of their trip to Holyhead Mountain. Isabel butted in on occasion, when Sarah became too excited, and finally, with a triumphant air, Sarah pulled the small canister from her bag.

"And you've not opened it?"

"No."

"Good. Then let's be overly cautious, shall we." Danny stood and dug a pair of blue latex gloves from his back pocket. "It might be OTT but we've so little evidence, I don't want to miss anything. Shall I go ahead?"

Sarah nodded and leaned forward, propping her elbows on her knees.

Danny unscrewed the cap and slid his fingers inside, retrieving a roll of the now recognisable cream paper. He read it quickly, then carefully flattened it out on the coffee table between them.

Sarah scowled. "No. Damn it!"

The paper contained one block of text.

V1. P12. L6. W15.
V1. P54. L28. W2.
V2. P102. L66. W10.
V2. P169. L40. W7.

"What the hell is that?" said Danny.

"That is another of my father's sodding cryptic clues."

"Calm down, we've got to think about this logically," said Isabel, fetching a notepad and pen from the shelf near the window. "You're good at this, Sarah, look what we've achieved so far. Get inside your father's head and try to think as he would."

Sarah snorted. "I'd rather not."

"I'm serious." Isabel sat down, unscrewed the pen. "Come on, think. What could they be? They're obviously references of some kind. But what …"

"Map references?" said Danny. "You know, longitude, latitude. Have you got an Ordnance Survey to hand?"

Isabel shook her head. "No. But they don't look like any map co-ordinates I've ever seen …"

"What about shipping charts?" said Sarah. "What are they like?"

"Not like that," said Danny.

Sarah closed her eyes, muttering the letters and numbers under her breath, seeking inspiration from somewhere, anywhere. There was a familiarity there. Again, almost so close she could touch it, but still it eluded her.

"They're more reference numbers, obviously," Sarah said, looking up at Danny. "The same as the biblical quotes?"

"They can't be." Isabel tapped the pen against her bottom lip. "There are no chapters. We couldn't just guess. That doesn't make sense."

Danny picked up the piece of paper, rolled it out and studied both sides. "I think you're right about reference numbers. What other reference books would your father use? Anything in his line of work, do you know, Isabel? Don't forget he wanted you here, perhaps for a purpose, this could be aimed at you?"

She shook her head. "I'm thinking. But no …"

Sarah punched the cushion beside her. "Oh, goddammit, Father. Why did you have to make everything so bloody complicated? Even as a child he loved setting treasure hunts, leaving clues hidden inside pages of books in the library – oh!"

"What?" Isabel said.

"The clue. Where's the original clue?"

"What do you mean?"

Sarah tutted. "The verse Dr Gillingham translated."

"It's in your handbag."

"Oh, sorry, it is. Hang on."

A dropped pin would have shattered the silence while Sarah shuffled through the junk in her bag, finally producing the printed translation.

"Let me see. Yes, here … *The end will be your starting point; the start may be your end. Close your mind to the modern day; Let The Mabinogion be your friend.*"

Isabel frowned. "After all that, I don't get it …"

Danny began to nod. "I think I do. Why mention *The Mabinogion*? That's what you're thinking, isn't it? It had nothing to do with any of the clues, did it?"

"But it must have a purpose," said Isabel. "We've overlooked that. It's something in one of the books, it has to be."

Sarah shook her head. "I've checked them and there's nothing hidden between the pages, I made doubly sure."

"They could be page numbers," said Danny.

Isabel slid the notebook onto her knee. "V1. P12. Oh! Yes, I see. This must be Volume One. Page twelve –"

"Exactly. Line six. Word fifteen," Sarah concluded with a smile as she peered over Isabel's shoulder.

"Great," said Danny. "It's worth a shot. So where are these books?"

Sarah's smile faded. "In my father's safe. Back at Charter House."

"Gran!"

Sarah stamped snow from her boots and closed the door.

Charter House was silent.

"Gran!" Sarah yelled louder.

The sound of Jim's whines turned into persistent yelps. It sounded like he was out in the rear garden.

"Go on through," she said to Danny and Isabel, pushing open the door to the sitting room. "I'll just sort the heating and see where Gran is, then I'll get the books from the safe. Good grief, it's cold in here."

In the kitchen there were hints of recent activity but no sign of her grandmother. On the cooker, a saucepan full of still-warm stewing steak with a layer of oil on the surface looked abandoned. In the sink, vegetable peelings floated in the water, and a mug of her gran's favourite chamomile tea was left untouched on the table. Sarah felt the mug. Cold. They were clearly having stew for dinner. But where was Gran now?

This wasn't like her. She wasn't an idiot; she'd lived alone for enough years, and was strict with rules about checking identity of callers. Sarah turned the key and opened the rear door. Jim bolted past her legs and took up residence on his new bed, trembling with cold.

Sarah bent and rubbed his ears. "You're freezing, little one. Did she leave you out there?"

Jim exhaled a pitiful whine, and with an expression of dismay and disgust, curled into a ball and tucked his nose under his rear leg, adding a few more shakes for effect.

Sarah got to her feet and gave the kitchen a final look. What if she'd taken unwell and gone for a lie down? Sarah unzipped her coat, hung it in the alcove, and headed for the stairs. She stopped, took a step back. Something was missing. Gran's best winter coat. It had been there when Sarah left, she remembered it clearly. So, if she'd taken her coat, then she must have left the house. But where the hell could she go in this weather?

Fear rose like a tide and Sarah began to shake. That creeping, buzzing feeling of evil … of wrongness. She couldn't explain, even to Dom, he'd cited stress levels. The first day she arrived at Charter House it had been here – and it was here again now.

She leapt into action.

"Gran! Where are you?"

She took the stairs two at a time, slamming each door open in turn. Every room was empty, cold. Her gran's room was pristine, undisturbed; her handbag stood on the dressing table chair where she always kept it. But she never left home without it. Never. It was all the proof she needed.

Danny joined her on the landing, red-faced and anxious. "What is it?"

"Gran. She's gone." She tugged on Danny's sleeve, pulling him to her gran's room. "Her handbag, see. She wouldn't leave it. But her coat's gone. Where is she?"

Danny held onto both Sarah's wrists. "Deep breaths. There could be a hundred explanations. I need you to be calm. Now think. Where?"

Sarah shook her head. "I don't know. We talked about it. She promised not to leave the house, to ring me if anything happened. Luke was coming round later …" Sarah deflated a little as the idea settled. "Luke. That could be it. He could have taken her somewhere."

"Good. That's better. Think."

"Doctors. Perhaps she's ill. But he'd have texted or rung. Perhaps I've missed a call. I need to get my phone."

Danny increased the pressure on her wrists, pinning her down. "Now, take deep breaths. Steady, lady. You're going to blow. Take it easy and we'll go downstairs. Ready? I'm certain there's an explanation. I take it you can ring Luke?"

"Yeah. Let me get my phone, check my messages. I'll call him. Please God … she's with him. I tell you I will kill her for this. What the hell is she thinking?"

Danny held her hand tightly as they took the stairs with care. Sarah knew she was shaking, felt the hysteria ready to explode like a geyser.

Isabel appeared in the hall. "She's not in the garden. I've checked everywhere down here. Why would she go outside?"

"Luke." Sarah mumbled, pushing past. "Let me get my phone."

As Sarah pulled her bag from the bottom banister, she noticed the red light flashing on the answer-phone. That was new too. There'd been no messages for days. She pressed the speaker button.

"You have one new message."

The machine hissed.

"Sarah, bach, it's your gran. I'm in a bit of a fix, see, but don't get in a panic, I'm okay …"

Relief swept through Sarah and she smiled. Gran was okay, she was fine, just in some sort of pickle knowing her. Probably realised they were out of parsnips and took herself off into town. She'd done worse …

"Look, I've been told I've got to read this …."

Sarah stiffened and the smile dissolved. She dropped to her knees on the hall floor, sensing the warmth of Danny's body behind her. Isabel took a seat on the bottom stair.

There was a whisper; a rustle of paper. Gran's voice was high and tight, and Sarah recognised she was near to tears.

"I'm to say that you're running out of time. That you're a disappointment … that's not me saying that, bach, you understand." A pause. "I'm to say that the game is getting boring and I'm to tell you that I'm the pawn ..."

More mutterings. Then her gran saying in a stage whisper, 'this doesn't make sense at all. No, I won't."

She cleared her throat. "That I'm the pawn in the game. You have to supply the winning ticket in the next forty-eight hours or you lose. I am to be exchanged for the winnings. You will hear from me again 7pm tomorrow with further instructions. Be ready with a progress report." Another pause, rustling. "You're close. But if you want to see me alive ag-again, you'll do as exactly as you're told and keep this from the police. You are being watched twenty-four-seven. Any hint the police are involved, any sign you break the rules, and it is game over."

Her voice shook. She paused. "An-and I'm to tell you the game of collecting corpses is getting too easy … and … quite happy to have me as his latest t-trophy."

She broke off with a tortuous sob that pulled at Sarah's soul.

"Sarah, bach, please, do whatever you must. Quickly. Please, help me. He's dangerous and –"

The line went dead.

Sarah sipped the drink she found in her hand, and grimaced. Brandy. Medicinal. Good for shock. And Christ this was shock at its most shocked. She couldn't stop shaking; her leg was bouncing like an old man watching football.

"Drink."

Isabel nudged the glass and tightened the arm around her shoulder.

"Why?" Sarah took another small sip. "Why my gran?"

Isabel shook her head. "I don't know."

"Who?"

"Sarah stop it." Isabel hugged her tight. "Let the experts sort this. We don't have time for analyzing. We have to do what Danny suggested, get the clue solved. Once you're up to it we'll take a look at *The Mabinogion*."

Sarah sniffed as tears rolled down her cheeks. "What did Gran ever do? This is nothing to do with her. If they hurt her, if anything happens to her … I will kill them!"

"It won't. She's strong and she sounded fine. You have to focus on the positives."

Sarah laughed. "And there's buckets of them around, aren't there?"

"Look … you stay positive because what's the other option? Eh? Your gran needs you now. You heard her beg you. Come on, Sarah, I know this is so hard. But you have to hold it together now."

"I know. It's okay. I know. Just let me settle a minute, then we'll crack on."

Danny's voice got louder and the kitchen door opened; his mobile in his hand.

"Sarah, does your computer send and receive MP3 files?"

She nodded. "Yeah. I use it all the time."

"Cool. I've got the techie guys on the phone, they've told

me how to record this message onto your hard drive and then I can email it over to them. See if we can pick anything up in the background noise. It won't be perfect but it's the quickest option."

He spoke into the phone for a few seconds, then took a chair opposite.

"Right. Plan of action. We have to be careful. I'm in a bit of a fix. If he knows who I am, and if he is keeping a surveillance on the house, it stands a good chance – then I'm stuck here. I've swapped cars, put mine in the garage and pulled the Jag outside. If he's not been around this afternoon, that might cover me, but I don't want to take a risk." He drummed his fingers on the table. "Lewis is back in the office and I've filled him in so he can be my eyes and ears. For now, we keep the curtains closed and the doors locked, and we crack on with this clue. Once we know, we can make decisions what to do in the morning. The techies have run a trace on the land line and from what we can see it's not bugged. So, only use the land line until further notice. He could have a scanner and it's much easier to pick up mobiles."

Danny pushed his chair back. "Right. I'll get this file sent. Your laptop still on the desk in your room?"

Sarah nodded. "Thank you for taking charge and I'm sorry I crumbled. But seriously, I don't know if I can do this anymore."

Danny squeezed her shoulder as he moved to the door. "You can. Dig deep. Do it for your gran and that wee nipper in there, eh? We're dealing with a bad guy, possibly a mad guy. I've dealt with hundreds, Sarah, and remember they are only human."

"But if anything happens to Gran; I've got no one else in the world –"

"Nothing will happen. Not while he needs her. It's a big gamble. Either he's desperate or it's a big prize. He thinks he's clever but we're clever too. Trust me."

Sarah looked down, blew her nose.

"Hey."

She looked up. Danny was studying her with a curious

expression.

"Do you trust me?"

"Yes." She gave the thumbs up. "Yes, I trust you."

"Good." Danny repeated the gesture, then carried on into the hall.

Isabel watched with eyes full of questions. "Ready then? Lean on me. Come on, by the time Danny comes down, let's have it solved. What do you say?"

Sara forced a smile. "Sure. It'll be easy."

It wasn't.

Half hour later they sat shivering, either side of the desk in her father's study. Their breath spiraled in white plumes as Sarah looked down at the open pages and the notebook in the centre of the desk. They had followed each code to the exact page, and line, and arrived at the four words it led them to.

Isabel shook her head. "More Welsh I don't understand."

Sarah tapped the biro on the desk, nerves still aflame.

"I think I do," she said. "Couple of the words at least. Can you pass me that Ordnance Survey map? And I need my laptop."

Danny appeared at the door as if summoned by magic. "All done?"

"Could you fetch my laptop down, please?"

Sarah waited while Danny's heavy footsteps rumbled on the stairs. The brandy had taken the sharp, painful edge off everything, rounded the corners enough so she could cope. Staying busy helped, thinking she could be making progress. But still her eyes flooded the second an image of her gran came to mind. Where was she? Locked in a room? Was she tied? Was she being fed? And her tablets. What would happen ...?

Enough.

Danny arrived, laptop in hand, and with a nervous anticipation, Sarah Googled a translation site and carefully typed in the words provided by *The Mabinogion* one at a time

TWR.

DU.

YNYS.

Y

MEOLRHAN.

Within seconds the computer produced results, and Sarah scribbled them onto the page under the original.

"Thank God for the Internet. I've translated it into English."

"What does it say?"

"Black Tower. Seal Island."

"What's that? Or where's that?" said Danny. "Do you know a Seal Island?"

Sarah nodded. "I think so. I used to sail quite a lot out of Moelfre, and one of my favourite spots was Traeth Lligwy. Lligwy Bay. And from memory this little island … here." Sarah opened the map, located Moelfre, and jabbed a finger at a small point just off the coast. "This is Ynys Dulas – or as the locals call it Seal Island. I remember watching the seal pups basking in the sunshine on the rocks there."

"Does it have a black tower then?" asked Isabel.

Sarah nodded, feeling increasingly sure they had the right spot.

"It's the stuff of local legends. A survivor of the Royal Charter had it built as a store for food and water for shipwrecked seamen. One of the local families who became suddenly rich after the shipwreck. Apparently, numerous ships went down on the rocks all around Point Lynas at that time, and the current washed many survivors up onto Seal Island. It was thought if they could survive the storm with food and shelter, there was more chance they could be rescued when conditions improved."

Danny met her eye and nodded. Clearly he thought the clue was solved too.

Isabel let out a deep breath. "So, you think the gold could be there - in this black tower? Is this finally the end?"

"I think so, Isabel. And for my poor, dear gran's sake, I really, truly, hope so."

Chapter Twenty

"It's really good of you, Huw," said Sarah, raising her voice above the rhythmic thud of Sea Goddess II's diesel engine. "Taking us out at such short notice, I mean. We're very grateful."

Huw the Boat wiped oily hands down the front of his overalls, then re-tightened his grip on the wheel. "Aye, is no trouble, del. Been givin' the engine a bit of an overhaul, so the run out'll do her good. Winter's a quiet time, 'specially January with the storms. Bit choppy today for her likin' but the old gal is up to it, don't fret. Not sure on your friends, like."

Sarah glanced across at Isabel and DS Lewis, both perched on the wooden bench at the rear of the boat. Lewis gripped the bow rail with whitened knuckles, and every few seconds puffed out his cheeks, while Isabel was making conscious efforts to control her breathing as recommended by Huw's guide to beating sea-sickness. Isabel met her gaze, rolled her eyes, and held a tissue to her mouth as a particularly large wave rolled the boat from side to side. Sarah stood, feet apart, relishing the power of the ocean and the long-forgotten adrenaline rush of riding the waves.

It had been a manic morning, with a queue to use the land line at Charter House, but finally everything was in place. Sarah sorted transportation out to the island with Huw, unable to use a police launch for obvious reasons. And for the same reasons, Danny had been forced to stay out of the picture, arranging for

Lewis to meet them at the quayside in Moelfre, dressed in jeans and a thick dark jumper as a make-believe deck-mate. A yellow waterproof coat supplied by Huw, which was several sizes too large, completed the disguise.

Everything was going to plan, but, although Sarah felt in safe hands, and trusted every word Danny said, her thoughts were filled with images of her grandmother and concerns for her safety. Nothing Danny could say or do helped quell Sarah's fears. First her father, then Dom, now Grandma Ruth. And she was powerless, controlled like a marionette by some evil lunatic.

"So, you want to be landing on Ynys Dulas, you say?" said Huw. "Not an easy task with the tide rolling on the ebb too. There's a cove round far side of the island from memory, probably easier to moor in there, out the wind. You want me to wait, I take it? Not planning an overnight stay?"

"God, no, Huw. I'm hoping we're on and off pretty quickly."

"Don't recall you saying what it was you wanted on the island? There's no one lives out there, you know?"

"No, I know. Like I say, we should be on and off in no time. Blimey, this wind's getting up," Sarah said, flicking her hair out of her eyes. Huw nodded in Isabel's direction. "Can't see your mates going nowhere, state of 'em. They're no sailors. This ain't no more than a five or six blow today. The Goddess has gone through waves twice as high and come out unscathed. But then if the bile gets you, it gets you good, aye."

Sarah nodded in sympathy.

"And how you keepin', del?" Huw turned his watery gaze towards her; his wrinkles deepened as he frowned. "I was talking to Conrad Hughes in town. Told me bout young Martin Cole. What a tragedy, aye. Like the good Lord hasn't given you enough to contend with. I dunno what's going on round here of late."

Sarah pulled up the hood of her waterproof coat as a fine mist rolled across Lligwy Bay. "I'm fine, Huw."

"Is it true, what they say? That he left a note sayin' he murdered your da? Conrad was tight-lipped, but it's all round the village.

Not that I hold with gossip, mind you."

"I think the police investigation is on-going. Sorry, I can't tell you more. It was a shock at the time, but I'm trying not to dwell on it."

"That's the spirit, del. Keep strong. And always remember to keep your friends close, enemies closer. And you'll do right."

Sarah contemplated Huw's words. Ynys Dulas, Seal Island, was visible now; a small mound rising from the water, its craggy sides shiny black and topped with the unusual shaped tower. It crossed her mind why she'd never thought to land on the island during the many hours she'd spent sailing these seas in her youth.

Huw broke into her thoughts as if reading them. "I only landed on the island once, for a dare it was. Little more than a lad I'd be, 'bout fourteen." Huw turned, his jaw set and face grim. "Supposed to be haunted, y'know. It's reckoned the island was piled high with washed-up bodies after the wreck of Charter. An' it's reckoned lost souls of long dead sailors linger there. It's said if you walk on Traeth Lligwy late at night you can hear em crying out, begging for release, so they say. Some of the locals to this day call it Island of Souls instead of Island of Seals."

"I never knew that. I was wondering why I'd never moored there, especially as I love seals and spent hours on these waters when I was younger."

"It's kept quiet, aye, tis true. Mind you, we have enough tales going round these parts to last a lifetime. Goes with the territory, I suppose. Seafaring folk always been superstitious. But there's some wouldn't set foot on the island, that's for sure. I don't hold with all that mumbo-jumbo, like. Though I've never been back since that first time. Always thought it a creepy place."

"What do you know about the tower?"

Huw stared at her. "More important, what do you know?"

"What do you mean?"

"Well, I suppose I was thinkin' your family history was the reason you wanted to visit the island."

Sarah shook her head, aware of a growing apprehension. Was it possible Huw knew about the hiding place of the gold?

"Well, I heard it was one of your ancestors what built the tower. With Charter gold money, so it's rumoured."

"Really? Why? I mean, how come I never knew?"

Huw shook his head. "No idea. Summat I've always known, since a lad. Tale went he was maddened with grief as he lost his wife and daughter in the sinking. Wasn't able to accept they were dead, like. So he built this tower and visited every week to make sure there was food and water for them in case they turned up alive. They never did, like, quite obvious they wouldn't. I wonder if he knew, but had the idea of keeping provisions for their souls." Huw sniffed and rubbed his face with a gnarled hand. "Tragic. Suppose we'll never know. I thought with all the research your da had been doing, you wanted to take a look at the island yourself."

They stood in silence as the island gradually appeared through the fog, its sides suddenly sheer cliffs, looming above them like skyscrapers. Ominous and haunting, like a scene from a pirate-ship movie, the noise of the ocean crashing against the rocks adding to the drama. Sarah's teeth began to chatter, a mixture of fear and cold, and a creeping sensation worked its way through her gut. How come she'd never known? Why had Father never told her? She shook her head. How many more family secrets lay hidden?

Sarah cleared her throat. "Thinking back, I never knew much about the tower, but I'd heard it was built by a rich local family who wanted to try to help out stranded seamen when ships were regularly going down round this part of the coast."

"Aye. In later years, no doubt that it were used for that. But my own da told me it were this Stewart fella who built it with his bare hands, and I believed him. Grief can do strange things to a man. Anyway," Huw continued, "best we concentrate on these rocks; let's see if I can remember where this inlet is, 'tis close on sixty years since I tried to land here."

Fear shone in Isabel's eyes as the boat lurched and rolled on the waves, jagged rocks appearing alongside like icebergs. Lewis gave a weak smile and thumbs up. Sarah returned the gesture, having every faith in Huw's seamanship.

"Sarah, del, think you remember the ropes? Could you pop up onto the bow, see those fenders there, can you lob three or four over the port side? I think I can get up close enough to those rocks there, to moor us safely. You'll find a boat hook and a bow line you should be able to secure us with."

Sarah made her way onto the port deck, picked up a coiled bow line and braced herself ready for landing.

* * *

Red dismounted his bike, and propped it against the fence. He tightened the straps on his rucksack and followed the path round the edge of the field, till the ruins of the farm cottage came into view. His senses hummed. Ears and eyes strained to the maximum, even sniffing the air for any rogue smells. But everything was as peaceful as ever at the old place. No one ever came out here. Not even the courting couples, who frequented the car park on the nature reserve, ventured this far into the woods.

He picked his way through muddy-coloured slush and piles of bricks and broken roof tiles and unlocked the barn door. There was the rustle of wings as he stepped inside and the resident doves took flight. He was greeted with the usual stench of their droppings. Yellow light from the windows of the caravan warmed the inside of the barn, creating shadows, which stretched across his feet. He closed the door on the last of the daylight, and stood still, listening for a moment. Everything was peaceful, just the tinny hum of the radio he'd left for company.

Approaching the touring van, he sorted through a heavy bunch of keys, selected two padlock ones, and undid both chains. He wriggled a smaller key into the lock on the caravan door, and pulled it open an inch at a time. The strains of Beethoven greeted him, but nothing else. He took the step and peered inside. The old lady was where he'd left her, fast asleep on the double bed at far end. With nothing but darkness outside her window, and the companionship of Classic FM, it was probably hard to differentiate night from day.

He stepped into the caravan, shrugged off the rucksack, and unloaded a flask and assorted pastries onto the kitchen work surface. There was a snuffling noise, as the old lady groaned in her sleep, pulled her coat up to her chin, and rolled over onto her side. Red stood poised, ready for her to wake. But within seconds, her breathing was rhythmical again. He checked the heater was still set to medium and that nothing had been tampered with which she might use to cause damage or aid an escape.

But no. She'd been as good as gold. Content with her Margaret Atwood novel. They'd talked in the car, well, he'd tried to reassure her – anything to stop the persistent bloody sobbing. They'd come to an agreement; she'd wash the dried tear stains from her face and quit the blubbing. And he'd leave her in peace as long as she did what he asked, when he asked. If all went to plan, he explained, time and again, no one would get hurt. He'd made it clear, however, with one glimpse of the pistol he carried, that any attempts at escape would be dealt with harshly.

So far, so good. It was the way with the elderly, he found. They'd survived wars. They were stoic and less prone to hysteria, more ready to accept who held the power and how to follow rules. Anyone below middle age wouldn't have handled this like Mrs Hughes. There'd have been anger, outrage, reprisals. And society wondered why there were so many murders? So many stories of sixteen-year-old kids killed in their local JD Sports? Simple. No one nowadays could accept taking orders. That was one of the main problems with the world today – sort that out and there'd be no riots, no revolutions. It didn't take Einstein to work out not everyone could be top of the tree.

Right, he had to make a move. The next part of the plan was

all important. Now, he'd made sure this trump card, or maybe he should call her his back-up plan, was alive and kicking – he could concentrate on the main game. And he couldn't wait! He zipped up his rucksack and backed out of the tourer, checking the window bolts were secure and the bathroom was undamaged. He was lucky. There was little chance this caravan would hold a young, fit male who was determined to escape. Martin Cole, for instance, was the type who would have ripped up the floorboards rather than stay imprisoned. But Grandma Ruth Hughes was a softy – the perfect hostage you could say.

It would break his heart if he had to kill her in the end.

* * *

Both women followed Lewis along a worn cliff path. He'd thought it safe enough to come with them, reasoning it was unlikely they were under observation out here. Sarah paused to take a few deep breaths after the steep climb, and waved down to Huw on the deck of the Goddess. He gave his toothless grin and bent to enter the cabin; the sound of music drifted on the breeze. The classical melody almost added a film soundtrack to the eerie scene. Isabel paused a little way along the path and waited for her to catch up. She'd pulled up the hood of her anorak; her eyes looked huge and scared in the smallness of her face, which still shone with a greenish tint.

"Are you feeling okay?" Sarah asked as she caught up.

"A bit better, just freezing. Let's hurry."

"Huw reckons there's a storm on its way. Lewis, hang on, we're coming, this path is icy."

The tower was on the northern most point of the island, but within ten minutes they'd crossed the sodden, bracken-covered hill and approached the incline that led to the front of the building. Lewis climbed the half dozen steps and stood in front of a heavy wooden door. He grabbed the circular iron handle, and turned.

Locked.

It took a while for reality to connect.

"No way," said Sarah. "Why …"

Isabel climbed the steps and slipped a large key into the lock. There was the sound of grating metal as she pushed the door open with her foot.

"What? Wh-where did you get that key?" Sarah managed to ask.

"It was the piece of the puzzle your father left with me."

"I don't understand …"

"I think it was his decision, he entrusted the safe code to you and this key to me."

"But why did you never say?"

"Because I had no idea what it fitted, obviously. I always intended telling you the minute we found a lock it fitted."

Sarah shook her head, hearing the words but not understanding their meaning. Her eyes met Lewis's worried frown. He blew on his hands and eased Isabel to one side, stepping into the gloom. Sarah waited at the bottom of the steps, fighting back indignation that swelled inside and threatened to erupt in fury from her mouth. She'd been honest with Isabel from day one. And despite having reasons not to trust her, she had. Implicitly. Was this the way Isabel repaid that trust?

Isabel looked down, raising her voice above the wind. "Come on, Sarah, be reasonable. Now isn't the time to be deciding if you can trust me or not. It's a little late for that."

Sarah frowned as she mounted the steps. "I've never kept anything back from you. You must see how this looks?"

"No, tell me." Isabel's lips were a thin line across her face.

"Well, how do I know it's the only thing you've not told me?"

"You don't. You either believe me or you don't. But I didn't tell you because I had no idea what the key opened. That's all. No other reason. But if you want to believe otherwise, I can't stop you. However, I don't think this is the time or place for such a debate. Do you?"

"It's such a shock –"

"Then I apologise. But we could be about to find treasure, Sarah. Together, we have come so far. Why would I do anything to jeopardise things now? Please … let's get on with it … Lewis is waiting."

Sarah shivered and nodded. Part of her didn't like this new Isabel; the hardness of her face, the edge to her voice and new-found confidence. But the rational side had to agree. They were on the edge of something big here. Besides that, they were in the middle of the ocean, on a remote island with a storm looming on the horizon, and in truth it was probably not the right time to have a discussion about moral rights and wrongs. Sarah followed Isabel into the dark interior of the tower, reaching into her bag for her torch.

The tower was no more than ten feet in diameter, with a rough stone bench chiselled out around the base of the wall. Two small windows high up offered a little natural light, and from the fluttering above them in the darkness, it also served as home to a collection of birds. She shone the light around the white-washed walls, and across the stone floor. The beam jerked as her hand shook, and finally came to rest on the only object in the room. A wooden crate, about the size and width of a coffin, but twice as high. The torch picked up Lewis's trainers and, as the light reached him, he bent to examine the box.

Isabel gasped. "God, what is it …"

"It's okay, I don't think it's a coffin, if that's what you're thinking," said Lewis, blinking in the torch light. "Looks more like an old-fashioned shipping crate."

Isabel nodded. "We should open it, why didn't we think to bring tools?"

"Well, it may prove useless but I do have an old Swiss Army knife," said Lewis. "Let me see how this lid is fixed."

He bent and rubbed layers of dust and bird droppings off the lid with his gloves. Sarah tried to stop the light shaking;

she stepped back onto the doorstep, and took deep breaths to clear her lungs of the musty air. It was a slow, painful process; Lewis's fingers, no doubt frozen, slipped as he tried to grip the tiny fixings, but eventually the lid was free, and, with Lewis at one end and Isabel at the other, it slid to the floor, landing with a crash and clouds of dust.

Sarah's heart hammered as she peered into the box. No glint of gold, no shaft of light reflecting off bullion. Instead, several other packages, wrapped in layers of brown paper and string, stacked concertina style inside the box.

"Paintings?" said Isabel. "They look like paintings."

"I don't know."

"Well, it doesn't look like gold bars, does it?"

"I don't know."

"Is that all you can say?" snapped Isabel.

Was it? Shock seemed to have taken over her body. Her hands and legs shook, and her mouth refused to formulate the required responses. Had it all been a big joke? Was the treasure nothing more than a few old paintings?"

Lewis lifted out one of the large packages, balancing it horizontally across the crate. "Let's open one and see what's in there. Okay, Sarah?"

"If you ask me, this is getting beyond a joke," said Isabel.

Sarah nodded and stood motionless. Isabel picked up the knife and slit the string, while Lewis pulled off layers of old wrapping paper. The edge of a wooden frame appeared, then the rear of a canvas. Lewis turned the picture towards them and held it under the light.

Sarah recoiled as she saw the images on the canvas. The painting was dark: white, grey and black. The distorted figure of a ragged child, on its knees, praying, while black tear drops slid down the girl's pale face. Lewis, almost reverently, stood the painting against the wall and lifted another from the box. With the wrapping removed, it showed a similarly coloured scene, this time wild seas tossing a small boat against a jagged cliff.

Bodies floated face down, some battered against the rocks, while others clung to wreckage among the waves.

Isabel unwrapped a further painting. This was coloured in ghostly pale greens and greys of a young woman dressed in rags, one hand plunging a bloody knife into her own chest. Her face was lifeless, bloated; her fingers blackened claws that tore at the material of her skirt. Sarah stepped forward and opened another. She gasped. A young girl, underwater, hair swirling around her face, eyes wide and scared, hands out stretched, begging for mercy.

"My God," she whispered.

Sarah shuddered, her eyes fixed on the black stare of the young girl in the last painting. She knew those eyes, had looked into that deadened stare. Hadn't she? She shook her head to repel the dizziness.

Lewis cleared his throat. "They're horrific. Good. But horrific. The closest I have ever seen are the Black Paintings by Goya, in a museum in Madrid. The person that painted these must have been in terrible pain."

"Or terrible madness," said Isabel.

Sarah nodded, noticing for the first time an envelope fixed to the inside of the lid of the crate. She tore away the staples, ripped open the envelope, and gasped as she recognised her father's writing.

Darling Sarah,

You have made it this far, cariad, but I fear this is not at all what you expected to find, and I can be in no doubt that you are as disappointed and saddened by me now as you surely have been for most of your life. However, I have good reason. I need your forgiveness my darling daughter. What despairing old man am I to be asking so much? Perhaps all I can ask is that you bear with me?

Before your disappointment deteriorated to the abhorrent odium of which I am now so used, I desperately wanted you to gain some small insight into my world. For it was not all bad, you see. Perhaps I have been successful in providing you with a glimpse of the passion I hold for my work, for our culture, and our heritage. I hope you gained something from the journey, darling. Not for me you understand, sweet, sweet cariad, but for your own dear soul. Please try and understand this old man. The love I feel for you overwhelms my every thought. Call it guilt, or remorse. Call it what you will. But believe that it is there and it is powerful - the like of which I have never experienced before.

Forgive me a little if you can, cariad.

In my first letter to you, I warned I had ruined lives. Some you were aware of, others you were not.

The paintings you find here are from your mother's hand. Created in the last months of her life. I imagine how that must sound to you, how unbelievable you may find it with the memories you hold of your mother so dear. I will never forget the abundance of life, colour, vibrancy in her work and in her beautiful soul. Never!

Sarah, I have told so many lies, so many deceptions, that I have grown to hate myself and at this juncture in my sad old life, I have no option other than total honesty. As hard a thing as this is to do, I fear there is no other way. I am sorry. With every worthless fibre - I am so very sorry. It's your mother, Sarah. Your dear mother did not die in a car crash.

I am sorry to tell you she brought an end to her suffering by leaping from the heights of the Menai Bridge. I hid this terrible reality from the outside world, her reputation being my only consideration. Only your grandma, Ruth, who I begged into silence, and of course, Dr Davies, know what really happened. Your mother's paintings may well seem to indicate a state of grief turning to madness and fault, of course, lies only with me. I have been too cowardly to ever admit this, but it is certainly true.

Sarah, this is so hard. But the truth, I must …

I never had a faithful heart. Not a single reliable gene. Always a wandering eye and a weakness of spirit. I am not proud. How *could I be? Drink deadened urges and dulled pain. I drink even now to numb the shame of such admissions to my darling daughter. Drink clouds the memories - that is the only good thing.*

Your sweet mother was nothing less than an angel. As a wife she was loyal, very loving and so strongly devoted. Sadly, this was not enough for me. Please believe that with my ignorance, I tried, but her innocence became a wound in my side, and hatred grew. I treated her badly. So, so, badly. I can see it now of course, and in truth I knew it then. She tried so hard, begging me not to leave her, promising she could ignore my philandering. Your poor mother prayed every night for the strength to keep her family intact.

Reflection is a damned thing. These days all I do is cry. Back then I was weak in every aspect. And a coward. Another woman captivated my wretched soul, and I have great shame in admitting that I forced your mother out of Charter House. It was the summer you lived mostly with your grandma, the summer of your mother's death. You were told I was working abroad, but I was here, with that other woman filling your mother's shoes, filling her life and her bed.

And so your mother painted. Painted to rid the pain from her heart. Painted to try somehow to cleanse her soul too, I believe. And here in this box you find the results. If you wonder why Grandma Ruth always hated me, you now have the answer. But to her honour, she has kept her word and I thank her for that.

That is everything, sweet cariad. No more secrets or lies. I say this as if enough damage has not already been done, when I can only imagine how much pain you must have. Hatred for an unacceptable father, terrible sorrow for the mother you lost. I understand and accept all responsibility. I only wish I could be there and somehow take that pain away, Sarah. You deserve none of this.

Please bear no hatred towards your mother. She was not of the soundest of minds at the last. I wish I could tell you she left a letter, left some special gift for her darling daughter. But she did not. All I ask is that you keep your memories close, the real memories of love and life.

The treasure you seek, I have been forced to move. I fear someone discovered the tower, damaged the lock. I pray from my grave that it remains safe. I want you to ask Grandma Ruth to show you our secret memorial. Go to your mother, my darling cariad. She needs you.

Remember, the end will be your starting point.

My dying love to you,

Dad x

Sarah dropped to her knees as Isabel snatched the letter. She heard Lewis speaking; the words making no more sense than a foreign language. Isabel began to cry, wind howled through the door, and a mewling sound, like an animal in pain, filled her head as it grew louder and louder. As tears began to flow in hiccupping sobs, she felt Lewis's hands on her shoulders, lifting her.

Sarah closed her mouth, realising the howling came from her own lips.

Chapter Twenty One

"Sarah, come on … please!" Lewis's voice cut through images of her grandmother's face, her mother's gentle smile, her father's drunken rages and Dom's tender kisses.

All interspersed with the empty eyes of a young girl struggling, deep underwater, trying to gasp one final breath into her lungs.

She lifted her face from her knees; her head had never felt so heavy. A drumming pounded through her skull. Lewis tugged at her arm, trying to drag her to her feet.

"Why?" she sobbed. "I don't understand. Why?"

"I don't know. I'm sorry. But we have to go, please, come on. Move!"

Sarah stood shakily, gripping hold of Lewis for support. "What about the paintings?"

"Leave them –"

"No!"

"Sarah, you're not thinking rationally. We can't possibly carry them. The weather is getting worse, they'll be ruined. We can lock the door and leave them as we found them. I know how you must feel, but the paintings will be safe here. We'll come back. Here, see, I'll stack them back in the crate."

Sarah watched, numb and shaking. "Where's Isabel?"

"I sent her back to the boat. The storm's getting worse. Come on."

Lewis took her hand and dragged her outside, pausing to lock the door and zip the key into his pocket. He pulled out his mobile, checked the display, and with a growl pushed it back inside his coat. A flash of lightning lit the island, followed by a distant rumble of thunder. They headed into the wind, ignoring heavy, stinging rain which hit them head on.

"Keep moving, Sarah," Lewis called above the wind, pushing back the hood of the yellow coat.

"I can't hurry. I can barely breathe. Did you read the letter?"

"Briefly. But you can't focus on that now. Hurry up. If the sea gets any rougher we might not get off the island."

Her feet moved, one heavy step after another, slipping and sliding, while her brain felt ready to explode. Her whole life had been a sham. She'd been lied to by everyone she loved, everyone she ever trusted. And worse, so much worse, abandoned by the mother she'd adored. It was clear her mother had loved her father much more than she ever loved her daughter – or there was no way she would have left like that.

They reached the cliff edge and Sarah was forced to ignore the waves of self-pity and concentrate on her footing. Lightning cut through the sky again in a jagged arch, and thunder rolled, this time overhead, loud and booming, echoing around the high cliffs and across the swollen tide.

The rain made the track down into the cove much more dangerous. Taking side steps, pushing back images of the day Dom died, she slithered down the rock face. Lewis paused every few steps, checking her progress. She squatted onto her haunches, fully aware of her pregnancy as the waistband of her jeans dug into her stomach. Gripping the coarse stringy grass, she let her boots slide across the rock, controlling the speed of the descent with her hands.

Lewis's breathing was heavy, and she could sense even he was beginning to panic. "Be careful, Sarah. Slow down, wait for me."

Eventually, they reached the shingle beach, racing across to the far side of the cove, gripping Lewis's hand as they climbed up onto the narrow shelf of rocks. There was no sign of Isabel or Huw on the deck of the Sea Goddess; presumably they were inside, preparing leave. Breathless, they jumped down onto the deck. The cabin was closed up against the elements, but a bright light shone out like a welcoming beacon against the gloom.

Sarah turned the handle and pulled open the door. Yellow light flooded the deck. A high-pitched hiss of a radio filled the air. Sarah bent and jumped down into the small room, her eyes taking in the half-drunk mug of tea and upturned chair.

"Huw?"

A figure stepped forward.

"Isabel. Thank God. Where's Huw?"

A hand tugged the sleeve of her coat. She glanced up at Lewis and followed his gaze.

Isabel stood feet apart, holding, in both hands, a small black pistol that was aimed directly at Sarah's chest.

"Sit."

"Isabel, what are you doing?" Sarah frowned. "Lewis, what –"

"I said sit," hissed Isabel.

Lewis tugged Sarah's arm; his face was grey and water dripped from his hair. He backed away, pulling her with him. "Let's sit down. Everyone, let's stay nice and calm."

"Isabel?" Sarah looked around the cabin as she slid back onto the bench seat. "Where's Huw? What's happening?"

"Did you read the letter?" Isabel asked, pulling the pages from the inside of her anorak with one hand, while straightening the gun's aim with her other.

"What?" Sarah frowned.

"Did you read the letter?"

Lewis squeezed her arm. "Answer her," he whispered.

Sarah swallowed, feeling the shakes start up in her leg. "Yes. You know I did."

"This whole thing. A fucking game. A fucking charade!" Isabel looked to the ceiling of the cabin as if yelling at a higher entity. "And I fell for it. What a fool. What a waste of the last six years of my life. What was I thinking?"

"I'm not sure that's what was said in the letter, is it?" said Lewis, clearly trying to maintain the voice of reason. "I only got a quick look but I'm sure it said the treasure had been moved for safety?"

"Ha," Isabel spat. "Yeah, right. And so we go there, and there's some other excuse. We move on, the same thing. No, it's all been a game. A sick twisted game by a sick, twisted, old drunk. What the hell did I expect from my worthless father!"

Sarah opened her mouth to respond, then closed it again, not wanting to correct Isabel when she had a gun in her hand.

She sensed Lewis looking at her, and turned towards him, trying to read his expression. He looked shocked and embarrassed. But it was she who should be upset, all this stuff about her mother's suicide, not to mention how this affected their chances of rescuing Grandma Ruth. On top of everything, who cared about treasure and phantom gold? Her whole life was in shreds. And, quite honestly, who gave a shit that Isabel seemed to have flipped?

Lewis cleared his throat. "Your mother –"

Sarah nodded, began to respond, but Isabel's voice drowned out her own.

"That's right, Mr Detective." Isabel smirked. "My mother is the whore in the letter. What did he call her?" She opened the pages. "Ah, yes … '*that* other woman … filling your mother's shoes, filling her life and her bed.'" Isabel flung the letter onto the small table, staggering as a wave rocked the boat and cups chattered on the shelf above her. "*That* woman. *That* woman whose life he ruined. *That* bastard!"

"Isabel?" Sarah made to stand, but Lewis's hand on her arm held her down. "I don't understand –"

Isabel laughed, but there was no humour. "No, that's about right. You wouldn't understand. Why would you? Poor, neglected, little cariad, who he loved more than life itself. Why would you understand, *dear sister*?"

The last words connected, tumbling through the entire length of her body until they slotted into place. Sister. Isabel was her *sister*? How could that be? Then, the letter began to make sense. Another woman. Not a one night stand. Not a fling with a student. But someone with whom he'd had a child. No. It didn't make sense. How ...?

And then, as if a gift from some other dimension, Sarah remembered the photographs in Isabel's flat. Thomas. The wise eyes and strong jaw. The blond curls. The connection she'd felt, that immediate recognition.

A family resemblance.

Her hand flew to her mouth. She turned to Lewis. His eyes confirmed her fears as his hand sought hers on the bench.

"At last. You get it now?" said Isabel, voice dripping sarcasm. "I was the bastard daughter. The one who barely got a mention in his Will, despite skivvying for him for the past God knows how many years. Trying to make amends. No. Trying to *make* him love me." She broke off, unable to continue.

"I didn't know." Sarah felt sick and giddy. "I never knew ..."

Lewis held up a hand. "You know, this probably isn't the time or place to do this, is it? Isabel, what's with the gun? Perhaps you should tell us what you want?"

Isabel ignored them, pacing now, back and forth. "The one whose son your father refused to meet or even acknowledge. His only grandson. How could he?" Tears rolled down her face. "The one who begged your father to meet a dying woman who never stopped loving him. Only to be rejected all over again." She took a deep breath. "Yeah, that's me. Nice to meet you, *sister dear*."

"Your mother?" whispered Sarah.

"Yeah. Sad cow. Poor, sad cow." Isabel breathed out. "Mom found out she had terminal cancer a couple of years ago. She had a mastectomy when I was in my teens. It came back, spread, the usual. She came over to visit, tell me in person, and begged to see Owen. He refused point blank. I had no contact with him for six months after. I hated him so much for rejecting us again. Then Mom died. And when I came back from the funeral, I said goodbye to Toronto for good, and decided then I'd get revenge."

"You found out about the Royal Charter –?" said Lewis.

"I saw everything through typing out his research and notes for his books. Of course, I thought it was the paranoid ramblings of a drunk to start with. But then I began to wonder. I worked my charms and started to fill him with drink as often as I could. But hard as I tried, he wouldn't give me all the pieces of the puzzle. That's why I needed you."

Isabel spat the last words at Sarah, who flinched under the hatred. The boat rolled and Isabel staggered, reaching out to balance herself against the table. Lewis stiffened beside her, but the gun was immediately straightened, inches from Sarah's face.

Sarah couldn't speak, all she could do was stare and shake her head as if this was nothing more than a tale of fiction. Deep down, though, she knew it wasn't.

"Besides, why should you get everything when the old sod died?" said Isabel. "I deserved my share and I was determined to get it one way or another. Wasn't it enough I had to listen to him weeping and wailing for hours on end how much he loved his Sarahs – how much he missed his Sarahs. How he wished he had his time over –"

A bump on deck interrupted the flow of vitriol.

Lewis tensed. "Did you hear that?"

"What was it?" said Sarah.

Isabel sniffed, seeming to regain her composure. "Just the boat hitting the rocks. Sit down!" The gun swung to her right as Lewis began to stand. He dropped back onto the seat.

A thought flashed through Sarah's mind. *She's lying.* Sarah knew from Isabel's expression she'd heard the noise at the exact same moment, yet her face was blank, her eyes deliberately vacant.

"Huw?" Sarah sprang to her feet. The boat lurched, and she stumbled backwards, grabbing the roof for support. Mugs slid from the table, smashing to the floor, cold tea splashed her boots. "What the –"

The cabin door crashed open, wind howled, and a tall hooded figure stepped down into the cabin.

"Huw?"

Large hands pulled back a black hood. Sarah screamed. For a second, all she saw was Luke, then chaos took over as Lewis leapt from his seat, pushing her to one side. He punched the man in the face as hard as he could, unbalancing him. Both men fell, stumbling against the table. Sarah looked round frantically for something to use as a weapon, if she could get one good swing …

Lewis jumped to his feet. "Sarah! Get out now! Get help!"

As the man crawled towards them, rubbing his jaw, Lewis grabbed her, propelling her towards the door. She fell against the frame, yanking at the handle, heart pounding.

A noise as loud as a bomb explosion ripped through the air; the cabin echoed with repercussions of the sound. A bang so loud, Sarah clutched her ears and staggered backwards under the assault. There was a curious burning smell in the air, a weight tumbled against her legs, then Isabel was screaming.

Hands grabbed Sarah's waist, lifting her, throwing her across the small space, away from the door. Her head smacked against something solid, pain blurred her vision and nausea spun inside her gut. Noise and commotion filled her head, whirling around her like a hurricane. But she felt strangely detached from it all.

"What have you done?"

More screams.

"Nothing." Sarah whispered. "Nothing."

"You stupid bitch! What have you done?"

"He's police."

Sobbing, shouting. Bumps and groans.

Isabel's voice. "I panicked! Where were you?"

"Jesus."

"Do something!"

"You stupid, stupid cow. Police? This changes everything."

"No. No. It doesn't. We-we can take the boat out, dump it overboard. No one will know. Please."

"I don't want any part of this. Shit."

"Please …"

Sarah rubbed her head and sat up. Lewis lay beside her on the floor, his head rested against her thigh. He stared at her, his piercing blue eyes trying to reach her. No doubt to calm her, reassure her. The usual Lewis. She thought of Danny, wished with all her heart he was here. He'd put this right. He had that sort of magic, just the same as Dom.

The argument continued above her head, above the table, out of her vision. But down here with Lewis was their world. It was her job to keep Lewis safe; Danny would expect nothing less.

She bent forward close to Lewis's ear. "We need to get out. I don't know what's happening. But we need to find Huw. Can you move?"

Lewis opened his mouth to speak, then shook his head slightly, and closed his eyes.

Sarah shook his shoulder. "Come on …"

He tried again. "Sarah … go," he whispered.

"I'm not leaving you."

Lewis began to shake; he opened his mouth. A bubble of deep cherry red appeared between his lips, burst and slid slowly down his chin.

Sarah screamed, reached out and touched Lewis's face.

He flinched and lifted a hand, touched the front of his coat. A bloom of crimson leaked through a charred hole in the front of the shiny yellow material. He examined his fingers, smeared with bright red blood. The arm flopped to his side.

Sarah gasped. "No!"

"Shush … shush …" Lewis opened his eyes wide, lifted his hand again, pointing to his coat. "Phone. Get …"

Sarah nodded. Trying not to touch the blood-soaked jumper, she slid her hand inside the coat, retrieved his mobile, and quickly transferred it to her own pocket. She grabbed a pile of towels from the floor and held them against Lewis's middle. Within seconds, streaks of red soaked through the grey material.

Reality hit Sarah like a goods train, clearing her head and heart in one solid impact.

"No!" she whispered again, dragging herself to her knees, and pulling Lewis's head into her lap. "He's shot. Please! He's bleeding. I think he's dying!"

More blood began to pool between Lewis's lips, dribbling down his chin in a steady torrent. He tried to speak, but Sarah held a finger across his lips. Tears and snot stopped her speaking; her breath came in ragged gulps. Lewis's eyes fixed on Sarah's for several moments, his breathing stuttered and he gasped for breath. Then as if a light had been extinguished in a bright room, his eyes emptied, and his head tilted to one side.

"No!" She shook Lewis's shoulders, already, despite her sick panic, recognising the futility. "Isabel!"

The table scraped to one side. A black hooded figured blocked out the glare of the overhead light. A face came towards her. An arm reached out and dragged her to her feet, pushing her hard. Sarah slid down the opposite wall, legs useless, arms held outstretched, hands sticky with Lewis's blood. The figure bent over Lewis, checking for breathing and a pulse.

Sarah forced each breath; dizzy and unable to stop herself shaking, she had a desperate need to pee but couldn't move. Isabel stood near the door, blocking any thought of escape, wringing her hands in front of her, almost in prayer. There was no sign of the gun. Isabel watched the two men, trembling almost as much as Sarah.

A minute later, the man stood and eased Lewis's corpse as far as he could under the bench seat, piling the soiled towels on top of the body. Sarah sobbed. The finality of the action was like drawing a solid line under any chance of her diagnosis being wrong.

The man took one step towards her. Sarah pushed herself

into the wall.

"He's dead. No point making more fuss. Get used to it."

Sarah studied the wide face and dark hair. Not Luke at all. The blue eyes, which should have been warm and gentle, were cold, calculating. Evil.

"You?" she whispered.

He grinned and shrugged off the long black coat. "Hello, Sarah."

"David?"

"Long time no see. Though most people call me Red nowadays on account of this fella."

He pulled up a blue tracksuit top, turning to reveal the tattoo of a huge red dragon on his back. Fire breathed into the nape of his neck, while a spiny, curled tail disappeared under the waistband of his dark jeans.

"Very patriotic," murmured Sarah.

"Ha. Thank you. Like to take a piece of the homeland with me wherever I roam."

"Where's Luke?"

"No idea. Why would I have anything to do with that loser?" He rubbed the grimy window as the boat lifted in the swell. "We've got to get away from here, get back to Moelfre. Anyone here can drive this bloody thing?"

No one answered. Sarah was shaking and too far inside her own thoughts. What was happening? Lewis was dead. Isabel had killed him. David Evans was taking charge of the situation. Sarah fingered the phone in her pocket. She needed Danny – she needed him so badly.

David slammed the door open and pulled himself up onto the deck. Isabel stood in the far corner; hiccupping sobs filled the cabin as the wind swirled through the door, lifting the edge of the towels. Lewis's legs, one bent, one straight, came into view. Sarah stared at the bottom of size nine hiking boots, tiny shells clung to mud wedged in the patterned sole.

David reappeared, putting all his weight against the door to force it closed. "Right. I've cut the ropes. Someone needs to get this thing started. You ..." he jabbed a finger at Sarah, "get up front. I remember you and Luke know about boats. Don't argue. Move. Now."

He grabbed Sarah's arm, lifted her to her feet, and pushed her towards the wheelhouse.

"Are you mad?" Sarah's voice came to life. "Don't touch me. I warn you! Isabel, ring the police. Call 999 –"

A stinging blow across her face knocked her backwards; she staggered and grabbed hold of the table.

"Shut it. Pregnant or not, I don't give a shit." A hard thump in the middle of her back. "Now move."

Sarah frowned. How did he know? The Sea Goddess began to twist and rock as the tide collected it into its grip, tossing it as easily as a model boat on a pond. Isabel groaned and bent forward, a rush of vomit splashed against her shoes. Sarah jumped back from the puddle; the room filled with a sour stench.

"Nice," David hissed. "Move."

Sarah held out an arm to Isabel as David manhandled her towards the wheelhouse. They made eye contact as Isabel wiped her mouth with a tissue, then quickly looked away. Why didn't Isabel do something? Where was the gun, why didn't she use it against David?

Nothing made sense ... nothing made any sense.

And then ...

Everything made complete sense.

David shoved her again.

Sarah span round. "Don't touch me. I warn you. If you want me to sail this boat, you best start talking. I mean it. I've got nothing to live for. How about you?"

She faced David down, fury speeding through her veins.

Isabel rubbed her face. "Me and Red. We've been working together."

David sighed. "Like the fuck we have time for this, let's cut to the chase. I heard rumours. Craig Davies owed me a debt; he helped pay it off by passing on information. He'd heard, through madam here, who no doubt he was shagging, that Owen was onto some stolen gold." He grinned. "I did my research and it seemed a possibility. But I needed an in. And she ..." he nodded, "was more than happy to let me in, if you know what I mean."

"Bastard," hissed Isabel.

The boat lurched, throwing Sarah and David together; a wave splashed against the side window. Sarah recoiled from him.

"Look, there's no time for this," said David, panic tightening his voice. "She has to sail this bloody boat, get us clear of the rocks."

"She? She? Don't *you* dare tell me what to do!" Sarah yelled, fists clenched at her side. "No one is going anywhere until someone tells me what the hell is going on here. Understand?" She spat the question at David; his face turned red and ugly.

Isabel reached out, pulling her away. "Don't antagonise him, Sarah. He has a temper."

"Yeah? So do I." Sarah was burning up with anger. "Okay, Isabel, where the hell is Huw?"

"I don't know." Isabel gripped hold of the seat. "I had no part of it –"

"He's safe," said David.

"That's not good enough. Where is he? If you want me to take his boat, then you better –"

As Sarah spoke, the boat tipped sideways, and a grating sound ripped through the cabin. All three of them tumbled to the port side as the gas ring, old transistor radio, cups and cutlery crashed to the floor.

"We've grounded. Oh God, we've hit the rocks," Sarah cried.

Isabel's face was ashen. "Do something, Sarah. Please, do something."

"Not until you talk. Tell me. Everything."

"But we'll drown!"

"I told you, I don't give a damn. I have nothing to live for," Sarah said calmly, reaching for her stomach. "Talk."

"What do you want to know?"

"Was it true, what you said about your mother?"

Isabel nodded. "Yes, she was a student teacher, over on an exchange from Canada. Everything I told you is true. We're half-sisters, Sarah. Surely that counts for something. I never meant for you to get hurt, for anyone to get hurt." She glanced at the covered form on the floor.

"Other than my father?" Sarah said. "I assume you were behind the poison?"

Isabel looked down. "I met Red, things spiralled out of control. I couldn't stop."

"And Martin Cole?"

David sneered. "A simpleton. So easy to manipulate. He was besotted with her, totally under her control. The only problem was he spent so much time hanging around your father's house, he saw and heard too much. He began to put two and two together. He became a big problem."

"So, you murdered him too?"

"No choice, I'm afraid. Shit!"

Sarah followed David's gaze down to the floor, where water had started to leak across the floor from the starboard side.

"And you thought you would kill two birds with one stone if you got him to confess to my father's murder at the same time. Now the meddling daughter was involved and a post mortem had proved you'd poisoned him ..."

"Clever, eh?" There was no sign of remorse in David's voice.

"And my grandmother? Where is she?"

"Safe and well as long as I remain so. Think of her as my winning lottery ticket."

"You evil bastard." Another thought shook her. "And Dom?"

Isabel nodded towards David. "If it's any comfort that wasn't intentional. It was an accident. We were intending to blackmail you. A fight broke out, Dom slipped. We had to make it look like an accident."

"I hate you so much I can hardly breathe," Sarah whispered.

"Pity you won't be getting away with it."

"Oh, but I think we will," said Isabel.

She lurched forward, throwing the small revolver across the room. David plucked it from the air and held it against the back of Sarah's head.

"I think the balance of power shifts now, eh?" said Isabel. She staggered and gripped the back of the chair as a wave lifted the boat. She waited for the deck to level before continuing. "Sarah, I don't wish to hurt you, that was never part of the plan. But there is no way, *no way*, we are going to fail now. We are so very close. I will not waste any more years of my life. I won't risk life in jail. Do you think Red will just let you go?"

"So, what are you going to do?" said Sarah.

"You are going to take us to the gold."

"B-but I don't know …"

"Don't lie!" shouted Isabel. "Enough lies. I read the letter back there. You know, or you have a very good idea. Either you take us to the gold, where we'll have no option to leave you captive just long enough for us to leave the country. Or …"

"Or … what?" Sarah asked, slipping sideways as the boat rolled again.

"Or there is yet another tragedy in the life of Sarah Morton. A boating accident … or perhaps people will think suicide is hereditary. Like your poor innocent mother. I did worry, all this talk of being haunted and ghostly girls, you're clearly not too stable. Share her genes, I bet. It would be understandable; you've had such a lot of trauma, haven't you –"

Sarah swung a fist at Isabel, but the other woman caught Sarah's wrist and twisted it hard.

"You bitch!" Sarah yelled. "Don't you dare speak my mother's name."

"Well, at last you show some backbone. Have you any idea how hard it has been to put up with your constant whinging and self-pity? Shame I no longer wish to hear it. Now, I suggest you do as Red says … and sail this boat!"

The gun nudged harder and Sarah decided she'd stalled as long as was safe. Part of her believed they wouldn't risk hurting her, not while they thought she could lead them to the treasure … but another part wasn't up for taking the risk. She pulled herself up two steps into the wheelhouse, and stared at the controls.

It was so many years since she'd sailed, and little here was familiar to the small yachts she'd known. Yes, she'd spent summer holidays helping out as a deckhand, but had never skippered an old boat of this size. She recognised a wiper switch similar to one in a car, and as soon as the cabin-shield cleared Sarah could see what peril they were actually in. Waves, ten foot high, loomed all around. The falling tide had dragged the boat a fair way out. Through heavy rain and dark skies, she could make out one or two orange lights on the horizon, land presumably. The brass compass to the right of the ship's wheel looked intimidating and unreadable, but at a guess they were faced in a northerly direction.

Sarah turned the ignition key. Nothing. She turned it a second time, and kept a grip on the key. There was a deep rumble as the engine started up somewhere below. Selecting forward drive, the boat began to move and she gripped the wheel, trying to look as if she were in control.

Sarah turned to look at Isabel and David, who were now both seated. Isabel with her head between her legs, whilst David rubbed her back with one hand. When he saw her looking, he lifted the gun, and gestured for her to concentrate on her job.

"I want to go back for Huw," Sarah called over her shoulder.

"No." David shook his head.

"Then I won't go any further. Your choice."

"Don't try to be clever. Besides, it will do you no good. He's dead."

"Dead." Sarah swallowed. "Dead?"

"Drowned. Fell overboard," said David, with a smirk. "Now sail the goddamn boat, get us back to shore as quickly as possible."

Poor Huw. Her hands shook on the wheel and her eyes flooded with tears. Another life lost. Her fault. No, she reminded herself. This was all her father's fault. Her father who could not help himself when it came to women. Who was a gullible fool all his life.

But then was she not just as gullible? Had she not fallen for Isabel's story, and her charms, too? Why had she never questioned why no one in Moelfre mentioned Isabel? Why had she not thought it odd Isabel hadn't been at her father's funeral if they were so close …?

So many questions.

But now wasn't the time. She had some serious decisions to make. How was she going to get out of this situation? Think. She had to stay alert and look for any means of escape. Sarah stifled a hysterical laugh. Not that there was much scope for a successful means of escape in a boat in the middle of the ocean at night. Was there anywhere on earth it would be harder to escape from? Now, come on! Think. What would Dom do? What would Danny …

Danny!

Sarah checked over her shoulder, both David and Isabel were deep in conversation. She wedged herself into the furthest corner, and carefully dug Lewis's mobile from her pocket. It took less than a second to access his contacts and dial Danny's number. The screen flashed and hung. No signal. Damn! She tried again. Nothing. Hardly surprising out here, but still it felt as if another of her nine lives had been cruelly snatched away. She pressed redial, and jammed the phone between two controls where it was hidden from sight.

As the wipers screeched across the small window, and waves battered the bow, she considered other options. Sail around until the fuel ran out. Take the boat into harbour and then try to out-run Isabel? Moor the boat somewhere and blag she knew where the gold was – but in the meantime somehow summon help? How? Without a mobile, did she intend to try smoke signals?

And where did this leave Grandma Ruth? She had to get help. Danny. He was her only hope.

Her gaze fell on the ship's radio. She flicked the 'on' switch, and the dials illuminated, casting a green glow across the controls. Sarah stepped to the right to block sight of her actions. Hoping neither of them noticed the glare, she picked up the handset, and took a deep breath. Whatever she did she had to be quick, there would be one chance, and one chance only.

Sarah pressed the transmit button, and winced as a loud hissing noise filled the cabin.

She kept her voice as low as possible, trying to enunciate each word.

"Mayday. Mayday. Mayday. This is Sea Goddess II. Off the north point of Ynys Dulas. We require assistance. Please. Anyone! Are you receiving? Over."

Sarah sensed movement as she switched the dial to receive.

Nothing but static.

She pressed transmit again. "Mayday. Help me, please! Are you receiving?"

Her finger wobbled as she pressed receive; a loud bump from behind shook the boat.

"Hello there. This is Holyhead Coastguard receiving –"

Bang!

Sarah screamed as the radio exploded in a shower of sparks. David stood back with a wooden oar in his hand. Sarah cowered as he brought it down repeatedly on the transmitter, grunting and sweating as he cursed. Eventually, the destruction complete, he turned towards her, fury blazing in his eyes. Sarah pushed herself against the furthest porthole, hoping it would smash, preferring the thought of the cold, black seawater.

"You clever bitch!"

He took two steps forward and pushed the oar across her throat, horizontally, pinning her head back against the glass. She began to gag. Choking, she clawed at the wood, desperate to push him away, but his grip was much stronger.

"Red! Stop. Enough." Isabel's voice.

The pressure released. Sarah opened her eyes, rubbed her throat. David's face hovered in her vision.

"Next time, I'll kill you," he hissed. "Understand?"

Sarah swallowed, nodded. She believed him.

"How much longer?" shouted Isabel from her seat. "Are we nearly back to the harbour?"

"Not much longer," Sarah croaked, rubbing her throat as David strode back to Isabel's side.

In fact, Sarah had no idea where they were. At that moment, she felt more inclined to drown them both than deliver them safely back to shore. After all, they were murderers. Did they have more right to life than Dom, Huw, Lewis or poor Martin Cole? What about her grandmother? There was no guarantee Danny had found her yet. She sobbed and rubbed her aching neck, taking her position back at the wheel, turning off the auto-pilot and manoeuvring the boat so she could try to pinpoint some navigable point, something she recognised.

'Please,' Sarah prayed silently, gazing through the windscreen at stormy skies and inky water. 'Please, God. Give me guidance. Get me though this.'

Anger writhed inside. Greed. All this through nothing more than greed and personal gain. She hated her father. She hated Isabel. David Evans. Once the loathing lodged itself inside, it refused to budge. Her thoughts were full of Dominic. Her beloved Dom. Fighting for her honour, plunging to his death. Of Lewis. Trying to defend her till the last. A red mist blurred her vision. As hard as she tried to find another solution, an escape, an opening, nothing would come. Sarah stared out at the blackness with unseeing eyes, riding the swell of the ocean, feeling its power.

And then a young girl's face appeared in her mind, long hair swirling around her face, fingers hooked like talons reaching out towards her as water pulled her deeper.

Sarah had her answer.

Chapter Twenty Two

Sarah's mind emptied as a huge flash of sea-lightning rolled across the ocean, illuminating the horizon and the recognisable outline of the cliffs at Point Lynas. It came as if a gift from the heavens. Proof that God had indeed been listening, and chosen to answer her prayers. Thunder boomed, loud enough to be heard above the noise of the waves, loud enough to drown out the resonant drum of the engine and thud of the wipers as they struggled to keep the small cabin-screen clear.

Isabel and David's voices blurred. The inside of the cabin diminished, squeezing in on her, forcing out her breath in short, sharp gasps.

Her focus was tunnel-visioned. Concentrating on the dark water, turning the boat to starboard forty-five degrees, heading towards Point Lynas.

Home of the resting place of the Royal Charter – watched over by Charter House high on the cliffs.

Sarah was coming home. Hadn't she already seen this moment? In every vision and nightmare. Hadn't Angelina Stewart done her best to save her? Every portent had shown in perfect clarity exactly where this would all end.

Hadn't her father said the same?

'Remember, the start may be your end.'

The pull was instant. Sarah could almost believe the Goddess knew her intention, accepted her fate. She pushed down on the throttle with both hands, all her strength, building towards a top speed of sixteen knots, according to the gauge. She set the steering lock and closed her eyes, mumbling a prayer. To God. To Dominic. To Angelina. To Martin … Huw … Lewis. Everyone who had perished through no fault of their own. If the Lord was on her side, she prayed she'd done enough and the Coastguard, already on alert, would arrive to rescue then. If not then their fate was in the lap of the Gods. Her fingers burrowed under the waistband of her jeans, stroking the soft downy skin. There was no more she could do; no point in high emotion, the decision was made. Final.

She thought of her mother. Her poor, sweet, innocent mother.

Perhaps it was true.

Suicide *was* hereditary.

From a hook at the side of the control desk, she quietly retrieved an aged life-jacket, and bending, slipped it over her head. She dropped to a crouch, easing herself into a small space between the desk and the hull of the boat, trying not to attract attention. The engine roared as it struggled to maintain top speed against the rough seas. The boat shuddered and lurched. She clutched her knees to her chest, tucked her head down low.

And waited.

Our father, who art in heaven. Hallowed be thy name. Thy kingdom come, thy will be done on earth as it is in heaven …

"Sarah? Sarah!" Isabel's voice. "What are you doing? Get back up here and drive –"

Sarah looked up, opened her eyes for a brief second. Isabel stood before her. *Her sister.* Swaying as she struggled to stay on her feet, her face was pale and frightened, arms outstretched. The whole boat shook now, hard enough to shake itself to pieces. Sarah braced herself with her feet against the desk and closed her eyes for a final time.

Give us this day our daily bread. And forgive us our trespasses, as we forgive those who trespass against us …

The impact was how she imagined the end of the world would sound. An explosion of noise, loud and booming. Almost beyond description. A tearing, juddering sensation that ripped the air from her lungs and rattled her insides. Then the coldness of water, rushing all around, coming from everywhere at once. Around her feet … ankles … knees.

Get up! Get up! Get moving …

She tried to stand, to pull herself upright, but staggered and fell. There was no way to tell which was floor and which ceiling. The boat was dragged and pushed, shattered into pieces all around her in a cacophony of ear-splitting noise.

Crashing … creaking … grating.

Screams, wild and scared, sounded like circling gulls.

Sarah knew she should open her eyes, but feared what she would see.

She screamed above the howl of the ocean, above the echoing destruction:

"And lead us not into temptation, but deliver us from evil. For thine is the kingdom, the power and the glory. For ever and ever. Amen!"

With a whooshing noise, Sarah was sucked out of the boat. She catapulted downwards. Invisible hands took hold of her ankles and dragged her deeper. Cold water engulfed her. Greyness swallowed her whole. She kicked out at the invisible grip, and swam for the hint of light above, knowing she could make it, feeling a rush of elation. She broke the surface, sucking mouthfuls of air. There was nothing but total blackness, nothing but the ocean and whistle of the wind.

The Sea Goddess had disappeared. How was that possible?

A massive wave washed over her, taking her by surprise, filling her mouth with acrid water. She choked, spluttered, tried to tread water, but again the invisible force yanked her downwards. The sane part of her brain knew it was the currents, the strong riptides, but in her paranoia she believed it was David. He'd come after her! She remembered his fury, his insistence he would kill her. No!

Again, she kicked out and her legs became entangled. She looked down. Through the murkiness, she could make out massive fronds of kelp, slithering around her ankles and calves. Sarah opened her mouth to scream; icy water rushed into her lungs. She gagged and spat, losing the initiative to swim, forgetting to use her arms. She panicked, her body trapped in the life jacket, twisting and turning as she was pushed and pulled by the combined forces of seaweed and tide.

Her energy began to slip away. It was palpable. She forced herself to breathe, to gulp another mouthful of air into her screaming lungs, and then again she was sucked beneath the surface. As she grew weaker, her kicks became more and more inadequate.

She was drowning.

The reality forced some last miniscule ounce of strength from her aching body. She pushed upwards, swimming with all her might. Cold air hit her – cool, wonderful night air. She panted and forced her eyes open. Splintered bits of wood, a tatty red cushion, and a lifejacket floated by. Then she recognised Isabel, face down in the water, motionless. With clarity of thought Sarah would never have believed, she reached out and caught hold of the yellow inflatable, tugging it over Isabel's head and twisting the still form onto her back. Her face was slack and grey, but there was a flicker of pulse under the taut skin of her temple. Sarah tightened the life belt and fastened the Velcro straps. Wedging open Isabel's mouth, she cleared her hair from her face, and tipped her onto her side. A torrent of grey water gushed from her mouth and she began to splutter.

Sarah gripped hold of Isabel's head, forcing her body to float, as she kicked water beneath them.

Isabel's eyes fluttered open, rested on Sarah, and closed.

Sarah controlled her breathing, teeth chattering with cold, and kept her focus on the distant twinkle of stars.

'Thank you, God. Thank you, Lord. Thank you. Thank you.

Thank you.'

It was cold. So very cold. Better to keep moving. She splashed with her hands, kicking out to the side, hoping she could see land. If she had a point to head for then they might just make it. She knew they'd crashed into cliffs, cliffs she knew well enough, what she didn't know was how far the current had chosen to take her. She turned a full rotation. Nothing. She kicked out and turned back the same way, scanning the surface for any sign of life. She knew now how those poor victims of the Royal Charter had felt, so close to land, within sight of life. And yet still claimed by death.

The waves rose around her, and when they dropped down into the swell, she was surrounded by nothing but walls of water. Waiting until they reached the crest of the next massive wave, Sarah used the opportunity to shout out as well as search the horizon. Her teeth chattered; her voice was weak, ineffective. The blackness total. Isabel's body was a leaden weight that made her shoulders scream in pain.

The cold numbed its way through her clothes, her skin, burrowing deeper. It was okay once you got used to it, comfortable at least. They could wait. The night would end; dawn would show her the way. The tide would turn; wash them up on some remote beach.

Carry them home.

Sarah stopped kicking, wedged Isabel's lifejacket across her lap, laid back her head and closed her eyes. Her teeth rattled and there was no feeling in her hands, arms, shoulders. Her legs ached, her trousers weighted like leaded balloons.

She needed to sleep. Just for a while. She was so tired.

She turned her face into the smooth, warmth of the lifejacket.

Closed her eyes.

Carry her home.

* * *

Danny felt sick. Things were going from bad to worse. And he only had one choice left.

He knocked sharply on the door and pushed it open without waiting for a response.

Thompson looked up from his computer; his open-eyed astonishment soon narrowing into an angry scowl.

"Forgotten your manners today, Buchanan?" he barked.

"I'm sorry, sir. I need your help."

Thompson twisted his seat forwards and nodded to the vacant chair opposite.

Danny chose to stand, gripping the back of the chair with white knuckles. "I think I might have fu- messed up, sir."

Thompson pulled himself straight. "Go on."

Danny gave a garbled account of the previous day. The kidnapping and his decision to send DS Lewis in his place were given priority. Thompson clenched his hands into one solid mass on the desk as Danny talked.

"Okay." Thompson leaned forward. "A bit of a balls up, I'll admit, and again you've taken on more than I would have chosen. But I can't see a major problem."

Danny sighed down his frustration. "They should have been back hours ago, sir. I've been trying their mobiles all day. Sarah's, er Mrs Morton's rings out, and DS Lewis's phone tried to connect and kept cutting off. About ten minutes ago it went dead altogether. But I heard, well, at least I thought I heard …"

"Spit it out, Buchanan."

"Screaming."

"Screaming?"

Danny nodded. "Like a child, sobbing and screaming. And now it's totally dead."

"Right. So you think … what?"

"I don't know. That's the thing. But I know Lewis. He wouldn't have left it this long to get in touch. Plus, I was checking on the local weather, and a storm has hit Anglesey. It's a force eight, I think. And it's bad enough here." Danny gestured to the window, where trees were bowing against the wind, rain beating a steady rhythm on the glass.

"Christ, Buchanan, why didn't you keep me in the loop, we could have called HQ and used one of our boats with proper communication channels to get out there. Last thing we need is more civilians involved because you choose to employ Captain Birdseye and a fishing fleet." He thumped the desk. "Let me think."

"It was the kidnapper, sir, he said he'd be watching …"

"I said let me think!"

Danny bit down on his lip, tapping his toe against the chair. Something had happened. He knew it. He *felt* it. And when he'd heard that sobbing child through Lewis's phone, sure in God's name … well, how he'd not shit himself. He'd never heard such a noise.

Thompson pulled his phone towards him. "Right. Let's scramble the Coastguard. Get me a map. You do know where this place is, I take it?"

Danny nodded, raced out into the main office, and yanked the Ordnance Survey map from his desk. A cold mug of coffee slid to the floor, shattering into pieces. It rolled under DS Mayou's desk, splashing his trousers with brown stains.

"Shit, Buchanan, you clumsy bloody oaf –"

But Danny was already in the corridor. Seconds later, the map was open on Thompson's desk. Danny pointed out the area of coastline. The DI was speaking slowly and patiently into the receiver. "Ah, yes, that's good, thank you. Yes, Lligwy Bay. And a small island called Ynys Dulas."

Thompson held his hand over the receiver, glancing up at Danny. "HQ is checking with the Coastguard."

Danny nodded, clenching his hands into fists. He was frozen, colder than he could remember. Fear flowed through his bloodstream and it was as much as he could do to stop himself shaking. If anything happened to Lewis, it would be his fault, sending his partner in his place. And if anything should happen to Sarah Morton, after all she'd been through ...

"Hello."

Danny focused.

Thompson spent a few moments listening, then looked up. "Do you know the name of the boat they've gone out in?"

Danny shook his head. "I don't think so ..."

"Christ, you either do or you don't. Is it the Sea Goddess? Get a grip, man!"

Danny tried to remember, overhearing Sarah's conversation with the old sailor, back in the hall at Charter House. He recalled her worried face; the slight hint of a smile as she'd given a thumbs up, slammed down the receiver and said ...

Danny nodded. "Yes. Huw the Boat. Sea Goddess. That's the name."

Thompson relayed the information, then replaced the receiver. His mouth was a thin red line scarring his face. He stood and pulled his jacket from the back of his chair.

"What?" said Danny.

"What, sir." Thompson shrugged on his coat. "They've had a Mayday call from a boat called the Sea Goddess about ten minutes ago. No details. They've already sent Holyhead and Moelfre Inshore boats out. I've politely requested they contact RAF Valley, get a helicopter out there too as it's quicker. I've explained we've got an officer in need of assistance."

Danny thought his knees might collapse. "Where are you going ... sir?"

"*We* are going out to Moelfre. See if this mess can be sorted. And you better be right about this. My reputation's on the line here."

Danny wanted to respond, to say, personally, he hoped he was wrong. One hundred percent wrong, and they were all back at Charter House, sharing out a bucketful of gold at this very moment. But they weren't. He knew as much, even if he'd no idea how. He forced himself to let go of the back of the chair, and hurried to catch up with Thompson's retreating form. He wanted to thank his boss for coming up with the goods when it most mattered. But there was no time, and besides, Danny had a sick feeling it might be too little, too late.

* * *

Sarah jolted awake. The noise of an engine, loud and drumming. She inched open her eyes; the glare of intense whiteness forced them shut again. She was trying to sleep, what the hell was going on? She became aware of a man's voice. Counting?

"Nine … eight … seven."

Was she dreaming? She had to be dreaming.

"Six … five … a tad to the right, guys. Lower, lower, lower. Slowly does it. Three … two … okay. Down. Down. Down. Got her!"

Strong hands grabbed underneath her armpits. Sarah waved an arm in a weak attempt to push them away. A hand grabbed her wrist and squeezed. Hard fingers pushed into her neck. She tried to struggle, tried to voice her pain, but no words would come.

More shouting.

"She's alive. And conscious. Just. Send down another wire. Cheers guys."

It was no good; there was no chance of sleeping through this. Sarah opened one eye, squinting against the bright light. She'd never seen anything like it. It was ethereal. Was this heaven?

"Am I d-dead?" Sarah whispered, trying desperately to stop her teeth rattling.

"What's that, lovely?"

"Is this h-heaven?"

A mumbled laugh. "'Fraid not. More like hell."

She continued to bob gently on the tide, the thudding noise grew louder, the light ever brighter. The strong hands were at work again, tugging at her clothing. Something warm tickled her ear; a voice loud and clear.

"Right. We're going to lift you now. You're clipped onto me, so you've nothing to worry about. I just want you to stay as still as possible. Nod if you understand, lovely."

Sarah nodded. She wasn't deaf. No need to shout.

"Okay, guys. Ready to lift in three. Three … two … one."

Suddenly, she was flying. It was amazing. She didn't care what anyone said, she had to be dead. Dead or dreaming. She couldn't fly. Not in the real world. The sea began to slip away and the sky got nearer and nearer. Wow, she really was going to heaven!

A hand on the back of her head pushed her face forwards into soft fabric, and she snuggled her cheek into its warmth. It was the softest pillow ever. A roaring noise filled her ears, an icy wind whipped around her head. But she felt safe. The strong hands gripped her. More strong hands lifted her, slid her backwards. More voices.

All she wanted, needed, was to sleep. With a giant yawn, she closed her eyes.

Sarah pulled the blanket up under her chin, and rolled onto her side. Her forehead bumped against something solid and she jerked awake. Her head throbbed and a loud thudding filled the small room. Everything seemed to be vibrating. The floor, the walls, her bed. Where was she? And what the hell was that noise?

She pushed her nose above the blanket. Before she could speak, hands were lifting her. A cup of something warm was pushed towards her face. She opened her mouth, swallowing down the hot honey-flavoured drink in grateful gulps. She coughed and spluttered, forcing herself to sip slowly. Sarah licked her lips as the drink warmed her insides. Someone wiped her chin, before lowering her head back onto the pillow.

She tried to move, but her arms seemed to be taped to her sides, legs bound in a similar fashion. She flexed her fingers and felt naked flesh on her hips and thighs. Pushing herself up onto her elbows, she looked down. She was covered from head to toe in tinfoil.

Her head hurt. It hurt to think. Everything was fuzzy, distorted. Turning carefully, she glanced around the darkened space. In the shadow, two people were hunched over a covered form, flat on a stretcher. One man, with a bright yellow crash helmet, pressed insistently with both hands, then bent every few minutes to give the kiss of life. Sarah watched the scene, understanding but not quite understanding. It was such an odd sensation, like she was drugged. Had there been an accident, and why could she not remember anything?

She took her weight on her elbows and turned to her right. Huw the Boat sat propped against the far wall, wrapped in a similar silver blanket. He smiled and Sarah smiled back as he gestured to the Bacofoil. He rolled his eyes and gave his trademark toothless grin. Sarah was glad to see he looked as ridiculous as she felt.

She dropped back onto the grey pillow, the effort exhausting. Was this another dream? God, she wished that bloody noise would stop. A headache pounded against her temples. A face appeared, blond hair, a square jaw, blue helmet. The man smiled. A nice smile, laughter lines crinkled round his eyes.

"Hello, lovely. I'm Sergeant Andy Henson. You probably don't remember but we met earlier."

Sarah smiled and nodded. But hadn't got a clue.

"We're on our way to Rhyl. Just to let you know we'll be landing in about fifteen minutes, okay?"

She nodded again.

"You're suffering from hypothermia, so we need to keep you tightly wrapped and give you regular fluids. How're you feeling?"

"Fine. I can't remember … where am I?"

"You're on a RAF search and rescue Sea-King helicopter."

"What?"

Sarah struggled to sit up. Firm hands pushed her down.

"Relax, lovely. You're in safe hands. None better. Flight

Lieutenant Gavin Morris is at the controls, and we're Rescue 182 squad from RAF Valley. We're the best, if I do say so myself. Award winning, in fact we are. So, you just lie back and enjoy the ride."

"What happened? Why can't I remember?"

"Short term memory loss is a common symptom of hypothermia. Don't you worry, lovely. Soon as your brain starts to thaw, you'll start remembering things. Probably some things you'd sooner then forget. Just rest, okay. We'll be landing at Glan Clywd Hospital before you know it. We've been diverted from Bangor. They have some emergency power failure in A&E, so apologies for the delay …"

His words drowned out. Hospital! Oh God, last time she was there …

Sarah gasped. "My baby!"

Sergeant Andy's face came up close. "Hey, you pregnant, lovely?"

She nodded, biting down on her lip, willing herself not to cry. Hating the feeling of helplessness, her fingers burrowed inside the tight layers of blankets, seeking out her stomach.

"Hang on there two minutes, lovely. I'll be right back."

Her fingers reached the tiny bump. It was still there! She stroked the cool skin, mouthing a prayer for her baby.

Seconds later, the tightness around her middle started to release. She breathed deeper, then yelped as something smooth and cold pressed into her stomach.

Sergeant Henson's smiling face appeared beside her again.

"Hear. Take a listen." He slipped an earpiece into her ear. There was a rhythmic gallop - thud-thud-thud. "That's your baby's heartbeat. Alive and well."

"Thank you," Sarah whispered, unable to stop tears rolling down her cheeks.

"It's my pleasure. My wife is pregnant, our first. This your first?" Sarah nodded and sniffed. He added, "I always have my stethoscope handy, lie at night in bed listening to his little heartbeat. Hey, you've one tough little boy or girl inside there. You make sure you look after them." He re-adjusted the blankets.

"It's a girl," she said.

"Congratulations," he replied. "I'm just going to radio ahead to the hospital; let them know we're on our way. Back soon, okay?"

"Sure. Could I get another of those drinks please?"

He made an okay gesture with his finger and thumb, then disappeared from view.

Sarah turned her face into the roughness of the pillow. She was stiff, uncomfortable, aching. Suffering from hypothermia, so the sergeant said. On a RAF helicopter... on her way to hospital ...

Something clicked inside her brain. An avalanche of memories cascaded, sweeping in and leaving her breathless.

She sat up straight.

"Huw!"

Huw opened his eyes, smiled.

"You're alive!"

"Aye."

"But ... but ... he said. David said ..." Sarah swallowed. Fear gripped her as everything came back. Everything. "Oh Huw, the Goddess. I'm so sorry –"

"That's enough now, del. You're suffering from the shock. You relax, there's nothing that can't be sorted."

"But the boat, there was a storm. It's wrecked. I-I wrecked it."

Sarah closed her eyes. Images swirled. Gun shots. Icy water. Crashing timbers. The feel of slippery hands on her ankles dragging her beneath the waves. Sounds and smells accompanied the flashbacks playing out on the inside of her eyelids. She groaned and pitched forward as a wave of nausea rose inside her. Tears sprang to her eyes and sobs echoed around the enclosed space, muffled by the thud of engine or rotor blades.

There was a shuffling noise and Huw's voice came from close by.

"Now, you stop them tears, you hear? They'll be thinking I've caused it. Do you want to see me thrown out for bad behaviour?" She tried to smile, sniffed. Huw added, "Don't get going over things in your head now, there's too much to take in. You're in shock. Just relax."

"You don't understand. The Sea Goddess is wrecked –"

"I know. I've seen and heard much of what's gone on. The boat's insured. You're alive. That's important thing. I can always buy another boat. Can't replace a human life, del. Always remember."

"But you loved that boat –"

"Aye, that I did. But I can replace her. I loved my wife too. When she died, I couldn't replace her. I learnt a valuable lesson that day. Mind you, perhaps it's time I retired. Use the insurance money towards a nice little bungalow, and enjoy the rest of my days."

"I'm so sorry about all this. I've been such a fool – Isabel!" All was quiet around the stretcher. "Is she …?" Sarah couldn't make herself say the word, but she remembered the grey face floating, lifeless, on the water.

Huw spoke gently. "I think it's touch and go, del, but they're keeping her alive."

"Oh, God."

Huw leaned against her; one nut-coloured hand stroked her arm. "Sarah, forget about all that's happened, just concentrate on getting well. There will be time for the inquest later. Police and whatnot."

Police. Lewis. Sarah groaned. Her stomach heaved and her mouth was full of the taste of salt water. "What a mess. Do you know if they found anyone else alive?" She looked into Huw's eyes, saw his expression harden. "Please tell me. I need to know."

"I heard the Sergeant talking earlier. He said Moelfre and Holyhead sent lifeboats to the scene. I heard they recovered a body."

Sarah shuddered. "Just one?"

Huw shook his head. "Sorry, del, I don't know."

Her mouth filled with the memory of bitter salt water and she retched.

Sarah cleared her throat. "What if … I mean, will the police charge me with murder if David and Lewis are dead?"

"I don't think you should be worrying your head about that. I'm sure the police will believe you. Why wouldn't they? You just make sure you get the story straight. How you weren't used to handling a boat, got hit by a storm, lost control and hit the rocks."

"But that wasn't how it was, Huw. I deliberately wrecked the Goddess. I knew *exactly* what I was doing. There was a flash of lightning, I saw Point Lynas and I knew what I had to do. I can't explain it. It almost felt as if I weren't really in control, that someone else was taking charge. But it was me. I could get charged, couldn't I?"

"Calm down, now. Like I say, best we get our story straight before we talk to the police. Best you never repeat that again, okay? With no witnesses, they'll have little choice but to believe us."

"God, I hope so," Sarah whispered.

"I promise you, del. Nothing to worry about."

"So, what happened to you?" she asked, needing to change the subject before her paranoia turned to hysteria. "He told me you were dead."

"Well, it wasn't nowhere near as dramatic as what you've been through, I'd imagine. Mind, left there much longer I think I'd have perished."

"Left where?"

"The lad, David … he tied me up, left me in a cave."

"How did he get you there? Did he hurt you?"

Huw shook his head. "No. He appeared on deck, banging on the door in a right state, jabbering he'd hit rocks, round in the next cove, and his friend was injured. Got me to follow him with some cock and bull story, and half way round the headland he pulled a gun on me." Huw paused. "Odd, you know, I figured I recognised him from the off. But you get old and your memory … pah. He forced me into a cave. I asked what was going on, where was the boat. And he just laughed and said there was no boat. Anyway, he tied me up. Said he was stealing the Goddess, but he'd notify the Coastguard once he'd put distance between us."

"Were you scared?"

"Aye, a little." Huw sighed. "I was more concerned about you and the other gal and that copper. To start with I thought it was a robbery. Then I figured it was too much of a coincidence, started to wonder about a connection. I'd managed an old trick of keeping my hands apart when he tied them, so it wasn't long afore I was free. And luckily, being a helpless old fella, he hadn't bothered to search my pockets."

"Why?" Sarah asked. "What did you have? A knife?"

"No." Huw smiled. "A mobile phone."

They both managed a laugh. "So, you called the rescue services. I thought my radio skills had worked. I tried to send a Mayday call from the Goddess."

"Aye, I called the Coastguard. But just as they were winching me on-board, a call came in that a boat had run aground on Point Lynas. I knew the minute I heard. Was almost like someone walked over me grave. I begged them to go to the scene, not to worry about me. I didn't need no hospital treatment, no fuss, so I did my best to explain my fears. And seems I was right."

"You probably saved my life. Thank you, Huw." Sarah leaned across and kissed his leathery cheek. "And in return, I wrecked your pride and joy …"

"I shan't tell you again. I don't want details. I trust you did what you had to."

"I wish I could say I did, Huw. I fear I lost my mind. You see, it was all lies, everything she told me. She took advantage of the fact I'd been separated from my father. She played on my past. And I swallowed it all. I'm such a fool."

"Now then –"

"No, I am. You have no idea. They were evil and I didn't see it. To think someone I grew up with could actually try and kill me … and he killed Dom …" Sarah shook her head. "I saw Isabel shoot Lewis. Pure greed. So many people died just because she wanted the gold all to herself. And she used me to help her find it. When in fact, I'm beginning to doubt the gold ever existed. What a mess. I can't believe it, really, I just can't believe it. "

"I can, del. Greed can do strange things to folk, turn them to do right wicked things."

"You can say that again …"

Huw smiled and shook his head. "They always say history repeats itself. Aye, that they do."

Sarah frowned. "How'd you mean?"

"Well, greed was the cause of so many deaths when the Charter went down, weren't it? Miners desperate not to lose the gold, strapped it to their bodies, and their families, and the weight sent 'em straight to the bottom."

"And now, hundred and fifty years later, how many lives has the same gold cost? My father. Dom. Martin Cole. Lewis. More victims of the Charter. And now … now …" Sarah choked as memories of how close she'd come to drowning filled her mind. "I thought I was going to die, Huw. I said a prayer, closed my eyes, and thought I'd killed my baby."

Tears rolled down her cheeks. Huw patted the lump in the silver blanket where her hand rested on her tummy.

"But you didn't, del. You fought. You did all you could to escape and survive. Who knows what might've happened otherwise. I don't think you have to worry about the police not believing your version of events. Not when you expose these two as murderers. You did the right thing, del. God was looking after you."

"I don't know. Perhaps, I got blinded by the thought of hidden treasure too."

"No, you were doin' what your da asked of you. No more. You

weren't driven by greed or evil. I have no worries on that score."

"Thank you, Huw."

Sergeant Henson reappeared with two steaming mugs.

"Take it you two know each other?" he said as he dropped down beside them and took a seat on a pile of boxes. "This would be one hell of a coincidence, otherwise."

Huw nodded, and winked at me. "Aye, I know this brave young woman. And proud to say I do at that."

"Yes, I know this man who saved my life with his selflessness."

"Then I think you should both consider yourself right lucky," said Sergeant Henson.

Sarah took a long gulp and worked up courage to ask the question eating away at me.

"Is she alive?" Sarah nodded to the stretcher.

"For now …"

"Any other survivors? Please, I really need to know."

"One body found so far. I've no details," he said, seeing the question on her lips. "Moelfre and Holyhead lifeboats are both still at the scene. They'll search at least till daybreak, probably most of tomorrow too. I promise they'll do all they can."

"God rest their souls," said Huw, making the sign of the cross.

Chapter Twenty Three

Wind swayed bare sycamore branches as Sarah made her way along the cobbled path, remembering the last time she'd walked here, supported by Dom's arms, kicking through piles of leaves. This was where it started, where she'd been approached by the solicitor, Adrian Carter, and his mysterious words about her father's bequest.

Remember, the end will be your starting point.

Now, perhaps Sarah really understood her father's words for the first time.

Llanallgo Church.

Its history with the Royal Charter, as well as with her family, was complex. Both her father and mother had been christened, married and buried here. And the majority of the victims of the shipwreck were interred in its churchyard. Why had she never considered its importance before?

The past week was one to wipe from memory as soon as possible. Another two-night stay in hospital in the next room to her grandmother. Grandma Ruth had been kept in for observation, following her rescue from a caravan hidden inside a barn on the Evans's land. Luke had led them there, realising his brother had been hiding out on the part of the estate left to him in their father's Will.

Sarah fought a constant battle against memories of how near she'd come to drowning, to dying. And, other than a late night trip down the corridor outside the window of the ICU, she hadn't been able to visit Isabel. She was still in a coma, doctors inducing the state to give her brain time to heal. They were hopeful, that was all they would say.

For Thomas more than anyone, Sarah hoped Isabel recovered. But as Danny pointed out, she'd be facing a life sentence if she did. Who knew which was worse for a young woman with a child?

She'd also faced another round of police interviews. Despite Huw's warning, she'd had to relate the real version of events out at Point Lynas, and how she'd wrecked the boat. Danny comforted and calmed her, and the bond between them grew.

There would be no charges. She was free to rebuild her life.

"If Lewis's body is never recovered, if the sea claims him, I think it would be what he'd prefer," said Danny, wiping away a tear. "He was always unconventional. A good man. By Christ, I'll miss him. One day I'm sure I'll stop blaming myself."

Sarah touched his sleeve. "It wasn't your fault. It wasn't Lewis's. He died protecting me. I'm the one who should feel bad. So many deaths, so much of it my fault."

"You will get through this, Sarah," Danny said. "I told you once; I'd lost the person I loved most in the world. Cancer. Dinah was only forty-one. I was her toy-boy. We'd laugh about that." Danny smiled. "We were together ten years. In the end, her pain got too much, and she took an overdose. I was there. I often think I should have stopped her, the sanctity of life an' all that, but I promised her I wouldn't. And I didn't. I'm fierce sorry she's gone and I miss her every day. I've never told anyone how it eats me up inside. So, I understand, Sarah. I do."

Now, Sarah found herself back among the gravestones where both her mother and father lay. She paused at a crossroads in the path. Could she go left, to her visit her parents' grave? Was she ready to accept her mother's betrayal? Yes, she understood. But accepting it was harder. Was she strong enough to face *him* yet? She shook her head. Not today. Not yet.

Had Sarah known the truth, the real truth, about her mother's death, she would not have forced her to spend all eternity lying beside her father, whose treachery still left Sarah numb. Perhaps the forgiveness he begged may come one day, but right now she could see no hope. The memories of her mother, that sense of unconditional love and security, had been the one thing that kept Sarah going, through both the worst days of her father's drinking, and the lonely days and nights when she first left home and faced the solitude of the big city. He had robbed her of every single memory. Now, they seemed a charade; a bitter web of lies and deceit that if allowed to flourish would ruin her life a second time over.

Remember, the end will be your starting point.

Sarah chose the right hand path. Today, she was here to discover the truth; this was no time for bitterness. No time for recrimination; no one to take her frustrations out on now. She could not let hatred burn her up. She could not let it ruin her future as easily as she'd allowed it to consume her past.

Her gaze sought out the gravestones lining the path; a mixture of small slate tombs and high granite obelisks. She was amazed, once her eyes registered the words, at the amount of references to the Royal Charter. Every other grave seemed to hold a victim of the shipwreck.

Sarah stopped in front of a large slate tomb, surrounded by a silver-painted fence. Gripping the spikes, she squinted to read the inscription.

'Sacred to the memory of the Rev-d
Stephen Roose Hughes A.M
for 20 years Rector of Llanallgo and Llaneugrad.
He was a faithful Pastor, a warm hearted friend,
and charitable to the poor.
He died February 4th 1862. Aged 47.
Blessed are the merciful for they shall obtain mercy.'

Warm tears welled as she read the words, and squeezed her nose with a gloved hand. She hoped those final words proved true.

She remembered from the research Hughes had spent months, years, trying to contact over one thousand relatives in Australia. No mean feat with the technology of the day. He'd spent many painful hours trying to identify the dead. The stress was said to have caused his premature death. Perhaps here lay the first victim of the Royal Charter, who had not actually been on the stricken vessel on that night in October 1859.

The first of many.

Sarah stepped back onto the path and followed it to the church door, ducking her head and standing inside the porch. Another sign she'd never bothered to read before caught her attention.

'Llanallgo Church together with its sister Church of Llaneugrad was originally built at the beginning of the 7th Century. It has become famous due to the fact that 140 victims of the wreck of the Royal Charter in 1859 are buried in the Churchyard and also for the ministry of the then Rector, the Reverend Stephen Roose Hughes to the bereaved.

Charles Dickens was instrumental in raising subscriptions for the Monument to the victims which can be seen behind the Church and an account of his visit to the Parish following the tragedy can be found in the opening chapter of his book 'The Uncommercial Traveller.'

The Church is always open for prayer and meditation and our hope is that you will experience God's Love, His Peace and His Blessing.'

She wasn't ready yet to enter. She returned to the cobbled path, followed as it curved around the side of the church. There, almost up against the far wall of the consecrated ground was the monument to the Royal Charter. Almost six feet tall, the four-sided obelisk seemed to reside over the rest of the churchyard with an imposing authority. Sarah had never been to this side of the church; it was at the opposite end to her parents' grave, and although in the past she must have known about the memorial, she'd never stood on this spot before, never bothered to read the words.

Sarah negotiated the muddy ground and read the first inscription.

'*This monument has been erected by public subscription to the memory of those who perished in the wreck of the ROYAL CHARTER off MOELFRE on the coast of ANGLESEY on her passage from AUSTRALIA to ENGLAND. Wednesday the 26th Day of October AD 1859.*'

She stepped round to the right, following the inscription in a clock-wise direction.

'*The Royal Charter. Steam clipper of 2719 tons burthe sailed from Melbourne, Australia, August 26th AD 1859. Bound for Liverpool having on board 371 passengers besides a crew of 107.*'

The third side read.

'*There lie in this Churchyard remains of 140 of the sufferers and 45 in the Churchyard of Penrhos Lligwy all of whom were buried by the Pious and Charitable Incumbents of Rev-d Stephen Roose Hughes and his brother Rev-d Hugh Robert Hughes.*'

The fourth.

'*The remains of many of the sufferers lie near the following Churchyards. Llanallgo: Llaneugard; Penrhos Lligwy: Llanwenllwyn: Llanfair Mathafarn: Llanbedrgoch: Pentraeth: Llanddona: Amlwch.*'

Stepping forward, she slipped off her glove and laid her palm flat against the dampness of the stone. She wondered if Angelina, or her mother, lay in one of the local churchyards, unidentified. Or if it were true Charles Stewart had searched in vain, inspecting every single body pulled from the sea, only to find his family still missing. How easy it was to understand the madness that drove him to build Charter House, and fight so hard to recover the gold he considered rightfully his. Not least because it had wiped out half of the beloved family he'd dragged across the globe to start a new life with its profits.

Had his genes, his insecurities, been passed down to her father?

Was there not a distinct similarity in the lives of the two men? Had they not caused the death of their wives, leaving one child to suffer the effects on their lives? Neither wore their scars well, neither coped quietly with their burden. The tales she'd heard of her father's paranoia in recent years, seemed to echo the lengths Charles Stewart had gone to defend his home and his fortune, leading them both to the black tower on Ynys Dulas. The pattern of both men's downfalls seemed frighteningly similar.

She could hear Huw's words. *'They always say history repeats itself. Aye, that they do.'*

"Sarah, bach."

A quiet voice broke her thoughts. She stepped back onto the path, peered round the monument. Grandma Ruth stood at the corner of the church. One hand gripping her walking stick, the other a navy handbag. She was dressed in her Sunday best, even though it was Friday. She looked scared, worried. Sarah gave her a smile, and made her way towards her, enveloping her frailness in a warm embrace. She looked over her shoulder. Luke hovered at the crossroads in the path, hands in pockets.

"I'll be right back," she whispered. "I'll meet you in the church, okay? We can talk there."

Her grandmother nodded, and Sarah supported her elbow as she climbed the steps.

"Luke," Sarah said. "Thanks for bringing Gran. I appreciate it." She paused. "Is it my imagination or have you been avoiding me?"

Luke looked down. "I can't do this right now, Sarah. There's so much I want to say but the guilt outweighs everything else. I should have known. He was living on our land, virtually next door to me. How could I not have known?"

"Quite easily. Your brother had an evil streak, Luke, that's for sure. But he was also very clever and manipulative. I don't think anyone connects him with you and I don't think you should think that way either. You came good in the end. Gran's safe. That's all that matters."

"Thank God I thought of the old poacher's cottage. I'd not been out that way in years, never knew about that caravan. He knew that, no doubt. I can't tell you what a relief it was to find your gran, safe and well. I couldn't have lived with myself if … well, you know."

"Believe me, in the guilt stakes, I'm way above you. But life goes on."

"I know. And I'll be around soon; time's a healer and all that. I won't be a stranger, don't worry. I've got to sort David's funeral, I don't want to, but he's still my brother and it's what my parents would expect of me. It's a cremation anyway, what he wanted." Luke breathed out. "Once that's over, I hope I can move on."

"I hope so, Luke. We need you."

He shoved his hands deep into his pockets. "Right, I'll leave you be. You have a lot to discuss with Grandma Ruth."

"Thanks. I think Reverend Thomas is meeting us here shortly. Not sure why."

Sarah frowned, remembering the tearful conversation with her grandmother at the hospital. It had been her grandmother's suggestion they met here at her church.

The door creaked as Sarah entered the church; footsteps echoing as she crossed the stone floor. It was eerily quiet and dim after the glare of the winter's sun. Grandma Ruth sat on the end of the third row of pews, eyes closed and hands clasped, while her lips moved in prayer. Otherwise, the church was empty. Sarah settled herself in the second row, and concentrated on the crucifix above the altar; its symbolism connecting for the first time in her life. Betrayal. How real it felt at the moment; how deep the pain inflicted by a modern day Judas.

A hand touched her shoulder. "Are you okay, bach?"

"Getting there. And what did Doc Davies say?"

"Clean bill of health. I don't know why all the fuss. I was in a caravan, hardly life threatening. Some folks choose it as a way of life."

Sarah smiled. "So, why are we here? Couldn't we have talked back at Charter House?"

Grandma Ruth looked up at the altar. "I'd always dreaded the day would come. A part of me perhaps hoping it never would, that I would carry the secret to my grave. But you can't change what's done."

"I saw the paintings." Sarah shivered; saw the flash of pain in her gran's eyes. "I can't believe she painted them. I can't believe she had that inside her –"

"She didn't!" Gran's voice rose. "He put it there. He bred it inside of her. And it festered and it festered. I thought painting would help, maybe ease the pain, fill her time at least." She sighed. "That summer, nothing I did seemed to help, seemed to make the slightest bit of difference. She would go for days without speaking a word. The only time she smiled was when she saw you, but then every smile ended in tears, and I was scared in the end to leave you alone with her."

"I don't remember any of this," Sarah said. "I remember living with you for a while. I think I thought they'd gone on holiday, and then I recall you saying Mother got some contagious illness. I thought it was measles or something. Nothing seemed out of the ordinary. Nothing stays with me until the morning you woke me and said Mother had been in an accident, and she was never coming home –"

Tears choked her. Nausea settled a vice-like grip on her stomach.

"Then at least in the normality, I managed to do one thing right by you, bach. For that same reason, I lied to you that day. And yes, there's been days I've hated and regretted that decision. But if I had my time over, I'd probably do the same again. I couldn't wreck your life, ruin your childhood or involve you in a bitter feud between me and your father. So, I lied. I lied and covered up for him. But I did it for you. Everything I did was for you. Not for him. I didn't care whether he lived or died. But I wanted you to have a good life, a happy life. Not one tainted by the suicide of your mother."

Her voice trembled on the word, and when Sarah looked up she was wiping tears from her powdered cheeks. "I begged and begged him to let me keep you after Sarah died. I didn't have his money but I knew I could have given you a decent life, and love you more than he ever would. It broke my heart when he sent you away to boarding school. Just so he could move in another of his floozies, no doubt."

The anger in her voice was unmistakable, even though she remained straight backed, fully in control.

Sarah cleared her throat. "He said he had to send me away because it hurt too much to see me growing up, looking more like my mother every day. I think he really did love her, in this own way. He said so in his last letter … " Gran gave a loud grunt. "And I never remember any other women at Charter House. I won't defend him, but I suppose that is to his credit."

"He didn't need to bring them home," Gran snapped. "I heard he had a flat at the university he kept for that kind of thing. I have no doubt he cheated on your mother all through their marriage, but it was only when this language teacher gave him an ultimatum that things turned ugly."

Sarah stared, shocked by the clear hatred in her gran's voice, even now so many years later.

In the same tone, she added. "Right enough, six months later, your mother was dead and the Canadian gone back to her own country, with a pile of his cash, so rumour had it. Her prayers were answered, and he got what he deserved. Not that it brought my Sarah back. But he had his own demons to contend with there, I knew that. I never spoke to him again, once he refused to let you live with me. I hated him so much I feared what I would do, truth be told."

"I can't believe I knew nothing about any of this."

"Think yourself lucky you didn't, bach. It can eat you up. Many a time, I regretted covering up Sarah's suicide. But I couldn't bear people knowing what depths he'd led her to." She put her hand over Sarah's. "You mustn't hate her. You must never for one second think she didn't love you. Oh, cariad, she adored you. But in the end, she wasn't really there anymore; she had no idea what she was doing. I don't want you to carry more burden for the rest of your life. Your mother loved you utterly. I promise you that."

It was as if her gran could read the thoughts eating away at Sarah's heart. Why? Why had Mother left if she truly loved her? Tears dripped from the end of her nose. She'd not even realised she was crying. Sarah wiped them away with an impatient swipe of her glove, and leaned over to plant a gentle kiss on her gran's tear-streaked cheek.

"Thank you," Sarah whispered, and could say no more.

A few minutes later, her gran added. "I said to you once, bach, that it was amazing what a mother would do for her child. I hope you understand now."

Sarah took a deep breath and blew her nose. "When I first heard, I didn't know what to think. Why you hadn't told me? Why everyone lied to me? But you said to me once that we do our best, what we think is right, and live by the results. So, yes … I understand."

"I think if you'd stayed around here as you got older, I would have told you. But I never got a chance."

Sarah unzipped her jacket, and from the inside pocket,

removed a creased sheet of writing paper and handed it across.

"This was the letter I found with the paintings. I think you should read it."

Grandma Ruth opened the paper carefully; its edges tattered, and ink smudged where it had dried out. She'd treated it with kid gloves since Danny retrieved it from a plastic bag of Isabel's personal effects at the hospital. Sarah heard Grandma hiss as she read Owen's words. She slipped off her glasses as she finished, and dabbed her eyes with her hanky.

"I hate that man so much," she whispered.

"Gran, don't upset yourself over him. Like you said, you can't get revenge from the dead. You can't change the past. We have to look to the future."

Grandma Ruth pushed her glasses back on her nose. "I know, bach. And I know forgiveness is a Christian belief. I am a Christian, so I'm not proud to say this, but I will never, *never*, forgive that man. Never."

"He mentions a secret memorial …?"

She nodded. "I'd not spoken to Owen in Lord knows how many years, fifteen or more. Then early last year, he turns up on my door step, saying he needs to talk. He looked like a tramp, no joke. His hair was long and he was unshaven, looked like he needed a right good wash. He'd walked miles in the rain and was soaked to the skin. And he looked old. Old and broken. And I couldn't find the will to hate him anymore. So, I let him in, more worried about what the neighbours would think with him hollering on the doorstep."

She paused, swallowed, and collected her thoughts. "I made him a pot of tea, and he seemed calmer. He kept thanking me for keeping our secret, saying he needed my help again. He was jabbering on about stolen treasure, how he'd found missing gold, and that someone was trying to kill him. He said he'd been out all night, moving the treasure as someone had found it. I started to get a bit scared. He was like a man possessed. He begged me to take him to the church, to the crypt, to store the treasure."

"And did you …?"

Grandma Ruth shook her head. "I did not. I wanted no part of his crazy fool plan. But when I told him so, I really feared he would hit me. He went berserk. He shouted so loud that Molly rang from next door. I told her it was the television. But I knew it was the only way to get rid of him, so I gave him the church key and the crypt key. And I told him if he hadn't returned them both by dawn I would call the police."

"And did he?"

"He did, barely. I sat up all night, waiting and praying. Wondering what on earth I was doing, trusting that man. But there was something about him, something I'd never seen before. Sincerity? And I believed he was scared. It was clear he feared for his life."

"So … the memorial he mentions in the letter?"

Grandma Ruth nodded, clasped her hands on her lap. "It had troubled me for years that Sarah had been laid to rest on consecrated ground under false circumstances. I was sure Reverend Thomas would have buried her regardless of her cause of death, but it never felt right her funeral had been a sham. I'd had a small crystal vase, with a picture of Sarah, in her room for many years. I asked Owen to take it with him, leave it as a memorial to her in her family crypt. I'm the last to be buried there – don't look shocked, all the details are in my Will, bach – so in some respects I shall be back with her again one day."

"And you've never been down there, or told anyone since? What happened when he came back the next day?"

"Who has cause to visit a crypt? No, of course not. When he came back he was pious, humble. He told me he would leave full details in his Will, so if anything happened to him you would know the truth about your inheritance. That's why I was so angry to find out he'd lied yet again."

"Why didn't you tell me?" Sarah asked.

Grandmas Ruth gave a gentle shrug. "Honour, I suppose. And if I'm honest a growing doubt he'd made the whole thing up. I never spoke to Owen again from that day. Never had no desire to."

"So, as far as you know, the treasure, if it exists, is still in your family vault?"

"Yes."

"My God."

"Although, do I believe Owen? I don't know. With the amount of drink he's soaked up in his lifetime, it could all be a figment of his addled brain. So, I'd not get your hopes up, bach."

"Surely not … not after everything he went through?"

Her gran shrugged. "There's a separate door round the back of the church that leads down steps to the private crypts. I'm not fit enough now; next time I go down will be in a box –"

"Gran!"

She held up her hand to silence her. "Have no fear, I'm going nowhere yet. I just got you back, and I've my first great grandchild to greet into the world. What was it the great Dylan Thomas said? *Do not go gentle into that good night. Rage, rage against the dying of the light.* That's my philosophy, don't you worry. But I know my limitations, bach. I've asked Reverend Thomas if he'll meet us here, he can take you down there. Let's see if Owen can try to redeem himself from beyond the grave, shall we?"

Sarah nodded, speechless.

"Here," she said, and pressed a large black key into the palm of her hand.

Was this really it? Finally?

Remember, the end will be your starting point.

Reverend Thomas flicked a light switch, and a large underground chamber appeared. There were lines of individual vaults, either built into the rock face, or segregated by iron railings. Sarah followed the Reverend's billowing cassock as he disappeared along a narrow aisle. He stopped about half way along the row of vaults, waiting for her to catch up. She quickened her step, a damp chill enveloping her body; her breath spiralled out before her as she hurried to reach him.

"This vault belongs to the Jones family. There are eleven bodies in here at the moment, nine adults and two infants, according to records. I understand you want to go inside, which is fine. There is nothing to fear, each body is separately entombed. I should just warn you though that you may wish to cover your nose, the smell for those not acquainted can be a little unpleasant." He registered her expression. "Oh, not the smell of decomposition, I should have explained. No, there can be a build-up of natural gases; some have said a sulphuric smell – probably being so near to the copper mines of Amlwch. But it can be a little overpowering until the air gets chance to freshen."

"Have you ever been inside this vault?" Sarah asked.

"Years ago, I presided over the funeral of your grandmother's sister, Bronwyn. Really, there's nothing to fear, I promise you."

Sarah wanted to tell him that she no longer feared the dead. She'd learned there was far more to fear from the living.

She removed the key from her pocket. The lock resisted as she turned it anti-clockwise, but then with a click it released and the tumblers turned.

"I'll wait in the main crypt area. I have a funeral here next week, so I just want to check the family's vault – make sure we can get access on the day. That happened once, frightfully embarrassing. Got all the way down here with the coffin, and they couldn't get the blasted gate open." Reverend Thomas broke off, blushed. "Anyway, just holler if you need me."

She waited until he disappeared and then pushed the heavy door open, closing her eyes for a moment. *Father, I hope this is the end. I don't care anymore about treasure or inheritance. I just want this over.*

There was no electric lighting inside the vault, so she switched on the heavy flashlight Reverend Thomas had given her. Taking a lungful of air before ducking to enter the low door, Sarah pulled up the neck of her polo-neck jumper and covered her nose, making sure she breathed inside the collar of her fleece.

She stepped over the threshold and shone the light around, taking in the dusty stone floor, and low ceiling, slick with moisture. Coffins were stacked on ledges to her right and left. Cobwebs clung to her face as she stepped forward, and a cloud of dust rose in the beam of torchlight. She coughed, even through her jumper, she could smell an unpleasant, rotten eggs type stench. She took small breaths through her mouth, and stepped into the centre of the room, turning a complete rotation.

All she could see was greyness. Slate coffins, stone walls. Dust and more dust.

And then, a glint. A tiny flash of brightness reflected in the beam of light. Down low, near the floor. Sarah stooped, brushed a layer of dust from the nearest shelf, and then she saw it.

A crystal vase covered with a gossamer layer of dust, and in the centre a photograph of her mother. Head back, laughing. Just as Sarah remembered her.

Below the bench, she saw a wooden box. Coffin sized, but definitely wood, not slate.

Her heart began to pound and a wave of dizziness came over her. She pulled in a long mouthful of air, fresher now, and dropped to her knees. She stood the flashlight on its end so it illuminated the room in an eerie semi-darkness, casting shadows from every corner of the vault.

Bending forward, she stopped dead; a yell hovering on her lips as something kicked her beneath her ribs. *Someone* kicked her in the stomach.

What the …? Reality dawned. Her first kick! Could the baby really be as excited as she was? Was she showing her pleasure, excitement? Or maybe her displeasure?

Sarah took a deep breath and gripped both ends of the wooden crate, tugging it out from below the stone shelf. It was lighter than she expected. She coughed and spluttered as the lid slid to the floor, and a cloud of dust hit her full in the face. Wasn't it odd there was no lock, nothing to secure the contents?

Her heart pounded in her ears, another kick above her

bladder made her groan. The anticipation had built for so long, she felt sick. With shaking hands, she pulled the box out further, hoisting the torch and leaning forward to get her first glimpse of the treasure.

The crate was empty.

"What?"

Sarah shone the torch beam into every corner. No treasure. No note. Nothing.

"No way. No, this can't be ..."

She slid the crate out fully and shone the torch along each side; noting on the side that had been hidden, nearest the wall, splintered wood and a smashed lock.

"Oh, no!"

Sarah dropped back onto her haunches, looking to the ceiling in despair.

Someone had got there first.

This whole nightmare journey had been for nothing. All the loss of life. Her poor Dom. And Lewis. Tears ran down her face. There was such tragedy here, and such irony, such bitter irony. The curse of the ship lived on. There would never be a happy ending with the legacy of the Royal Charter. It was the way of things and always had been.

More innocent lives lost in its name.

And all for what?

An empty wooden box.

Epilogue

Today

Nine months on, Sarah stands at the edge of the high cliff. Holding back hair that whips across her face, she shields her eyes from the sun and stares down at the crashing tide below. Gulls circle above her head, their cries echoing above the noise of the waves, swooping down to the ocean for food.

Today, with threatening grey storm clouds on the horizon, the rocks at Point Lynas look deadly, and her mind is transported back in time to 26th October 1859.

She imagines the scene then. Lifeless bodies washed up against the cliffs. Screams and shouts filling the air. The stricken vessel rolling on the tide, dragged down to the depths by the weight of its cargo. Helpless bystanders lined up along the cliffs, powerless to prevent the tragedy unfolding before them.

A cry catches her attention, and she turns, lifting her daughter from the pram. She yawns and tiny fists rub her eyes. Sarah tucks in her arms, wraps her tight in the crocheted shawl, and turns her face seaward. Her small body fits into Sarah's arms as if she's designed to fit - and stay there forever. Sarah sighs; she will never let her go.

"See, here, Angelina. This is where lots of people died,

drowned because of greed. It's a lesson to us all. But it's also the place your daddy died. And he died protecting me … and you. He was a wonderful man who would have loved you so very much. I'll tell you all about him one day - and this is the place we will always come to remember him."

Sarah kisses the delicate forehead, tracing tiny veins beneath translucent skin with her fingertip. She touches a nose that is so like Dom's, gazing into eyes as vividly blue as his. A gentle smile twitches Angelina's lips, and Sarah's heart surges with a love so powerful it makes her gasp.

They walk along the cliff path, Angelina tight in her arms, the sun trickling shadows across her face. They reach the cove and watch the tide surge along narrow gulleys; the sound like an angry roar. There is a flash of movement, behind the furthest rocks. Sarah blinks, watches. A shadow crosses the beach, pauses and raises a hand against the sun. And for a second, Sarah sees a young girl. Dark shawl, buffeted in the breeze. Sarah blinks again, waves – and the image has gone. The beach empty. And a sense of peace settles itself deep within her soul.

Was it a shadow? Or was it something more.

She doesn't know, but she doesn't need to know.

Sarah begins the walk back across the field, pausing to settle Angelina under the yellow blanket in her pram. Her life has changed so much in the past year. Finally, she is beginning to find comfort in her surroundings. No more nightmares, no more ghostly apparitions. And no more evil. She owes the young girl, Angelina, her life. But there is tranquillity now. If her ghost is still here, she is at peace. Charter House is safe. Sarah is sure of that.

Her future will be here, with baby Angelina, Grandma Ruth, not forgetting Jim, and hopefully Isabel's boy, Thomas, if the adoption is successful. She will pass her days writing travel books, maybe some fiction. She remains great friends with Danny, and Luke is a constant companion. One day, she hopes she can find the forgiveness in her heart to visit Isabel in the secure hospital.

But not yet. Not for a while yet.

Sarah may not have found treasure, but she has found peace. And that is so much more important. Perhaps for the first time in her life she can stop running. She can write books about Anglesey, study her latest love of archaeology. She can explore and enjoy the historical beauty she turned her back on in her youth. She has time on her hands now, and a future that, although unplanned, she can do with as she so desires.

And the Royal Charter to thank for the journey that led her here.

THE END

© *G E Hamer 2012*

Coming next …

CLOSURE

The university town of Bangor is in lockdown, following a series of student abductions. When the investigating officer's favourite cousin becomes the first known murder victim, the case becomes a whole lot more personal.

The police hit a series of dead ends. Are they dealing with a random serial killer or are these attacks part of a bigger picture? If they could find a motive or connection between the victims, they might be able to find the answer.

DS Chris Coleman believes there is a pattern, and works with pathologist, Susan Connolly, to examine every minute detail of the recovered bodies – the only evidence they have.

Two hundred miles away in Stratford-upon-Avon, Helen West is coming to terms with her husband's death and trying to cope with her six-year-old son's grief. Jake suffers from nightmares, and visions of what he calls his 'other life'. He talks about a boy called Jacob and a place known only as 'the island'.

Helen's journey to find the source of Jake's torment leads them to North Wales. Whilst there, Jake reacts to a local television news bulletin about the latest student abduction. What could his 'other life' possibly have to do with these crimes?

With the clock ticking, will Helen be able to convince North Wales CID to let her son help? And will it put an end to the strangeness controlling Jake's life?

Also from Triskele Books

BEHIND CLOSED DOORS

Suicide – the act of taking one's own life.
Homicide – the act of taking someone else's.

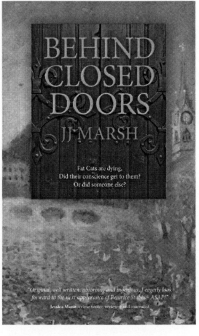

An unethical banker suffocates. A diamond dealer slits his wrists. A media magnate freezes in the snow. A disgraced CEO inhales exhaust fumes. Four unpopular businessmen, four apparent suicides. Until Interpol find the same DNA at each death.

Beatrice Stubbs, on her first real case since 'the incident', arrives in Switzerland to lead the investigation. But there's more to Zurich than chocolate and charm. Potential suspects are everywhere, her Swiss counterpart is hostile and the secretive world of international finance seems beyond the law. Battling impossible odds by day and her own demons at night, Beatrice has never felt so alone.

She isn't. Someone's watching.
Someone else who believes in justice.
The poetic kind.

"Original, well written, absorbing and ingenious."
Jessica Mann, crime writer, reviewer and journalist

Also from Triskele Books

SPIRIT OF LOST ANGELS

Her mother executed for witchcraft, her father dead at the hand of a noble, Victoire Charpentier vows to rise above her poor peasant roots.

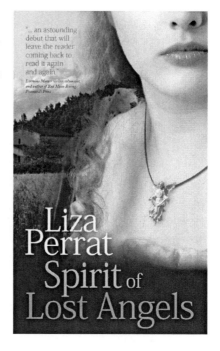

Forced to leave her village of Lucie-sur-Vionne for domestic work in Paris, Victoire suffers gruesome abuse under the *ancien régime*. Can she muster the bravery and skill to join the revolutionary force gripping France, and overthrow the corrupt, diabolical aristocracy?

Spirit of Lost Angels traces the journey of a bone angel talisman passed down through generations. The women of *L'Auberge des Anges* face tragedy and betrayal in a world where their gift can be their curse. Amidst the tumult of revolutionary France, this is a story of courage, hope and love.

"... an astounding debut that will leave the reader coming back to read it again and again.

Lorraine Mace – writer, columnist, and author of Bad Moon Rising, Frances di Plino

Lightning Source UK Ltd.
Milton Keynes UK
UKOW050225150512

192564UK00001B/7/P